Nikki Soarde

Redeeming Alec

What the critics are saying...

"Ms. Soarde has written a really suspenseful story in Redeeming Alec [...] the suspenseful twists and turns in the story kept me on the edge of my seat, always rooting for Alec and Kira to find some resolution before something even more horrible happened. The supporting characters add a lot to the story, especially Lauren and Rachel. This is one story that the reader will have a hard time putting down, I know I did."

~ *The Romance Studio*

"*Redeeming Alec* is a heart wrenching book [...] However, these two characters work through their problems albeit many years later and is able to come through it stronger than before." ~ *Fallen Angels Reviews*

"All in all, Redeeming Alec will hold your attention and have you rooting for Alec and Kira to get past their differences and work things out." ~ *Romance Divas*

"The story is written beautifully. The emotions are raw and honest. The skill in which she deals with each and every character's dark past has you crying and laughing right along with them. The plot, with tautly crafted twists and turns, leaves you with a page-turner—hooking you from the very start and gasping and teary-eyed when it comes to a shocking end." ~ *Coffee Time Romances*

A Cerridwen Press Publication

www.cerridwenpress.com

Redeeming Alec

ISBN 9781419955969

Edited by Sue-Ellen Gower.
Cover art by Willo.

This book printed in the U.S.A. by Jasmine-Jade Enterprises, LLC.

Electronic book Publication January 2006
Trade paperback Publication May 2007

Cerridwen Press is an imprint of Ellora's Cave Publishing, Inc.®

Also by Nikki Soarde

ℬ

Legacy of Sin

Mortal Wounds

If you are interested in a spicier read (and are over 18), check out her erotic romances at Ellora's Cave Publishing (www.ellorascave.com).

And Lady Makes Three *(anthology)*

Balance of Power

Duplicity

Ellora's Cavemen: Legendary Tails III *(anthology)*

Jagged Gift

Package Deal

Phobia

Roguish Hearts

Wild Oats

About the Author

ℌ

Nikki lives in a small town in Ontario, Canada. In the midst of the chaos that comes with raising three small boys, working part-time as a lab tech in a hospital blood bank, and caring for her ever-adoring husband, she dreams up her stories. Nikki's work is an eclectic combination of romance, mystery, suspense and humor with characters that have plenty of room to grow. To learn more about her and her work visit her at www.nikkisoarde.com.

Nikki welcomes comments from readers. You can find her website and email address on her author bio page at www.cerridwenpress.com.

Tell Us What You Think

We appreciate hearing reader opinions about our books. You can email us at Comments@EllorasCave.com.

Trademarks Acknowledgement

&
The author acknowledges the trademarked status and trademark owners of the following wordmarks mentioned in this work of fiction:

Amoxil: Beecham, Inc.

Animaniacs: Time Warner Entertainment Company

Armani: GA Modefine S.A

Beretta: Fabbrica d'Armi P. Beretta S.p.A.

Big Bird: Muppets, Inc.

BMW: Bayerische Motoren Werke Aktiengesellschaft

Cap'n Crunch: Quaker Oats Company

Chrysler Neon: Chrysler Corporation

Count Chocula: General Mills, Inc.

Crown Royal: Joseph E. Seagram & Sons Limited

Double Bubble: Hardman Incorporated

Ford: Ford Motor Company

Glock: Glock, Inc.

GQ: Advance Magazine Publishers Inc.

Haldol: McNeil Laboratories, Incorporated

Juan Valdez Coffee: National Federation of Coffee Growers of Colombia

Kool-Aid: Kraft Foods Holdings, Inc.

La-Z-Boy: LZB Properties, Inc.

Magnum: Smith & Wesson, Inc.

McDonald's: McDonald's Corporation

Mercury Capri: Ford Motor Company

Montreal Expo: Montreal Baseball Club Inc.

Naugahyde: United States Rubber Products, Inc.

Nissan Altima: Nissan Jidosha Kabushiki Kaisha TA Nissan Motor Co., Ltd.

Pinky and the Brain: Time Warner Entertainment Company

Prozac: Eli Lilly and Company

Ralph Lauren: Polo Ralph Lauren Corporation

Rohypnol: Hoffman-LaRoche, Inc.,

Scrabble: Hasbro, Inc.

Smith & Wesson: Smith & Wesson, Inc.

Styrofoam: Dow Chemical Company

Tylenol: Tylenol Company, The

Velcro: Velcro Industries B.V

Versace: Gianni Versace S.P.A

Waterford: Waterford Wedgwood Plc.

WD-40: WD-40 Company

REDEEMING ALEC

ﻌ

Prologue

ꚙ

Melissa shivered. The spring breeze that teased the curtains through the open bedroom window was warm and scented with lilacs. And yet she couldn't seem to shake the chill that had settled over her like a dark, damp mantle the moment she stepped into the house that night.

She flicked a switch and flooded the space with light. The room was just as she had left it. The bed was heaped with chintz pillows. The woodwork gleamed with fresh polish and every knickknack and perfume bottle sat exactly as it had for the last two years.

She told herself that she was just being silly. She'd spent too many lonely nights listening to local news stories of brutal rapes and gruesome murders. The idea of some villain having designs on someone like her was ridiculous. Besides that, she had a state of the art alarm and security system. And that window opened out onto a two-story drop. She was perfectly safe and—

The ring of the phone pierced her like a steel icicle. She snatched it up. "What?"

Silence.

Her knuckles whitened around the receiver. "Tony, if that's you, you slimy, two-timing son of a—"

Click.

Dial tone.

With a low growl and a shaking finger, she clicked off the cordless phone and glared at it, entertaining a fleeting image of her ex-husband, eviscerated and dangling by his gonads from the top of the Peace Tower on Parliament Hill. That thought brought a small smile to her thin lips.

He had been harassing her with pleading phone calls ever since the divorce had been finalized. But in the last week the calls had dwindled down to annoying episodes of heavy breathing and heavier silences.

Of course, she didn't know for certain that it was Tony. She just assumed. Who else would want to harass or molest, or pay any attention at all, for that matter, to the likes of her? To Melissa with her small eyes and unremarkable bone structure? To Melissa with her big feet and bigger bank account? *Poor little rich girl.* A trite but true cliché.

A gust of wind billowed the curtains into the room, and sent a fresh chill shimmering over her skin. Still clutching the phone in a sweaty palm, she crossed the room and pulled down the sash. She snapped the lock back into place, and tried to recall if she had left the window open that morning. Or perhaps the cleaning woman had opened it to air out the winter mustiness that still clung to the inside of the house after the long months of a typical Ottawa winter hibernation.

She lifted her eyes to gaze out the window at the winking lights of her hometown, which glittered off the glasslike surface of the Rideau Canal.

Suddenly she wanted to be a part of it. She wanted out of this house with its cavernous rooms and torturous memories. The vast emptiness of it pressed in on her so she couldn't breathe. It almost seemed alive. She could feel its malevolence like a presence.

She fought for breath as fingers of panic unexpectedly wrapped around her throat and sank into her soul.

"Stop it!" she shouted.

She wasn't sure whom she was addressing—herself or some intangible evil. But it didn't matter. Absurd or not, the sound of her own voice eased her tension, and a nervous giggle swelled up from her chest.

She shook her head in self-deprecation but, even as she did so, she had to acknowledge her need to get out. A bunch of her friends were meeting downtown for drinks. Melissa had declined the invitation, pleading a headache and sore feet. But now her desire for companionship outweighed her desire for a hot bath and a box of chocolate chip cookies.

She needed a lift. She needed to feel sexy and desirable and like she was part of the human race. Maybe she'd wear one of those slinky cocktail dresses her ex had picked out for her but she had refused to wear for fear of actually drawing attention to herself. Determined to rise above the pall that had settled over her in the last hour, Melissa strutted over to her huge walk-in closet and pulled open the door.

She barely had time to register surprise before the hand clamped across her mouth and strong arms pinned her hands to her sides.

His gloves filled her nostrils with the scent of fine calfskin leather as his hand tightened painfully across her jaw. Melissa's eyes were wide with terror and her heart pounded furiously as he dragged her toward her bed and hissed in her ear, "Life's just not fair, is it?"

She whimpered in a muted plea for release.

"Nope. It's not fair and you'd better get used to it. We all have to learn the lesson…eventually."

He lowered her to the bed, his body heavy and oppressive. Belatedly, she remembered the phone still clutched in her hand. But she was only able to hit two buttons before he wrenched it from her and dropped it to the floor.

He gently brushed a wisp of hair from her cheek. "I'm sorry, honey," he whispered, and she almost thought he meant it. His eyes behind the ski mask were at once sad and fevered. "But we can't let you call them." He ripped open her blouse. "Not quite yet."

Chapter One

ஐ

The evening sun glittered through the brilliant ruby liquid. Alec lifted the glass to catch as many of the fading rays as possible. The light danced and swooned within its dark, rich depths, struggling in vain to escape the seductive allure of the provocative French Merlot. He drew the glass to his lips and breathed deeply the delicate notes of lavender and vanilla before taking his first tentative sip.

The wine swirled across his tongue and caressed his senses. He allowed his eyes to drift closed, losing himself in the experience. He even imagined he could feel its healing touch on his tattered soul. Few things in life these days could give him as much pleasure as a truly refined glass of wine. He had spent the last several years educating his palate and perfecting his technique so he wouldn't look the fool whenever the topic came up in casual conversation. Here in Bordeaux, one of the most renowned wine regions in France, that was a foregone conclusion. One could no more avoid discussing grapes and French oak than one could avoid water in the Seine. His education had begun as a work-related necessity but, somewhere along the way, he had fallen in love.

"Mon Dieu!" exclaimed the sultry figure who had coiled herself around a huge cushion on the expansive satin-sheathed mattress. *"Je pense que tu préfères le vin à moi."*

"Speak English," he said evenly, his eyes now riveted on the scenery outside the wide picture window. Row upon row of neatly trimmed vines, their limbs heavy with blossoms, stretched to the horizon. "That's the only way you'll learn."

She quietly muttered a few unflattering names before sighing and speaking in halting English. "Mm…You like the wine…better than me, I think."

"Perhaps."

"I should fire you immediately for being so…so…" She struggled with her limited vocabulary.

"Insolent?"

"*Oui!* That's it. You, sir, are a bastard."

He chuckled quietly. He found it very interesting that that particular epithet had found its way into her repertoire. He took another leisurely sip before turning his gaze on his charge. A black silk peignoir encased her figure like a shimmering second skin. Her long, black mane flowed over her shoulders and spilled down her back. She watched him with enormous brown eyes fringed by a cloud of dark lashes. She was strikingly beautiful, and even more strikingly rich. She was intelligent and exciting, if occasionally petulant and moody. She was his employer and he was sleeping with her, but that didn't mean he had to like her.

"Go right ahead," he challenged. "I had at least three offers of employment last night at the party. Some of them were even richer than you." *And younger,* he added silently.

She raised her hand and with a practiced arm threw her empty glass squarely at his head. He avoided it with a small step to the side and the glass shattered against the marble fireplace behind him.

"You really are a spoiled brat, *ma chèrie.*" He drained his glass and moved toward her. "I should make you clean that up. You overwork your staff mercilessly, and waste perfectly good Waterford in the process." He shrugged out of his tux jacket and dropped it on the floor as he settled down beside her on the bed. It had been another tedious afternoon at the gallery.

She flushed crimson. "Y-you have no right to speak t-to me like that," she finally sputtered. "You are merely hired muscle—a mindless brute that I pay to keep me safe and amuse me between the sheets. You are little more than a…a…gold-plated gigolo." She tossed her hair back defiantly.

His hand lashed out and latched around her fragile wrist. "You may pay me to protect you from your imaginary enemies, but you do *not* pay me to sleep with you," he hissed.

"Let go of me," she commanded.

He ignored her. "I sleep with you because it amuses me. And because, if not for that little diversion, and the gallons of Pinot Noir and Chardonnay that you provide for my entertainment, I would be bored stiff."

She tried to wrench her wrist away, but it was a futile attempt. "You…" she whined.

He continued, the frustration and rage of the past few years bubbling up unexpectedly. Suddenly he needed to vent, and Sylvie Pierrot was vulnerable and handy. She also embodied everything about this damn country that he abhorred.

"Do you know how much I hate this country?" He didn't wait for a response. "You people make me sick. I've never known such a group of arrogant, pompous snobs. You, who think your language is more pure and more eloquent than any other language on Earth. You, who think you are the only ones who know how to make fine wine or fine cheese. You, who must rely on immigrants to stabilize your population because the native French can't be bothered with having children!" He finally dropped her wrist and wiped his hand on his trousers as if she carried the plague on her skin. "And you—*you* take the cake. You squander your family's money on frivolities like a bodyguard that you have absolutely no use for other than to elevate your social status. You think of no one but yourself, barely take an interest in the business that puts clothes on your back and champagne in your bathtub. You treat your employees like dirt…and your friends no better."

He tired of looking at her face with its gaping mouth and wide incredulous eyes. He stood and whirled away from her. He stalked to the bathroom and slammed the door behind him, amazed that he didn't hear the crash of another wineglass shattering against the oak. He rolled up his sleeves and ran cold water into the sink. He splashed his face as if that could wash away the film that he had gradually been accumulating ever since he had come to this damn country.

He studied himself in the mirror as water dripped off his chin. Who was he? He didn't know anymore. The crooked nose, jade green eyes and jutting jaw were familiar. The scar that made a jagged L beneath his left eye wasn't strange. The unruly mane of auburn hair and fine spattering of freckles across his high cheekbones were just as they had been since he was twenty. The face in the mirror hadn't changed in the past fifteen years. He still boasted the charming combination of boyish innocence and rugged austerity. Someone had once told him he was a quirky cross between Ron Howard and Clint Eastwood…with a French accent.

He was certainly no fashion model, but women seemed to find him appealing regardless. They seemed to be drawn to the enigma that was Alec Robert Frechette. He used to get a kick out of being an *enigma*. He used to get a kick out of a lot of things. He used to have a sense of humor. He used to have other things that were more important to him than a BMW and Brie. He used to feel like he mattered.

He heard the bathroom door ease open. Without looking at her he taunted, "Looking for more abuse? There's lots more where that came from."

"How can you judge us so harshly? Your grandmother was born right here in Bordeaux, *non?* You cannot deny the trickle of French blood in your own veins." *Trickle of French blood.* He knew she had chosen the word deliberately as a slight to his lineage. However, she was surprisingly calm considering the torrent of insults that he had unleashed.

He snorted and grabbed a plush, monogrammed towel. "I most certainly can deny it. My grandmother abandoned her heritage, and while I may have been born in Québec that does *not* make me *Québecois.*" He scrubbed his face and hands dry. "And it certainly doesn't make me *French.*" He sneered the word, relishing the opportunity to scorn the coveted French bloodlines, just as the French scorned their lowly Quebecois cousins. He tossed the towel in the tub and headed for the door, but she blocked his path.

"Where are you going?" she asked.

"I'm leaving. I assumed I was fired."

"Mais non!" She shook her head in frustration, before correcting herself in English. "You assumed wrong." She backed up the statement by reaching for the buttons on his shirt. She managed to undo four of them before he gathered his wits about him enough to respond.

"I just insulted you and your entire country, and you still want to keep me on?"

Her fingers were already caressing his chest. *"Oui.* You remind me of the..." Again she struggled. *"...le loup."* She smiled seductively and he wanted to vomit.

He batted her hands away and shoved her roughly aside. "I'm no wolf," he spat. "And if you're not going to fire me, then I quit."

Her eyes turned feral again. "You cannot quit. You signed a contract."

"Just watch me."

He had already wrenched open the door to the third-floor bedroom suite when her voice reached him again. "Where will you go? I will make sure no one in Paris will touch you!"

He stopped and turned around, studying her silhouette in the evening sunlight, which had now taken on a warm golden hue. He hadn't thought about that until just that moment, but the answer was all too obvious. In fact, it was long overdue. He had been running long enough.

"Home," he said simply. "I'm going home."

He slammed the door behind him.

Chapter Two

"Kira?" whispered a tiny voice. It was the kind of voice Kira had always imagined a fairy or an elf might have—soft and sweet and brimming with innocence. A pair of pale, delicate arms reached up in a silent plea for comfort. "Up?"

Her patient's treatment now complete, Kira North bent low and allowed those tiny arms to wrap around her neck. They gripped her with surprising strength, considering their owner barely weighed thirty pounds. Perhaps Cassie *was* a fairy—an incarnation of stardust and moonlight. Her existence was most certainly as sparkling as those ethereal substances...and just as nebulous.

Kira stood and nuzzled her cheek against the smooth skin that had once been adorned with a cascade of shimmering golden waves. Four-year-old Cassie Eldridge had lost her hair weeks ago—a side effect of the chemotherapy drugs that were pumped through her fragile system. The IV bag, now empty of its lifesaving contents, hung from the pole, looking withered and forlorn—much like her patient.

"How are you feeling today, honey?" whispered Kira, carrying her charge from the chemotherapy suite out to the waiting room.

"Okay," Cassie mumbled against her throat.

Cassie was always *okay*. Even when she was so weak she could barely walk or swallow, even when she was so consumed by nausea and vertigo that she could only sit up in bed with assistance, even when she looked up with those huge brown eyes that were so full of sadness and misery that it made Kira want to cry—even then, Cassie was always *okay*.

Kira couldn't discern which type of patient was more painful to deal with—the brave little troopers like Cassie, who stayed strong because they couldn't bear to see their mothers cry, or the little monsters who whined and complained every step of the way, fighting the hands that were struggling so desperately to help them.

They had every right to be miserable. They had every right to fight. Whether they fought silently, or screamed loud enough for the whole world to hear, it didn't matter. More than debilitating drugs, or invisible rays of radiation, a fighting spirit was the only thing that stood between these children and the dark, menacing abyss that pulled at them with such fierce determination.

Kira was merely one of the many guiding lights who helped them across the gaping pit. Many made it to the other side, some virtually unscathed, many with scars. But even the ones who didn't make it at all left her with memories to treasure—memories that helped to fill the hole in her soul.

Many nurses looked at her with undisguised amazement for her choice of specializing in pediatric oncology. She often joked that she had gone into it because the hours were good—she worked with outpatients, so rarely had to stay past five o'clock. But the joke fooled no one. It took a very strong and special person to deal with these tiny, fragile beings whose pain and tenuous existence tore at the fabric of humanity. Children simply weren't meant to face this sort of torture. It wasn't normal. It wasn't right. It made people too aware of their own mortality, and of the risks inherent in having, and loving, their own offspring.

It took a very special person to face them day in and day out—Kira heard that constantly. She heard it from parents and colleagues, friends and acquaintances, but she didn't believe it for a minute. She wasn't so special. She wasn't so strong. She was as weak as anyone, perhaps weaker. However, she did have her reasons, but they were intensely personal. She had no intention of sharing them with anyone.

Out in the waiting room Cassie's mother sat, rigid and thin-lipped. Like the children, there were several different categories of parent, each type dealing with their child's pain in their own way. Cassie's mom dealt with it by not facing it. She rarely, if ever, sat with her daughter during the infusion, deferring that responsibility to the capable, trained hands of the nursing staff. Kira didn't judge her for that. Seeing your child in that setting was unnerving and went against the strong maternal instinct of protecting your young. There was nothing to do in there, other than to hold a hand, read a book, or hold a cup of water, while every fiber in your being screamed at you to pick up your child and run, screaming for safety.

Cassie's father was another story entirely. He accompanied his daughter whenever possible and, when he did, he was exactly the icon of strength and comfort that his daughter needed. He told stories and sang songs, stroked cheeks and tickled toes. He did whatever was necessary to distract Cassie from the cold, stark environment and the pain of needles and drugs. But Kira had unwittingly come across him once, when he had excused himself for a few minutes to go to the washroom. She had gone into the supply room and found him there, huddled in the corner, his shoulders shaking as he wept in great heart-wrenching sobs. Kira had slipped out again, unnoticed, and had never spoken of it to anyone.

"Here we are," she said as she seated herself beside Cassie's mom. She hugged Cassie tightly in farewell before handing her over to the waiting arms of the tall, slim woman in the chrome and vinyl chair. Emma Eldridge had lost more than twenty pounds since her daughter was diagnosed with Acute Lymphocytic Leukemia. Their ordeal had begun a mere four months ago but Kira had no doubt it seemed like years.

Emma settled Cassie on her lap, and checked her over thoroughly. "You feeling okay, peanut? You up to a little drive to pick up Daddy?"

"Can we stop for ice cream?" cooed that fairy voice.

Emma smiled, her tight mouth relaxing slightly. "Okay, but no grape flavor this time. Last time it melted all over your best white T-shirt." Emma looked up at Kira. "Even pure bleach couldn't get that stain out."

"You could always dye it purple," suggested Kira with a smile.

"Yes, I guess I could at that." Emma glanced down at her daughter, who had snuggled tightly into the circle of her mother's arms. "I guess we have to make the most of what we've got." The moment stretched as both women watched the soft rise and fall of Cassie's chest and her eyes fluttered closed. Emma took a deep breath and shrugged off the mood. "Any instructions, Kira? And when's our next appointment?"

Kira and Emma spent the next ten minutes discussing the finer points of the next phase of Cassie's treatment. By the time they were finished, and Kira had ushered them out the door, the chemo suite was almost devoid of patients, and the clock was approaching five.

"How's Taylor doing?" she asked her colleague, who was poring over charts at the nursing station. Taylor was another acute leukemia who had joined them within the last few months.

"The drip's almost done. He should be out of here by five-thirty." Jean Elliott never lifted her eyes from the pages before her. Her small, ample frame remained hunched over the desk. She pushed her oversized glasses up her nose and continued reading.

Kira gritted her teeth before saying as smoothly as possible, "Would you like me to check on him for you? Cassie's gone and I've got a few minutes."

"That's not necessary," replied Jean, even more tight-lipped than usual. "Why don't you clean up and leave on time for a change? Let me worry about my own patients."

Kira stifled her reply that Jean didn't seem to *worry* about her patients at all. She treated them like they were on an assembly line—admit, IV drip, consult with oncologist if needed, discharge. She seemed determined to forget that these children were human beings with needs and feelings—that they were weak and vulnerable and needed every ounce of human compassion that their nurses could wring from their overworked bodies. Maybe that was how Jean chose to address her own turmoil and the pain of dealing with these shadows of childhood. Perhaps it worked for Jean, but, tragically, the children paid the price.

Jean was also from the old school. She insisted on wearing the traditional nursing uniforms in stiff, starched whites, complete with duty shoes. Her only concession to current trends was that she had retired her cap. The rest of the staff, in an effort to make the children's time in hospital less like a time in hospital, wore jeans and bright T-shirts. Kira's uniform closet consisted of a variety of shades of denim and T-shirts that sported the likes of the Animaniacs and Pinky and the Brain. Dressing in street clothes put the children more at ease, and even managed to draw the occasional smile. They were lucky that Ottawa General Hospital was progressive enough to allow the unorthodox attire.

"I don't mind," persisted Kira. She took a step toward Taylor's cubicle. "I'll just see if—"

Jean was already brushing past her. "Go home, Kira," she ordered.

Kira propped her hands on her narrow hips as she watched Jean waddle away. Well, if Kira's interfering ways prodded Jean to pay a little more attention to her patients, Kira was willing to weather Jean's withering looks and sharp tongue. There were much worse things in this world.

She turned back to the desk to make a final check of her charts and generally tidy up before calling it a day. She was almost finished when she sensed a presence behind her.

"Do you ever go home?" lamented a velvety baritone very close to her ear. His breath ruffled the fiery red fringe of hair that brushed the collar of her T-shirt. She had tired of bothering with braids and ponytails, so had finally taken the plunge and had her hair trimmed in a short, funky style several months earlier. It was the smartest thing she had ever done.

She rolled her eyes and tried in vain to contain her smile. Mike LaRocque, the resident pediatric oncologist, had a legendary bedside manner. He was warm and funny with the children, and open and honest with the parents. However, the joke among the nurses was that to really appreciate him you had to experience him *in* the bed rather than *beside* it. Mike had mischievous blue eyes, wavy blond hair and a physique that even a lab coat had trouble camouflaging. And he pursued Kira relentlessly.

"I go home occasionally," she replied. "I like to watch *ER* on Thursday nights. That's my social highlight for the week."

Mike glanced at the calendar. "Well, what do you know. It's Thursday and I'm free."

Kira dropped the last chart onto the cart bound for medical records. "That wasn't an invitation."

He raised his eyebrows. "No? Maybe you'd learn by example then. How about dinner?" He spread his hands, palms turned toward the heavens. "See how easy that was? Three simple words that eloquently deliver an unmistakable invitation for a meal and…"

Kira grabbed her purse. "And what?"

"And whatever." His eyes and the twitch at the corner of his lips communicated all too eloquently what *whatever* meant.

"Sorry, boss. I've got a hot date with a dialysis patient."

He grabbed her arm as she tried to move past. "That neighbor of yours?"

"None other." She tried to sound flippant.

"Honey, you gotta slow down. You can't save everyone you know."

Those words stung more deeply than he could imagine. "I'm just stopping in for a game of Scrabble to help her pass the time. That hardly qualifies as saving the world, does it?"

He sighed and let go. "No." But he didn't sound convinced. "You just seem to have so many causes, so many friends with problems and you spread yourself so thin. You need to take time for you." He dropped his voice to a whisper. "Even I take a vacation occasionally, and I freely admit to being obsessed with my work. Take a break. Come to dinner and I promise I won't make a pass."

Kira scoffed. "That's like a bull promising he won't gorge the matador if he relinquishes his cape."

Mike just kept gazing at her. The concern in his eyes made her uncomfortable. She wasn't used to anybody worrying about her. She was the one who did the worrying. "Thanks, Mike," she yielded a little. "But I really did promise Rachel I'd keep her company."

He shrugged. "All right. But consider it an open invitation. Whenever you need a break just give me a call. You've got my beeper number."

She granted him a knowing smile. "Oh, I've got your number, all right." She picked up her purse and slung it over her shoulder.

"Just be careful, okay?"

"Careful?"

"When you go home tonight. It might be late, and I hate the thought of you walking into that dark house all alone. Especially lately."

"Don't be ridiculous. I can take care of myself. Besides, I've got nothing worth stealing."

Mike's blue eyes darkened with concern. "You know that's not what I mean. The Rideau Rapist just chalked up victim number four, and it wasn't that far from your neighborhood."

Kira plastered on a mask of composure. The last murder had unnerved her. It was a little too close to home for comfort but, thus far, she had managed quite nicely to keep those fears and worries under wraps. Lately her cozy little bungalow had taken on almost cavernous proportions. And it had felt more empty and unappealing than ever. But she wasn't about to share that with Dr. LaRocque. "I've got a can of pepper spray, and a ferocious guard dog."

"He's a Chihuahua."

"He'd annoy an intruder to death."

"This isn't funny, Kira. You're very vulnerable there. You should get a security system or…or something."

She smiled. "Like a bodyguard?" Her smiled wilted as that unintentional reference dredged up unwelcome associations. She rushed to fill in the awkwardness that only she felt. "The women who were attacked had security systems and Dobermans out the wazoo. It didn't help them. Besides, his targets have been the rich upper crust of the Ottawa jet set. I hardly think I fit the profile." She turned to go.

"I hope you're right," muttered Mike as she stepped out into the hall. "But I reserve the right to worry about you anyway."

Kira's cross-trainers padded across the sterile hospital flooring. By the time she reached the bank of elevators, she had already pushed Mike's concerns to the back of her mind. There were so many other immediate problems to occupy her mental processes. Worrying about the unlikely possibility that she could be targeted by a maniac was ludicrous. There were a few hundred thousand women in the Ottawa area who were possible targets. She was probably taking a bigger chance when she put the key into the ignition of her Chrysler Neon.

She stabbed the glowing white button that summoned the elevators. Tapping her foot nervously, she watched the numbers slowly count up to eight. Dialysis was down on five. She could take the stairs. She really should take the stairs. She knew she should do *something* to improve her fitness level. She got so little exercise, and on top of that she didn't eat properly. In fact, her diet was so poor that she had lost almost ten pounds over the last year.

Her previously lean five-foot-seven figure was verging on gaunt, and her muscle tone had dwindled down to nothing. At least her problem wasn't an addiction to junk food. She actually had an aversion to greasy snack foods. Her problem was that cooking for one always seemed so pointless, maybe even a little pathetic. She usually just grabbed an apple or a bagel for her supper, and munched while she cuddled Cujo on her lap and watched a rented movie or pored over the latest medical journals.

The elevator arrived and she stepped into the cramped tin box. As the doors closed and the winch whined to life, an uncharacteristic wave of claustrophobia washed over her. Suddenly the thought of spending the next hour surrounded by pumping, chugging machinery, bustling medical personnel, and the harsh scents of alcohol and iodine, was intolerable.

Rachel was a lovely young woman, and her mother was a dear friend of Kira's. Normally Kira enjoyed helping Rachel pass the time on her four-hour dialysis run with playful gossip and mindless games, but tonight she just couldn't face it.

It was early summer and the skies outside had looked clear and inviting. The grass was lush, and no doubt the breezes warm and balmy. Tonight she had the urge to take a long walk along the canal. Perhaps she'd stroll through the Byward Market and pick up some fruit and cheese for her supper. The large open-air market near the downtown core was a favorite and there were almost always a few wide-eyed tourists and struggling musicians lining its streets, eager to amuse her. Maybe she'd even pay one of those well-toned college students to take her for a rickshaw ride. It was always a treat to watch a nice set of *gluteus maximus* in action. She smiled to herself. It didn't happen very often, but tonight she felt like treating herself.

She would stop in on Rachel and Lauren, and make her apologies. Maybe she'd pop by later tonight for a cup of tea and one of Lauren's brownies. Yes. That was exactly what she would do.

A little fresh air would do her a world of good.

* * * * *

Lauren Nickle flipped through the copy of *Canadian Living* she had picked up at the hospital gift shop on her way in. She barely glanced at her surroundings. The dialysis suite had become as familiar to her as her own living room. But it would never become comfortable.

"Mom?"

She lifted tired blue eyes to look at her daughter, reclined on the large vinyl La-Z-Boy. Lauren ignored the enormous needle poised over her daughter's iodine-stained skin. She ignored the bulge of the fistula that marred her daughter's perfectly formed limb but was necessary to allow for the efficient transfer of huge volumes of blood in and out of Rachel's body. Rachel barely flinched when the needle pierced her skin and the requisite vials were filled before her blood began circulating through the life-saving machine.

Lauren ignored all that, and instead focused on her daughter's eyes, which were the color and shape of almonds. Those beautiful eyes that she had inherited from her father. She had also inherited his wide, easy smile and mischievous sense of humor.

Lauren had bequeathed her daughter a set of high cheekbones, a heart-shaped face, and a delicate chin. Rachel's hair was a hybrid. She had gotten her father's unruly waves, and the deep midnight hue had come from her mother. Lauren was pretty sure her daughter had inherited her stubborn streak from both sides of the family tree.

"Mom," said Rachel again, once the run was under way. "I wish you wouldn't insist on coming with me all the time."

Lauren sighed. "We've been over this, honey. I *want* to. I *like* spending time with you. I'm your *mother*. It's my *job*."

Rachel rolled her eyes. "I hate it when you talk in italics."

Lauren heard the nurse snicker quietly. "Oh, shut up, Debbie. I take enough abuse without adding my daughter's nurse to the mix."

Debbie held up a hand in contrition. "Okay, okay. But you do have a tendency to *emphasize* certain words—when it *suits* your *purpose*."

Now Rachel was giggling. Lauren couldn't take the ribbing seriously, especially if it made her daughter smile. She chewed on her tongue to keep from spewing an insult that would no doubt get her into even more trouble.

Rachel controlled her laughter. "I know you're my mother. God knows you won't let me forget."

Lauren opened her mouth to respond, but Rachel ignored her and continued blithely on, "But I'm nineteen! I'm an adult. I can handle this on my own. Honest. You can't hold my hand forever, Mom."

Lauren sighed. She took a moment to watch the blood being pumped out of her daughter's arm, watched it disappear into the mystical maze of machinery that cleansed her daughter's blood of toxins and waste. She watched as it was pumped back into Rachel's body, only to start the process all over again. Three times a week, for four hours at a time, her daughter sat in that damn chair and trusted her life to a hunk of metal and plastic.

How could she explain such things to her daughter? How could anyone who didn't have a child of their own understand? In many ways, Rachel was grown. She had faced things in her brief time on Earth that most people didn't face in a lifetime. But that was all the more reason for her parents to feel the need to protect and nurture her. How could they let her strike out on her own when her life was so fragile? Or maybe it was selfish. Maybe they needed to spend time with her, because for so long they had lived with the fear that each moment might be her last. Lauren and Tim Nickle also lived with another fear that they would never share with their daughter. Perhaps they would never even share it with each other, even though each knew exactly what the other was thinking.

"I may not be able to hold your hand forever," Lauren conceded. "But I can certainly give it a darn good try." Rachel shook her head in frustration and Lauren picked up her hand. "You're going to be leaving us soon, sweetie. Heading off to college and a whole new world that won't include us. Just allow us this little indulgence for the time being."

"Maybe I'll get a transplant and then we won't have to argue about this anymore at all," said Rachel, her eyes sparkling with hope. Talk of a possible kidney transplant never failed to bring a flush to her cheeks and a curl to her lips.

"There's no *maybe* about it. You're advancing steadily on the list, honey. I'm sure you'll get that call any day."

"I second that motion," cried a familiar voice from the doorway.

Rachel's smile widened. "Kira! Thank God you're here. Mom and I were just running out of things to talk about."

Kira scoffed, "Huh! I don't believe that for a moment."

As Kira settled down into her usual chair, Lauren got the immediate and distinct impression that Kira was uncomfortable. There was a tightness to her shoulders and a set to her lips that screamed *tension.* That was very odd. Lauren had known Kira for four years. They had become almost as close as sisters. They were nothing if not comfortable with each other.

"You two could talk circles around Lucy and Ethel," Kira teased.

"Who?" asked Rachel with a raise of her eyebrows.

Lauren and Kira locked eyes and groaned in unison.

"Oh, God. We're over the hill, Kira."

"Speak for yourself, sweetie." Kira threw back her shoulders and ran long, dexterous fingers through her brilliant red hair. "I've still got ten years on you. I'm practically a baby."

"Isn't thirty-five middle age?" asked Rachel with the tactlessness of youth.

Kira clutched at her gut. "Oh, you are a cruel wench."

Rachel giggled. "Are you up for Scrabble? I want to play in French today."

Kira didn't answer, and Lauren could swear she was squirming in her seat. "What's wrong with you?" laughed Lauren. "Spill it before you wear a hole in your jeans."

Kira twirled her ring around her finger. "Uh," she muttered at last. "Can I take a rain check? I—uh—"

Rachel perked up. "You got a date?"

Kira's shoulders sagged. "Why is everybody trying to fix me up? Tim tried to sucker me into a blind date with a friend of his last week. It's a conspiracy!"

Lauren kept her mouth shut. She didn't want to admit to Kira that she was the one who had suggested the match to her husband. However, Tim had been just as disappointed as she was when Kira adamantly refused the date.

"Well?" persisted Rachel. "Do you?"

"No. It's—it's just that I should really take Cujo for a walk."

Lauren scoffed. "Don't give me that! A walk around the kitchen exhausts him. If you need a break just say so. Heaven knows you deserve it."

"You know me so well," sighed her friend. "But I promise we'll play next time." Kira stood and planted a kiss on Rachel's forehead. "But you can forget the French idea. You think I'm stupid? I can hold my own in downtown Montreal, but ask me to spell *au revoir* and I melt like Camembert in the sun."

"Chicken," taunted the teenager.

Kira flashed her a sample of pink tongue before heading for the door. "You watch your mouth, young lady. I don't care if you are nineteen, I can still paddle your behind."

"Just try it!"

"Call me if you want a cup of tea tonight," called Lauren.

Kira smiled warmly. "Definitely. But right now I need a nice long walk along the canal."

"With Cujo?"

"Yeah, all warm and snuggled in a backpack." She waved and was gone.

Rachel pondered the empty doorway. "It's too bad she never had any kids. She would have been a great mom."

"Yes," said Lauren thoughtfully. "I think you're right. It's a shame no man ever snapped her up."

"So, Scrabble for two?"

"You got it. But I think we should play in Latin."

"*Latin*?"

Chapter Three

ꟾ

Kira stepped off the paved walkway that ran the length of the Rideau Canal. She toed off her shoes and wallowed in the long lush grass that was already laden with dew. Cujo yapped at a scull that glided past them. Its occupant rowed expertly, barely leaving a ripple in his wake.

"Shhh." She reached back and patted the tiny pecan-colored head that poked out of the top of her specially designed knapsack. Momentarily mollified, Cujo licked at her fingers, which were still sugary from the beaver tail pastry she had decided to treat herself to at the halfway point of her trek.

It was nine o'clock, but the sky still clung to a hint of gray. In two weeks they would hit the solstice and summer would officially be here.

This city was unparalleled for the distractions it offered its residents and tourists. In the summer, the canal was a popular venue for rowers and tour boats. Its banks boasted a steady stream of strolling lovers and fitness buffs. Each Sunday morning two of the main city streets were closed off to allow for bikers and joggers. There were carriage rides and rickshaws, museums and restaurants, galleries and exhibits, parks and mansions. In the summer, Ottawa was a lush and eclectic mix with something to suit every taste.

It was only surpassed by Ottawa in the winter. Despite the bitter cold and biting winds that descended upon the Ottawa region, Winterlude drew tourists and artists by the thousands. Stunning ice and snow sculptures sparkled in the clear, starlit nights. Skaters packed the canal—the longest stretch of groomed ice in the world. Hot chocolate and Beaver

Tails were served along the length of the waterway, warming the hands and tummies of young and old.

Kira had grown up in Ottawa. She didn't know what had ever possessed her to leave it, even if it had been but briefly.

She continued her walk toward home. The only thing that marred the experience was the yellow police tape that circled one particularly lavish Tudor-style home along her route. The latest murder.

Then she wondered if *murder* was technically correct. The latest victim of the Rideau Rapist had been alive when she was found. She had been ravaged and beaten, and was technically alive. A poorly placed bullet to the brain had failed to kill her immediately. It had rendered her comatose, and tests had eventually revealed that she was brain-dead. A day later the machines had been turned off and her suffering had ended.

Kira shivered. She suddenly had the irrational feeling that she was being watched. What if the rapist regularly surveyed the Canal walkers and joggers looking for potential victims?

But then she shook her head in self-deprecation. She hardly fit the profile of the rich young women who seemed to be his preferred targets. The police were saying very little, but Kira suspected robbery was a partial motive for the assailant.

Then she scolded herself and dragged her mind away from such macabre topics. She hadn't come out here to scare herself silly. She had come out to relax and reflect and gaze at the heavens.

She allowed her eyes to drift upward as she stood on her front step and fumbled in her pocket for the key. The sky had shifted to a deep midnight blue dappled by a legion of dazzling jewels. She let the beauty and serenity of it seep into her soul, but the mood couldn't last.

The moment she stuck her key into the lock Cujo began yapping in excitement. Kira glanced next door expecting to see a flicker of movement. But it seemed that none of the Nickle family had yet arrived home. Tim often worked late to make up for the time he spent with Rachel at the hospital, and Lauren and Rachel had likely stopped for ice cream or a latté on their way home.

Cujo hadn't let up. "Quiet, Cujo!" she scolded as she stepped through the door. She slipped off the knapsack and allowed the animal to scuttle across the entryway floor, his nails clicking against the terra-cotta tiles. He headed immediately for his food dish and finally shut up as he munched and scattered crumbs over the floor.

She tossed the sack in the closet and strolled to the refrigerator. Maybe she'd make herself a sandwich for once. The walk had actually given her an appetite. Her head deeply ensconced in the maze of pickle jars and leftovers, she was annoyed when Cujo began another round of yapping.

"What now?" She grabbed the ham and straightened up. "You know Cujo, I'm seriously considering having your voice box—"

An arm wrapped around her waist and a hand clamped across her mouth.

For just a moment, her breathing caught and terror gripped her insides. But that was short-lived. Within seconds, adrenaline and old reflexes kicked in.

Aiming for the wall behind her, her elbow blasted back into her attacker's ribs. Simultaneously she raised her foot, thankfully shod once again in her heavy cross-trainers, and drove it back into his kneecap before raking cruelly down his shin.

He grunted and loosened his hold as she twisted out of his arms. Acting purely on instinct, she reached for the coffee can beside the sink. His hand latched onto her shirt and he tried to drag her back, but she managed to slip off the lid and reach inside. Her sweaty palm latched around the butt, and she just managed to get a firm grip as he hauled her back against him.

Their eyes met as she shoved the Glock firmly against his crotch. She clicked off the safety and hissed, "Let go of me or I'll blow your dick off."

Then the unbelievable happened. He laughed. The skin around a pair of jade green eyes crinkled in amusement.

She blinked. "Alec?"

"I'm flattered you remember." He had not yet let go.

She set her jaw. "Didn't you hear me? Let go."

He ran a finger along her jaw. "You couldn't really hurt me."

"Wanna bet?" She shoved the gun a little further down. "I may be out of practice but I think even I could manage to hit that *tiny* target at this close range."

Reluctantly he let go and stepped back, his eyes still laughing at her. "Do you really hate me so much?" he said with that annoyingly suave French accent of his.

"More. Now what the hell are you doing breaking into my house and sneaking up on me like that?"

"I heard about the rapist. I was worried. I wanted to see if you could still take care of yourself." He bent down and inspected Cujo as he munched on his food and growled at the threat to his dinner. "Your choice of guard dog leaves something to be desired."

She flipped the safety back on and deposited the weapon in the canister. She turned to the sink and ran warm water over her hands—more to hide the fact that they were shaking, than to clean them. "Well, as you can see, I don't need a guard dog. I'm perfectly capable of taking care of myself. So you can go now. Go back to your life of women and parties and international intrigue."

He didn't respond, merely studied her as he leaned back against the counter and rubbed absently at the rib she had bruised.

She grabbed a towel and dried her hands, annoyed that those verdant eyes of his were following her every move with practiced precision.

Her hands now dry, she leaned back against the counter opposite him and stuffed her hands in her jeans pockets, silently communicating her total disdain for his presence. They had always been very good at silent communication. Unfortunately they had been lousy at the verbal kind.

In a cruel mimicry of her actions, he stuffed his hands into the deep pockets of his pleated linen slacks. It was cruel of him to look so fit and dapper. From the tailored cut of his trousers that hugged a trim waist to the broad shoulders that strained at the green silk of his Armani shirt—from the top of his tousled auburn head to the tips of his expensive Italian loafers, he just screamed out *Look how well I've done without you!*

They had faced off like boxers in a ring.

"Why are you still here?" she taunted.

"I've missed you."

"Huh! I've been watching the tabloids and reading *People*. You've been working nonstop. *Protecting* one glamorous debutante after another. One of them even had ties to the royals, from what I gather. You've been attending balls, sipping champagne like Kool-Aid, hobnobbing with the rich and famous, and no doubt sleeping with your share. How could you possibly have had time to miss me?"

"You're far more interesting than any of those spoiled little rich girls."

If his eyes weren't so serious she would have assumed he was joking. "Really?" She pulled her hands from her pockets and crossed them over her stomach in an unconscious attempt to shield herself. "Why the sudden interest now? You certainly didn't seem to find me that interesting seven years ago."

His jaw tightened and his eyes darkened. She had hit her mark.

When he didn't respond she continued to drive the knife home. "Besides, that's no way to talk about your gravy train. Isn't that looking a gift horse in the mouth? Biting the hand that feeds you? Cutting off your nose to spite your face? You are obviously doing quite well to afford a thousand-dollar outfit just to break in on an old girlfriend. I'm sure your employers are to thank for your success."

"True," he conceded, his expression once more controlled. *The Ice Man*. He rarely lost control. Rarely showed more than a flicker of emotion, and when he did he usually covered it with a joke or off the cuff witticism. Full-fledged rage for Alec Frechette consisted of clenched fists and a tic at the corner of his mouth. He laughed easily, but the chuckles were carefully measured. And she had never seen tears in his eyes—except once.

"Financially I'm quite secure," he continued. "And I have them to thank. But I'm tired of that scene."

"So I'm your latest diversion?" Unconsciously she began to twirl the one lone ring that she always wore around her right ring finger.

"You were always more than a diversion, Kira. You know that." He glanced at her hands. "You still wear my ring."

She looked at her hands as if seeing them for the first time. "Yes. Believe it or not, it still means something to me." Alec had given her the princess-cut emerald on the one-year anniversary of their first date. He had said it was supposed to remind her of the color of his eyes—that he was always watching out for her, always with her. It was a beautiful ring but she still found it odd that, even after all these years, she couldn't bring herself to take it off. She tore her eyes away from the shimmering green fire on her finger. "But that doesn't give you the right to burst in on me like this."

"Maybe not. But I still have to keep the promise that came along with that thing." He looked her up and down. "For starters, I think you've lost weight. You apparently need me to cook for you again." He moved toward the refrigerator.

She groaned in exasperation. "What do I have to do to get rid of you? You can't just waltz in here after seven years and pick up where you left off."

He rummaged through the assortment of wilted lettuce and moldy cheese. "This is hardly where we left off."

That was true enough.

"Whatever. But regardless of that, I don't want you here. Besides, I have nothing for you to cook with. Even my eggs are probably stale…"

Her voice trailed off when he magically withdrew a bag of tomatoes, fresh onions and garlic, chicken breasts, a wedge of Brie and a bottle of wine.

"What the…"

"I did a little shopping before I arrived."

"You were already in the house when I got here?" she sputtered. He was just as arrogant and inconsiderate as ever.

He just shrugged and pulled a cleaver out of her knife block. "I knew I'd find your cupboards bare. You never could cook worth a damn."

"Things have changed since you left."

He merely raised his eyebrows and glanced at her fridge. *"Je pense que non."*

"I don't care what you think, and you'll get your shirt all dirty." She was grasping at straws.

"Then I guess I'll have to take it off." He set down the cleaver and reached for the top button.

In a heartbeat, she had crossed to him and closed her hands over his. "Don't you dare," she breathed.

His hands stilled. In fact, the whole room seemed to descend into suspended animation. Even Cujo was quiet.

Kira knew instantly that it had been a mistake. She should have just let him remove his shirt. She could easily have ignored a set of flexing pecs and sculpted abs. But touching him was another matter. It always had been.

Even a contact as innocuous as her hand on his had the power to reduce her to ash. She could try to blame the fact that she hadn't had a serious relationship since he had left. In fact, it had probably been a year since she had been thoroughly kissed. But in all fairness she had to admit that that wasn't it at all. Well, maybe part of it. But certainly not all.

It wasn't just the physical contact of their skin, or the luminescence in his eyes. It was all the history and turmoil that went with it. It was both love and hate, trust and betrayal, joy and grief. It was everything that bound them together but had driven them apart.

Maybe most of all it was a shared guilt neither of them could face. Not that any of the reasons mattered at that particular moment.

She couldn't seem to stop herself from running her fingers delicately over the strong, familiar lines of his knuckles and the pulsing veins on the back of his hand. She felt him shiver as she caressed the muscles of his forearm. His biceps tightened beneath her palm.

Strength. That was what she had loved about him. Perhaps it had been the naïveté of youth that had led her to read his stoicism as strength. She had needed someone strong and solid. She had needed someone to help her keep her perspective, keep her distance. She had always been so vulnerable to the worries and trials of those around her. She felt their pain as if it were her own. She had needed Alec to keep her sane, to help her keep her distance, to keep her from being sucked into a vortex of emotion.

But when she had needed his strength the most, he had abandoned her. Or perhaps they had abandoned each other.

He closed his eyes when her fingers reached his shoulders. And suddenly all the walls crumbled. "Alec," she whispered, "why did you leave?"

She could feel the vibrations as his heart thudded against his chest and his muscles hummed with tension. "You know why."

"No." She cupped his jaw in delicate fingers. "No, I don't. I needed you and you left me."

His eyes opened. He looked at her and his gaze held more sorrow than that of an orphan without family or friend, or a place to call home. It was a peek at his soul that she had never glimpsed before. "You never needed me, Kira. God knows I wanted you to…but you never did."

He stepped away and the wall was back up, the ice fortress had crystallized once again. He glanced at the food on the counter. "On second thought I'll have to take a raincheck on dinner. But I promise to cook for you in a couple of days." With every phrase he took another step back, another step toward the door. "I'm back to stay this time. I got a position with the Governor General's office." His hand was on the doorknob. "Sorry if I scared you. I promise I'll make it up to you. My chicken *primavera* is second to none." He stepped outside. "I'll call you." And he was gone.

If Kira didn't know better she could have sworn he was running away. And what the heck had he meant by that cryptic phrase? Of course she had needed him. He was the one who had deserted her. But why had he looked so pained at that moment? Had he been sincere? Or was he just trying to hurt her…again?

And he was working for the Governor General? Mansion security? That was pretty tame, considering what he was used to. The Governor General was an aging political appointee with no real power and few enemies. He didn't even throw decent parties. So why would Alec work for him when he could have probably gotten a position working for the Prime Minister himself?

One thing was certain, Alec Frechette was just as much a puzzle as ever. And she hated to admit it, but if he hadn't run off she had a feeling she would have made love to him right there on the kitchen floor.

Some things never changed.

* * * * *

Alec walked.

Thankful that he had decided to take a cab to Kira's, he walked until he reached the canal. He hit the footpath and walked a little faster. The evening was cool but sweat glazed his face. His silk shirt began to stick to his chest, so he ripped it off and cast it in the water. The air felt good against his bare skin.

Why had she touched him like that? It was the same nightmare all over again. The beginning of the same cruel cycle that had tormented him so many years ago.

And why had he gone there in the first place? But that was a stupid question. He knew perfectly well why.

His fists clenched and his blood pumped. He found himself walking faster, as if he were trying to outrun something, he just couldn't say what. Maybe it was Kira. Maybe it was the past. Maybe it was himself.

He broke into a run. His feet pounded the pavement in a steadily increasing tempo. The exertion and the rush of adrenaline as his muscles were pushed to their limits thrust everything else from his mind. He had always been good at ignoring his feelings. After years of practice, he had it down to a science. Feelings were dangerous things, they reeked of vulnerability and weakness.

To put it succinctly, they were scary as hell…and Alec didn't like to be afraid. He liked to be in control. He liked to *act*, and have his actions make a difference. Except that, ever since leaving Kira, he hadn't *acted* at all. He had drifted through life, barely making a ripple in the lives of those around him. For a time he had thought that was exactly what he wanted. Lately he wasn't so sure.

Exhausted, he flopped down in a patch of lush grass. He lay back and savored the feeling of cool dew against hot, aching muscles.

He looked up at the stars winking down at him mischievously. He spotted the Big Dipper and Orion's belt. Involuntarily his eyes followed the familiar lines of the constellations until they settled on one particularly bright star. It twinkled and sparkled, teasing him with its rare and irrepressible beauty, taunting him with its false promise of wishes fulfilled and joys untold.

And a single tear slid down his cheek.

Chapter Four

ȣ

Alec scanned the titles on the assortment of leather-bound tomes. The oak shelves in this elaborate library overflowed with classics by Mark Twain, Emily Brontë, Margaret Atwood and their peers. Understated wealth and elegance hung in the air like the subtle perfume of apple blossoms in the spring. This room was truly one of the jewels of the Governor General's mansion.

A set of windows spanned the far wall, the glass stretching to the full height of the twelve-foot ceilings. From here he had an unhindered view of the expansive grounds and lush gardens. In the distance, Alec thought he heard the chiming of the Peace Tower clock on Parliament Hill.

He picked out a book at random and flipped idly through the pages. His fidgeting didn't stem from nervousness so much as annoyance. He wasn't accustomed to being kept waiting. He was here to begin his assignment and he wanted to get to it. He needed something else to focus on—something to occupy his time and keep him from dwelling on the images and emotions that his visit with Kira had dredged up. He would have to face all that sooner or later, but honestly he favored later. Much later.

Already bored, he stuffed the book back into its niche. His eyes roved to the portrait that hung behind the substantial desk, crafted of Canadian bird's-eye maple. Jonathan Cromwell, the latest in a long line of British royal emissaries to the Canadian Parliament, stared out at him with eagle eyes and a brittle smile.

Alec had accepted the position graciously because it had suited his purpose. But he secretly scoffed at the absurdity of the office. The Governor General was technically the British monarch's representative in Canada. And his or her approval was needed on every bill that was passed into Canadian law. But the elaborate expense of keeping up the office and the mansion and the salary of the figurehead was an exercise in futility. It had been close to a hundred years since the Governor General's office had held any significant power. It had been close to a hundred years since the office was even held by a British subject. All appointees to this office were full-blooded Canadians. And every one of them stamped approval on anything set before him because, if he didn't, he would have to face some very irate and powerful politicians—politicians who had put him in this mansion in the first place.

But Canada cherished its ties with Britain, and Alec supposed this was a small price to pay, even for an obsolete monument to an outdated Canadian tradition.

At last the carved oak doors swung open and a small party of men dressed in finely tailored suits and silk ties entered the library. Alec recognized Cromwell instantly, but the other two were strangers to him. He had accepted this position solely on the basis of correspondence, references and his reputation, and therefore had not yet met any of the Governor General's staff.

Cromwell approached him without hesitation, and extended a gnarled hand. "Monsieur Frechette?"

Alec clasped the older man's hand and shook it firmly. The grip that greeted him was warm and solid. "Mr. Cromwell," he responded. "It's an honor."

To Alec's astonishment, Jonathan Cromwell laughed. "Don't bullshit me, Frechette." He motioned Alec to follow him toward the desk. He indicated an overstuffed leather chair, which Alec settled himself into as Cromwell rounded the desk and occupied the plush leather recliner opposite him.

"I wasn't lying, sir," said Alec with some puzzlement. "I've heard—"

"I'm sure you've heard that I'm a doddering old fool who can barely stay awake through dinner. You've probably also heard that I'm Chretien's lapdog, and will do whatever I'm told so long as it keeps me in this plush mansion and puts Newfoundland rock lobster on my plate."

Alec chewed on the inside of his cheek to keep from smiling. "I didn't believe a word of it, sir."

"Well, you should have."

Alec raised his eyebrows.

"I absolutely adore Newfoundland lobster." Cromwell smiled broadly, his brown eyes dancing despite the wrinkles and bags. "However, the rest of it is bullshit, pure and simple."

"Apparently."

Cromwell snorted and leaned back in his chair and studied his new employee. His probing stare examined Alec thoroughly—scanning him from head to toe and back again. Alec wondered if this was how those poor lobsters felt, swimming around in their tank, as their potential murderers hovered beyond the glass scrutinizing their next victim. He shifted slightly in his seat.

Finally Cromwell spoke. "I like you, Frechette."

"Gee, I like you too, sir."

Cromwell grinned. "I've read the tabloids and seen the pictures. I didn't believe a word of it."

"Well, you should have."

"Good. I'm glad you didn't deny it."

"Was that some sort of test?" Alec's fascination with Cromwell's odd approach was rapidly turning to confusion.

"Of sorts. I'm taking a chance on you, young man. I know your reputation with the ladies, but you've also got a sterling reputation as a bodyguard and police officer. Along with the tabloid reports I've seen the Interpol file on you, and I had a feeling you were exactly what I needed. I just wanted to see if you were honest enough to admit to your weaknesses."

"And what exactly is it that you need me for, sir?"

While the banter was entertaining and the man intriguing, it was beginning to wear on Alec. The correspondence had been somewhat vague as to exactly what his duties would encompass. He was anxious to get the details and get to work.

"You will be looking out for my granddaughter while she stays here at the mansion for the next six months. After that, I'm sure a more permanent position can be found for you, if you're interested."

Alec blinked. "Granddaughter?"

Cromwell motioned to one of the men standing off to his right. They had blended so completely into the woodwork that Alec had almost forgotten they were there. A thin, mousy man with tortoise shell glasses and a receding chin nodded and quietly left the room.

Cromwell continued, "Yes. Her name is Darcy." He grimaced. "Why her father chose such a hideous name I will never understand. My wife still shudders every time she has to write out a birthday card."

"That name has actually gained popularity in recent years, sir," Alec teased. "We must keep up with the times, mustn't we?"

Cromwell scowled. "You have absolutely no respect for this office, do you, Frechette?"

"None, sir." But Alec allowed a small grin to creep across his face. "But I'm gaining a measure of respect for you."

"Good. That's good to hear," said Cromwell with approval. "Because I'm going to be counting on you. Darcy is staying with us temporarily because she had a small brush with disaster while attending university, and has come here to recuperate. However, the recent rash of murders has us all very concerned, especially since she would seem to fit the profile quite neatly."

"I'll take very good care of her."

Now Cromwell pointed an arthritic finger at him. "You damn well better. I'm paying top dollar and I expect value for my money." He dropped his hand and fixed Alec with a steely stare. "However, if I catch the slightest whiff of impropriety with my *very young* granddaughter, rest assured, Frechette, I will personally cut off your balls with a butter knife and feed them to you through your nose."

Alec recovered quickly from the unexpected threat. "I don't doubt it for a minute." And it was the truth. Cromwell was tilting on the far side of seventy, but there was an intensity and energy about him that many men half his age lacked.

"That said, however," grinned his boss. "Tell me honestly…"

Alec frowned. "Sir?"

"Are Sylvie Pierrot's boobs silicone or the real McCoy?"

Alec couldn't contain his laughter. He finally managed to squeak out, "One hundred percent saline, sir. I saw the bill myself."

Their male bonding ritual was interrupted when the heavy oak door behind them swung open, and Alec heard the click of chunky heels against the hardwood floor. He stood and turned to greet his new charge.

She was, indeed, young. He wondered if she had even hit the landmark twenty-one. She was tall, however, and carried herself with the bearing of one who is sure of herself and her station in life. The tight jeans and baggy T-shirt couldn't mask her regal air, nor could they hide the pleasing, if somewhat ample, curves of her figure. A swathe of blond hair was fastened loosely at the nape of her neck, and a pair of small wire-frame eyeglasses magnified the thoughtful blue depths that studied him from head to toe.

Cromwell had stood and rounded the desk. He kissed his granddaughter's cheek possessively. "Darcy, I'd like you to meet your new built-in security system. This is Alec—"

"Frechette," she finished for him as she extended her hand. "I've seen your picture in the tabloids. Does associating with you automatically lead to one's name being dragged through the mud?"

Alec was impressed with how confident and well-spoken she was. But, considering her lineage, maybe he shouldn't be surprised. He took her hand and brushed his lips across her knuckles in his finest rendition of the traditional European greeting. He allowed her hand to linger in his for just a moment as he spoke to her across her knuckles. "I beg to remind you that I am rarely the focus of such attention. I'm merely along for the ride." He relinquished her hand. "I actually try to fade into the woodwork whenever possible."

She snorted. "If you can fade into woodwork, Monsieur Frechette, then I could double for Demi Moore."

"Never say never," teased Alec. "Demi is vastly overrated." He was pleased to see that his greeting had brought a faint blush of color to her cheeks.

Cromwell had been watching the exchange with amusement, but now he interrupted with details of the business at hand. "Darcy, you are to defer to Monsieur Frechette's judgment in all matters of security. He won't be available twenty-four hours a day, but he is to be consulted about any and all outings and activities."

Darcy addressed herself to Alec. "Just as I suspected—*bodyguard* is a euphemism for *chaperone*."

Cromwell tsked. "You know there's a dangerous homicidal rapist on the loose. This is a reasonable precaution."

"How do you know *he's* not the one the police are looking for?" She directed her words at her grandfather, but her half-lidded gaze continued to rest on Alec. "He looks rather *dangerous* to me."

"Oh, Darcy," sighed her grandfather. "Now, believe it or not, I have work to do. So out with the lot of you."

With that quick and unapologetic dismissal, he turned away and headed back to his desk. "Come, Ted," Cromwell approached the tall fair-haired man who had begun riffling through a calendar on Cromwell's desk. "We have to get ready for the Premiere's visit."

The mousy man motioned for Alec and Darcy to precede him out of the room.

"Your grandfather is not what I expected," mused Alec as they walked.

"I'm willing to bet I won't be either." Darcy's eyes barely grazed across his features before turning straight ahead once more.

They crossed the threshold and paused as Mousy Man closed the doors behind them. That done, he turned and spoke for the first time. "Miss Cromwell, why don't you go about your business for the next hour or so while I give Mr. Frechette a tour of the grounds and a rundown of your itinerary?" The rich, deep timbre of his voice surprised Alec, considering the man's rather unremarkable physique.

"All right." She turned to Alec. "I'm having dinner with a *friend* tonight. I'd appreciate it if you would try not to frighten him off. I haven't had a date in months."

"Am I so frightening?"

"I have a feeling, Monsieur Frechette, that you can be just as frightening as you need to be." She whirled away and headed for the broad staircase on the other side of the room.

That was a surprisingly astute observation for one so young. There had even been times when he had managed to frighten himself. But that had never been in his capacity as a bodyguard. That had been something entirely different.

Alec turned around to face the mystery man.

With a raise of his eyebrows above the rims of his glasses, Alec's tour guide queried, "Shall we?" And he motioned Alec to join him.

"I never caught your name," hinted Alec.

"Carl Stuart. I'm afraid Cromwell sometimes forgets the protocols of introducing his underlings." He didn't even bother with a smile to dull the knife-edge sharpness of his words. "The other gentleman was his personal assistant, Ted Bridges. I'm in charge of mansion security, and you will report to me."

"I was under the impression I reported directly to Cromwell."

The muscles in Carl's jaw twitched. "Ultimately, yes. Directly, no."

"I see." They had reached the doors to the ornate ballroom. They stepped inside and Carl closed the doors behind them. Alec frowned. "Is there a party scheduled in the near future?" He failed to see why the ballroom was something that he needed to be acquainted with at this point in time.

"Look, *Mister* Frechette," hissed Carl Stuart, "I may as well tell you right out front that I resent your presence here. Cromwell was attracted to you because you're a well-known name, and he figures the office could use the publicity…questionable though it may be."

"But you think you could handle things," observed Alec coolly.

"Of course I could. Darcy is a spoiled brat who needs a good, sound spanking a hell of a lot more than she needs a bodyguard. And I resent the intrusion on my domain."

"I see." Alec kept his tone deceptively even.

"I really doubt that you do. You've got your duties, and I'm powerless to do anything about that, but if you so much as raise an inappropriate eyebrow, or step on my toes in any way, rest assured you will live to regret it."

Alec nodded thoughtfully. "Understood. However, I feel the need to point out to you, Mister Stuart, that if you step on my toes, or in any way interfere with my mandate, rest assured you *will not* live to regret it." He smiled cheerfully. "Now, do I get my tour, or not?"

* * * * *

"You seem awfully distracted today, Kira."

"Hmm?" She looked up from the blood work results she had been studying.

Mike waved his hand in front of her face. "Hello? I said you seem distracted. Is everything okay?"

"Yes, yes, of course. I—I just didn't get enough sleep last night."

"Mm." Mike obviously wasn't convinced.

"I can't be *on* all the time, you know. I have a right to my off days." She glanced back at the computer screen, willing the colorful numbers and letters to make sense to her befuddled brain.

"It's a man, isn't it?"

Kira's head swiveled around to face him. "What?"

Mike tapped his chin and gazed at the ceiling. "Let me see...you completely forgot to send the samples down to the lab this morning. You forgot all about Mrs. Rock's special request to have *Tarzan* available for her son to watch during his treatment. And this is the third time today I've caught you with that faraway look in your eyes." Mike focused on her and a frown clouded his face. "In my experience, there's only one thing that can put such a kink in a woman's day."

"Well, I certainly defer to your superior knowledge of the female psyche," commented Kira wryly.

Mike hitched his hip up on the desk beside her. "Come on, Kira. Something's obviously bothering you. I like to keep abreast of my staff's personal lives, you know. I want to be supportive."

"You don't mind a woman crying on your shoulder?"

"No, not at all. It makes me feel very needed and useful." To Kira's amazement, he kept a straight face.

She raised her eyebrows. "I bet you even rub her back and talk in soothing tones."

"If it seems appropriate."

"Possibly press a kiss to a troubled temple?"

The mischief danced in Mike's eyes. "Possibly."

"A warm embrace, perhaps?"

Mike held up his hands in protest. "Please stop. You're getting me all hot."

Kira returned her attention to the computer screen. "Maybe you should take a cold shower. I can look after things here."

"Nice try, but I'm too smart for you."

"Smart?"

"You're trying to change the subject, but I'm not biting. Now what's wrong?"

Kira sighed. Mike was nothing if not tenacious. "It's really none of your business. I'm just fine."

"You're not fine." Mike's jaw clenched. "Dammit, Kira, why won't you lean on somebody for a change? You don't always have to be the strong one, the one everybody turns to when they have a crisis. You're allowed to have your own crises, for God's sake. You're allowed to need other people. Let your friends help you for once in your life."

Kira's mouth had dropped open at his tirade. "Is that really how you see me? As some pathetic Florence Nightingale wanna-be?"

Mike's shoulders slumped. "That's not what I meant, and you know it."

Kira rubbed at her temples. Mike was absolutely right, of course. She hadn't been lying about not getting enough sleep the night before, but it had hardly been a typical case of insomnia or too much caffeine before bed. Alec's return had shaken her more profoundly than she liked to admit. For years she had told herself repeatedly that she was better off without him. They were too different. They had nothing in common and Alec's new career choice had merely underscored their incompatibility.

And yet she had found herself habitually scanning the tabloid headlines for any mention of his jet-setting associates. Alec's name rarely made it to the bold-face type, but he was invariably on the arm of the subject of some outrageous gossip. The women were always beautiful and glamorous and filthy rich. Everything she was not. Thank God.

But if his tastes in women had changed so drastically—if he got his kicks by playing hero and bedmate to wealthy, paranoid women while raking in a six-figure salary and guzzling designer wine, why had he bothered coming back? And why had he offered to cook her dinner?

And why did she care?

Mike was still studying her. She looked at him and found these words tumbling past her lips, "Okay, Mike. Why not?"

"Huh? I didn't ask a question, did I?"

"How about dinner tonight?"

He frowned. "You're on the rebound, aren't you?"

"Is that a no?"

The frown transformed into that famous *"You want to sleep with me, don't you?"* grin. "No, merely an observation. There's a great new Italian place down in the Byward. I heard a bunch of nurses talking about it. Pick you up at seven?"

She nodded and forced herself to smile warmly.

Mike raised his index finger and added, "But there's one condition."

"Oh?"

"Cujo eats at home."

Chapter Five

ꙮ

Alec straightened the crease in his trousers and crossed his legs. His foot bobbed as his gaze swept over the rack of outrageously priced cocktail dresses. His practiced eye had already discerned that nothing on that rack would be to *his* taste. He preferred simpler, less trendy fashions. However, judging from the length of time Darcy spent lingering over each piece, she was very close to choosing one or two for a final appraisal in the spacious change rooms at the back of the boutique.

He stifled a yawn. He had spent far too much time in fashion boutiques and lingerie stores in the past seven years. He had browsed through so many shoe stores and leather shops that he had completely lost his taste for the scent of calfskin. He had been faced with too many fashionably light lunches that consisted of wafer-thin sandwiches and ridiculously expensive tap water. He had lost count of the number of times he had gorged on burgers and fries after a day of starving himself alongside his anorexic charge.

Darcy held a dress against herself and gazed into a full-length mirror. At least Darcy ate like a human being. That was one point in her favor.

She turned back to the rack and continued pawing through the silk and rayon creations, and Alec mused that the price tag on some of those dresses equaled the national debt of any one of several small African countries.

He glanced at his watch and was stifling another yawn of boredom when an anxious voice caught his attention.

"But the price tag said fifty dollars last week!" A young girl in a miniskirt and thick-soled shoes stood at the cash counter. She appeared to be close to tears.

The clerk behind the counter barely acknowledged the young customer whose age Alec estimated to be around twelve or thirteen.

"The handbag sale was last month," said the clerk absently. "The end of the month was two days ago. The sale is over."

"But..." the girl gazed longingly at a rack of purses that hung far out of reach behind the clerk, "but I've only got fifty-five dollars. I saved for a whole month!"

"So, save for another month." The young woman with the heavy mascara and dark brown lipstick seemed to be losing patience with this no-commission customer. Jet-black hair pulled back off her face and tied in a tight knot at the back of her head exaggerated the severe look, and honestly made her resemble something out of a teen horror flick.

"But..." the girl sniffled, "but my mom's birthday is *tomorrow*!"

"Listen, little girl." The sales clerk gazed at her with contempt. "I've got other *paying* customers. I don't have time—"

"Excuse me."

"What!" Those Morticia Addams eyes swiveled in Alec's direction.

He leaned against the counter and tossed the girl a reassuring smile before focusing his attention on the clerk. "Are you *sure* that sale wasn't extended a couple more days? I could have sworn the sign out front still advertised a sale on handbags."

The clerk's eyes flitted over his face, down his torso and back again before she deemed him worthy of a response. "I guess I forgot to take it down. But the sale *did* finish two days ago. The dates are on the sign."

"I'd say that sounds a little like false advertising," said Alec through a fractious smile.

"Look, honey, are you her dad or something? Because if you're not, I just don't see what—"

"Look, *sweetcakes,*" Alec leaned a little further over the counter, "if you would just *listen* for once in your life, you would hear what I am *saying* to you."

The clerk raised one eyebrow and Alec glanced at the young girl to reassure himself that she hadn't wandered off. But she stood, still as a statue, her eyes riveted to him and her mouth just slightly agape.

He turned back to the clerk. "I think that if you were to double check your policies you would see that as long as a sign is posted then you are bound to honor the terms on the advertisement." He covertly slipped a hand inside his jacket and pulled his wallet out just far enough for the clerk to identify what he was doing. "Surely this young lady who is trying so hard to give her mother a nice birthday present deserves such simple consideration?" He raised his eyebrows and winked meaningfully.

The clerk studied him as the hidden meaning of his words gradually sank through the layers of foundation and eyeliner. A moment later, she nodded understanding. "Oh…uh…yes, of course. I suppose we could do…that." She smiled broadly and turned to the little girl. "Okay. Fifty-five dollars even. Just for you."

The girl beamed as the clerk got out her hook and slipped the coveted handbag off the rack.

Alec felt a dainty hand rest lightly on his arm. He smiled and bent low in order to lessen the distance between them. "Yes?"

She curled in her lips and chewed on them for a moment as she gained the courage to speak. "Thank you, Mr. Frechette."

Alec's eyebrows lifted in surprise. "You know me?"

She nodded. "My mom has your picture in her nightstand."

Alec chuckled. "Are you sure she'll like the bag?"

"Oh yes. She was in here last month and she just loved it but she couldn't afford it. I had some money left over from Christmas and I saved my allowance for a whole month to get it for her."

"I think she's a pretty lucky lady to have a daughter like you."

The girl shrugged, obviously pleased by the compliment. But a moment later Alec was startled to feel a delicate finger on his cheek.

The girl's smile had disappeared. "Why are you crying?"

Damn! *Where the hell did that come from?* "I-uh—"

"A-hem!" said the clerk with a marked lack of tact. "You gonna pay me anytime soon?"

Grateful for the interruption he straightened abruptly and waited while the girl paid her fifty-five dollars. With her mother's gift clutched tightly under her arm, she tossed him a sappy grin as she floated out of the store toward home.

He didn't allow himself to dwell on the cause of his emotional disturbance as he settled up the difference. He tossed in a miserly tip for the clerk's trouble, but he also suggested in no uncertain terms that the sign be taken down immediately. The clerk sneered at him as she strode toward the front of the store.

He turned around and almost bowled over his charge. "Darcy!"

She smiled sweetly. "That was a lovely gesture." Her words were laced with irritation.

He sighed deeply. She had every right to be angry. He had left her alone far too long. Considering his mandate, the lapse was inexcusable. "I'm sorry, Darcy. This was sort of a special case. It won't happen again."

"I hope not. While I'm sure your heart was in the right place, my grandfather is paying you to be *my* guardian angel. Nobody else's. I won't tolerate incompetence, even from the French Connection himself."

Feeling like a family pet faced with a rolled-up newspaper, Alec remained silent.

"Is that clear?"

"Like I said," he said tightly, "it won't happen again." He bent low and whispered in her ear, "But I will not be chastised in public by you or anyone else." He straightened and tossed her his own sweet smile. "Is *that* clear?"

To his surprise, she smiled back—a bright, genuine smile, without derision or contempt. "Yes, actually. I think we understand each other quite well. Now can I please finish my shopping? There's something else I'd like to do before my date tonight, and the clock *is* ticking."

Feeling just slightly off balance by the entire series of events, he followed her back toward the change rooms. But as the afternoon progressed he found his mind being repeatedly drawn back to the little girl with the thick shoes and the big heart. Her mother was a lucky woman indeed. He doubted that she really grasped the depth of her good fortune. Few parents did.

* * * * *

"Did you have to hover like that?" Darcy ascended the sweeping staircase ahead of him. Still clad only in jeans and T-shirt, her presence somehow managed to command the room like Scarlett O'Hara reigning over Tara.

"Definitely. Hovering is quite essential." After his lapse in the first boutique he had stuck to Darcy like white on rice. Three stores and twelve outfits later she had finally decided on a purchase. She had joked that he would have accompanied her into the change rooms if she had let him. He had just smiled, neither denying nor confirming the allegation.

"You sound like my mother," she teased.

"Good. Just think of me as your surrogate mother. I'm here to keep you all safe and cozy."

They had reached the doorway to her suite. She turned around and traced a finger down the elegant line of his dove-gray lapel. "My mother never packed a shoulder holster."

"No? Perhaps she was partial to carrying a .457 Magnum in her purse?"

She chuckled quietly. "Does my grandfather pay you to entertain me as well, Monsieur Frechette?"

Half of his mouth curled up. "Actually he was quite adamant that I *not* entertain you."

She nodded sagely. "You got the butter knife speech."

Alec nodded, trying to hide his disappointment at hearing that he was not the first to be graced with the threat. Here he had thought he was special.

"Gramps loves to throw his weight around. He likes to protect his womenfolk. Sweet and old-fashioned…but annoying." She used her key to open the dead bolt that her father had ordered installed as an added precaution, and was about to step inside when Alec latched onto her wrist. She rolled her eyes in exasperation. "You want to check my suite first?"

"You're finally catching on." He preceded her across the threshold and made a thorough sweep of the sitting room, bedroom and bath. Satisfied that there were no intruders and no cause for alarm, he came out of the bathroom, but drew up short upon taking in the sight of Darcy, casually surveying her latest acquisition, which she had laid out on the bed before her.

Her jeans were already in a heap in the corner, and he watched in fascination as she casually removed her glasses, drew her T-shirt over her head and added it to the pile. That left her clad only in a black lace demi bra and a sheer black thong. Her ample breasts spilled over the lace in luscious curves and the sheer fabric of the underwear barely concealed the coveted wedge of flesh between her thighs.

He licked dry lips. "I can wait in the sitting room while you get dressed."

She carelessly unsnapped the front clasp of her bra and, still holding the pieces in place, sauntered over to him. "That won't be necessary."

He held his ground, the words of her grandfather ringing in his head, vying futilely for his attention against the flagrant display of feminine flesh being flaunted before him. She stood mere inches from him.

"I like a man who doesn't let people walk all over him. And that display with the little girl was very endearing." She released her hold on the bra and allowed it to fall from her shoulders, revealing taut flesh and hard nipples. "I like you, Alec. You're even more exciting than I expected."

He heard her but the words barely registered as he watched her sensuous movements. With provocative expertise, she touched the hollow of her throat and traced elegant fingers down her chest, finally swirling around her own breast with hypnotic precision.

He swallowed as she took his hand and covered her breast with it. Electricity sizzled through his fingers, up his arm, and right down to his groin. "You have a date in less than an hour," he whispered.

"This won't take long." Her hand covered his erection through his trousers.

He moaned involuntarily. "But your grandfather—"

"Will never know."

She kneaded him firmly, and he found his other hand reaching beneath the tissue-thin fabric between her thighs.

Already silky wet, she rubbed herself against his fingers. "God, you're incredible. I've wanted you ever since I was sixteen and I saw your picture in *The Enquirer*." Her hands had already loosened his tie and undone half his shirt buttons.

His mouth found her throat and he mumbled, "I really shouldn't do this."

"But you will anyway. You always do."

She knew him better than he would have believed possible.

Darcy and he shared nothing. Intellectually and emotionally, they had little in common. She was too young for him, and far too wrapped up in herself. He felt nothing for her beyond professional responsibility and a tenuous respect. He had been warned explicitly to avoid this very situation. He was risking his job and his self-respect. But he would go through with it nevertheless.

He could no more deny his nature than a lion could turn vegetarian. Why bother to even try? He was a shallow, moneygrubbing, hunk of male flesh for hire. The fact that he carried a gun merely validated his social position. Perhaps Sylvie was right after all. Perhaps he was little more than a "gold-plated gigolo". He shrugged mentally. What did it matter? He had nothing else in his future, and he had no desire to dwell on the past. He may as well enjoy the present.

"Condom?" he asked, assuming she would have one handy. He was hardly planning on such a tryst.

"I'm on the Pill."

That wasn't why he had asked. He merely looked at her and arched one expressive eyebrow.

"Under the pillow," she said with an impatient sigh.

He nodded understanding even as her fingers threaded through his hair.

"You're not what I expected," he observed as his lips moved down to her breast and she arched against him, drawing him toward the bed.

His trousers were already open and they dropped to his ankles as he fell on top of her across the wide expanse of imported linen.

"I told you so," she moaned as he ripped away the thong and her hand closed around his cock. "I told you so."

Engrossed in their mutual gratification, neither of them noticed the soft click as the bedroom door was pulled quietly closed from the outside. Neither did they hear the softly retreating footsteps from the sitting room beyond, or the click as the dead bolt was turned back into place.

His eyes fierce and his expression smug, the intruder dropped the master key back into his pocket and walked away.

Chapter Six

ꟾ

Kira stabbed a piece of tomato coated in raspberry vinaigrette. She brought it to her lips but hardly tasted the burst of flavor as her teeth sank into the ripe, juicy morsel. She tuned out the subtle tones of the Mozart sonata that wafted across the crowded restaurant. She hardly noticed the flickering candles and hushed voices of the other patrons. The open-air feel of the Mediterranean-style decor with its marble flooring, high ceilings and thickly upholstered wrought iron chairs held little interest for her. Even the enticing aromas that emanated from the kitchen couldn't break through the fog of introspection.

Mike's voice drifted to her through the haze of memories and questions. "Perhaps after dinner we could go skinny-dipping in the canal. I hear there's a great spot for it downtown, right near the Westin Hotel. I'm sure some of the guests would enjoy the show immensely."

"Mm." She chewed methodically. "Sure, I guess we could do that."

Mike rolled his eyes. "Kira!"

She shuddered slightly as the fog cleared and her mind was wrenched back to the present. "What?"

"You just agreed to swimming naked with me in public," said Mike with a grin.

Kira blinked. "I did?"

"Yes, you did." He cocked an eyebrow. "I think maybe there's something on your mind. Now, will you tell me what's going on?"

She sighed and studied her salad. "You're right, Mike, and I'm sorry. But it's very personal. I don't like talking about it."

"Was I right about it being over a man?"

"Partly. But there's more to it than that." *Oh God! So much more.* To her amazement, she was battling a swell of tears.

Mike tore off a steaming hunk of sourdough bread. "Do I have to pry it out of you with thumb screws?"

Kira examined another piece of tomato as if she were reading her future in the pattern of the seeds. "You've never asked me what I did before I came to work in oncology."

Mike blinked, then seemed to remember the chunk of bread in his mouth and chewed before responding. "No, I guess I haven't. I guess I always assumed you had worked elsewhere in the hospital, and just transferred there. I'm not privy to the hiring process."

"I worked for one year on surgery before moving to oncology. That was my first nursing job."

Mike frowned, obviously doing some mental calculations. "You're what—about thirty-six?"

"I thought you knew better than to ask a woman her age."

He rolled his eyes.

"Yes, I'll be thirty-six next month," she conceded.

"And you've been in oncology for two years..."

She nodded again, allowing him to sort through the information himself.

He frowned again. "Nursing school is three years."

"Four. I got my degree."

"That still leaves a good chunk of your life open for another career. You don't have any kids hanging around, so you weren't a stay-at-home mom." He slathered some butter on another piece of bread. "And I can't see you as a receptionist or on welfare."

"Gee, thanks."

He shrugged. "So, what did you do? Bum around Europe, meet the wrong man, get married and divorced all within the span of seven years?" He chewed thoughtfully. "That's it, isn't it? Your ex-husband showed up and wants you back."

They were interrupted by the waitress's arrival with their entrées. She set down a plate of pillowy gnocchi in front of Mike, and a small serving of chicken *primavera* before Kira. She gazed at her steaming plate of chicken, pasta and sautéed vegetables. "No, I never married. And I've never been to Europe." She skewered a hunk of chicken and nibbled at it tentatively.

"Okay, so what did you do?'

"I worked as a police officer in Montreal."

Mike had just stuffed a fluffy potato dumpling laden with Alfredo sauce into his mouth, but it took a full ten seconds before he had the presence of mind to chew it. He swallowed. "A cop? As in, walking a beat? Doing take-downs and apprehending thugs?"

"Yes. Exactly like that."

"That's…uh…that's fascinating."

She allowed herself an ironic smile. "Not quite fit in with your image of me?"

"Well…"

"Oh, you should have seen me back then," she said as she toyed with her broccoli. A ghost of a smile haunted her lips. "I worked out four times a week. I used to do two hundred sit-ups at a time, and could bench press a hundred and thirty. I was all toned muscle and boundless energy."

Mike was watching her, his fork poised over his plate, completely spellbound by her reminiscing, and likely by the image she was painting for him.

"I practiced on the firing range until I was in the top ten percent of the department for accuracy. I knew I had to work harder than the men to be considered equal with them. But I didn't mind, I thrived on it."

"I've never seen you so animated, Kira. Your eyes are sparkling."

She chuckled. "Really?"

"Yes, really. What else did you love about it?"

"Oh, I liked the excitement of ferreting out the scumbags and the occasional chase or take-down, but I was always best with the victims."

Mike nodded knowingly. "Of course."

"Especially the women—the rape victims, and the women and children who lived with domestic violence. They seemed comfortable with me. I was always able to put them at ease, and I almost always convinced them to cooperate and press charges."

"What made you give it up?"

But she didn't hear him. For just a moment, she lost herself in her memories—the *happy* memories that for seven years she had tried so hard to pretend didn't exist. "And then I got hooked up with a new partner and, impossibly, it got even better."

Mike skewered another fluffy dumpling and played along. "Oh?"

"He was a transfer from another part of the city, and we got hooked up because my partner had thrown out his back. I also needed a partner who was fluent in French, since my linguistic skills have always been somewhat lacking." She blew out a slow breath. "We seemed to be a perfect fit, and we hit it off immediately."

"I take it the relationship moved beyond the squad car."

She avoided looking at him, suddenly unsure what on Earth had made her share her story. She had known Mike for two years, liked and respected him. He was pleasant to work with and had a decent sense of humor. But he wasn't exactly a kindred spirit and yet, here she was spilling a story to him that she hadn't shared with anyone in almost seven years.

"Yes," she finally admitted quietly. "It took all of two weeks before we were sleeping together." *Sleeping together.* It sounded so innocent, so...pure. But pure and innocent did not begin to describe their first few weeks together. And they had done just about everything *but* sleep. The very first encounter between her and Alec had occurred against his kitchen counter and had left the floor littered with—she glanced nostalgically at her plate—hunks of vegetables and raw fusilli. For an encore they had headed for the bedroom, but hadn't quite made it. They had copulated like bunnies on the half flight of stairs that joined the living area and the bedroom level at Alec's old condo. They had laughed and moaned and devoured each other in a flurry of arms and legs and indescribable need. She never knew it could be like that. She had never been happier. "We moved in together three months after that."

"How long were you together?"

"A few months after we moved in together we requested new partners for patrol. It seemed...prudent."

"But you lived together for—"

"A little over four years."

"You never wanted to get married?"

She set down her fork and reached for the glass of Chardonnay that Mike had poured for her. She sipped delicately before answering. "No. Things sort of got in the way."

"Things?" asked Mike as he sipped from his own wine and studied her across the shimmering golden liquid.

"It's complicated." She lifted her fork, and then decided there was no way her stomach was accepting any more tonight. She set the fork back down and concentrated on her wine. "He left and I hadn't seen him since." It was amazing how deceiving a phrase could be. Those words made it sound as if they had parted amicably. But in reality Alec had stormed out after a fierce argument. His eyes had been wild with a rage that she had been unable to comprehend. He had abandoned her at the lowest moment of her life, and left her to fight her way out of a bottomless pit of despair all alone. He had walked out of her life, and away from a promising career. He had thrown everything away to pursue a future that was the polar opposite of everything he had ever believed in—everything they had both believed in.

"Until recently, I take it," prompted Mike.

"Yes. Last night he showed up out of the blue."

"Where was he all this time?"

"Europe mostly. That is, when he wasn't jetting over the Atlantic, or down to Egypt or Australia for a holiday."

"How does a Montreal cop afford such extravagances?"

"He's not a police officer anymore. He now handles personal security."

Mike's fork froze in midair. "What?"

"He's a bodyguard for the rich and famous. He caught the eye of the French Ambassador when he was helping with security for a press conference in Montreal. She offered him a position, and I guess he decided it was an offer he couldn't refuse. He's been quite sought after ever since. He's like the hottest fashion accessory for the woman who has everything." She rolled a mushroom around her plate. "I'm sure his rakish good looks and sophisticated accent have absolutely nothing to do with his success."

Mike set down his fork and stared at her, his expression incredulous. "Are you telling me that you used to live with Alec Frechette?"

Her eyebrows arched heavenward. "Oh, so you've heard of him too?" The fact that Mike was familiar with Alec's reputation didn't exactly instill her with confidence for the future of this relationship.

"Of course I have! Christ! He's living every man's fantasy. Women fall over themselves to hire him. He gets paid handsomely to carry a gun and save damsels in distress whom, I have no doubt, show their gratitude in many innovative ways." He turned his attention back to his plate. "I heard a rumor that he was in Ottawa, but I didn't believe it."

"Believe it."

Kira practically jumped out of her skin at the familiar baritone that reverberated from a position just behind her left shoulder. She whirled around to face the intrusion. "Alec! What are you doing here?"

"Working," he said with a grin. "It's just work, work, work, all the time. Never a moment to myself."

Kira craned her neck to scan the restaurant. "Is the Governor General here?" That hardly seemed likely. Somehow trendy Italian food didn't fit with his image.

"No. I'm in charge of his lovely granddaughter—and her date."

"Right. How silly of me. I was having a little trouble picturing you fawning over an aging, overweight politician."

Alec's jade eyes flared white-hot, but cooled almost instantly. *Ice man.* "I don't fawn," he said evenly before making a smooth transition and offering his hand to Mike. "Alec Frechette."

Mike and Alec shook hands cordially and Kira grudgingly danced the social waltz. "Alec, this is Dr. Mike LaRocque. I work with him at the hospital."

"It's good to meet you," crooned Mike. "I couldn't help but follow your career over the last few years." There was an unmistakable glint in Mike's eye, and Kira thought she might be sick.

"Thanks. I do try to live an entertaining life." Alec snatched a roll out of their basket. "But it's good to be back in Canada again. And it's good to see that Kira has gotten over me," he said with unrepentant impertinence. "And she's snagged a doctor, no less. Quite an improvement over a lowly cop, eh, *chéri*?"

Kira clasped her hands together to keep from madly twirling that ring around her finger. "Not really. But a definite improvement over you. Of course, that's not saying much."

Alec's expression was one of mild amusement, and it irritated the hell out of her. "I see your tongue hasn't dulled over the years. You always had a special knack for slicing right to the heart."

Kira decided to put an end to the festivities. "Aren't you neglecting your duties, Alec?" she said tightly. "What if a kidnapper makes off with your charge?"

Alec glanced at a booth in the far corner, and Kira caught sight of a buxom young woman and a starstruck young man with dark curly hair and puppy dog eyes. He was already head over heels in love. He'd find out soon enough how painful that could be.

"Don't worry," said Alec as he took a step back. "I've never lost anyone yet."

"Oh, I don't know about that," said Kira wryly.

Mike had leaned back in his chair. Arms crossed, he watched the exchange with rank fascination. "I'd ask you to join us but I'm not sure my date would approve."

Alec chuckled, and Kira refused to acknowledge the warm glow that laugh still kindled in her gut.

"You have a keen insight, *mon ami*. I'll be on my way. After all I do have a job to do." He turned to go and called back, "Perhaps you'll like my chicken *primavera* better, Kira. You never could resist *my* cooking."

Kira watched the broad, strong lines of his retreating back. She wanted to feel outrage and betrayal, anger and resentment—she wanted to feel *something*—but all she felt was a deep, aching emptiness. Alec symbolized all the things in her life that she had lost, and could never recoup.

"He's going to cook for you?" asked Mike as he stuffed a gnocchi into his mouth.

"He seems to think he is. I'd rather he didn't, but he has a knack for getting into places where he's not wanted." *Like countries and houses…and women's hearts.*

"Fascinating character," mused Mike as he watched Alec settle at a table within a stone's throw of the giggling girl and her date.

"Not really. To me he's pathetically transparent." She crumpled up her napkin. "Would you mind if we have coffee and dessert elsewhere? Suddenly I find the atmosphere here a little stifling."

* * * * *

Alec peered over the top of his open menu. He was having extreme difficulty focusing on the assortment of pastas and salads. Instead he watched as the doc took Kira's hand and helped her out of her chair.

Even considering the weight loss, the graceful lines of Kira's body hadn't changed. She still moved with the same poise and self-assurance as she had when they had shared a beat and a bed. Her hair was shorter, but he found the style flattering. She still dressed with the same sense of understated elegance. Tonight she was wearing navy khakis and a white silk camisole. He watched with regret as a pair of perfectly kissable shoulders were obscured from view by a neatly tailored white blazer. He wrenched his mind away from such pointless memories, but he couldn't help reflecting that she had really changed very little, considering the ravages of time and circumstance. The only really significant difference was in her eyes.

The color was the same—chips of emerald caught in a sea of amber. He had always loved her eyes, both the color and the fire. But now the fire was gone—extinguished by a lethal mix of grief and disappointment. Her current career choice had apparently done little to rekindle the embers of her soul.

He had checked into her situation almost immediately upon arriving in Ottawa. She was living alone and working in pediatric oncology. *God!* She had picked one of the most emotionally demanding and draining areas of nursing. Was she punishing herself? Of course she was. Just like he was. They were just coming at it from different angles.

And now that he thought about it, the fire had gone from her eyes years before he left. In fact, he could pinpoint the exact moment that it had died—the exact moment that she had stopped loving him.

His eyes continued to follow Kira as she and her esteemed colleague headed for the exit doors. The dear doctor placed his hand on the small of her back and guided her outside. Was she serious about this guy? Had she been serious about anyone over the last seven years? Was she happy? And, after the hell she had put him through, why did he care?

He was ripped away from his reverie by raised voices off to his left.

"How did you find me?" Darcy cowered behind her date in the corner of their raised booth.

A very irate man in jeans and a leather jacket was leaning across the table, his finger pointed accusingly. "It hardly took a genius to figure out you'd come running to Grandpa, you vindictive little bitch."

Alec launched from his chair, cursing himself for allowing Kira and her social life to distract him from his meager duties. He had let memories and sentiment distract him and get in the way of his work. He had to get a grip on himself! He had to get a grip on his life, period.

He placed a restraining hand on the man's shoulder and dragged him away from a fuming Darcy.

"Well, it's damn well about time you showed up!" she hissed.

Her date just sat there looking confused and uncertain.

"Get your hands off me!" ranted the assailant. He was several years older than Darcy's current date. Apparently her taste in men spanned several generations. "Who the hell do you think you are?"

"I actually think I'm the one who should be asking that question." Alec didn't release his shoulder. In fact, his grip strengthened until the man stood immobile, wincing under the pressure.

"I—I just wanted to talk to her," he whimpered. "I just wanted to know why—"

"Alec," interrupted Darcy with soft authority. "Dan here has already disrupted our meal enough. I'd appreciate it if you would get on with this so we can order our dinner."

Alec flashed her an irritated glance, but addressed himself to *Dan*. "Well then, if you want to talk I suggest you pick a more suitable spot for a rendezvous and refrain from screaming and threatening her." He slowly released Dan's shoulder. "Now, why don't you just toddle on out of here before this turns into a scene."

Dan stared at him for a moment before a burst of laughter erupted from his lungs and drew the attention of the entire restaurant. "A scene? You've got to be kidding. You think I give a shit about making a stupid little scene in a goddamn fucking little restaurant?"

The vehemence and the desperation in his voice startled Alec. He didn't want to hurt Dan, so he silently debated how to handle the situation while the man continued his tirade and the rest of the patrons watched in mute fascination. "My whole life is fucked up beyond belief and you think I give a damn about making a scene and embarrassing the likes of *her*?"

Alec decided he didn't have much choice. Either he'd have to remove the ranting lunatic or restaurant security would beat him to it. "Come on, Dan, old man," he said tersely as he grabbed Dan's arm and moved to drag him toward the doors. "Let's not make this worse than it already is."

Dan's voice reached a fever pitch. "Worse? You think it could get *worse*?"

Alec had had enough of talking. He pulled on Dan's arm and was astonished when an angry fist came sailing directly toward his jaw. Old habits and good instincts kicked in and saved him a square hit. He shifted away and Dan's fist barely grazed his cheek. But, unfortunately, Alec had always had trouble controlling those habits and instincts. He felt a rib crack under his retaliating blow, and Dan grunted and doubled over in pain. An uppercut to Dan's jaw sent him reeling back against Darcy's table, and he slid into a boneless heap on the floor.

"Shit!" lamented Alec as he towered over the unfortunate slob who was moaning and complaining softly to no one in particular.

"Well, you sure do put on a good show," commented Darcy from the corner. "I think you might just deserve a bonus for that one." The edge to her voice and the lascivious glint in her eye aggravated Alec's already overstimulated adrenal glands.

He refrained from telling her to shut up, however, and bent down to assist Dan to his feet. He motioned to a nearby waiter. "Can you call a cab for this guy? I'll deposit him on a bench out front."

Once on his feet Dan batted away Alec's hands. "Leave me alone, asshole." He cast an accusatory glance at Darcy. "You'll be sorry, little miss rich bitch. And one of these days you won't have a fancy bodyguard around to save your pretty little heinie."

"Get lost, Dan." Darcy's expression was contemptuous. "You always were full of hot air."

Without looking back, and with a hand held to his rib cage, Dan meandered toward the front doors. Alec watched him go, all the while wondering what on Earth would inspire a seemingly respectable man in his mid-forties to resort to such behavior in a public place.

After the door swung closed behind Dan, Alec returned his gaze to Darcy, but she had already immersed herself in the adoring gaze of her starry-eyed date—apparently unfazed by the harsh words and questionable activities that had just taken place around her.

He seated himself back at his table but vowed that Darcy wouldn't get off so easily. She might technically be his employer, but he had some questions for her. And he damn well intended to get the answers.

Chapter Seven

ꝏ

Kira slipped the key into her front lock and, even before the dead bolt clicked open, Cujo began his familiar greeting routine.

"God," moaned Mike. "I don't know how you stand those things. They're yappy and annoying, and look more like a drowned rat than a dog."

"You're just bound and determined to wheedle your way into my heart, aren't you?" quipped Kira as the door swung open and a tiny projectile collided with her ankle.

"Yup, you landed a real sweet-talker when you landed me."

Smiling, Kira scooped up Cujo and cradled him in her arms as she slipped out of her pumps. "Would you like a coffee? I'd offer you some wine, but I know you have to drive…very soon."

"Is that a hint?"

"No. I was trying to be quite blatant about it." She set down the dog, filled his food dish and reached for the coffeepot.

Mike chuckled as he settled himself on a stool at her breakfast bar. "Okay, I won't outstay my welcome." He watched the dog nibbling at his food. "I take it back—I think the drowned rat thing was insulting. To the rat."

Kira couldn't restrain a burst of laughter. She turned around and leaned against the counter as she studied her guest. "Somehow *sweet-talker* doesn't do you justice. How does this approach work when it comes to coaxing your dates into bed?"

"I use different approaches as I see fit. Every situation is unique."

"I see," she nodded sagely. "And you figure I like to be insulted."

"You certainly handed out your share tonight. If that was how you two related, it's small wonder it didn't work out."

Kira was surprised by the instant and intense reaction she felt to that little jibe at her and Alec's past. She found herself clutching at the edge of the counter, her fingers straining against the Formica as she struggled to contain her temper. She took a deep breath and turned back to the coffeepot. "Alec and I are none of your business, Mike. I think I already told you more than enough."

"I don't know," he mused as he steepled his fingers. "You told me a little, but there are still an awful lot of holes in your story."

"Holes?"

"Yes. Like you never explained why he left. You never explained why you quit police work, and you never explained why you chose such a notable career change. Actually, come to think of it, you both did." He remained quiet while Kira finished pouring the water into the unit and flipped it on. "Did something happen on duty that turned you both off police work, and ended up coming between you?"

Suddenly a mind-numbing fatigue settled over Kira like a heavy wool blanket. All she wanted to do was to crawl into her high sleigh bed, snuggle between a set of crisp percale sheets and dream her troubles away—alone.

"Can we drop this, please? I know that as a doctor you're used to digging for answers and finding the reason for an illness, but this is a little different. Sometimes the past is better left buried."

"And sometimes things that are buried have a habit of rising from the dead and haunting us."

Kira decided it was time to turn the tables on her nosy boss. She leaned against the breakfast bar, her eyes mere inches from Mike's. "How about you, Mike? I don't know anything about your past. Were you ever married? Divorced? Kids? Do you hate your parents? Did you pull the wings off flies as a kid? If it's a night for secrets, then it's only fair for you to share a few too."

"If you must know, I used to torture Chihuahuas just for kicks."

Kira's chuckle was interrupted by the chime of the doorbell.

"Whew!" exclaimed Mike. "Saved by the bell."

"I'm not that easy to distract," said Kira as she headed for the door. "You're not getting off so easy." She opened it to reveal the familiar figure of her neighbor, Tim Nickle. His honey-blond hair was windblown tonight and sweat had plastered his jogging pants and T-shirt to his body, revealing a lean, rangy physique. He hardly looked like a successful investment counselor. But then again, even on his best days, he barely resembled the majority of his finely manicured colleagues.

Despite appearances, Tim's business was flourishing. Kira often wondered if people felt a little more comfortable with a rumpled, slightly shy businessman, rather than with the typically sleek and polished members of the profession. Maybe they felt like Tim understood how precious their hard-earned money was, and thought he would treat it with the respect and care that it deserved.

That was one thing that Tim Nickle knew about. He knew what was precious. Surely every one of his daughter's dialysis runs reminded him of that very fact.

"Hi, Tim," she said warmly. "Out jogging a little late tonight."

He smiled hesitantly and glanced over her shoulder. "Hi, Kira. Sorry to interrupt. I know you don't have dates very often."

Kira chuckled. "Thanks for pointing that out."

Tim blushed. "Oh—sorry. I...uh...didn't mean it like that."

"That's okay," called Mike from the kitchen. "You're right. She's a social outcast."

"Yeah, and just look at the winner I finally manage to bring home," she said dryly.

"I heard that!"

She ignored him. "What can I do for you, Tim?"

"Well, it's just that Lauren is out tonight. I finally convinced her to go out with the girls, you know."

"You're one in a million, Tim. Does Lauren rent you out?"

He chuckled nervously before continuing. "Anyway, when I came back from my run I found Rachel huddled in bed with a fever."

Alarms immediately went off in Kira's head.

"She says she's fine," continued Tim. "But I always get so nervous when she gets sick. I know it's late, and I hate to impose, but I was wondering—"

"Say no more." Kira couldn't comply fast enough. The thought of Rachel shivering with fever, her body's systems already compromised by her renal failure and constant exposure to the ravages of dialysis, was all it took to release a rush of adrenaline into Kira's bloodstream. "Just let me get my stethoscope." She turned around and almost banged her nose against Mike's chest. He had come up behind her during the last bit of conversation. "I'm sorry, Mike. But I'm sure you understand."

He frowned. "Why don't I come too? I *am* a doctor, you know. Maybe I can help."

Kira was already loping toward the bedroom where she always hung her stethoscope. "No, no. That's okay. I'm qualified to see if she needs a trip to the hospital. I don't want to impose." She grabbed the familiar piece of medical equipment and draped it around her neck as she hustled back toward the front door. "Besides you were going home soon, anyway. I'll—"

She broke off when she noticed Mike standing alone by the front door.

"Where's Tim?"

"I told him to head on home, and that we'd be right over."

"Oh. Well, like I said. I can handle this myself—"

"Dammit, Kira! What is your problem?"

"What?"

"I honestly don't know why you bothered with nursing. You should have gone directly into a medical practice. Nursing is geared to people who are willing to cooperate with each other—with other nurses as well as with doctors and other professionals. Doctors are the ones who have the reputation for wanting to control and do everything themselves."

Kira was astonished at the fierce intensity behind his eyes. "But even the doctors who are like that are generally seen as assholes—even by their peers."

"What on Earth are you saying?"

"Why won't you let anyone help you? It is *not* an imposition. I *want* to help. But you are just bound and determined to do everything yourself. To take on the whole load even if it kills you. You think I don't see how you act around the other nurses? Most of them put up with you because you're a damn good nurse, but..." He paused and grabbed her shoulders, as if holding her in place to force her to listen. "But Kira, you're annoying as hell."

"Why?" She found herself on the brink of tears. This speech was all too familiar, and she didn't like it any more than she had the first time she heard it. "Because I care about my patients, and my friends and neighbors? Do people hate me because I care enough to go out of my way, and make sure things are done right? If they don't like it, then to hell with them. Maybe they're the ones with the problem."

Mike dropped his hands in exasperation. "You just don't get it, do you?"

She poked his chest with a stiff finger. "No. You just don't get it. I like you, Mike. You're a nice guy and a good doctor, but I don't *need* you. I needed somebody once and he let me down. I don't ever want to be put in that position ever again."

"That's a sad existence, Kira." Mike's voice was sad but his eyes were fierce.

"Maybe. But it's mine." She poked herself in the chest. "And no one can take that away from me." She reached for the doorknob. "So thanks for the offer, Mike. But I'll pass. I can look after things myself just fine, thanks." She stopped in the doorway and turned around to add, "And please don't kick the dog on your way out the door."

Mike watched the door slam behind her. "Damn you," he muttered. "And damn Alec Frechette." How exactly had Alec let her down? Not that it mattered. All that mattered was that Alec had left a broken woman in his wake. Normally Mike liked his women a little on the needy side. But he liked them to know they were needy. And he liked them to, very specifically, need *him.*

Kira was a new experience for him. She needed him but refused to acknowledge it. That was a challenge. But he'd win her over eventually. One way or another, he always got what he wanted.

He grabbed his jacket and stalked out the front door. Perhaps tonight he hadn't landed in the bed of his choice, but there were always alternatives. If there was one thing Mike enjoyed it was variety. It was the spice of life, after all. And tonight he had one very particular flavor in mind.

* * * * *

Alec held his glass to the light. He always examined the rich, red depths before taking his first sip. There were secrets hidden there—secrets that needed to be explored and exposed. The color and bouquet were the beginning of the quest. The tasting was the culmination. When a fine wine hit the tongue, the secrets burst across the taste buds, filling the senses and ripping away pretense.

He had once heard someone say that a fine wine was much like a woman—beautiful to look at and heady to the senses. Only in tasting it fully could one unravel the mysteries. But that was woefully inaccurate.

Tasting a woman didn't unravel her secrets, it merely added to them. Intimacy with a woman was a labyrinth of conflicting images and emotions. It could strip a man raw and leave him a confused, befuddled shadow of himself.

It was safer to admire from afar. Tasting was far too dangerous.

He raised the glass to his lips and sipped delicately, allowing the ambrosia to make love to his senses.

What he had done with Darcy that afternoon had not been making love. It couldn't compare to this. That hadn't been intimacy. He hadn't *tasted* Darcy Cromwell. They had shared recreational sex. It had been little more than a ride on a hormonal roller-coaster. It had been invigorating and exciting—a regular thrill a minute that left his knees weak and his stomach rolling. But love and intimacy had about as much in common with that kind of sex as Shakespeare had in common with a dime-store romance.

"What the hell are you still doing here?"

The accusing voice interrupted his private moment. Alec looked up to see Carl Stuart coming in through the back kitchen door. He looked tired and haggard. But perhaps that was to be expected considering that it was two in the morning.

Alec remained seated at the counter and took another leisurely sip before answering. "Just making sure my lady's little friend doesn't abuse her hospitality and, you know, murder her in her sleep or anything."

"She brought a man up to her room?" asked Carl.

"Yes. But I get the distinct impression that it isn't all that unusual."

Carl snorted as he opened the refrigerator, and appeared to think that was all the response that was warranted for that little observation.

Actually, Alec's real reason for waiting around was that he had hoped to have an opportunity to talk to Darcy after her *friend* left. But it had soon become apparent that lover boy wouldn't be leaving until the wee hours of the morning, so Alec had decided to treat himself to a glass of merlot before tottering off to his cold, empty apartment.

Alec watched as Carl pulled a beer out of the fridge and had already brought it to his lips before the refrigerator door had snapped shut. He guzzled thirstily, and Alec could swear his hands were shaking.

"Rough day?" Alec asked politely.

"None of your fucking business."

"I take that as a yes."

Carl just glared at him as he wiped a hand across his mouth. "Why don't you take off, Frechette? You know you don't have to watch her every move while she's in the mansion, so why don't you go pick up some cute little whore and a have a little fun before you have to come back to work in the morning."

"Thanks for the kind social tip, but I think I'll pass." He shifted on his stool and studied the surly figure in the wrinkled suit. He wondered idly what had brought Carl here at this time of night. But then he recalled Darcy mentioning something about Carl conducting unannounced spot checks of the security systems. Alec shrugged and decided he really didn't care how Carl spent his time. The less he knew about Carl Stuart the better. Despite that decision, however, he was curious about one thing. "I get the distinct impression that you don't like me very much, Stuart."

"No, not at all. You've got me all wrong." Carl paused for another swig of ale. "I hate your damn guts."

"And what have I done to deserve such profound loathing?" Alec swirled the wine around in the glass and sniffed the musty aromas of oak and currants. Already Carl Stuart was boring him.

"Just being you is enough."

"Please, do tell me more."

"Guys like you give bodyguards a bad name. You carry a weapon and look around every once in a while, but you're more of an affectation than a serious shield against a potential threat."

"You have no idea as to my qualifications, Stuart." Alec kept his voice smooth and low, but the words kindled his temper. Perhaps it was true that many of his clients hired him more for appearances than for protection, but that didn't negate the fact that he was good at what he did. His senses and reflexes were as sharp and quick as ever. He was sure of it.

"Huh! I know enough. Even when you were a cop, you were a lousy one. I know what really happened, *mon ami*. I know the real reason why you left the Montreal force. I know that…"

The back of Carl's head crashed against the door of the huge stainless steel fridge. Alec tightened his grip on that scrawny little throat, and watched with satisfaction as Carl's eyes bugged out and his face flushed red. The beer can had clattered to the floor and Alec could hear the soft *glug-glug* as the contents leaked out all over the gleaming Italian marble floor.

"You listen to me, asshole," hissed Alec as Carl's fingers clawed in vain at Alec's hand latched around his throat. "You don't know squat! I don't care what you *think* you know, you have no idea why I left the force. Nobody does. That little incident had nothing – *nothing* – to do with it. And your boss must know that or he wouldn't have hired me."

Alec let go and Carl sagged, rubbing at his throat and glaring at his assailant. "What, are you an idiot?" he rasped.

"Shut up, Stuart."

Carl laughed mirthlessly. "He didn't hire you because his granddaughter needs protecting." He shrugged. "Or at least, that was only a small part of it. Just think about it, Frechette. You're a smart boy. You'll figure it out." His smile was lecherous as he bent down to retrieve his beer.

Alec stood there, seething, restraining himself from pummeling Carl into a bloody pulp. He didn't like what Carl was implying and refused to face the possible truth in his words.

Carl continued blithely on, oblivious to the precipice over which he was dangling. "Don't get me wrong. I don't give a shit about that crap. *Use 'em and lose 'em*. That's my motto. Most of these rich bitches got it way too good. If somebody like you can get them to spread their legs, or better yet down on their knees, then more power to you. They need some reminding of who's the stronger one – who's really in charge."

Alec's breathing and heart rate had settled down to a manageable level as he'd listened to Carl's medieval ranting. "You sound like you don't exactly respect the women in positions of authority who pay our wages."

"Huh! Respect? How am I supposed to respect somebody who curls her eyelashes and shaves her armpits?"

"Right, of course. Those things are incompatible with decency."

Carl scowled and waved a shaky finger at Alec. "Don't get sarcastic with me, buddy. If you respected 'em, you wouldn't screw 'em every chance you get. You and me are more alike than you know."

Alec chose to ignore the accusations and the implications of Carl's semi-coherent ravings. He tossed back the remainder of his wine and staunchly walked out of the kitchen. "You and I are nothing alike, Stuart. You have more in common with the dog shit I scrape off my shoe than you do with me."

Alec was mildly surprised when a bullet didn't come whizzing by his head. He made it outside unscathed, got into his BMW ZX3 and revved the engine to within an inch of its life.

Flying down the highway at a hundred and forty clicks, he determinedly kept his mind focused on the road. He refused to think about the barbs that Carl had flung that had hit home.

He had nothing in common with Carl Stuart. Absolutely nothing.

* * * * *

Lauren Nickle slipped in through the front door, careful to ease out of her high-heeled boots and not make any undue clatter against the tiled floor.

The multilevel house was dark and silent. It might have been ominous if she hadn't known that her husband and daughter were sleeping, safe and sound, in their rooms upstairs.

So as not to disturb anyone upstairs, she slipped into the main floor powder room to make use of the facilities. The nachos had been spicy, and it had taken a significant amount of beer to wash them down. God, when was the last time she had done something like this? It had to be more than a year since she had gone out with a group of women and just had fun. They had seen a Mel Gibson flick, during which they had oohed and aahed and whistled without remorse or consideration for the seven other patrons in the theater. Maybe Mel's popularity wasn't what it once was, but his body was holding up pretty good for a man approaching fifty. Or was he past the fifty mark?

She giggled to herself, still feeling the effects of the beer and the general silliness of the evening. After the movie, they had gone to a local bar and told dirty jokes and complained about their husbands into the wee hours. At least the others had complained about their husbands. Lauren had had very little to say on that subject. She had nothing to complain about.

Finished with her business, she ran her hands under warm water before drying them with the monogrammed towel hanging by the sink. That towel had been a wedding present more than twenty years ago. The first ten years she hadn't used any of the set because it seemed too nice to soil with dirty hands. At last Tim had said it was ridiculous for them to be gathering dust in the linen closet. They should be taken out and used and appreciated. So what if eventually they lost some of their sparkling newness? Loved things should look a little rough and worn around the edges—just like their marriage. God knew the two of them had taken their share of knocks. They might be a little worse for wear but they were still together, and still desperately in love.

She flicked off the light and stepped out of the washroom. She was just about to head up the stairs when she heard a faint noise. It sounded like someone was in the kitchen.

Frowning, she made her way through the gloom toward the back of the house. Their kitchen had wide patio doors that looked out onto the backyard and a park beyond. The moon was full tonight, and it cast the table and chairs in a silvery glow.

"Tim?" she asked quietly.

He was sitting at the table, gazing out at the moonlit landscape. He cradled an empty glass in his palm. "Hi, honey. Did you have fun?"

"Yeah. I almost felt like I was in college again." She moved over to him and rested her hands on his shoulders. "I even flirted with the waiter," she teased.

He rested a cheek against her knuckles. "Good. I'm glad I made you go. You don't get out nearly enough."

"Is something wrong? It's after two, and I know you have a meeting at nine."

He sighed, and she knew the answer was yes, but she waited patiently while he sorted through his thoughts. Tim never spoke without carefully considering his words first. He rarely lost his temper, and never raised his voice. It was part of what made him a success with his clients…and with the women in his life. "It's nothing really. When I came back from my run tonight, Rachel had a bit of a fever."

The euphoria of the evening left Lauren as if someone had pulled a plug and it had drained out of her. "Is she all right? Should we take her—"

Tim reached up and grasped her hand. "No, no. She'll be fine. Kira came over and checked her over for me. Rachel's throat is a little raw, that's all. Kira suggested that if the fever doesn't come down by morning, maybe we should take her in to see the GP, but with Tylenol she should be okay until then."

Lauren let out a breath that she hadn't even realized she had been holding. "Good." Then she hesitated and stroked her husband's wavy hair. "But if she's okay, why are you up so late?"

"I couldn't sleep." He set the glass down on the oak table beside him. "Maybe it was because I was alone with her, but when I felt her forehead it just brought everything rushing back again."

Lauren didn't have to ask what he meant. He was referring to the day thirteen years earlier when Rachel had become deathly ill. They'd had barbecued burgers a few days earlier, and served them with just a hint of pink in the center—just like always. How were they to know? The strain of E. coli bacteria that wreaked havoc with Rachel's body, almost killed her and then doomed her kidneys to fail at the age of seventeen, had been virtually unheard of back then. It was very shortly after that doctors and health officials had begun preaching the importance of cooking hamburgers completely, and of being scrupulously careful with raw meat and chicken.

But the warnings had come too late for Rachel. Her brush with death had been a nightmare that they had never wanted to repeat. But then Rachel had gotten better, and the world had been rosy. Her parents had breathed a sigh of relief. It had been a tough lesson and it had been well learned, but things would be fine. And they had been…until she started to get sick…again.

"I'm just so tired of it, Lauren. I'm so tired of worrying and wishing on stars that don't hear me. And it's only been two years. Some of those people have been on dialysis for close to a decade. I just…" His voice trailed off into mute desperation.

"I know, honey," she said as she continued stroking his hair. "I'm tired too. But maybe there's an end in sight. She's young, and a good candidate for a transplant. I'm sure—"

He didn't seem to hear her. "How can I make it up to her? She trusted us to look after her, to keep her safe. That's what parents are supposed to do, right?" He looked up at Lauren, and she touched his cheek. "And what did I do? I fed her poison! Goddammit!" He stood and walked heavily to the patio doors. He leaned against them, looking so alone and forlorn.

Lauren tried to swallow past the lump in her throat, but no words would come.

"And then God has to punish me further. I'm a perfect match for my daughter! I could give her a kidney, and maybe make up for everything. Wow! Isn't that great?" His voice was as bitter as wormwood tea.

The words were familiar to Lauren. She'd heard them before, but he seemed to need to work through it again. "Tim, it's not your fault."

"Sure it is!" The angry edge to his voice startled her. But almost immediately it evaporated, and he spoke more quietly again. "I'm the one who cooked that damn burger. And I'm the one who totaled my car when I was eighteen, damaging the kidney that should have gone to my daughter."

She moved over and wrapped her arms around him. She squeezed tightly and willed his heart to stop its furious pounding against his chest, wishing she could ease his suffering, and maybe hers along with it. "Please don't do this to yourself," she pleaded, resting her cheek against the soft cotton of his T-shirt. "If anyone's to blame, it's the both of us together." She looked up at his brown eyes, so full of anger and remorse. "You're a wonderful father, and you've done the best you can. We both have."

"I hope so," he murmured, resting his cheek against her hair. "I really hope so."

Chapter Eight

ꙮ

Kira nibbled on a French fry dripping with gravy. The noise in the cafeteria was tolerable since she hadn't made it down until after one o'clock. The noon rush hour had passed, leaving only a few stragglers behind to eat with the second, smaller lunch shift. She generally lunched alone, since staffing in oncology didn't allow nurses to take breaks in groups, or even pairs. She often brought a book and ate outside in nice weather, but this morning she had been wandering around the house in a funk. She had even forgotten to pack the crackers, cheese and fruit that she usually toted along to fuel her through her rigorously long day.

So today she had decided to splurge and get the healthiest thing on the cafeteria menu—fish and chips, with a side of gravy. She picked up the cake of fish and regarded it dubiously. She shrugged and drowned it in the thick, dark liquid. She nibbled and shrugged her shoulders. Who said she wasn't a creative cook?

"Oh my God, Kira!" Startled, she looked up to see a familiar, smiling face. "What on Earth are you eating?"

"Fish and gravy," she said through a greasy grin. "I'm thinking of selling the idea to McDonald's and making a million."

"Don't quit your day job," quipped her colleague. Patty Kellerman settled her ample frame down across from Kira. Her tray was heaped with fries, cherry pie, a low-fat yogurt and a diet cola.

"Does the grease and the low-fat stuff cancel each other out?"

"Yeah," said Patty with a straight face. "Usually I have a stick of celery with it, because I figure that puts me into the negative calories. But they were out today." She shrugged and grinned. "So I'm living dangerously."

A moment later, two other nurses joined them—Kira's cohorts from her days on surgery. They were a fun crowd and she occasionally missed them…but not enough.

"So, how do you like working with the chemo kids?" asked Patty as she hammered at the less-than-flaky pastry adorning her pie. Apparently Patty didn't hold to the convention of eating dessert last.

"They're wonderful," said Kira fondly.

Elly MacNeil sighed. "I'm sure they are, but I don't know how you can bear to grow fond of them, knowing full well that some of them won't make it."

"Even in surgery there was always that chance," reasoned Kira. "There are no guarantees."

"Yeah," said Patty. "But we see our patients for a couple of days—a week max. Even if things go bad, we haven't really had a chance to bond with them." She shook her head thoughtfully. "Your kids are tougher. Don't try to deny it, Kira. It's different and you know it."

Kira studied her last fry. "Yes, I know. But they give so much back…" She sighed. "It's worth it."

"Jeez," moaned Simone Hopkins, the last of the threesome. "You guys sure are on a downer. How about a happier topic?"

"Like what?"

"Did you hear that there was another rape?" Simone's voice was conspiratorial.

Patty laughed. "Now there's a pleasant topic of conversation."

"When?" asked Elly.

"It happened last night. I've got a friend who works the ER over at Civic. I guess she was brought in VSA," Kira vaguely recalled that that stood for *vital signs absent,* "but they managed to resuscitate her."

"Is she okay?" asked Kira.

"Nope. Brain-dead."

"Christ," lamented Patty. "For once in my life I'm actually glad to be a working stiff."

"Sure beats just being a stiff."

"Elly!" moaned the group.

"What?"

Simone continued sharing her ill-gotten information. "Elly's right though, you know. She was another jet-setter. Lived out near one of the embassies. They found her in her bedroom, just like the others." Simone slurped some soup from her bowl. "But there's one good thing."

"What could possibly be good about it?" said Patty with a frown.

"She's a donor. I think the harvest team is there right now. She had signed her card and everything."

Kira instantly thought of Rachel. But there were so many *ifs*—so many uncertainties when it came to organ donation. And just being in the same city didn't guarantee that you got an available organ. There were protocols and criteria that had to be met. It was a cruel game of Russian roulette, in which somebody had to lose big so that one lucky recipient could win. Or, in some cases, the organs might be distributed among several recipients. However, for Kira, there was really only one who mattered.

"That still doesn't negate the horror of what she went through," said Kira quietly.

"No, of course not," said Simone quickly. "I didn't mean that at all."

"We know you didn't." Patty shot an irritated glance at Kira. "Don't we, Kira?"

She looked up at the others. "No, I didn't mean to hurt Simone," she said quickly. She toyed with the last of her fish. "I guess I'm just on a bit of a downer this week. That's all."

"Oooh," crooned Patty. "I know something that'll give you a kick in the hormones. I heard that the French Connection himself is in town."

"French Connection?" asked Kira.

"Yeah, you know, Alec Frechette. That French bodyguard that all the women cream over."

Contrary to poor Patty's good intentions this topic did little to lift her spirits.

"Really?" drooled Elly. The word *horny* may as well have been tattooed across her forehead. "He's in Ottawa?"

"Uh-huh. A friend of mine saw him down at Alonzo's the other night."

"I'd take my chances being rich if I could have him watching over me." Simone's eyes were dreamy.

"Oh yes. I definitely—"

"I'm done." Kira had heard enough. The thought of other women salivating over Alec shouldn't have bothered her—especially after this many years. But it did, and she certainly had no intention of revealing her reasons to this crowd. Or anyone. "I've gotta get back."

"Okay," said Patty warmly. "It was good to see you again. If you ever feel the need to change catheter bags and dress infected sutures, just let us know. We'd love to have you back."

"Don't hold your breath," called Kira as she headed for the tray depository. "I'm definitely hooked on caustic chemicals." *And tiny arms that wrap around my neck in silent gratitude.*

As she made her way back to oncology, she silently mused how the human race was so prone to want what they didn't have. People perpetually wished for the moon, for things and relationships that seemed to hold all the answers or all the excitement but, once they actually had it in their possession, it usually turned out that they were better off before. The fulfillment of such wishes often brought on a whole new set of problems, sometimes bigger and more complicated than the ones that preceded them.

Just ask the million-dollar lottery winner who suddenly discovered dozens of cousins crawling out of the woodwork. Just ask someone who divorced and married their illicit lover, only to have that relationship fail as well.

Would Kira's life have been better if she had never met Alec? No. In all fairness, she couldn't imagine her life without him. He had caused her a lot of pain, but he had also given her the greatest gift of her life. If nothing else, she had to at least acknowledge that.

She walked through the familiar doors on 8B. Her colleagues Jean and Alyssa were in a huddle, talking in excited tones. When Kira sat down, they immediately stopped and turned to look at her with stark amazement.

Kira frowned. "What?"

Nothing.

Then she laughed. "What is it? Do I have broccoli in my teeth?"

"Cassie is here," said Jean slowly. "Her mom thinks her port may be infected, but she wanted you to look at it yourself."

"Uh-huh." Many of the children had permanent portacaths or "ports" installed to allow easier access to their circulatory system. It saved them from a painful IV setup every time they came for treatment, and prevented the formation of harmful scar tissue. But the ports had to be watched closely for infection and relocated if problems arose.

None of this was unusual or warranted these odd looks. She nodded suspiciously. "Is there something else?"

"Just go on in. You'll see."

Completely baffled, Kira shook her head as she headed to the examination room. She opened the door, stepped in, and felt as if someone had socked her in the gut. It took her a full ten seconds to suck in enough breath to speak. "Alec?"

Her former lover, clad casually in black jeans and a blindingly white golf shirt, was sitting there in *her* examination room with *her* patient on his lap. He looked up at her, and she didn't know him. The expression on his face was foreign to her. His smile was more warm and tender than she ever remembered, and his eyes glistened with a happiness that seemed to spill directly out of his soul.

She had never seen him like that before. Then she corrected herself. She had seen that look on his face one other time. But that had been so very long ago.

"What are you doing here?" she breathed. "Where's Cassie's mother?"

"Emma had a friend to visit somewhere in the hospital. The others said you'd be a while, and when I said I knew you and offered to look after Cassie, she didn't even hesitate." He smiled a smile that was familiar to her. "I haven't lost my old charms."

Cassie tugged on his shirt. "Alec," she said quietly. "You weren't finished your story."

"Oh yeah, that's right. But Kira's here, so maybe—"

"Please?" pleaded that fairy voice. "She was so pretty. Mommy has a book with pictures of her, and I like to look at it sometimes. Mommy says she cried when she died."

Kira was holding her breath. The whole thing was surreal, as if painted by an artist with a twisted sense of irony and a knack for cruel imagery. "Who are you talking about?"

"Princess Diana." He said it so casually, as if it were nothing—as if he wasn't flaunting his success in her face just to be cruel.

"You knew Princess Di?" she demanded.

"Well, not in the biblical sense," he said with a twinkle. "But I did meet her briefly at a fund-raiser. She was quite charming."

"Yeah, I'll bet."

"Actually I do know her bodyguard fairly well, though. Poor guy," he lamented. "He's still taking it pretty hard."

Kira was startled by a voice behind her. "Thank you so much, Monsieur Frechette," said Emma as she swept into the room. "I can't tell you how much I appreciate you looking after Cassie." Cassie's mom stopped in front of the unlikely pair and turned to Kira. "I didn't know you knew him, Kira. You've been holding out on everyone."

Kira swallowed dryly. "I—I'm a little surprised you left Cassie with—" She hesitated, not wanting to insult Emma's judgment.

"With a stranger?" asked Emma with raised eyebrows. "If you can't trust a bodyguard, I can't imagine who you can trust." She turned back to Alec and her eyes were warm. "The papers don't lie, Kira. He's very charming, and Cassie took to him right away. But surely that doesn't surprise *you*."

Alec shrugged. "What can I say? I have a way with women." He tickled Cassie under her chin. "All women, big and small."

Cassie giggled and snuggled in tightly. "Can Alec hold me while Kira looks at my thingee?"

Emma smiled and Kira found herself fighting an urge to pound Alec with a sound right hook. This was her turf, her life—the life she had carved out without him. He had no right to invade it and look so at home here. He had no right to make her begin to care about him again.

"Sure, honey," Emma was saying. "That is, if Alec doesn't mind. He might be a bit squeamish about that sort of thing."

"Good grief," he groaned. "I've seen things that would make Stephen King toss his cookies. I think I can handle a little infection."

"Where would he throw them?" asked Cassie with knitted brows.

"What?"

"His cookies."

Alec laughed and hugged her. "You're pretty special," he said with a chuckle. "I might have to visit you again."

Kira stood there taking in the tableau while a rock the size of Gibraltar settled in her stomach. She was astonished when an unusual seriousness settled across Cassie's features. Cassie reached up and bracketed Alec's rough cheeks between her tiny palms. "You're special too. Maybe you should have a little girl of your own someday. I bet you'd be a good daddy."

To his credit, Alec's smile barely faltered. The only thing that belied the wrecking ball that Cassie had just launched at him was a momentary tightening of his jaw muscles, and the dying of the spark in his eyes. He swallowed and looked at Kira who was fighting an urge to hug him for the first time in seven years. "I think we should get on with this, right, Kira?" he said after a momentary hesitation.

Kira nodded mutely as she headed for the sterile gloves.

"Because," he continued, "when she's done with you I get to talk to Kira for a few minutes."

Yes, thought Kira. They definitely had things to talk about.

* * * * *

"What the hell are you doing here?" spat Kira, half an hour later.

"Gee, it's nice to see you too, sweetheart." Alec had meant that to come out all sweetness and light, but instead it came out harsh and sarcastic. He was still reeling from his encounter with Cassie, and from the tiny little darts of caring that she had shot directly at his heart. Lately his heart seemed particularly vulnerable, and his emotions particularly volatile. He was used to controlling his reactions and measuring out his temper in manageable doses. But somehow his return and his exposure to Kira had tipped his whole world on its end. He felt like little bits of him were constantly leaking out through the tiny holes in his soul that his experiences in Montreal had left behind. He thought he had patched them all up, all neat and tidy, but apparently he was wrong.

This latest encounter had left him feeling particularly drained and raw, and he just wasn't in the mood to deal with Kira's accusations and temper. "For once in your life could you *try* to be civil. We did share a bed for four years, you know. I thought we even loved each other once."

Kira's jaw was tense. "Maybe. Once."

Alec closed his eyes in frustration. Who was he kidding? He had tried to convince himself for years that she had loved him but, the more objective he became, the more distance he could put between himself and the events of seven years ago, the more convinced he was that her love had been a lie. Maybe she had been lying to herself as much as to him. Maybe she honestly thought she had loved him, but that wasn't love. Or, if it was, then that wasn't the kind of love he wanted to be a part of.

Kira's voice cut through his reverie. "So? What did you want? Why are you here?"

"Why indeed?"

"Alec! I have work to do."

Why the hell *was* he here? Did he have some hidden masochistic tendencies? Did he crave abuse, just like he seemed to crave women who used him?

No. He was here for closure. There were things that needed to be said before he could get on with his life. And Kira was the only person to whom he could say them. He tried to blow out his tension in a long slow breath. "I was hoping to cook that dinner for you, and I thought you might actually appreciate it if I talked to you in advance instead of ambushing you at your house."

"Well, will wonders never cease?"

"God, Kira! What's your problem? I'm bending over backward here to be civil and meet you halfway. I just wanted to talk to you." *I've missed you. Dammit, I need you again, and I can't figure out why.*

"Why?" she asked suspiciously. "Why now? You ran out seven years ago. You could have talked to me then, or a half-dozen times since that I know you visited Canada. Why now?"

He looked away, gazing out the huge picture window that graced the end of the long sterile hallway. Through it, he could see lush greenery and the swirling brown waters of the Ottawa River. The green roofs of the Parliament buildings were visible in the distance. This might be a beautiful city, and Kira's home, but it wasn't his home. Maybe he didn't have one. "I don't know. It just caught up with me, I guess."

"What caught up with you? I didn't realize you knew the meaning of regret."

He snorted with derision. "Regret? Lady, I wrote the book. Now, how about dinner? Tomorrow night. It's Saturday and I know you don't work weekends and hardly have any social life. You've got no excuses."

She frowned. "Doesn't the Governor General's granddaughter have a party to go to or anything?"

"Actually, she's having dinner with her family, so I'm off the hook."

"Well..."

"Dammit, Kira. Don't make me beg. All I'm asking is one night, and if you still hate me you never have to see me again."

She sighed and stuffed her hands in the pockets of her jeans. "All right."

"Good. And don't forget I'm cooking."

"Are you kidding? That's the only reason I'm letting you through the door."

He forced a chuckle as he reached up to caress her cheek. "Ah, *ma chère* loves me after all." Her eyes immediately mellowed and he dropped his hand. He definitely hadn't lost his touch. Well, at least that was something, he thought bitterly. If only that wasn't all there was.

He turned and walked down the hall toward the elevators. "I'll come and start cooking at five o'clock sharp," he called back.

She didn't answer. Her silence was answer enough.

It always had been.

* * * * *

Carl Stuart was doing what he did best—blending into his surroundings. He watched with mute disgust as Darcy Cromwell allowed that skinny, whiny college kid to grope her breasts during a lengthy and particularly sloppy kiss. Their lips slapped and smacked together like a pair of water snakes in heat. In that sound, he could hear the echoes of what their naked flesh must have sounded like as they copulated voraciously upstairs in her "boudoir".

At last she pushed the poor slob playfully away, her sultry laugh echoing across the cavernous side entrance of the mansion. Her lover stepped outside and the door closed behind him. She leaned back against it, a self-satisfied smirk plastered to her face as her eyes closed in obvious rapture at the memories of her latest conquest.

Carl withdrew even further into the alcove concealing his presence. He heard her sandals click across the marble, and breathed a sigh of relief. However, his relief was short-lived when her calm, regal voice reached his ears. "Did you enjoy that, Carl?"

He silently gritted his teeth and seethed, willing her to just go away and leave him alone.

But she stopped just outside his little foxhole and continued as she inspected her fingernails. "I don't really mind you watching, just as long as you know that you don't have a hope in hell of ever feeling my hands on your dick."

Resigning himself to his fate, Carl stepped out of hiding. Through tightly clenched teeth he muttered, "I have no designs on you, Darcy." He struggled for an adequately respectful response that wouldn't land his ass on the unemployment line. He hated having to be subservient to these people. The Right Honorable Jonathan Cromwell was one thing. But his granddaughter was quite another. "I was merely concerned for your safety."

She grinned devilishly. "Yes, I'll bet you were." She ran fingers through the mane of blonde hair and adjusted her glasses as she studied him like she might study a fly in her Chardonnay. "Were you also concerned for my safety yesterday afternoon, when you came into my room without my permission?"

Carl blinked. *Shit!*

"I wondered if you wanted to watch Alec and pick up a few pointers. I have no doubt at all that you could use them."

He swallowed dryly as the word *Bitch!* repeated in his brain with mind-numbing speed. "I—I didn't realize you had come home. I heard a noise and thought there might be a burglar."

She laughed, and he fought the urge to smack that smile off her face. "Oh, come on, Carl. You can do better than that."

"All right," he said evenly. "The truth is I was concerned that our dear friend Monsieur Frechette wouldn't heed your grandfather's warning. I know how...vulnerable," he almost choked on that one, "you are, and was concerned that he might take advantage of your innocence."

She nodded approval. "Better. Much better. I could almost believe you, except that you and I both know what a load of bullshit that is." She brushed a strand of hair off her face and let her fingers trail provocatively down the deep vee of her T-shirt.

Carl wrenched his eyes away with some difficulty.

"But why you did it is irrelevant. I don't care if you're just into voyeurism or if you're insanely jealous of your colleague. What matters is if I tell Grandpa that you snuck into my room and watched me get naked, it won't matter whether I was screwing the Prime Minister himself, you'll be looking for work in Whitehorse. I'm sure they need people to shovel all those tons of snow." She tapped her chin thoughtfully. "Or perhaps you'd be better qualified to clean up after the dogsled races. The shovel is smaller and, I have no doubt, much easier to handle."

Bitch! Bitch! Bitch! "I am getting the impression that I am about to be screwed over quite soundly myself, Miss Cromwell," he said sweetly.

She granted him a half smile. "How witty! I had no idea you had it in you, Mr. Stuart."

"What do you want?" he growled.

"Oh, not too much. All I am asking for is your discretion. I don't want to hurt poor Grandpa—his poor little ticker hasn't been quite itself lately."

"I wouldn't have said anything anyway. You can count on my silence."

"Good." She turned away and Carl breathed a sigh of relief. He hadn't sunk too far into the manure pile after all. But then she stopped and turned around. "Oh, I almost forgot. There is one other *tiny* thing." He felt himself sinking deeper as the manure gradually crept up to cover his exposed throat.

* * * * *

Alec trudged up the long, sweeping staircase. Darcy was demanding his presence in her room. He hoped to God she wasn't in the mood for another afternoon *snack,* with him served up *au jus.* He just wasn't in the mood for more female manipulation.

Then he rethought it. That wasn't entirely fair. Kira didn't manipulate him. She just hated him, and maybe with good reason. Sometimes he just didn't know anymore. Maybe it had been his fault. Maybe he hadn't tried hard enough. And maybe politicians made it to heaven.

He stepped through the door into Darcy's sitting room.

"Well, it's damn well about time you got here!"

"Gee, it's nice to see you too," he said dryly. Didn't that line sound familiar?

"You're late."

He checked his watch. "Two minutes. Care to dock me an entire week's pay? What's wrong, are you missing a big sale at Eaton's?"

"Shut up!"

He was astounded to realize she was close to tears. He could swear she looked scared. "Why?" His tone instantly turned coolly professional. "What happened?"

"Didn't you notice my car on the way in?"

He frowned as he considered the question. "No," he said slowly. "I didn't come that way. I parked by the front doors because I knew we'd be leaving, and I thought you said you wanted me to drive my car." She had apparently creamed over the thought of riding around in his Beemer.

She sniffed demurely. "Oh. Well, somebody trashed it."

"What?"

"Somebody took a screwdriver or some sort of big tool and scratched it up."

Alec shook his head in disbelief. "Isn't it parked in the garage? The *locked* garage."

"You ever hear of picking a lock, Mister Ex-Cop?"

"No need for sarcasm, Darcy. That garage is a fortress, what with your grandfather's antiques in there. Did they trash any of the other cars?"

"No. Just mine."

He sat down on the damask love seat and studied his charge. "Why? Who's got it in for you?" But then he stopped and nodded knowingly. "Right, of course. Dear old Dan."

"Maybe." She sat down beside him and wrung her hands.

"Okay, then the next logical question is *why?*"

"He just hates me, that's all. I broke it off with him and he hates me. He's warped. That's why I ditched him."

Alec narrowed his eyes. "You know what, Darcy? I don't believe you. Judging from the way he ranted last night, there's more to this story. Lots more." He paused and leaned back, with arms folded across his chest. "What did you do to him?"

"Nothing! I didn't do anything to him that he didn't have coming. And then he goes and scrawls *bitch* all over my car a dozen times over. He broke the windows and ripped up the seats. He's sick, pure and simple."

Alec tried to modify his breathing as the stress of dealing with Darcy's evasions tightened across his chest. "What did the cops say?"

"I don't want to call the police."

He frowned. "But even if you don't prosecute, there's the insurance."

She stood and walked impatiently to the door to the bedroom. "I don't care about that. I can afford to fix it. I just want to forget about it." Now she pointed a finger at him. "And I want *you* to make sure it doesn't happen again."

"So now I've got to baby-sit your car too?" He stood and approached her. "I don't think so, *chèrie.* I need to know what's going on here. I need to know why this guy's got it in for you, so I know what I'm dealing with."

"All you need to know is what I tell you," she said fiercely. "Now, I want to go look for those shoes for my visit with the Prime Minister," and she whirled to head into the bedroom for her purse.

His hand snaked out and latched around her arm. "We're not going anywhere until you tell me what the hell is going on!"

* * * * *

"Shit!" cursed Jean under her breath.

"What?" asked Kira as she settled down beside her colleague at the nursing station desk.

Jean glanced at the clock. "It's been so crazy around here this afternoon, I completely forgot about Jeremy's request for a checkers set." Jean shook her head regretfully. "His session's almost over. It's just so hard to keep track of everything and still do those special little things..."

"Don't worry about it. I got it for him an hour ago."

Jean's pen froze over the chart she had been working on. "You did?"

"Yeah. I happened to notice him looking a little forlorn as I walked by, that's all. And I remembered how much he loved checkers, so I went ahead and got it." She shrugged noncommittally. "No big deal."

"Thanks," said Jean grudgingly.

Alyssa came around behind the desk and started slamming drawers and charts in a frantic search for some mysterious item. "Where the heck did I leave those requisitions?"

"Requisitions?" asked Jean.

Kira continued pulling the charts for the patients who were due on Monday. She generally checked over each one, to familiarize herself with the kids who were expected, just in case there was someone with a particular need or special request. She did it for all the patients, not just the ones for which she was personally responsible.

Alyssa finally plopped down in a nearby chair. "I was in the middle of filling out the requisitions for Sherry Wells' drug levels when I got a phone call. Now, I swear they've disappeared."

"I finished them," said Kira absently. "I already sent them down to the lab."

After a moment, Kira realized that it had suddenly grown very quiet. No one had spoken or moved for almost a minute. She finally looked up to see Jean and Alyssa staring at her with irritation. "What? I was just helping out."

Jean drew in a breath and was about to speak when Mike came sweeping up to the desk. He dropped a folder down in front of Kira. "Would you mind filing these? I'm supposed to meet somebody for supper and I'm late already."

"Sure, Mike," said Kira warmly. "Where are you going?"

"Zeke's Diner. I'm bound and determined to try their mile-high apple pie."

"They're not kidding, you know."

"Trouble is I always fill up on the burgers and—" He cocked his head. "Shoot! There's my phone." He checked his watch and shrugged. "Oh well, I'm late already. What's two more minutes?" He rushed back into his office and closed the door.

"You know, Kira," said Jean coyly. "I've got a hot date tonight, too." She dropped a couple of charts in front of Kira. "Jeremy's the last one and he's almost done. I'm sure you wouldn't mind finishing up with him and filing his chart?"

"Yeah," continued Alyssa with a yawn. "I'm beat. You'll lock up for us, won't you?"

They both grabbed their purses and sauntered out while Kira watched in mute fascination.

"Fine," she muttered. "I was just trying to help." She got up and stretched before heading into Jeremy's room to disconnect his IV and speak to his parents about the next session of chemotherapy.

Half an hour later, the suite was empty. Charts were filed and requisitions were ready for Monday's clinic. She glanced around the rooms quickly to make sure everything was in place before she locked up. Rachel was on dialysis again that night, and Kira wanted to pop in, and maybe play that game of Scrabble with her and her mother.

She was just about to shut off the last of the lights when she realized Mike's office door was closed. He never remembered to lock when he left, probably because he was always in such a rush to go somewhere. Either that or he was just plain lazy. She chuckled to herself. If there was one thing Mike LaRocque was not it was lazy.

She checked the knob just to be sure and, as predicted, he had been delinquent in his duties. She reached around to lock it from the inside, but stopped when she realized there was still a light on by the desk. She stepped inside.

"Mike?"

His back was to her as he gazed out the window that overlooked the river, but she could see the top of his head over the back of his high-backed, leather office chair. He didn't move. "Oh, hi, Kira. You still here? I thought everyone would have left by now."

She stepped a little further into the room. "Everyone else has. I thought you had a dinner date." She paused. "I assumed you left."

"I changed my mind. I just wasn't in the mood." His voice was flat and dull, and he still hadn't turned to face her. "You go on home. I'll lock up."

Kira took another step toward him. "Is something wrong?"

She heard him sigh deeply. "Nothing you can fix."

Feeling a pull to him as strong as a paper clip to a magnet, she stepped around the desk so she could see his face. His square jaw seemed slack and his skin pale. His perpetual dimples were noticeably absent, and there was no life in those blue depths that gazed out over the trees. "What is it, Mike? Was it that phone call?"

"You don't have to worry about me, Kira. You've got enough on your plate to deal with, what with Alec back in town." She had confided in him earlier about Alec's visit to the hospital and the planned dinner the next night.

"I can't help it," she said softly. "I worry about my friends. Maybe I can't do anything, but I can listen." She leaned back against the window frame and watched him intently. He looked up at her and the look in his eyes tugged at her heart.

After an endless moment he finally spoke. "That was my ex-wife."

Kira raised her eyebrows. She had no idea Mike had been married. But she remained silent and allowed him to continue.

"She's getting re-married in a couple of weeks." He raked his fingers through his hair. "Not that it should matter. I mean, we've been divorced for close to five years. So what she does with her life is none of my business."

"But I'm sure it hurts anyway," said Kira softly.

"Yeah, well—it's not just that she's getting married, you know. It's the fact that Lisa's gonna have somebody else to call 'Daddy'."

Kira swallowed against a sudden thickness in her throat. "You—you have a daughter?"

"Yeah. I don't talk about her much because…because I try not to think about her. They live in Australia. The other side of the goddamn world!" Unexpectedly his voice gained in intensity, but just as quickly the anger was snuffed, only to be replaced by a quiet bitterness. "Sorry about that. I only get to see her once a year for a couple of weeks as it is. She hardly knows me. And now she's going to have a new daddy." He suddenly stood and paced to the other side of the room. "That's just fucking great!" He kicked at a filing cabinet and then leaned heavily against it, raising his eyes to meet Kira's at last. "Isn't it?"

"No. No, it's not. I'm sure it hurts like the devil."

He didn't respond, just sighed and stuffed his hands deeply into his pockets. "Yeah, but that doesn't change anything, does it? Nothing at all."

"Do you regret divorcing her mother?"

Mike frowned. "I sure regret marrying her, but I don't regret divorcing her. She lost interest in our marriage pretty damn quick."

"Was it her decision to move to Australia?"

"Yes," he said hesitantly.

"Was there any way you could have had full custody of your daughter, or prevented her from moving?"

Mike pulled his hands out of his pockets and raked his fingers through those ash-blond waves again. "Where are you going with this?"

"Just answer me."

"Well…no. Tracy had been home full-time with Lisa since she was born. She was best equipped to care for a child. It was the least disruptive and best decision for Lisa. I didn't fight it. As for Australia—" He walked to the window again, propping himself against the frame right next to Kira. "I guess I could have fought it, but honestly I was tired of fighting."

"Then you have no regrets."

"Other than not seeing my daughter grow up?"

Kira picked up his hand and her voice was low but earnest. "You made decisions that were difficult, but were best for your daughter. Maybe it wasn't easy, but you did the right thing. You made sacrifices for your child." She squeezed his hand as she fought against her own demons. "Someday she'll see that. And you have the satisfaction of knowing that you were the best father you could be, even if it was from a half a world away."

Mike looked at her for a long time, the late afternoon sun casting his features in a golden relief. After a few moments he shifted slightly so that he was facing Kira directly, and he took her face in his hands. Quietly, he whispered, "Kira North, will you marry me?"

Laughter bubbled up from her chest, and the smile that was returned to her was warm and genuine. "No," she said after she had gotten the giggles under control. "And I have a date in dialysis right now, but I would love to have coffee with you later."

"Is this a sympathy date?"

"Definitely."

"All right." He shrugged. "I'll take it any way I can get it."

"You're that desperate?" she teased.

"Maybe." The twinkle in his eye was back, but an instant later it mellowed, and he reached out to caress her cheek again. "Got a kiss for a desperate, lonely doctor with an ongoing identity crisis?"

A witty retort formed on Kira's tongue, but it held there as he dipped his head down toward her. Her pulse throbbed heavily in her throat as she allowed his lips to caress hers in a slow, languorous kiss. It was brief but sweet. And when he pulled away he left behind a warm, tingling sensation that spread outward from her mouth to her toes.

She licked her lips before moving away. "Uh…I have to go. Rachel's waiting."

"Okay," he said. "Pick you up at eight and we'll get some of that mile-high pie."

"It's a date." She smiled and slipped out of the office and then the suite as quickly and efficiently as possible.

Confusion and chaos ruled over her senses as she walked briskly toward the dialysis unit. Maybe Mike was exactly what she needed in the face of her current upheaval. Alec's presence was throwing her whole world askew. What she needed was a solid, responsible influence. She needed someone she could depend on. Someone who knew the meaning of sacrifice and commitment.

Maybe what she needed was Mike LaRocque.

* * * * *

Dr. Mike LaRocque watched the door close quietly behind his little angel of mercy. After she left, he grabbed up his briefcase and jacket, and sauntered out the door with a self-satisfied smirk plastered across his face.

He strode down hall toward the elevator, his steps resolute and certain. "You think you're gonna lure her back to you, Frechette?" he murmured to himself. "Well, if you do, then think again. I know just what our little lady needs." He stabbed at the down button. "What she needs is a man who needs her. And that's exactly what she's going to get."

Chapter Nine

ꟾ

"Hi ya, kiddo," said Kira with enthusiasm as she sauntered into the familiar dialysis suite. "How's my favorite invalid?"

The sniffle caught her completely off guard. "Okay, I guess."

Rachel was obviously not okay. Her eyes were red and raw from crying, and there was a wad of tissues in her lap. "What's wrong, honey?" Kira settled down in the chair beside her, and grasped a pale hand. "Did they have trouble accessing your shunt again? I think maybe—"

"No, no." Rachel shook her head. "It was nothing like that." She coughed and blew her nose before attempting a weak smile. "I just blew off a great new kidney so I could entertain this pesky virus."

"Oh, Rachel." Kira's heart was in her shoes. "Wasn't there any possible way?" As soon as she asked it, she knew what a ridiculous question it was. Of course there wasn't. These decisions weren't made lightly. The immediate welfare of the recipient was paramount. Surgery was risky enough for a healthy patient. Respiratory illnesses almost always ruled out a trip to the OR.

Rachel was shaking her head. "No, my fever was too high. They couldn't risk it." She plucked a fresh tissue out of the box and crumpled it in her fist without using it. "But that's okay. Easy come, easy go."

"It's okay to be upset about it, Rachel. Your whole future is hinging on a new kidney. But it will happen. You just have to be patient."

"It's not really me I'm worried about, you know." Rachel gazed at her hands.

"No?"

"It's Mom and Dad."

At first Kira thought she was just making a brave attempt to deny her disappointment, but then Rachel looked up and Kira saw the sincerity in her eyes as she continued. "But especially Dad. Mom handles it better, somehow. Dad takes it all so personally."

"You're his daughter, Rachel. He can't help but take it personally."

"I know that, but I think he blames himself for everything. And he tries so hard to make up for it." She shook her head and swiped at a fresh swell of tears. "You should have seen his face when we got the page..." she swallowed, "and then when we found out I couldn't undergo surgery..." Her sigh was far too heavy for someone so young. "He seemed angry for a moment. I almost wondered if he was mad at me."

"Oh Rachel, you know he—"

Rachel shook her head. "Oh, I knew he wasn't really. It just seemed that way. Just for a moment. And then he got so sad I was mad at myself for even thinking such a thing. I hate that my illness hurts him so much." She gazed down at the tissue in her hands. "I just hate it."

Kira didn't know what to say. How could she comfort Rachel? How could she tell someone else that she cared too much? That she needed to stop taking on the loads of other people's problems, when Kira was so guilty of that offense herself?

"I just want him to stop hating himself and to start loving me," whispered Rachel, more to herself than to Kira. "That's all I want."

Kira reached out and stroked Rachel's arm. "Have you tried telling him that? Maybe that's all he needs to hear."

She was startled to feel a presence behind her. "I've tried," said Lauren. "He just smiles and agrees with me, but he doesn't really hear it."

Feeling restless, Kira stood and walked to the window. "At least he's the type who feels a responsibility for his children. From what I hear men like that are few and far between."

"Yes. You've definitely got a point there." Lauren handed her daughter a ginger ale. "You keep drinking, kiddo. I don't care what they say, your throat needs the fluids."

"Thanks, Mom." Rachel sipped from it, then set it down and picked up a novel that was lying beside her. "Uh, you know, I'm really into this book. The sex is finally getting good." She smiled mischievously. "I'd kinda like to read for awhile, so why don't you two go have a coffee or something?"

"Are you trying to get rid of us?" asked Lauren suspiciously.

"Maybe."

Lauren tucked a strand of Rachel's dark, silky hair behind her ear. "All right. I could use a dose of caffeine after all the excitement." She turned to Kira, who was watching the exchange wistfully. "How about it, buddy? Caffeine and pastry?"

"My two favorite things in life." Kira smiled and stepped over to squeeze Rachel's hand. "Hang in there, trooper."

Rachel nodded mutely and shooed them out the door.

Kira and Lauren walked down the hall to the elevators, their footsteps echoing on the cool blue-tiled floor. Lauren punched the down button a couple of times before speaking. "She wanted to be alone so she could cry some more."

"Yeah, I kinda figured that."

The bell dinged and they stepped into an empty car. Lauren leaned heavily against the elevator wall. "You can't know how difficult it is to see your child in pain, Kira. To see them face such blinding disappointment, and to worry about whether they'll live to see their twenty-first birthday."

Kira stared at the blank elevator doors and blinked back tears. "Yes, I do."

Lauren shook her head. "I know you work with those kids upstairs, but it's different when they're your own. It's so very different."

"I had a daughter, Lauren," she said softly. "I do know. I know exactly what it's like."

* * * * *

The four-inch thick oak door slammed shut with an ominous thud of finality.

Jonathan Cromwell looked up from the papers on his desk that he and Carl Stuart were studying. "Monsieur Frechette?"

Alec stalked toward him, ignoring the daggers that Carl Stuart was casting at him with his eyes. Alec approached the imposing desk and its equally imposing occupant.

Cromwell frowned as Alec halted directly across from him and regarded him with a steady stare. He arched his eyebrows. "Is there something I can do for you, Alec?"

"You can cut the crap, Your Honor."

"Watch it, Frechette," growled Stuart.

Cromwell raised a hand in silent reprimand before addressing Alec in measured tones. "And to what *crap* would you be referring?"

Alec settled himself comfortably in one of the leather armchairs that were situated across from the Right Honorable Governor General. "It would seem that you were not completely forthright with me about your reasons for hiring me."

"I believe I hired you to watch out for my granddaughter," said Cromwell with a puzzled frown.

"You said you were concerned because of the recent string of rapes in the area, but I now believe there is considerably more to her story." Alec continued without giving Cromwell a chance to cut in. "I want to know exactly what happened at Queen's University. Darcy has been hesitant to share her story with me, so I came to you." He leaned forward, bracing his elbows on his knees. "I want to know exactly what I'm dealing with here. And if you won't tell me I will walk out that door, contract or no contract. I don't take this kind of shit from anybody—not even the Queen's emissary to Canada." Alec leaned back again and crossed his arms…and waited.

Jonathan Cromwell tapped his pen on the desk as he regarded Alec thoughtfully. "Carl, would you excuse us please?"

"I am perfectly aware of the situation, sir," he replied tightly.

Tap, tap, tap. "Of course. But I'd still like a moment alone with Monsieur Frechette."

Carl scowled at Alec as he stepped away from his boss. "All right." He headed for the door and said over his shoulder. "Just let me know when you're ready to go over the agenda for the Premiere's visit."

Except for the irritating tapping of his pen, Cromwell remained silent until the door had closed and he and Alec were alone.

Alec became impatient. "Can we get on with this? I have a very restless lady upstairs who wants to go shopping for this big dinner of yours." Alec had to admit that part of his irritation stemmed from the fact that he hated playing escort on these endless shopping trips. He'd seen enough sling-backs and stiletto heels to last him a lifetime. But this was his lot in life. This was his role in the grand scheme of things and, dammit, he had better get used to it.

Cromwell finally laid down his monogrammed, gold pen and steepled his gnarled fingers. "Darcy was involved in something of a scandal at Queen's. It was regretful that she allowed herself to become involved with a certain, less than morally responsible young man. She made some poor choices, but she's young and I hope she's learned from them."

Alec felt his eyes making a desperate attempt to roll toward the ceiling. He restrained the gesture with some difficulty. "What was the scandal?" he said succinctly.

Cromwell took a deep breath and dropped his hands. "She and this young man were caught in a somewhat...compromising position in a faculty office. It came out later that he had had a crush on her for some time. They dated a few times but she refused his advances. Apparently he didn't take *no* for an answer. He drugged her with this date rape drug..."

"Rohypnol?"

Cromwell's hand was inching toward that damn pen again. "Precisely. He lured her to his office and gave her the drink so that he could seduce her more easily." He took a deep breath as if he were drawing to the end of his narrative. "I'm afraid he may not be taking the consequences too well. Darcy came back here to recover and I hired you to help assure that he wouldn't accost her or try to seek some twisted brand of justice."

"Justice?" Alec narrowed his eyes. "That would imply that *he* had been wronged in some way. Not the other way around."

Cromwell's jaw tensed. "You read too much into the word. He was the only one who believed he had been wronged."

Alec shook his head in frustration. This family was very adept at telling stories with lots of holes. "All right." He measured his words carefully. "What were these *consequences* that you mentioned? Was he expelled? Were there criminal charges?"

"There was insufficient evidence to warrant criminal prosecution, but he lost his position on the faculty."

Alec's eyebrows shot up, but then he thought maybe he should have seen that one coming. "He was a professor?"

"Yes. And Darcy was in one of his classes. It made the whole thing quite reprehensible." He picked up the pen and tapped it once on the blotter for emphasis.

Alec was incredulous. Could this relatively intelligent, well-read, accomplished diplomat really be so stupid? Alec had discounted Carl's reference to Darcy as being a spoiled brat, but now he was beginning to wonder. He licked his lips before plunging in. "Has it occurred to you…sir, that perhaps Darcy was not the victim in this scenario?"

Tap, tap, tap. "I'm afraid I don't know what you mean."

"Is it possible that it was Darcy who had the crush on her teacher? And Darcy who seduced him in his office?"

Tap, tap, tap.

"Has it occurred to you that this business about the Rohypnol came out *later* because she had to come up with it to save her butt and push the blame elsewhere? And that perhaps that is why there was no police prosecution?"

Tap, tap, tap.

"That would also explain why the man I saw in the restaurant the other night was so angry and desperate, and why he would be seeking *justice* from your granddaughter with such zealous dedication."

Tap, tap, tap.

"It pains me to point out to you, Mr. Cromwell, that your granddaughter hardly strikes me as the type to resist the advances of a reasonably attractive man who could do positive things for her grades."

Tap, tap—Cromwell vaulted from his chair and crossed to the window. "That's quite enough, Monsieur. I will not have you disparaging my granddaughter to me. It's true she has always been something of a free spirit, but that does not excuse this man's actions. He was in a position of authority, and I would expect better from him."

Alec blinked, then leaned back in his chair once more. "Are you saying that, because he was a professor and made the mistake of getting involved with a student, he deserved to have rape accusations thrown at him?"

Cromwell gritted his teeth. "What I am *saying* is that you now know the story, and this subject is now closed. I expect you to fulfill the terms of your contract without further discussion or questioning of my instructions."

"I see," said Alec slowly. "So it is with your blessing that the damage to her car is taken care of...privately? Without involving the authorities?"

"Yes," said Cromwell with exaggerated authority. "We don't want to expose Darcy or this office to any further scandal. But I want you to be especially careful with her safety."

With gritting teeth and long, slow breaths Alec got up and headed for the door. "I'll fulfill the terms of the contract but you can rest assured, *Your Honor,* that I will not be choosing to stay on when my six-month term is up."

"Frechette!" Cromwell's voice stopped Alec with his hand on the doorknob.

He turned around to meet the other man's gaze with hooded eyes.

"I do hope you took my warning the other day to heart. I will not tolerate your taking advantage of the situation with Darcy. She is vulnerable to men of your charms, and I won't see her exploited."

Alec just managed to stifle a loud guffaw. "You'll forgive me for asking then, if you are so worried about my influence over her, why did you hire *me* of all people?"

"Just do your job, Frechette. That's all I ask. Do your job…and nothing else."

Puzzled and disappointed with the man he had thought warranted his respect, Alec stepped out of the room and closed the door carefully behind him. He was startled by a voice very close to his left ear. "You know why he hired you, don't you?"

Alec whirled around. "What? What is it, Stuart? Why don't you just spit it out? Say what you mean for once in your life."

Carl smiled evilly. "He hired you because she begged and pleaded for you. He may have wanted her protected, but she just wanted a juicy hunk of beefcake."

Alec clenched his fists, but was having trouble refuting the accusation. "Why would he give in to that kind of pressure if he knew what she wanted?"

"Because he's a sap where his family's concerned. Didn't you see that flaunted in your face just now? She has him wrapped around her little finger. He can't bring himself to deny her anything. So he knows full well that she'll be doing everything in her power to get you in the sack, but he expects you to be the martyr and turn her down." Stuart straightened his tie and pushed his glasses up his nose. "But I suppose that's asking too much, isn't it, Frechette?"

Alec narrowed his eyes. How could Stuart know what had transpired between him and Darcy already? Were there hidden cameras in the bedroom? Or was Stuart just fishing?

"I suppose," Alec said slowly, "that you had better watch your mouth or you'll be picking pieces of your teeth out of your nostrils." He whirled around and headed up the stairs, barely seeing the sweeping oak banister through the crimson haze of rage that had settled over his eyes.

"The truth hurts, doesn't it, Frechette?" taunted Stuart. "All she wanted was a tight butt and broad shoulders to flaunt to her friends and entertain her in the sack. Face it, you're just a walking hormone with a shoulder holster."

The insults barely registered in Alec's seething cerebrum. Maybe that was all Darcy wanted. Maybe that was all she saw when she looked at him. But maybe she was going to get more than she bargained for. Alec would see to it.

* * * * *

Kira had passed on the cafeteria pie, opting to wait for the more appetizing creation at Zeke's. She had, however, braved the coffee. She poured a third dollop of cream into her mug. The cafeteria coffee could strip paint off a rusted-out Ford but she couldn't tolerate sugar, so loaded on the cream in outrageous proportions. She picked up the plastic spoon and stirred, hoping she wouldn't pull out a grisly stub.

"I am so, so sorry," sighed Lauren. "I—I just had no idea you had a child."

"Don't be silly. You had no way of knowing. In fact I've been very deliberate about not telling people."

"Why?"

Kira sipped and grimaced as the hot caffeine seared its way down her throat. "I guess because I was trying to put that part of my life behind me. You can't just say *'Oh, my daughter died of a congenital disease'* and leave it at that. It invariably demands an intimate discussion over coffee with lots of regretful words and sad looks."

"Oh," was all that managed to squeeze past Lauren's tensed lips.

Kira managed a sympathetic smile. "I'm just teasing."

"No, no. You're right. That's an incredibly personal story, and I don't blame you for not sharing it with every Tom, Dick and Lauren that comes along. If you don't want to—"

"No." Kira's voice was soft but emphatic. "It's time I did. In fact, there's never been a better time. I need to confide in someone or I feel like I'll explode."

"Why? Why now?"

"After Cherisse died, her father and I split up. I hadn't seen him for seven years—until two days ago, that is."

"Cherisse," mused Lauren. "That's a beautiful name."

"She was beautiful," said Kira wistfully. "She had the most brilliant red hair." Kira touched her own short-cropped mane. "Even brighter than mine. And the most beautiful waves. Her eyes were an intense shade of green—exactly the color of her father's. She smiled and laughed so easily, she..." Her voice trailed off into nothingness as she gazed down at the emerald on her finger. Then she whispered, "Cherisse was Alec's grandmother's name. He insisted."

"Alec? He was your husband?" Lauren took a tentative bite of her Danish, and Kira began to absently twirl the ring around her finger.

"No, we never married. We were just talking about it when Cherisse was diagnosed." She shrugged heavily, suddenly feeling the old familiar weight of a thousand pounds of sand on her shoulders. "After that, it seemed ridiculous to talk about getting married in the face of our daughter's illness."

"It was degenerative?"

"Mm-hmm. She was born perfectly healthy. The first year of her life was a fairy tale—for both of us."

"This Alec, was he a good father?"

"He tried." Kira smiled slightly at the memory. "He obviously loved her and he really tried, but he was hopelessly inept when it came to changing diapers and bathing. I breast-fed, so he couldn't do much there. I handled most of the day-to-day stuff, but I didn't mind."

"Mmm."

"He played with her some and, when she started to walk, he was more in his element." Kira felt the smile slip off her face. "But that was when we noticed the change."

"How old was she?"

"Just a little under a year. She had started to totter around furniture, and hold onto our fingers to take her first steps, when suddenly she just sort of stopped developing. Within a couple of months, she had stopped walking altogether. A few months after that she even stopped crawling."

Lauren silently sipped her coffee and allowed her friend to tell her story uninterrupted.

"It took months for them to diagnose her properly. G-M-1 Gangliosidosis is quite rare."

"Wow," said Lauren softly. "That's quite the handle. It sounds—"

"Daunting. Intimidating. Terrifying." Kira completed Lauren's thought for her. "Hopeless." She gazed into the cream-laden depths of her coffee. "And that's exactly what it was. Hopeless. It's a degenerative condition with no cure, and very little in the way of treatment other than to keep the patient comfortable as long as possible. They rarely live past the age of five. Cherisse died three months after her third birthday."

"Dear God," whispered Lauren.

"I quit work to look after her. She needed constant attention."

"In what way?" asked Lauren. "How does the disease manifest?"

Kira sighed deeply as she sifted through the information she had gleaned from the reams of literature she had read on the subject. She had struggled to understand the disease in as much detail as was possible for a layman with little medical training. As a nurse, she now understood it even more fully.

But she wanted to keep it simple and to the point for Lauren's benefit.

"You see," she said at last, "Cherisse's body lacked the enzymes that are necessary to break down the fatty tissue that builds up around the brain and spinal cord. Initially everything worked fine but, as she grew, and more and more fat built up, it began interfering with her central nervous system functions. She began to lose motor control, and eventually basic functions like swallowing and breathing became affected." She managed to choke down another swallow of coffee. "Eventually she needed a special wheelchair—oxygen occasionally. I had to feed her through a tube. There were seizures, and endless trips to the hospital." Kira stopped, suddenly exhausted and overcome with images from those days. She had watched her precious little girl wither away to a fragile husk right before her eyes, and had been powerless to stop it.

"Did she feel pain?"

"I don't know," answered Kira honestly. "It's hard to know how much cognitive function she retained, especially in the later stages. But she *did* know me. She seemed calmer, more at peace, somehow when I was with her. Somehow it helped to know that…at least a little."

"What about her father? Did she know him?"

Kira just shrugged, hesitant to address that question. Alec had been with her so little, and yet…

"Where was this?" Lauren's voice interrupted her thoughts. "Here in Ottawa?"

"No. I had moved to Montreal for…my career." She just didn't have the energy to go into the whole cop story. It was irrelevant here anyway.

"So you were far from your family," mused Lauren. "Did Alec help with her care?"

"Not really. I think the illness scared him. He worked around the house—you know, did the cleaning and the cooking. He actually got quite good at it. But then he started spending more and more time at work." Again, she picked up her coffee, which was growing tepid as she gazed at it and told her story. "He claimed we needed the money for her expenses, but I don't think he could bear to see her like that."

"So he left you with the rigors of caring for her." Lauren frowned and popped the last piece of Danish into her mouth. "Did you ever get a break?"

"Not very often. There are agencies with qualified nurses who exist just to help high-needs families like us. But honestly, I could hardly bear the thought of leaving her with a stranger, no matter how attentive and qualified." She looked up at Lauren, her eyes earnest and intense. "I only had such a short time left with her. I wanted to have every possible moment I could, no matter how exhausted it left me."

Lauren covered Kira's hand with her own. "Yes," she said quietly, "we have something in common there. I believe Rachel has many years ahead of her, but I can't shake the feeling that our time with her is so precious. Every moment should be treasured."

Kira nodded and took another sip from her coffee. That comment required no response.

"So, is that why you went into nursing?"

Kira nodded. "I had already learned so much in order to take care of Cherisse. It seemed like the logical thing to do."

"And Alec? I know a lot of marriages don't survive losing a child. I can't say I'm surprised."

"He left the day before the funeral."

Lauren blinked. "He didn't attend his own daughter's funeral?"

"It was the day after she died when we argued." She blinked furiously, refusing to cry over Alec Frechette. She had shed far too many tears and broken far too much crystal because of him already. "I confess, I said some hateful things. But so did he. He stormed out in a rage.

"I knew we were both stressed to the limit with everything and I assumed once he cooled off and figured out that we weren't ourselves when we said those things, that he'd be back. But I never saw him again." The coffee mug made it halfway to her lips before she set it back down again, untouched. "And now he's back, and I just don't know what to say to him. I see him and all I feel is anger." *And emptiness.*

"At him? Or at what he represents—the death of your daughter."

Kira looked sharply at her friend, but now that the words were said she knew it was true. "I guess both."

"Where was he all that time?"

Kira briefly considered lying about Alec's identity. She didn't know if she could tolerate any more oohing and aahing and drooling over Alec's burnished auburn hair and impish grin. Then she realized that Alec was going to be at her house the next night, and Lauren might very well see his arrival. Or what if he barbecued in the backyard? That would prove awkward as well. She might as well get it over with.

She took a deep breath and blurted out, "My ex-lover is Alec Frechette."

"Mm-hmm. And what did he do since he left you?"

Kira blinked slowly. "That name means nothing to you?"

"No." Lauren looked pensive as she thought it over again. "Should it?"

Kira chuckled as relief washed through her. She had worried for nothing. "No, of course not. He—he went into personal security, and worked in Europe. He just came back to Ottawa a couple of—"

Lauren's hands had flown to her mouth. "Oh my God! *That* Alec Frechette? You've seen the French Connection in the buff?"

So much for the heart-to-heart chat. Alec had a way of ruining everything.

Chapter Ten

ꟗ

Already stifling a severe attack of irritation, Kira stepped through her front door. Her nostrils were immediately overwhelmed by a bouquet of aromas—garlic, onion, basil and grilling chicken. Alec had already made himself at home.

It had been more than twenty-four hours since she had exchanged insults with him at the hospital. Apparently round two was about to begin. She was up for it.

She gently extricated herself from the knapsack, which had served Cujo well for another lengthy walk along the canal. She opened the zipper and lifted him out for a brief snuggle before setting him down and allowing him his freedom. His tiny nails clicked a rapid Morse code as he skittered across the tiles toward his food and water dishes. She was amazed at the absence of accusatory yaps when he found the intruder in their kitchen.

She walked in and Alec didn't even look up as he spoke. "Well, it's about time you got here," he said good-naturedly.

Kira just stood there and silently stewed in the enticing vapors that whirled about her kitchen.

Alec finally turned away from the skillet on the stove to look at her. He lifted a glass of white wine to his lips and regarded her with those hypnotic green eyes. "You're late. I decided to start without you." He raised the glass toward her. "Wine?"

"How did you get in here?"

"I picked the lock. You really need a decent security system around here."

"Have you no scruples at all?"

He cocked his head and managed to look as guileless as Opie Taylor caught with his hand in the cookie jar. "What I had was a carload of groceries that I didn't want to bake in the driveway."

"You could have waited five minutes."

He sighed heavily and Opie disappeared. "Do we have to start things off like this?" He turned around to stir whatever concoction was sizzling in the skillet. "I'm making you a nice dinner. Let's at least enjoy the food before we start on each other's throats."

Kira watched him in silence. It was a familiar scene—Alec in faded jeans and a ratty T-shirt hovering over a stove while she looked on from the adjoining room. And then she had a brief flash of Mike, as he stood at the counter in his kitchen and poured her a glass of Irish Cream liqueur on the rocks.

Kira had gone back to Mike's for a nightcap after their coffee and mile-high apple pie. They had chatted until almost one a.m. Kira had learned more about Mike's marriage and daughter, and had been amazed that she had overlooked his warmth and charm for so long. She had decided it was high time she allowed herself a little male companionship. She chose to ignore the fact that she happened to have come to that decision within days of Alec Frechette's return. Perhaps thoughts of Mike would help her to keep her distance and get through the evening with Alec without sacrificing too much. She didn't really believe that, but she had gotten very good at deluding herself.

"All right," she yielded grudgingly. "I'm sorry I was late. It was just such a beautiful afternoon, I lost track of time on my walk."

"Apology accepted." He turned around again. "And I'm sorry for committing B&E." He held out a second glass of wine. "Truce?"

She accepted the goblet. "Truce." She sipped it and examined his creation. "It smells good. What is it?"

"It will be chicken and pasta *primavera*. Which reminds me—would you mind flipping the breasts on the barbecue?"

Kira headed out the patio doors to her deck. "Still a breast man?" she asked playfully.

"Yep," he called. "But they have to be done just so. I don't like them all dried up and crusty."

Kira performed her duty and stepped back inside. "I guess you're not interested in mine anymore, then."

He peered at her from the corner of his eye. "Well now, I wouldn't say that."

Kira decided this line of conversation had gone quite far enough. "This is good wine."

"It's a Niagara Chardonnay. Not bad. But I guess I've developed a fondness for the French imports." He sipped and she watched as he closed his eyes and savored the golden nectar. "But still," he mused after he had swallowed, "not bad at all."

She settled down at the kitchen table. "Who are you now, Alec Frechette? I don't believe I know you anymore."

He dumped a load of pasta into a huge pot of boiling water. "That was your trouble, Kira. You never did."

Kira thought she should have been angry at that. A cutting retort would have been quite appropriate, but she just couldn't bring herself to say it. Maybe he was right. "Maybe we never really knew each other," she said at last. "Were we too young, Alec? We weren't ready for what happened. Maybe if we had been a little older, a little more mature—"

"Nobody's ever ready for that, Kira. Never." He stirred the pasta. "This is getting way too serious, way too fast. Let's leave the heavy stuff for after dinner."

Kira nodded agreement. "Right. It's much better to fight on a full stomach."

"Much."

* * * * *

There was a soft knock on the door to room 905. With a covert glance behind her, Darcy got up from her position on the antique love seat and sashayed through the lush suite. The Château Laurier was a landmark in Ottawa. An original of the internationally renowned chain of CP Hotels, its rooms were well appointed and the service unparalleled. Her bare feet swished across the deep burgundy carpet and she pulled open the polished brass knob.

Professor Dan Peters, complete with leather jacket and suspicious scowl, stood in the hall. "What the hell is this about, Darcy?"

"I thought we should talk."

Dan peered over her shoulder into the suite. "Where's your watchdog?"

"He thinks I'm at a family dinner. I told everybody I had a headache and snuck out the back." She stepped aside to invite him in. "It's just the two of us. No intrusions."

His frown deepened. "How do you know I won't slap you around? After what you did, you certainly deserve it."

Darcy allowed an evil twinkle to glint in her eye. "Maybe that's exactly what I have in mind."

She could see a flush of color in his cheeks, and his breathing altered slightly at the insinuation. But he still didn't step across the threshold. "I don't know. I'd be nuts to trust you."

"Ah, come on, Dan. I'm sorry for what happened. I had no idea things would turn out like that. I panicked. I—" She reached out and tugged on his jacket. "At least come inside. The last thing you want is more people talking."

With a glance down the hall, he relented and stepped inside. She closed the door behind him and led him by the hand to the love seat. He sat down, his spine rigid and his brown eyes wary. "Okay, so what did you want to talk about?"

"I've missed you," she crooned. "I was hoping to make it up to you." She pushed his jacket back off his shoulders and breathed in his ear. "I know what I did was inexcusable, but maybe you could find it in your heart to forgive me."

She rubbed her breasts against his chest and sensed the frantic pounding of his heart. *God,* men were so pathetic. They were as predictable and malleable as a wad of playdough. Show a little thigh, or rub in just the right spot and they were reduced to a wobbling mass of flesh with a woodie. Their minds became so focused on sex that everything else was wiped clean. Throw in a little money and influence, and a beautiful woman became invincible. Darcy had learned the game early and well, and she knew exactly how to win it.

"You—you're crazy, Darcy. I—"

She molded her lips to his and drew his hand to her breast. "Please," she murmured. "Just once more. For old time's sake."

His protests were soon muted as his mouth was filled with her flesh. She whispered in his ear, "Come in the bedroom, Dan. I've got something a little different in mind."

He followed her like a lovesick puppy, his tongue practically dragging on the floor in drooling anticipation. As clothes were peeled off and bodies became slick, he managed to croak out, "What were you thinking?"

She sat down and scooted back on the bed, lying down with arms and legs outflung. She fingered a set of soft, Velcro straps that were attached to the bedposts, and silently communicated her wishes.

A slow, disbelieving smile spread across his face like a stain. "You're kidding."

She merely shook her head, and he needed no more convincing. *Pathetic,* she mused. *Spineless wimp.* He deserved everything that had happened to him, and was about to happen to him.

The straps were on and his lithe, naked form was hovering over her.

"Now," she whispered. "Put your hands on my throat."

He frowned in confusion. "What?"

"Haven't you heard how that heightens orgasm? I've always wanted to try it," she purred. "Please? It'll be fine."

He thrust into her and complied with hesitant enthusiasm. Within moments, however, he was lost in the rush of a forbidden experience. Sweat had plastered his hair to his forehead and his eyes were closed in rapture. So he was taken completely off guard when her voice cut through his utopia. "Carl!" she shouted. "Get this moron off me."

"Huh?" Dan opened his eyes and was astounded to find a firm hand pulling him back and away from the subject of his fantasies.

"Come on, sucker," scoffed Carl Stuart as he tossed a robe to Darcy and handed Dan his clothes. "You're done here." He rolled his eyes. "Thank God."

"What? What the hell?"

Darcy pulled on the robe and slid off the bed. Carl had already undone the straps to free her. "Did you get it all?" she asked with a glance at the video camera on the bedside table.

Dan's eyes fell on the camera. Then they darted back and forth from Darcy to Carl. "You bitch!" he hissed and took a step toward her.

To Darcy's delight, Carl pulled out his small semi-automatic pistol and shoved it in Dan's stomach. "I would suggest, *sir,* that you get your clothes on and get the hell out."

"And don't bother me again," said Darcy evenly. "That stunt with my car was the last straw. If you come near me again, I'll mail copies of that tape to every university in Canada."

Dan's face was stricken. "You—you wouldn't." Then something new washed across his features. "Car? What the hell are you talking about?"

"You can drop the innocent act, Dan." Darcy grabbed her clothes and headed for the bathroom. "Just take the warning to heart. You keep this up and everyone will know you for the sick, twisted pervert you are." She grinned evilly. "Not that I'm complaining. It was fun." She began to pull the door closed. "For a while."

Carl watched Dan pull on his underwear and jeans. "You may as well learn now, lover boy. Stay away from the rich ones. They're all witches, but give 'em money and they sprout horns and a tail. They chew you up and spit you out as soon as fuck you blind."

"Shut up, asshole," muttered Dan as he pulled on his jeans. "Just leave me the hell alone."

* * * * *

Kira pushed her empty plate to the center of the table and sighed contentedly. "Your skills have improved."

Alec grinned. "In many things."

She leaned forward and propped her chin in her hands. "Are the stories true? Do you really sleep with all your clients?"

Alec's grin faded. "You're not wasting any time."

"No, no." She shook her head. "I'm not judging you. Just curious. I couldn't help but follow the stories about you, and I know you can't believe half of what you read, but I had to wonder..."

He drained the last of his Chardonnay and regarded the empty glass regretfully. "Let me put it this way, I can't exactly sue *The Enquirer* for defamation of character."

Kira was surprised at the knot that formed in her stomach upon his admission. But what had she expected? Had she expected him to be faithful to a bunch of painful memories? Or did the anxiety she felt stem from the look of raw suffering on Alec's face? She would have expected him to boast over his conquests—not look like his virtue had been compromised.

"I see," she said finally.

"No, you don't." He stood and gathered the empty plates. "But it doesn't matter because I don't think I do either."

Kira's confusion was mounting at his odd comments and puzzling demeanor. But then she glanced at the clock and cursed. "Shoot! I almost forgot."

"What?"

Kira had to grit her teeth at the next words that were destined to come out of her mouth. She stood and cleared the remainder of the dishes from the table. "I need to ask you a favor."

He smiled. "Oh yeah? This I gotta hear."

"It's not for me. It's for a friend."

"Of course. It always is."

Kira fought the urge to kick him in the shins. "I'm serious. My neighbor found out who my guest was going to be this evening and she begged me to bring you over to meet her teenage daughter."

Alec groaned. "Oh, God! Spare me."

Kira decided to be tolerant. No doubt Alec got his fill of young women pawing at him and hanging on his every word. Men just hated that sort of thing, she thought sardonically. "This is different, Alec. I'd really like you to see her. She had a big disappointment this week, and could use a lift. Otherwise her mother wouldn't have asked." After Lauren had apologized profusely for her outburst over Kira's revelation, she had humbly made the request on Rachel's behalf. Rachel had had a crush on him since she was sixteen, and meeting Alec Frechette might be just what she needed to lift her spirits. Kira could hardly say no.

"Oh yeah?" Alec popped a last morsel of bread into his mouth. "Did she get passed over for head cheerleader or something?"

"No," said Kira slowly, already relishing what this would do to him, and hating herself for it. "She got passed over for a kidney transplant because she had a bad infection. She's a nineteen-year-old dialysis patient, and I think you could go out of your way for her, just a little."

Alec stared at her, his expression stricken. "You enjoyed that, didn't you?"

"No." To her surprise, she meant it. "I thought I would, but I didn't." She watched him rinsing the plates. "So, will you?"

"Yeah, sure. It's what I live for."

"What is?"

"Forget it." He dried his hands and made a grand gesture with his hand. "Lead the way."

They headed out the front door and made their way across the lush carpet of greenery that Tim cared for with such selfless dedication. Kira rang the doorbell and, within moments, the paneled oak door with the beveled glass windows swung in to reveal Tim Nickle in jogging shorts and T-shirt.

"Hi, Tim," said Kira brightly. She turned to introduce Alec. "Tim, this is Alec Frechette."

Alec extended a hand. "Good to meet you. I'm afraid it's been a while since I had a neighbor. I'm glad Kira has some good ones."

Tim accepted his hand and managed a brief shake. "Yeah," he said curtly. "We do try and look out for each other."

Kira was astounded at the iciness in Tim's tone. She had never known him to be anything but warm and friendly. But then she thought maybe she knew why, and she silently cursed her enormous mouth.

Tim stepped away from the door and motioned them inside. "Come on in. Rachel's been in a dither ever since Lauren broke the *big news*."

Kira threw Alec an apologetic glance as they followed him down the stairs to the living room, but she wasn't sure if he noticed.

They reached the bottom of the stairs.

Alec stopped and a slow smile spread across his face. But it was quickly replaced by a look of stark amazement. *"Mon Dieu!"*

Rachel had stood up from her carefully arranged position on the couch. She was wiping her palms on her jeans and smiling uncertainly, but Alec's exclamation wiped it cleanly away. "What?"

Alec shook his head and stepped over to her, taking both her hands in his and stepping back to take in the full view from head to toe. "Kira lied to me. She said I was going to meet a nineteen-year-old girl, but that simply wasn't true."

Rachel began to get a hold on his train of thought. A ghost of a smile was back. "Oh?"

He turned to Kira. "This is no girl. This is one of the loveliest young women I have ever laid eyes on." Then he frowned and turned back to Rachel. "No, that's not right either. Lovely doesn't do you justice." He leaned in and Kira saw him whisper something intimately into Rachel's ear. The color that sprang to her cheeks told the tale well enough.

"Monsieur Frechette," said Lauren, who had come up behind Kira and was watching the events unfold with a mother's approval. "Are you sure filling her head with such tales and so many compliments is wise?"

Alec frowned but didn't take his eyes off Rachel. "Tales? Hardly. I've known women from here to the Mediterranean, from France to Bermuda and back again, and I have seen few who could hold a candle to the ravishing beauty that stands before me."

Rachel's color deepened. "You're teasing."

He glanced back at Kira. "Do I tease?"

"Not about that."

He turned back to Rachel. "See?" Then he leaned in and whispered another mysterious nothing, and Rachel nodded. He moved around and draped an arm across her shoulders. "Is the audience really necessary? I came here to see Rachel. I hardly remember selling tickets."

Lauren chuckled and motioned for Kira and Tim to follow her to the kitchen. "Let's leave these two to their own devices."

Tim followed, but not before a lengthy, appraising glance in Alec's direction. "If you need anything, Rachel, don't hesitate—"

"Daddy!"

He frowned and silently followed the women up the stairs.

Kira placed a hand on his arm and said lightly, "Don't worry, Dad. He won't ravish her in her own living room."

"Mmm." He didn't sound convinced.

The threesome settled around the kitchen table with a carafe of coffee and a plate of cookies. A giggle trickled up the stairs from the living room.

"It's good to hear her laugh again," sighed Lauren.

"Alec is very good at making women feel special—and safe," she hastened to add. She was startled to realize she wasn't fabricating. She had always felt exactly like that when they were together. *Special. Safe. Cared for.* Maybe that was why his abandonment had hurt so much. She missed feeling like that.

"A bit too good, if you ask me," grumbled Tim.

Lauren covered his hand with hers. "I think Daddy's feeling a little overprotective."

He didn't answer, merely stirred his coffee with unparalleled vigor.

Kira suspected that wasn't quite all there was to it, but she had no intention of broaching the subject. She had forgotten how freely Lauren shared things with her husband. Good communication was a definite asset and helped build a strong marriage. But it did have its downfalls.

They nibbled and sipped in silence for a few moments, allowing the occasional giggle and murmur that drifted to them from beyond the doorway to fill in the blank spaces.

"Why is he back?" asked Tim finally. "What's he after?"

"Tim!" scolded Lauren. "He might not be *after* anything. He and Kira have a history." She glanced at her friend. "Maybe the chapter just isn't quite closed yet."

"It was for me," murmured Kira into her mug.

"Maybe it wasn't for him."

Kira looked askance at Lauren again. She had been getting odd vibes from Lauren ever since their conversation in the cafeteria. It was almost as if Lauren wasn't completely sympathetic to Kira's predicament. She hadn't exactly taken up Alec's cause, but Kira had gotten the definite impression that she wasn't convinced of his culpability.

"What is it, Lauren? Is there something on your mind? Do you think I'm to blame somehow for his running out? For him running away like a spoiled child from his responsibilities to me and our families?"

Lauren sighed. "I'm not sure. I just would like to hear his side of it."

Kira felt betrayed and slighted by the one person she had assumed would be her advocate no matter what. After all, look at all Kira had done for Lauren's family. The least she could expect in return was a little loyalty. "I'm not convinced he has a *side*."

"Everyone has reasons for the things they do," mused Lauren to no one in particular. "They're not always the right reasons, or the most noble ones, but there are always reasons. There is always a story. And I'm not convinced you know Alec's."

"I lived with him for more than four years. I can't imagine there's much about him I don't know. Or at least there wasn't back then."

"You might be surprised."

Kira was startled to realize it was Tim who had spoken.

He looked at her and his eyes swirled with emotions she couldn't begin to name. "You might be very surprised at the secrets a man can hide in his heart."

Lauren broke in. "There were things I didn't know about myself, that I was astonished to find out when we were faced with Rachel's illness." She grasped Tim's hand again. "That kind of personal struggle is hard to acknowledge to yourself, let alone share with a spouse."

"You two seem to have managed just fine."

"It hasn't been easy," murmured Lauren.

"Are we interrupting something?"

The trio looked up to see Alec and Rachel standing hand in hand in the doorway to the kitchen. Rachel was positively glowing.

"Just a little sharing of our souls," said Lauren lightly. She stood and walked over to her daughter. "Did he treat you well? Or should Tim take him out and thrash him to within an inch of his life?"

"Oh, Mom," moaned her daughter.

Lauren laughed and wrapped an arm around Rachel's shoulders. "Join us for coffee, Alec?"

"I would love to but—"

"But you and Kira have some business together."

He looked at Lauren with surprise and admiration. "Yes, we do. But I thoroughly enjoyed meeting Rachel." He bent to kiss her lightly on the cheek as Kira rose to join them. "Promise you won't forget me?" he said softly.

Rachel shook her head and her eyes glittered with youthful awe and gratitude. "Never."

Alec smiled warmly and Kira's heart melted. He used to look at her like that. He used to look at Cherisse like that. Suddenly she missed it all so much her chest ached.

"Ready?" she asked, her voice annoyingly brittle.

"Ready." Alec nodded toward Lauren and Tim. "It was nice to meet you, and I hope—" He suddenly seemed uncomfortable. "I wish you all the best."

Tim didn't rise from the table. He only managed a terse "Thanks" before Lauren ushered them to the front door.

Alec and Kira stepped out into the cool evening air. Dusk had settled and a few hesitant stars were just winking into existence. A slight breeze was whisking away the humidity of the day.

"I know you just had a long walk with Cujo," said Alec. "So how about just sitting on the deck with a glass of wine?"

Kira glanced at the sky. "And watching the stars come out?"

"Yeah." He moved away from her toward the back of the house. "Something like that."

She followed a few paces behind, noticing the rigid set of his shoulders beneath the old Montreal Expos T-shirt. Her sneakers padded up the stairs to the deck and Alec called back, "Just sit down. I'll get the wine."

She settled down in a padded deck chair and listened to Alec rummaging around in her kitchen. He seemed to know instinctively where she kept everything. Did he really know her that well? Or had she unconsciously mimicked him in her culinary habits?

The patio door slid open and a glass was placed delicately in her hand. "Red this time?" she asked.

"A merlot. One of my favorites."

She studied the crimson liquid, then she studied him as he took a languorous sip. "Thanks for being so nice to Rachel. It really seemed to cheer her up."

He shrugged. "She's a lovely girl. It was no trouble." He took another sip. "Her father was a little cool to me, though. I guess he's read *The Enquirer* too."

"I don't think that was it."

"No?"

Kira didn't know why she felt the need to share this with him. She could have let the *Enquirer* comment go, and he would have thought nothing of it. But now she was committed. "I-I mean—" She took a sip of wine, and allowed the warmth of the alcohol to fortify her. "His wife is a good friend of mine. I told her some…things about us. And I'm afraid she shared them with Tim."

Even in the subdued light, she could see his jaw tense. "What…*things* are you talking about? What did you tell her?"

"The truth."

He took a measured breath and Kira fought the urge to squirm in her seat.

"Could you be more specific?"

Okay, this was her chance. This was her chance to throw all the accusations, and hurl all the insults she had harbored for the last seven years. She should relish the opportunity to cut him down to size. She should dive right in, head first, and wallow in the satisfaction of it. So why was she hesitant to even dip in her toes?

Despite her reservations, she tested the waters anyway. "I told her how you left me alone with Cherisse so much. I told her how you started to spend more and more time at work, and how I thought maybe you couldn't bear to see Cherisse like that." Once her toes were wet, the water sucked at her like quicksand. "I told her how I was left with all the day-to-day care without your support. And then I told her how you ran off, leaving me all alone to face a funeral and two grieving families."

"Oh," he said tightly. "Is that all?"

She continued, ignoring the sarcasm in his voice, but the twirling emerald ring belied her agitation. "Tim is very protective of Rachel. He's very involved with her welfare and care. I'm afraid he may have judged you something of a cad based on what Lauren told him."

"No," he growled. "You think?"

"Alec—"

"Is that really what you think? You think I worked more because I was afraid? Afraid of facing her illness?"

"Well, if that wasn't the reason, what was? We didn't need the money that badly. It was a flimsy excuse. You—"

"Dammit, Kira! I told you, over and over, what the problem was, but you refused to hear me."

"What? What are you talking about?"

He stood and walked to the railing of the deck, his hands clenched on the rail as if he were trying to choke the life out of it. "I wanted to help. I tried..." He shook his head in frustration. "Time and again I asked you to let me help you...to teach me what to do so I could have a part in her care."

"But you did help. You looked after the house and the meals so I had time to—"

He laughed bitterly and met her eyes. "You actually think that should have been enough, don't you? You actually think that cooking and cleaning and paying the bills brought me closer to the daughter that I barely had three years to get to know?"

There was a knot in Kira's chest that was beginning to constrict painfully around her heart. She couldn't answer.

"Do you know how hard it was to watch you feeding her, kissing her, comforting her, and not to be *allowed* the privilege of being a part of that?"

"I-I didn't think you really wanted to get involved in the feeding tubes and the diapers. It was all so...messy. Even when she was a baby you—"

"Even when she was a baby you shut me out!" He didn't bother to hide his rage. "If I didn't do it *your* way, it was wrong. If I didn't hold her head just so in the tub, you panicked. If I didn't powder her bum, you scolded me. It was your way or no way, Kira. Eventually I gave up. I couldn't live up to your expectations." He turned away and whispered into the night. "I still can't."

The knot in Kira's chest had swelled until it was pressing on her throat. It couldn't be true. Certainly, she remembered him offering kindly to help, once or twice. But she had always thought... She had always assumed... *Oh God.*

She had complained to Lauren that he left her with all the care, but had she really wanted his help? Would she have accepted it gracefully if he had really been willing and eager to learn? She didn't want to dwell on those thoughts that chafed painfully at old, scabbed-over wounds. So she latched onto something else.

"But you got to look after her that last night, didn't you? And you didn't wake me up!" Now she stood and clenched her fists at her sides, all the anger and the pain of that night focused on the man before her. "I had fallen asleep, and you knew she wasn't going to make it through the night. And you didn't have the decency to wake me and let me say—" Her throat constricted again. "You didn't let me say good-bye."

He looked at her. His eyes were full and his breathing was choppy. He spoke slowly and deliberately, every word vibrating with emotion. "You fell asleep because you were so damn exhausted you couldn't keep your eyes open another minute. God help me but I took advantage of that. When the alarms went off, I went to her and—" He sucked in lung full of fragrant night air. "And for the first time in weeks, and for the last time in my life, I held my daughter, and tried to let her know that I loved her. I didn't wake you, and I'm not sorry. You would have tried to take that away from me too."

"But—"

"I loved her so much, and that was my last chance to be with her. I knew you'd hate me for it, but I didn't care. When you threw your accusations at me the next day, I decided I'd had enough. You were never going to let me in after that. You weren't going to let me share your grief," he turned back to the railing, "or your life. So what was the point in even trying?"

Kira sat back down, feeling drained and raw. She just sat there, staring at his tensed shoulders and whitening knuckles. She sat there and, for the first time in her life, wondered if it had all been her fault.

She wasn't sure how much time passed. Her mind was so focused on the days of drugs and seizures and tears that she barely noticed him kneeling in front of her.

"That's what I had to say. That's why I came back." He picked up her hand and caressed her knuckles, and the familiar warmth traveled up her arm, quelling all the fears and doubts. "I had to try to convince you that I wasn't what you thought."

Those green eyes and the fine spattering of freckles hadn't changed since the day she had met him eleven years ago. The scar beneath his eye was a vivid reminder of the days when they had shared a beat. They had been chasing a young runaway and Alec had slipped on an oil slick in an alley. He had landed amidst shards of glass from a broken beer bottle, and had come away with the vivid reminder to take it slow and watch your step. That was exactly why they hadn't rushed into marriage. They had wanted to take it one day at a time, and be certain that they knew what they were getting into. But, despite their caution, they had been so sure.

They'd had something special back then. There had been a reason why she fell in love with him. Maybe she was gradually remembering what that was.

When she didn't respond, he continued, "So did I? Did I convince you?" His knuckles brushed her cheek and she closed her eyes and soaked in the tenderness.

A moment later, she was startled to feel his lips against hers. The anger and doubt evaporated on the heated waves of longing that washed over her. She returned the kiss and her hands strayed to his chest, clutching at the worn material of his T-shirt with an urgency even she could barely fathom. Suddenly she needed him as much as she ever had—maybe more. She needed the closeness and the safety of his embrace. He had always been her refuge against the suffering around her. She hadn't felt sheltered like that—safe like that—in a very long time.

The kiss became voracious. His tongue sought hers and his arms wrapped around her back, drawing her in against that broad, muscled chest. Her breathing quickened and her blood flashed to the boiling point.

"Do you still want me, Kira?" he whispered. "Even after all this time, do you still want to make love to me?"

His hand found her breast and her soft moan was answer enough. She moved against him in an urgent search for intimacy.

And then he was gone.

He had ripped his lips from hers, and torn her arms from around his neck. He stood over her, breathing heavily and staring at her with the eyes of a predator. "But I was always good for that, wasn't I, Kira?"

"What?" She felt dazed and disoriented.

"I wasn't good for much else. I got pretty good at cooking and cleaning and running the house, but the one thing I really excelled at—the one thing that I was absolutely essential for—was to satisfy your physical needs. I couldn't be trusted with our daughter, but I was always good for a post-seizure fuck or two."

"Alec! That—that wasn't how it was!"

"Mais oui," he said with a vicious sneer, "that was exactly how it was. Well, I bet you were hardly surprised when I found my niche in the world, were you? You had seen my potential long before. I must have been an idiot to think I ever meant anything more to you," he raked clawed fingers through his hair, "or anyone."

Uncertainty and guilt banded her chest and made her feel like she was sucking water into her lungs instead of oxygen. She couldn't speak.

He backed away. "I just had to make sure I hadn't lost my touch." He saluted her. "Thanks for everything. I couldn't have gotten where I am without you." He turned around and slipped into the night. Two minutes later, she heard the squeal of tires on the street out front as his BMW sped away from her house.

Belatedly she closed her eyes and whispered to the stars and the breeze, and no one in particular, "God, Alec, I had no idea. I'm so sorry. For everything."

Chapter Eleven

ഇ

Alec slammed his car door and stalked up the walkway to the side door of the mansion.

He had barely restrained himself from driving his BMW through the streets of Ottawa at a hundred and fifty kilometers an hour. A high-speed chase with a couple dozen cruisers on his tail would have felt pretty damn good tonight. He wanted to hit something. He wanted to kick something. He had driven past the National Art Gallery and had indulged fantasies of storming through the brass-and-glass building with a twenty-pound sledgehammer, wreaking havoc and leaving a trail of carnage in his wake.

And then he had asked himself what the hell he was upset about. There hadn't been any surprises with Kira. He had said exactly what he had planned to say and she had behaved exactly as predicted. It had played out exactly as he had imagined it a thousand times.

Maybe that was why he was angry. Maybe he had secretly hoped she would surprise him. Maybe he had secretly hoped that he was wrong. Maybe he had secretly hoped... *Dammit!* He had no business hoping anything. He had said his piece and now it was time to go back to the real world. It was time to accept who he was and stop dreaming of things that never were, and never would be.

So he found himself here.

He slammed through the kitchen on his way to Darcy's room, but drew up short when he saw Carl Stuart sitting at the counter slurping from a glass of beer.

"What the hell are you doing here?" growled Carl. "You're not due in until the morning."

"None of your damn business, Stuart. I needed to see Darcy. We have something to discuss."

"Oh, yeah?" taunted Carl. "I bet you'll be doing lots of *talking*."

"Shut up, Stuart. One more word and I'll make good on that promise to see you picking teeth out of your nose."

"In a bit of a snit?"

In a heartbeat, Alec had hauled Carl off his stool and was clutching Carl's lapels in his fists. "I feel a real need to hit something right now, and you're just about as good a target as I'm gonna get. So I'd advise you to shut the fuck up before I lose my cool."

A cold rage washed across Carl's features, but a moment later, his expression cooled. He silently appraised his colleague, allowing the wrinkles to set firmly into his jacket before speaking. "So you do know some four-letter words, Monsieur Frechette. I believe your *cool* was long past lost before you walked in here." He shrugged. "Maybe there's something to you after all. I was beginning to think you had ice water in your veins."

Alec took a few deep breaths before dropping his hands and stepping back from those gaunt, sunken features. "Normally I do. But you've got a knack for irritating me." Alec was furious with himself for revealing anything to the likes of Carl.

Carl cocked his head. "I hardly think I'm the cause. In my experience there's only one thing that can make a man lose control like that."

Alec eyed Carl's beer but said nothing.

"A woman. I've had some experience in that arena myself."

"Gee, your insights astound me, Stuart." His words were for Carl but his eyes remained riveted to the booze. He'd had several glasses of wine, and had driven, knowing full well he had enough of a buzz on to mean he shouldn't have. But suddenly it wasn't enough. He wanted to dull his senses. He wanted to sink into oblivion. He didn't want to feel anything when he went up to confront Darcy Cromwell because he was afraid he knew exactly what she'd say. "But my problems are nothing a little Crown Royal wouldn't cure."

"You asking to drink with me?"

"No. I'm just asking for a drink before I have to head into battle with the opposite sex. Is that so much to ask?"

Carl straightened his jacket and considered the request briefly before heading to the liquor cabinet. Alec sat down at the counter and dropped his head into his hands. Suddenly everything seemed so pointless. He had no direction, and nothing to look forward to. All that stretched out before him was years and years of parties and traveling and expensive wine and gourmet food. It was nothing but fun, fun, fun. So why did the mere thought of it set his stomach to churning?

Carl slammed down a tumbler that was half full of glistening amber whiskey. "That's a good start," mused Alec.

Carl grinned and raised the bottle. "There's lots more where that came from." He poured a shot glass for himself. "Lots."

* * * * *

Kira shivered slightly as the evening breeze ruffled the wisps of carmine hair about her face.

Cherisse's hair had been red, even more brilliant than her mother's. Hardly a surprise, considering Alec's lineage. With his auburn mane, and Kira's red tresses, their children were doomed—she stifled a tiny sob that welled up along with that thought. *Doomed.* Of course, their children were doomed. *All of them.* And there would be no more. *Never.*

"Kira?"

Startled, Kira looked toward the stairs to the deck. Lauren stood on the bottom step, a light jacket wrapped about her shoulders, and her eyes full of concern.

When Kira didn't respond, Lauren braved the invisible boundaries and ascended the remaining stairs. She pulled up another chair and settled down facing her friend. "You want me to get you a jacket?" asked Lauren. "It's chilly tonight. You have goose bumps."

"Do I?" If it was cold, Kira certainly wasn't aware of it. She hadn't moved since Alec had left. She had sat there going over it all again and again in her mind—going over what Alec had said, and his accusations, and the events of seven years ago. And now she was numb. She was to blame. It was all her fault. She had taken on too much and it had cost her something. How was it that caring too much could cost so much?

Lauren touched her hand. "What? What is it, honey? I heard Alec squeal out of here, and when I saw you still sitting on the deck an hour later I knew there was something wrong."

Kira just shook her head.

"Did he say something to hurt you?"

To Kira's amazement, she laughed at that. It took her several seconds to get the slightly hysterical giggles under control. "God, no! All he did was rip my world out from under me."

"What does that mean?" Lauren's tone was gentle and coaxing. She was such a good friend. Kira thought she'd be lost without her.

Kira looked at Lauren, studying her intently, trying to see beyond. "You knew, didn't you?" she asked quietly.

Lauren frowned. "Knew what?"

"You knew why he left. Somehow, without anyone telling you, you figured it out. How did you do that? Why couldn't I see it?"

"You were too close to it." Lauren paused and pulled her jacket a little tighter. "He left because you wouldn't let him help, right? He felt shut out of his daughter's life and, when she died, he felt shut out of yours." Lauren gazed at the stars. "Just the little bit you said sounded so familiar. My sister out west went through something similar with her husband. Of course, they didn't lose their child, but they almost lost their marriage over her inability to trust him with the most basic responsibilities of caring for their baby. It took him threatening to leave for her to figure it out, and let him find his own way to do things." A moth fluttered noisily against the yard light, casting eerie shadows across Lauren's face. "But a lot of men just give up and let their wives do it. It's easier than fighting. But I think maybe it was worse for Alec because he knew the stakes were so high. He couldn't push too hard. If he did he was probably afraid the whole thing would shatter."

Kira nodded miserably, acknowledging the truth in everything Lauren had said, but realizing there was more. She was hesitant to share the rest of it. She was afraid to face the other truths that pointed out such brutal flaws in her own character. She had always prided herself on being a pillar, someone for others to lean on, beyond reproach—perhaps even above the crowd. But how wrong she had been.

"Yes," she said quietly. "I think you're right about all that. But—" She took a deep breath. "But there was more."

"Yes?"

Kira took a moment to formulate her words perfectly, but what came out of her mouth was a complete surprise, even to her. "Men live for sex, right?"

Lauren laughed. "Yeah, I guess so. But what does that have to do with anything?"

"Near the end—the last year, when Cherisse was at her sickest, I so cherished my time with Alec at night. We made love more than we had the first year together. I was exhausted, but somehow making love to him rejuvenated me. It let me focus on something else besides Cherisse, and it was the only time I felt close to him." She hesitated. "Is that strange?"

"Well…maybe it wouldn't be like that for a lot of women, but the way you say it, it makes sense."

"I always assumed Alec was having the time of his life. Lots of great sex. I would often initiate it. And I didn't even bother with cuddling after. I would just fall asleep beside him." She was watching Lauren's face for any sign of disapproval or understanding. But her face remained passive and analytical.

"Yes?" prompted Lauren.

Kira sighed, feeling disappointed, and then foolish. "He told me tonight that—" She didn't even want to say it, but Lauren saved her the trouble.

"Oh, my God," she whispered. "He felt like you were using him?"

Kira nodded miserably. "I didn't think it was possible for a man to feel like that. They're just sex machines. That's what everybody says. But I guess—" Her voice wavered.

"But it's probably different when your child is dying."

"Yeah. That changes a lot of things."

"He felt like that was all you needed him for—all he was good for?"

Kira cradled her head in her hands and moaned, "And that's why he left police work and went into…this. I always thought it was because of something else, but now I'm not so sure."

"You're not responsible for his choices, Kira. Maybe you made some mistakes, but he had plenty of options."

"Did he?" She gazed steadily at her friend. "I'm not so sure."

"Kira. You can't take on his problems. You can't— "

"No!" It was all so clear, and she couldn't pretend not to see it. "Maybe I can't take on his problems, but I have to acknowledge my responsibilities. I'm partly to blame, and I can't whitewash that. Maybe I did use him. Maybe I was fooling myself to think any differently. Men are supposed to be the strong ones—the ones in control. But I put him into the roles that I wanted for him, and I never thought to consider his needs."

"Men have been doing that for eons, Kira."

"Maybe. But that doesn't make it right, does it?"

Lauren leaned back and closed her eyes. "No. It certainly doesn't. You've got some work cut out for you, honey, if you want to turn that man's life around and make up for past mistakes. I hope you're up for it."

"So do I," she said softly. "So do I."

*****

Alec pounded on Darcy's door. Still clutching a finger of Scotch in his hand he leaned heavily on the doorframe and waited while the world spun around him. He hadn't sat with Carl that long, at least he hadn't thought he had, but maybe it was the combination of the wine earlier, together with a few shots of whiskey—whatever it was, he was feeling more drunk than he had since...since whenever. His mind just couldn't work that hard.

The door opened and a bed-tousled Darcy in an oversized T-shirt and probably a thong, gazed up at him through those John Lennon glasses that made her look like she was all of sixteen. She smiled at him. "You're drunk."

He bowed grandly. "Out of my mind, and proud of it."

She stepped back and motioned him inside. "I don't recall summoning you tonight."

He stepped through and managed to walk with a minimum of difficulty to the bedroom. Darcy followed quietly. He tossed back the remainder of his drink and placed the glass precisely on the floor at his feet as he sat down on the edge of the bed.

Darcy regarded him with interest. "You're taking liberties tonight," she said critically. "I wasn't expecting you until tomorrow."

"Maybe I'm tired of taking orders. Maybe *I* want it for a change." He heard the slurring of the words and didn't care.

"Well." She propped a hand on her hip and drew herself up to her fullest regal bearing. "I don't know if I like *that*."

Suddenly feeling as powerful as a Titan, he grabbed her wrist and dragged her to him. "I don't recall giving you a choice in the matter."

To his annoyance, she giggled. "All right. I'll play along. I can do the submissive thing as well as anyone."

He ignored the churning sensation in his stomach. He ignored the little man of conscience screaming in his ear—screaming that he was demeaning himself, and that he should walk out that door immediately. He ignored the voice that pleaded with him to take charge of his life and take up his old ideals. Instead, he sought confirmation that he was exactly where he was meant to be—in a gilded gutter. "I came to ask you something."

Darcy blatantly settled herself on his lap, straddling him, and wrapping her legs around his hips. "Ask away."

"Did you specifically ask your grandfather to hire me?"

She ran her fingers through his hair and whispered in his ear. "Yes."

He allowed the explorations as a matter of course. "Why?"

"Does it matter?"

"No. But I want to know anyway."

"He was bound and determined that I have security. I agreed to a personal bodyguard, on the condition that it was you." She nibbled on his ear and her hand massaged him to full erection.

"But why me? Was it because of my qualifications or because of my reputation?"

Her lips descended to his throat and her hands worked his T-shirt free of his waistband. "It was because you've got a body that could stop traffic." She raised her head and met his gaze, smiling slowly. "And I checked references."

The combination of bitterness, lust and booze was conspiring to strip Alec of the few inhibitions that he had managed to hang onto up until this point in his life. He peeled her T-shirt off and his quickly followed. "What does that mean?" he finally asked as his thumb traced a path from her throat to her breast.

She shuddered slightly, her nipples already swollen and erect. "It means I called some of your old employers, just to make sure you weren't highly overrated."

Alec thought he should have been angry at that. He should have been livid that his stud qualifications had been more of a concern that his professional ones. But he felt oddly detached, as if he were watching the festivities from another realm, and he was completely powerless to stop it, or affect it in any way. "And?" was all he said as his hand slid between her thighs.

She shifted to allow his fingers through the damp nest of curls. "Mmm." She sucked in a swift breath. "And I have no complaints."

He suddenly grabbed her shoulders and threw her to the mattress, straddling her and gazing down at her with a feral intensity. "So I'm exactly what you wanted—a walking hormone with a shoulder holster." Carl Stuart's taunt had stuck with him like a bloodthirsty leech.

She grinned at the joke. "It helps that you look damn good in a tux," she said as she wriggled under his weight. "You got a problem with that?"

"No." The world swirled around him again as he stripped off his jeans and fell into the familiar role of paid lover and protector. "Just checking, that's all."

He tortured and teased, kissed and stroked.

She clutched at his back and moaned his name.

He felt her fingernails drawing his blood, and he whispered into the pillow, "I hate you, you bitch." She giggled, believing it was all part of the game. But even as spasms racked his body, he knew that he meant it. He meant it with every fiber of his being. But the worst part was that Darcy Cromwell wasn't the only person in that room who deserved his loathing. "I hate you. I hate you. I hate you!"

Chapter Twelve

ꟹ

Alec tried to bat away the pick ax someone was wielding at his temple. Or was it a medieval lance? Something big and intense and sharp had been driven right behind his eyes. He moaned and tried to fight his way back to consciousness.

He'd never had a hangover like this. At least he couldn't remember having one—or maybe his brain was playing tricks on him. The pain was so intense as to drive everything else from his mind. He was thirsty and his limbs felt like lead.

He managed to crack open an eye and suddenly remembered where he was. Darcy's room. *Shit!* Big mistake. He had better get out of there before someone realized he hadn't come in at his appointed time. Before someone—like the Governor General—realized he had spent the night. If only he could move. He groaned again when he managed to lift a hand to his face and rub his forehead.

He frowned. His hand was sticky. He opened his eyes a little further and studied his hand in the late morning light that filtered in through the curtains. That was odd. There was something… *Jesus Christ!*

The realization struck him and, despite the pain, he sat bolt upright in bed. He looked at his hands and knew he was right. Both of them were covered in blood. He looked around and it registered that the sheets were spattered with it as well.

And then he saw her.

Fighting nausea and panic he scrambled off the bed, and landed with a thud on the plush, Persian carpet. Despite his best efforts, his stomach heaved, but there was nothing there.

Dry, racking spasms wrenched at his stomach until he collapsed in an exhausted heap on the floor.

She was dead. She was so very dead.

Sucking in oxygen in great gulping breaths, he struggled to his feet and forced himself to look at her. He had lain beside a dead woman. She was on her back, naked, unseeing eyes gazing toward the ceiling, arms flung above her head, two gaping bullet holes—one in her chest and…*oh God!*…one in her forehead. The dark brown stains of drying blood surrounded her like a gruesome corona.

He looked at his hands, sticky with her essence, and another wave of nausea washed over him. He rushed to the bathroom, ran water in the sink and began frantically to scrub her from his skin. But as he stood in front of the mirror, he realized she was spattered all over him. Splashes of red adorned him like an ugly, malignant disease.

He stood there staring. What had happened? He had passed out. Had Professor Dan somehow gotten in and killed her while he slept? He had never slept that soundly in his life. How could he have slept through a struggle and two gunshots? Even with a silencer that struck him as beyond the realm of reality.

Then he realized he had to call the police. He had to inform her family. He rushed back into the room and pulled on his jeans. He was just reaching for his T-shirt when he spotted his gun amidst the sheets. *His* gun? But, if he had slept through an attack, how had his gun gotten here? He didn't even remember bringing it upstairs. He thought he had left it in his car. He assumed he had. The whole evening—everything since drinking that whiskey in the kitchen—was so hazy.

With complete disregard for all his police training and common sense, he picked up the gun and examined it. It was loaded. He expelled the clip. Two cartridges had been discharged.

He went cold. Icy fingers of fear skittered up his spine and wrapped around his stomach. He tried desperately to remember. He closed his eyes and gritted his teeth. But nothing would come. He vaguely remembered screwing Darcy's brains out, but after that he had passed into oblivion. There was only blackness—a great gaping hole where his memory should have been.

What if he was blocking it out for a reason? What if—

"Darcy!" Someone was pounding on the door.

He swallowed dryly and pulled on his T-shirt, realizing too late that it too was spattered with her blood.

"Darcy!" More pounding. Alec wanted out. He needed time to think. He couldn't have done it. It didn't make sense. But then again, what in his life did?

He heard the click of a key in the lock and voices in the outer room. He was trapped. He made a choice, knowing full well it was probably the wrong one. He stuffed the gun in the back of his jeans and stepped toward the door.

He almost ran right into Jonathan Cromwell himself, followed closely by his perpetual shadow, Carl Stuart.

Jonathan drew up short. "Alec? What on Earth are you—" A strangled cry erupted from his lips and he shoved Alec aside in his haste to reach his granddaughter.

Alec breathed deeply and regarded Carl, the man who stood between him and freedom. "Move, Carl." His voice was low and deadly.

"I don't think so. You're not going anywhere." Carl reached inside his jacket and pulled out his Beretta.

Alec took a step back, assessing his situation and considering his options.

Jonathan's anguished cry raked across his nerves like fingernails on a blackboard. "You!" He took a shaky step toward Alec, his gnarled finger pointing in accusation and judgment. "I hired you to keep her safe, and look—" He sobbed. "Look what you've done!"

Alec shook his head emphatically, trying to keep his breathing and his heart rate under control "No. It—it wasn't me." He licked his lips, and fingered the gun in his belt. "I didn't kill her. I couldn't—"

"Liar!" shouted the Governor General of Canada. "Her blood is on your clothes! You raped her, and murdered her, and I'll see you hang for it!"

Alec made his decision. He pulled the gun from his jeans and lunged for Jonathan. He heard the blast and felt the searing pain in his side just as he wrapped an arm around Cromwell's throat and pressed the gun to his temple. "God, I'm sorry, Your Honor," he said, even as the pain flared and he felt the warmth of his own blood soaking his clothes.

Jonathan's eyes were wide with terror.

"But I'm innocent and—" Alec winced and fought the urge to let go and press a hand to his wound. "I have to get out of here," he rasped.

"Let go of him!" shouted Carl, his arms outstretched, and his gun pointed at Alec's head. "You're insane, Frechette. You'll never get out of the mansion, even with him in tow."

Alec knew he didn't have much time. There would be cops there within minutes and he'd pass out soon if he didn't slow the bleeding. "Toss down your gun, Carl. And get out of the way. I'll shoot him if I have to." He blinked and started toward the door. "I'm just desperate enough to do it."

He pressed the gun a little more firmly to Jonathan's head and his hostage squeaked, "Do it, Carl. He's insane. He'll do anything."

"Now!" shouted Alec, on the verge of exploding.

Carl licked his lips and tossed down his gun. Alec scooped it up and, still holding on to Jonathan, edged toward the door. Carl watched him warily and moved aside just far enough to let them pass.

Alec moved past him but, as he did so, he mustered every spare morsel of energy, and every moment of training and every ounce of determination at his disposal. With an effort of raw will and precise timing, he cracked the butt of his gun against Jonathan's temple and kicked Carl Stuart in the balls. As Carl doubled over in pain, Alec pistol-whipped the back of his head with one, gut-wrenching blow.

For barely a moment he was standing over two prone, unconscious men—but only for a moment. The next moment, running on pure adrenaline, he rushed from the room. Clutching a hand to his side, he headed for the safety and freedom that his BMW embodied.

He met no one on the stairs. A maid glanced at him as he rushed, barefoot and bleeding, through the side door, but no one stopped him before he got to the car. He was relieved to find his keys in the pocket of his jeans and, as he thrust the key into the ignition and the engine purred to life, he wondered where the hell he was going. Where could he run? He needed sanctuary. He needed time to prove that he hadn't done this thing. He *couldn't* have done this thing.

As he roared down the long, winding driveway, the answer came to him. In a single flash of lucidity, he knew exactly what he had to do. Now he just had to get there. And he had to do it before he bled to death all over his calfskin leather upholstery.

* * * * *

"Aaah." The first scalding sip of coffee of the day. God knew she needed it. Kira had barely slept the night before. She had tossed and turned and wrestled with demons into the wee hours. Finally, at around four a.m., she had drifted off. But her sleep had been fitful. She had been plagued by dreams of Alec in bed with a string of beautiful women with flowing hair, perfect thighs, fangs and claws.

She had dragged herself from bed a little after ten, had tried to cleanse herself in the shower and now she sat with a full pot of coffee, a pitcher of cream and her regrets.

She had to see him. She didn't know what she would say, or do, but she had to see him. And she wanted to do it today. Maybe after she finished this pot of coffee she'd have the energy to call him. But not quite yet.

Cujo, curled up on his pillow, watched her with unblinking eyes as she took sip after sip of the Juan Valdez specialty.

"What?" she said irritably.

He didn't answer and all of a sudden the house seemed unbearably quiet. She flicked on the television on the corner of her cupboard and tuned it to one of the few morning shows that weren't pre-empted by Sunday morning cartoons. She was just settling into the banter when the doorbell rang.

She muted the sound, set down her coffee cup, and with a casual glance at the clock on the stove, headed to the door. She didn't often get callers at eleven a.m. on a Sunday.

Mike LaRocque stood on her front step holding a box from a local bakery, a sweater of Kira's draped over his arm, and a wide grin on his face. "Good morning," he said brightly.

A dull "Hi," was the most enthusiastic response she could muster.

His face fell. "That bad, eh?"

"Worse." She motioned him inside and closed the door behind him.

"Rough night?"

She rubbed at the back of her neck. "Sorta. But it's nothing a cherry Danish can't cure."

"Well then, I'm just in time." He held up the box. "Just what the doctor ordered. You got coffee?"

"Oh, an ocean full or so. Follow me." She led him to the kitchen.

Once they were seated and she had pulled a second mug out of the cupboard, she asked, "So, what brings you here? I hope you didn't come to bask in the warmth of my smile because I'm afraid I'm not up to my usual level of radiance today."

He chuckled. "No. You left your sweater at my place Friday night. I decided against dropping it off last night, considering you had a…guest."

"So, you're checking up on me? Here to see if Alec spent the night, or if he left me raw and bleeding?"

"Yeah," he said sardonically, "something like that." He sipped from his mug. "So, which is it? You don't look too wanton or well used, and I don't see any bandages, so—"

"Oh, I don't know about that. I may not have any open wounds but I am feeling pretty raw. But probably not for the reasons you would think."

"Oh?"

At that moment, Kira decided she was not in the mood to share the trials of her soul with Mike. He would, no doubt, be supportive and listen attentively to her troubles, but she had no desire to rehash her visit with Alec yet again.

She was just coming up with a convincing way to deflect his questions when she was saved by the bell. "Busy morning," she said as she scouted the countertop for her cordless phone. She got up and listened again. "I must have left it in the bedroom." She sprinted for the back of the house. "I'll be right back."

She found the phone on her nightstand, and just beat the answering machine to picking up. "Hello?" she said breathlessly.

Silence.

She frowned. "Hello?"

She heard a hint of a breath and then, "Kira?"

"Yes." She measured her words as she puzzled over the whispering voice. "Who is this?"

"It's—it's Alec. I—" She heard a sharp intake of breath that cut off his words.

"Alec? Wh-what is it? Is something wrong?"

"Merde!" he swore, and then rasped out in a short but torturous monologue, "I called because I was going to ask for your help." He sucked in another breath and she waited, holding her own breath as if it could help him speak. "But now I know I can't do that."

"Help? What's going on, Alec? I'd be glad to help you. It's the least—"

"No!" He managed more volume than he had since the conversation started, but she still had to strain to hear him. "You don't owe me anything. I just want you to know…"

Again an agonizing pause. Kira's heart rate and breathing had reached critical levels. She had never heard him like this. There was something very wrong, and she felt so powerless, so useless. She hated feeling like that. She had never been able to get used to it. "Know? Know what? Talk to me, Alec."

"That I loved you. Maybe I didn't say it enough, but I did. And…and I didn't do it. I hope."

Tears of frustration were brimming in her eyes. "Do it? Do what?"

He hung up, and there was only dial tone. "Alec?" she whispered into the deserted phone line. His words had sounded so final, so foreboding. The pit of her stomach was filled with lead and the hairs on the back of her neck were standing on end. Still holding the phone to her ear she whispered, "What is it? Please, let me help you."

"Kira?" She almost jumped out of her skin at Mike's voice. She quickly clicked off the phone, and turned to face him. He was standing in the doorway, looking concerned and puzzled.

"Yes? Sorry I took so long. I—"

"Come with me for a minute," he said, motioning her to follow. "Quickly. There's something you need to see."

His expression was so intense that she didn't question him, merely followed his brisk gait down the hall. They reached the kitchen, and Kira quickly understood the reason for Mike's sense of urgency.

A harried-looking reporter stood in front of the Governor General's mansion. In the background they could see a fleet of police cruisers, and Kira thought she heard helicopters overhead.

But it was the reporter's words that almost knocked the breath out of her. "As of this moment there is a full-scale manhunt in operation for the well-known bodyguard, Alec Robert Frechette."

Kira sank into a chair, the bones in her legs having suddenly dissolved.

The reporter continued, oblivious to the lunacy of his words. "I have just received confirmation that Darcy Cromwell, the Governor General's granddaughter, was murdered. She was found shot to death in her bed."

Murdered? No. No. That's impossible.

"Police are not releasing many details, but the body bag was just seen being removed from the mansion." He looked back toward the mansion, his eyes sad and the pause meaningful. "Darcy was a young woman of barely twenty-two years. She had hired Monsieur Frechette to keep her safe in the face of the recent string of rapes in the city."

He shook his head mournfully and Kira had a fleeting image of that reporter with his microphone sticking out of a most unpleasant orifice.

"Apparently, Darcy's trust was woefully misplaced. It is alleged by sources from within the mansion that Frechette was seen fleeing the scene earlier this morning after being found in the room with the victim. He is injured, but still presumed dangerous, and is in possession of at least two handguns. Police are asking that anyone believing they have seen him, or know of his whereabouts, not approach the suspect. They are asking you to call their hotline at—"

Kira punched the power button and the reporter vanished. *Dangerous?* Alec—a fugitive? The world had gone mad!

"Who was that on the phone, Kira?"

The tone of Mike's voice startled her. She looked at him sharply. "Why?"

"Was it him? Before you came in, they said he had been shot."

Shot? Her stomach clenched at the thought of a bullet ripping through Alec's flesh, and she began to fight a rising panic.

Mike continued, "It would be logical for him to come to you, a nurse, for help." He paused and his jaw tensed. "Did he?"

"No," she said slowly, and at that moment she knew exactly what she had to do. Alec was injured and in trouble. And he was wrong. She did owe him something. She owed him everything. And it was high time she paid that debt.

She straightened her shoulders, leveled her gaze at Mike, and lied through her teeth, "No, that wasn't him. It was just Jean asking if I could cover a shift for her."

She glanced at Mike and knew he wasn't convinced. She had to get rid of him, but she didn't want to be obvious about it. She couldn't let him in on her plans. Not yet. Maybe she could trust him, but she wasn't sure. She wasn't sure if she could trust anyone.

Alec, a murderer? It was beyond comprehension. It was beyond reason. But what had he said? *"I didn't do it. I hope."* What the hell did that mean?

Mike was shaking his head. "Such a shame. My father was a pediatrician. He treated Darcy frequently as a child. He always said she was a sweet girl. Maybe a little headstrong, but still…" He sighed. "My dad and Jonathan Cromwell go way back. He'll take it hard." Mike's tone had been soft and reflective but abruptly his voice sharpened as he focused more directly on Kira. "Who would have believed it? Alec Frechette—my hero. What a joke. Did he seem okay to you last night?"

"Yeah, yeah. He seemed fine. We had a little discussion, and he left early." She turned on Mike, at last focusing on his train of thought, and not liking it one bit. "You mean you actually believe that he did it?"

"Come on, Kira! He was in the room with her when she was found. He fled the scene. That sounds pretty damn incriminating to me."

She backed away from him. "Maybe, but you don't know him. He could never hurt anyone. He was a good cop, and a bodyguard, for God's sake. That's just insane." She paused and twirled her emerald ring frantically around her finger. "There's obviously something we don't know. There's got to be an explanation." She was mouthing the words even as her mind flew in a hundred other directions. "There's just got to be. "

"Lots of cops go bad. Surely you know that. What if he was upset after leaving you last night? What if…" He shook his head and reached for her hand. "There's no point in arguing about this. But you should be prepared. I predict the cops will be here within a couple of hours. They'll figure out he was here last night, and they'll want to know everything."

God! He was right. She had to get out of there before she got tied up with cops and questions for hours on end—before she had to lie to a group of people she respected and valued. She would hate to do that, but Alec was hurt and in trouble. He needed her and, for once in her life, she was going to look after *his needs.*

"Do you know where he might have gone?"

Yes. Yes. Now that Mike had asked the question it was obvious. If he were seeking sanctuary—if he needed someplace isolated and out of the way, she had a pretty good idea where he would have gone. And now she had to get there too.

For Mike's benefit, she frowned. "No. But if he's hurt, don't you think he'd seek medical attention?"

"Not unless he's insane or stupid. And somehow, I doubt that Alec Frechette is either of those things."

"No," she said quietly, "Alec is definitely not stupid."

Mike was silent for a moment and, when Kira looked at him, she realized he was watching her very closely. "I don't know about that, Kira."

"What do you mean?"

"Alec walked out on you. That doesn't exactly make him a genius in my book."

Despite herself, and the insanity of the situation, Kira melted, just a little. "That's sweet."

"It's the truth." Mike sat down heavily on one of the kitchen chairs. "Maybe I'm a bit on the stupid side as well."

Kira chuckled despite herself. "You mean I seem to have an affinity for stupid men?"

Mike's smile was sad. "Maybe. But what I meant was that I was probably pretty stupid in my marriage as well."

Kira put her hands on his shoulders, suddenly torn between soothing Mike's troubles and kicking him ruthlessly out of her house. "It takes two people to make a marriage fail."

"True. But it also takes two people to make it work, and I'm pretty sure I didn't pull my weight. I was so caught up in my career—in building up my practice and my reputation—that I'm pretty sure I neglected Tracy."

Kira's heart went out to him. They both shared similar regrets. Perhaps she and Mike LaRocque shared more than she had ever imagined. "I can't deny that's a possibility. Neglect is probably one of the worst sins in a relationship." *I know. I know now, and I should have known then. Maybe I was the stupid one.* "But maybe if you learn from it—"

Mike stood suddenly and turned to face her, cupping her face in long, agile fingers. The mischief in those smiling blue eyes had been replaced by an intensity that startled her. "I did. You have to believe me, Kira. I'll never take my...partner for granted like that again."

"All right," she said on a breath of surprise. "I believe you."

Then he was kissing her. There was a pleasing warmth to his kiss as his lips cajoled and his tongue teased. She responded to it, exploring the sensations, and savoring strong arms around her. But it didn't take long for her to discern that the warmth lacked fire.

Maybe she was too distracted by Alec's situation. Maybe she was too drained from lack of sleep and pining over things she could never change. Maybe, eventually, she could stop seeing Mike as a friend, and see him as a lover. But at that moment she knew that kiss could go no further.

She slowly withdrew her lips from his, and disengaged herself from his arms. "You've convinced me," she said lightly.

But he didn't smile. "Be careful, Kira."

"What? What does that mean?"

"You're worried about him. I knew it the second you turned off the television. You're worried about him, and distracted, and that's going to get you into trouble."

She stepped back in the face of the sudden wave of hostility that she had sensed from Mike. "I don't know what you're talking about. Of course I'm worried. I did love him once, but I wouldn't do anything stupid."

Mike stuffed his hands in his pockets. "I hope not, Kira. I really do. Because helping him now could have dire consequences. He's a murderer. If you're convicted of aiding and abetting—"

"He's not a murderer!"

Mike shook his head in wonder. "See? I—"

"I think you should go now." Her body went rigid.

"Oh, Kira. Don't be like that. I'm just concerned, that's all."

"Well, if you care for me, you won't say those things around me. Now, honestly, I'm still very tired. Maybe I won't be able to get any sleep, but I'd like to lie down and sort through all this."

"But what if—"

She held up her hands in protest. "I'll be fine. If the cops come, they won't want to talk to you anyway."

"That wasn't who I was worried about."

She took a slow, calming breath, as a strange rage washed through her. "Alec would never hurt me. And he would never intentionally endanger me by dragging me into this."

"I don't know..."

"I know you don't. You don't know him at all. Now, I appreciate everything you've said, Mike, but I'd really like to be alone."

He regarded her skeptically, but finally drained the last of his coffee and set it on the counter. "All right. I'll see you at work tomorrow. And don't forget what I said."

"What?" she said, allowing a trace of sarcasm to creep into her voice. "The part about a man I care about being a cold-blooded killer?"

"No. The part about me not taking you for granted." He touched her cheek again. "You'd be my world, Kira. I guarantee it."

She watched in mute fascination as he made his trek toward the front door. He was outside and had closed the door before she had completely regained her faculties. Or maybe it was the incessant yapping at the patio doors that had drawn her attention.

"Cujo!" she exclaimed. "Jeepers. I'm lucky we don't have a wet spot on the carpet." She pushed open the doors and allowed her killer watchdog to pee on the petunias. "Okay, Cujo," she whispered as she heard Mike's car rev to life and pull away. "I've got to come up with a good reason to ask Lauren to look after you, and then Mommy's got a bit of a drive ahead of her." In her mind, she listed everything she needed to do and pick up before she headed out into the countryside, to the ramshackle cottage that her parents had been trying to sell for the last five years.

She and Alec had spent a month there their first year together. It had no heat, and the roof leaked, but it had been one of the most romantic and passionate retreats they had ever shared. That was where they had conceived Cherisse because Kira had forgotten her birth control pills. Alec had laughed and said that they should be reckless, and let life take them where it would. If only he had known the road to hell that they had embarked upon that day. And it seemed that the trip wasn't quite over yet.

She rubbed at her temples and whispered to a frail, red-haired ghost, "I'm so sorry, honey. We didn't know." She watched, unseeing, as Cujo merrily dug up the rose bush she had just purchased two weeks earlier. A rose—so beautiful and delicate and fragile, destined to bloom and enrich lives with its bold color and subtle fragrance. But it lived for such a short time.

She whispered again in a ritual of lament and self-torture. "But maybe we should have, honey. Maybe we should have."

Chapter Thirteen

ꙮ

Detective Sergeant Genevieve Turcotte rubbed her eyes with the heels of her hands. She pressed hard enough to spark little bursts of light against the backs of her eyelids. She sighed in ecstasy.

She hadn't even been on this case a full day, and already her nerves were raw and her eyes felt like they had sand beneath the lids.

"Hey, Gen!"

She cracked open one small brown eye. "Yeah? What is it, Will?"

Her partner, Will Ridgers, stood in the doorway to the office they shared at Ottawa's Royal Canadian Mounted Police headquarters. If there was ever a quintessential Mountie, it wasn't Will Ridgers. He more closely resembled the junkies they occasionally dragged in off the streets than the crisply pressed, stereotypical, "always-gets-his-man" Mountie. He was skinny, with perpetually unkempt blond hair and a two-day growth of beard that never seemed to change. Gen sometimes wondered if he had a razor that he could set to shave a millimeter off the skin. Otherwise, how could the beard never get any longer, and his face never be clean-shaven? With his gold hoop earring and gap-toothed grin, with his razor-sharp wit and irreverent attitude, she couldn't figure out how he had been so successful in the highly rigid and political world of the RCMP. Despite having worked with him for three years, Will remained an enigma to her.

She also couldn't figure out how he had snagged a wife, let alone one as beautiful as Paige.

Will grinned and his gray eyes twinkled with impiety. "I was just going to get a coffee and a Danish. You want anything? Like maybe a dozen eclairs or so?" *Twinkle.*

Will knew full well her weakness for pastries and coffee with extra cream. "You're treading on thin ice, Will. I'm heavy into PMS today and I might not be able to stop myself from shooting that damn grin off your face."

"You'd feel a lot better if you quit with the stupid diets," he chided. "You're gorgeous just the way you are." *Twinkle. Twinkle.*

Gen rolled her eyes and silently scoffed at that. Her mousy brown hair, Roman nose, short legs and ample hips did not fit within the definition of *gorgeous.* Her only redeeming feature—her wide, full mouth—usually did her more harm than good. "And you should be on the cover of *GQ,*" she quipped. "Now go get me some coffee with *milk,* and help me sort through these statements."

With a mocking salute, Will exited stage left and left Gen to her gruesome photos.

In a ritual of self-torture, she flipped through photo after photo of Darcy Cromwell's torn, tattered body. She allowed herself to dwell on the Governor General's anguished cries and grief-stricken sobs. She recalled the image of Darcy's parents' arrival at the scene. In her mind she heard the grating vibrations as the zipper on the body bag was slowly drawn up, sealing the fate of a girl who should have had so much life to look forward to.

All of that usually served to motivate and energize Gen in her quest for justice. The outrage that seeped into her through all those images was a tonic through the long days and nights of a murder case…or a manhunt. But this time it wasn't working.

A Styrofoam cup appeared on her desk. The aroma reminded her more of diesel fumes than of the rich brew that Colombia was famous for. But she sipped it anyway.

"Any word on our fugitive?" asked Will as he settled one scrawny butt cheek on the corner of her desk.

She shook her head. "No. Nothing. But I'm sure it won't be long. He's wounded. There was a lot of his blood at the mansion. He'll have to seek help eventually. And when he does…" She blew out a long slow breath and braved the coffee fumes to take another sip.

"We nab him." But Will's voice was pensive. "What's wrong, Gen? You haven't exactly been attacking this with your usual zeal. You've been hovering over those photographs and statements long past your usual ten minutes. I would have thought you'd be dragging me out to the car for our own independent search by now."

Gen sighed. After three years, maybe Will knew her better than she thought. He obviously knew her better than she knew him. "I don't like it."

"Well, that's good to hear. I would hope rape and murder wouldn't be right up there alongside raindrops on roses and whiskers on kittens in your list of favorite things."

Gen gritted her teeth and tamped down her irritation. "What I *mean* is I don't like the way the case is playing out."

"What's not to like? He was caught in the room with the victim. The semen matches his blood type, of which we found plenty on the floor and under her fingernails, all of which points to rape. The bullets came from his gun. He took a hostage in order to facilitate flight. Shall I go on?"

"See? It's too easy."

"Oh." Will nodded knowingly. "I see."

She set her jaw at his tone. "And what does that mean?"

"You have a crush on dear Monsieur Frechette. You don't like to think that he's capable of murder. You don't think he's guilty."

Gen restrained herself from pouring her coffee over his head. "I thought you knew me, Will," she said tightly. "I admit

I find Alec Frechette attractive—I am a heterosexual female, after all—but I would never allow that to affect my judgment on a case."

"No? Then why would you try to complicate such a straightforward scenario?"

"Because it's too straightforward, and because it just doesn't ring true." She continued before Will could interrupt her with his own skewed sense of logic, "Frechette may have a tight ass and honkin' shoulders, but that doesn't mean he doesn't have any brains. He used to be a police officer, you know. He used to be a good one. He knows the ropes and he's not stupid. So why would he get himself into such a dismal situation?"

"Crimes of passion rarely make sense. Besides, you know how he left the Montreal force. There are still some unanswered questions about that incident. He had a difficult home situation. Maybe he snapped. And maybe he just snapped a little harder this time."

"Then why does this MO fit with the other murders?"

"That question is pending investigation," Will answered easily.

Gen shook her head. "I don't need to investigate to know it's damn unlikely that he's the Rideau Rapist. He wasn't even in the city when the other murders took place. And how would he know to mimic the MO—*except* for leaving ample semen for DNA fingerprinting *this time*—and why would he even try to make it look like the others?"

"It wouldn't be the first time there's been a deviation in MO, you know."

Gen blinked at him. "What?"

"I've mentioned this before, but you never seem to hear me."

Gen was genuinely baffled. "Mentioned what before?"

Will sighed in disgust. "Forget it. Let's just focus on Frechette."

"That's what I'm *trying* to do." Sometimes Will went off on tangents that left her head spinning and kept her from focusing on the essentials. "I *said*, 'why would he try to make it look like the others?'"

"He *is* an ex-cop, Gen. Maybe he still has sources within the force that spilled the beans about the murder details. Maybe he mimicked them very intentionally. Maybe he was planning to kill her, and leading us to believe it was the Rideau Rapist to throw us off the scent, and keep him off the hook. Maybe the plan went bad and he was discovered before he could carry it to completion." He paused and twirled his earring as he thought. "Or maybe he was in town and we didn't know it, and he really is the guy we want." He nodded emphatically. "I definitely think we should check and make sure we have the exact date he left France, and exactly where he has been since."

Gen shook her head. "You go ahead but I think it's a waste of time. He's not the Rideau Rapist. And I'm not convinced he killed Darcy. It's all too pat, and it just doesn't fit with his profile."

"You're a criminal psychologist now?"

"Jeez, Will. I've been doing this for twelve years. I think I've learned a little bit about the criminal mind." She glanced meaningfully at him. "After all, I've been hanging around you for three years."

Will's hand flew to his heart. "Oh!" he groaned. "Cut to the quick."

She tapped her fingers on the desk. "First thing we need to do is find that old lover of his. Kira North might just be able to shed some light on this for us. If not on the case itself, then on his character."

"She's a nurse, you know," said Will softly.

"And she's an ex-cop. She wouldn't be that stupid."

"I don't know. It seems to me that Alec Frechette has a profound effect on any woman he touches." Will picked up one of the photographs, and his eyes scanned the bloody evidence. "He touched Darcy, and I believe he touched Kira North plenty." He dropped the photo. "He might just be able to convince her to risk helping him."

Gen glanced at the photo of Alec Frechette that they had obtained from a local newspaper. He just might at that.

* * * * *

Kira glanced sharply at the tote bag on the car seat beside her before returning her attention to the winding road that meandered through dense bush and wetlands.

She ran her mental checklist one more time—disinfectant and topical antibiotics, sterile saline and a syringe for irrigating the wound, gauze four by fours and thicker ABD pads for packing, standard bandages and "cling" for wrapping the wound, a thermometer, acetaminophen. She was pretty sure she had everything. She might or might not need all of it depending on the severity of the injury and the depth of the wound. She had even obtained a prescription for an oral antibiotic at a pharmacy on the outskirts of town. She had called from a pay phone, claiming to be from a local doctor's office. She had given them the prescription over the phone, and said that *Mrs. White* would be picking up her husband's Amoxil shortly. There wasn't even a murmur of suspicion from the pharmacist at the request.

Knowing the system certainly had its advantages.

If Alec had a gunshot wound and if he refused to go through official channels, at least she could protect him from infection this way. She would have loved to bring along something stronger than Extra Strength Tylenol to deal with whatever pain he was experiencing, but obtaining a prescription for a narcotic or other heavy-duty painkiller was a little more complicated than getting one for a simple antibiotic or wart cream.

She shuddered again at the thought of Alec being shot. But surely it couldn't be as bad as the press had made it out to be. With a little luck, the injury was minor and the report had merely been sensationalized because of Alec's reputation and notoriety. With a little luck, she would find him lounging in front of a severely smoking fireplace, eating cold beans out of a can, and cursing the damp, cold fog that had rolled into the area in the last hour. With a little luck, she would wake up any minute to discover this was exactly what it seemed to be—a wicked, torturous nightmare.

Alec couldn't be involved in a murder, and most certainly not of a young, helpless girl. She could see him leaping to some young woman's defense in the face of an attack or burglary. She could see him firing on some perp who lunged for his charge, or even shooting in anger as a dark figure ran away after performing some dastardly deed. But she could not see Alec raising a hand, a fist or, God forbid, a gun to someone as fragile and vulnerable as Darcy Cromwell.

It was all an enormous cruel, ironic mistake. And she would do everything in her power to see it corrected.

I didn't do it. I hope.

She pushed those words from her mind, refusing to acknowledge the implications of those two simple phrases. She refused to acknowledge the desperation and confusion that had been evident in his voice when he had spoken them.

She would deal with all that when she found him, she thought as she pulled into the familiar lane shadowed by arching maple and oak trees. As she pulled up in front of the ramshackle cottage with the curling shingles and the peeling blue paint, she experienced a flutter of anxiety. She was worried and apprehensive, but she had to confess she also felt a tingle of excitement. It had been a long time since she had felt that way. And, if the truth be told, part of her missed it.

In spite of the circumstances, she smiled to herself. If there was one thing Alec Frechette could never claim to be, it was boring. Unpredictable, reckless and charming, perhaps. But never boring.

* * * * *

Alec could feel himself slipping. The pain, the fatigue, a nagging thirst—everything seemed to be conspiring to throw him into a downward spiral. And he knew full well what was at the bottom of the swirling helix.

What was it those damn Klingons used to say? He used to watch that show occasionally, in the Cherisse years. After the dishes were done and the bills were paid and the floor was swept, he would flake out on the couch with a six-pack and watch whatever re-runs happened to parade across the twenty-one-inch screen in their family room. Sometimes he would turn it up loud enough to drown out the wheeze of oxygen and the whimpers of his daughter. Later there was nothing loud enough to drown out the sounds or the anguish of his own helplessness. Then he would head out to the deck and gaze at the stars.

He closed his eyes and sorted through hazy images that seemed to flit through his mind with no regard for logic or reality. *Oh yeah!* "It is a good day to die," he muttered to himself.

Those Klingons were idiots. He had always thought so, and now he knew it for certain. Now that he was this close to cashing it in, he could say without a doubt that it was never a "good day to die". Anybody who thought so needed to have their cranial ridges examined.

He considered getting up and getting a drink, but then he shifted on the bed and felt a new surge of warmth against the skin of his abdomen. "Or not," he whispered, again to his unseen companion.

He had tried to dress the wound and apply some pressure to slow the bleeding, but it was in an awkward spot, and the pain limited his ability to contort his body. He chuckled soundlessly.

He remembered playing *outlaws* as a kid with his best friend Nathan Rich. They had made numerous trips to the jail in their own imaginary version of Dawson. Oh, they had been a pair of wily, young varmints. They had left a swathe of carnage in their wake, stealing horses and gold, and leading the posses on wild-goose chases through deserts and mountains and old, rickety mine shafts. But every once in a while, the old, crotchety sheriff would catch up with 'em, pump 'em full of lead, and toss 'em in the clink. And there, on an old rickety bunk, in a dirty cell with only day-old bread for sustenance, they would pull shrapnel from their wounds while they bit on bullets and doused themselves with whiskey. Where they had managed to get bullets and whiskey while incarcerated still remained a mystery but, despite the inconsistencies, they had always enjoyed their time behind bars, even as they hovered at death's door.

It was amazing how much fun bullet wounds were when you were eight years old. Everything was better when you were eight. Except, of course, for sex.

He laughed at his own twisted thought processes, and instantly regretted it as fresh pain lanced through him. There was no way he was pulling this bullet out himself. He wasn't even sure if it was still in him. It might have ripped right on through, leaving its own swathe of carnage in his body.

He just wanted to rest a little bit longer. He was so tired. Surely a little sleep would rejuvenate him. He'd get up soon, look at it again, dress it better, and get a drink of water. Very soon. But just not quite yet.

He let himself drift as he fingered the cool, smooth comfort of the Smith and Wesson stashed under his pillow. No one could find him here and, even if the cops did burst in on him, he would be an idiot to defend himself. It would be suicide. But the gun's presence was a comfort nevertheless. He mused that he had never fired it on another human being. He hoped he would never have to. But his hopes had an irritating and repetitive habit of being dashed.

And despite his wishes to the contrary, there was a first time for everything.

* * * * *

The fog had thickened to the consistency of French Canadian pea soup, making Kira's skin damp and plastering her hair to her forehead in thin, wet tendrils.

She lifted the tarp that covered a suspiciously familiar form behind the cottage. The burnished silver of Alec's BMW gleamed despite the overcast skies and concealing cover. She folded the tarp back just enough to peer in the driver's side window, and her stomach sank to her toes.

A huge portion of the pale gray leather bore the evidence of Alec's ordeal. From shoulder level to mid-thigh, the supple calfskin bucket seat had been stained dark rust.

"Oh God," she breathed as she dropped the tarp back into place. Obviously, the reports had *not* been mistaken. She leaned against the car for support, taking a moment to suck oxygen into her lungs and to calm her thudding heart. She had stalled long enough, it was time to get inside that cabin and assess the damage like the professional she was. She was a nurse, and a former police officer. Blood was nothing new to her. The fact that this particular hemoglobin belonged to Alec Frechette shouldn't make an ounce of difference. It shouldn't...but it did.

She picked her way through dripping weeds and knee-high grass until she reached the front door. She was hardly surprised when the battered hunk of pine resisted her efforts. Obviously Alec had locked it. But how had he gotten inside in the first place? He couldn't possibly have a key.

She slapped her forehead with an open palm. He had picked the lock on her house—what made her think he couldn't handle a thirty-year-old rusted-out dead bolt?

Kira rummaged around in her pockets until she found the key that she had reclaimed from the back of her jewelry box. She was still amazed that she had hung onto it for all these years—through the upheaval of Cherisse's illness, the separation from Alec, and especially the move back home from Montreal. Even through all that, that ancient, little key had retained its special spot between the gold hoops and pearl studs.

It slipped easily into the lock and the dead bolt clicked open, and she mused that perhaps that little key, in a very real way, represented the key to her heart. Her time here with Alec was one of her last happy memories with him. It was one of the last times that she had felt so completely loved, and free of the burdens of the world.

Cherisse's birth was the only memory that could outshine this one. The euphoria of seeing that healthy, pink little bundle writhing in Alec's arms, looking up at him with those big blue eyes that said, "So, you're the ones in charge, eh?" had only been surpassed by the smile on Alec's face when he had kissed Kira on the cheek and said, "Not bad, *chèrie*. I think we'll keep her." And then he had whispered that he loved her, and her world had been complete.

She didn't quite see how it could ever be that again.

She stepped inside and quietly closed the door behind her. "Alec?" she said quietly, not wishing to startle him in case he was asleep. She clutched the tote bag a little more tightly and headed past the kitchen, which had cobwebs across the window and a ragged mouse hole in one of the cupboard doors.

She glanced toward the living room, which sported a crumbling fireplace and two threadbare couches. The whole place smelled of dust and mold and age.

At last she reached the bedrooms at the back of the structure. She remembered the largest one was the last one on the left, right next to the washroom. No doubt Alec would want the luxury of the queen-sized mattress for his six-foot-two frame.

She passed the other two bedrooms and, as expected, the doors were standing open and they were empty. The last door on the left was shut tight. Quietly, hoping still to find him asleep, she tried the knob and only the creak of the reluctant hinges announced her arrival.

She caught sight of him, flaked out on the lumpy mattress barely a moment before a deafening crack blasted through the stillness of the forest. Thanks to very old reflexes, she dropped like a rock, and skittered backward to the safety of the hall.

"Alec!" Her voice was high and shrill with adrenaline and panic. "Alec, stop it! It's me...Kira!" She quickly checked herself over to make sure she hadn't been hit and, when she found no blood and no evidence of injury, she breathed a hesitant sigh of relief and tried again. "Alec?"

A low moan was her answer.

She swallowed a lump of fear and peered around the corner. "Alec?" she said more softly, hoping her voice sounded more familiar to him at that pitch.

"Kira?" he rasped. "Oh, Christ! I didn't..." She heard a thud, and focused on the semi-automatic that he had just dropped on the floor. "Are you okay?"

"Yeah, I'm fine," she said as convincingly as possible. "Your aim still sucks swamp water." She thought she heard a strangled chuckle as she collected the tote bag and headed to the bed.

He was on his side, facing the door. His face was ashen, and his auburn hair plastered to his forehead with sweat.

She sat down gingerly beside him and touched his forehead. "You look like shit, Frechette." And he was burning up. She should have gotten here sooner.

"And your bedside manner sucks swamp water," he mumbled as a ghost of a smile flitted across his face. "Now, get lost. You shouldn't be—"

"Shut up, Frechette." It was odd how she found herself reverting to the way they used to talk to each other when they were partners. Neither of them had ever been critically injured on the job, but somehow it felt natural here. It also helped Kira to keep her emotional distance—to keep her from dissolving into tears of fear and pointless remorse.

"Ah," he breathed. "Still a sweetheart."

"Where is the wound?" she asked coolly, professionally.

"Right side."

He was lying on his right side. "Roll over and let me see."

Only his eyes moved. They lifted to meet her gaze and, despite the glaze of pain that was camouflaging it, she could see the emotions roiling in their depths. "You can't do this."

"The hell I can't. Don't argue with me on this. You're in trouble, and I'm here to help. That's my job, and I've been very lax in my duties. It's about time I got my act together."

"But you'll be an accessory."

"Bullshit!" She saw him smile, and knew he was still amazed at the reserves of cuss words that she was able to call upon when needed. "I know exactly what I'm doing. Give me a little credit, okay? I'm not an accessory because you're innocent. And I'm here to help you prove it."

He closed his eyes and said nothing. She took the opportunity to check his pulse. It was rapid and thready. "Please, Alec." She allowed a note of concern and worry to creep into her voice. "You're already fevered. Let me help you. Roll on your back so I can take a look."

Grudgingly he did as he was told and she heard him stifle a moan of pain. He had tied some rags—no, they looked like torn-up sheets or pillowcases—around his middle to try to stanch the bleeding, but they were soaked through. In fact, the mattress beneath where he had been lying seemed to be saturated as well.

"You've lost a lot of blood."

"No. You think?"

"Don't get sarcastic with me, or I'll…"

"What? You'll shoot me?" He managed a wry grin, despite the pain she knew he must be experiencing.

"I'll sic Cujo on you."

"Don't make me laugh." His voice was thick.

She began untying the rags. "No. You're right. That was always your job." It was true. Alec was always the one with the easy laugh and the off-the-cuff quips and quick-fire insults. He had always been the one to make her laugh. He had always been the one to hold her when she was hurting. He had been the one to feed her when she didn't want to cook or eat.

Unexpectedly, tears welled up. What, exactly, had she ever done for him? How could she have overlooked his needs so completely? She had been so damn busy looking after everybody else around her that she had completely ignored the one person who should have been her first priority.

She wiped her eyes on her sleeve and pulled away the last of the bloody rags. The wound immediately began to ooze. "Oh, Alec," she whispered. "This is out of my league."

"Then leave."

"Don't be such a stubborn mule. You need a doctor." His right side had been torn open. A hunk of flesh had been ripped away, and she suspected a major blood vessel was involved, considering the amount of blood loss. "You have to get to a hospital."

"No. They'll lock me up."

"But you're innocent!" she pleaded. "You just need a chance to explain what happened."

"You don't understand. It's not that simple."

"What I understand is that you need intravenous antibiotics, some major suturing, possibly even surgery. I'm sure you should have a transfusion and bed rest in a sterile environment for several days. If you don't get that—"

"I'll be fine."

Kira reined in her temper and decided on blatant scare tactics. "You could die, Alec."

"I could get eaten by mutant skrill from Andromeda Four too. Every day is a risk."

She rolled her eyes and stifled a grin. "You're impossible. And you should stop watching that sci-fi crap. It'll rot your brain."

"I think it's too late." He was trying to be flip, but she saw him grimace. She was pretty sure it was from pain, but whether or not it was physical was unclear.

She sighed heavily. "What if I called an ambulance? In your condition you could hardly stop me."

He was silent for a time, studying her through hazy eyes until she became uncomfortable. "You won't."

She looked at his face. Then she looked at the wound that was in desperate need of professional medical attention. But when she looked back at his face again she knew he was right. "All right, I won't—unless you go critical on me. Then I won't care if they send you to the electric chair. There's no way you're dying on my shift."

He closed his eyes and the muscles in his face and neck relaxed. "Thanks, Kira. Did you bring any Merlot with you by chance?"

She reached for her tote bag. "I thought outlaws used whiskey to cut through the pain." She was startled by an odd, hoarse sound that issued from his throat. "Are you laughing?"

He waved her away. "It's too hard to expla— Christ!" She had dabbed at the wound with antiseptic.

"Finally I figured out how to shut you up," she quipped. But she bit back any further jibes when the sweat began to bead on his forehead, and his knuckles turned white from gripping the sheets.

"I did bring some pain killers. They're not that strong, but maybe if you take a triple dose..."

He nodded. "I'll take what I can get."

"Maybe I'll get them now. I'm going to have to pack the wound and that won't be easy on you."

He was silent as she rummaged for the drugs.

"And then I'm giving you some antibiotics. You're walking a fine line, Alec. I really wish—"

"How did you find me?"

"Oh, come on. You're so predictable. I knew instantly where you would head."

"No one followed you?"

"No. I'm quite sure." She paused with a half dozen tablets in her hand. "What happened, Alec? How did things go so bad?"

"Later. I'll explain later."

She accepted that silently and went to work. She coaxed him to take the pills, and got him to drink some water. She cleaned and packed and dressed the wound, and helped him move to a bed that wasn't saturated with blood.

She watched over him until he fell into a deep, restless sleep.

She bathed him with tepid water and kissed his forehead and wished she could turn back time.

They did it in those sci-fi shows all the time. It was so easy for them. It was the poor, wretched, twentieth-century humans who had to live their lives one day at a time, making mistakes and living with them, and maybe, just maybe, learning from them.

With a little luck, you didn't make the exact same mistake twice in your life.

With a little luck…

* * * * *

"Can't you shut that damn dog up?"

"Take it easy, Tim. You know what the doorbell does to him." Lauren allowed Cujo to scuttle off her lap and got up from her position at the kitchen table to answer the door.

"That's okay," called Rachel from the hall. "I'll get it."

Tim finished pouring his mug of coffee and leaned against the counter. He raked stiff fingers through his already mussed hair. "I'm sorry. I'm on edge. And I'm worried."

Lauren joined him at the counter and replenished her own supply of caffeine. "I know. Me too." They didn't have to verbalize what they were worried about. They had been together long enough that they couldn't help but employ a little mental telepathy now and again. Finishing each other's sentences and instinctively reaching out when the other needed comforting was habit-forming. It was at once comfortable and exciting. It was what marriage was all about.

Kira had seemed anxious when she dropped Cujo off. Her voice had been thin and her story thinner. Then they had seen the story on the news, and already reporters had begun hovering around Kira's bungalow. Lauren wouldn't have dreamed of questioning Kira's excuses, but she suspected that they were just that—excuses. Kira was tied up with whatever trouble Alec had gotten himself into, and there wasn't a damn thing she or Tim could do to help her. Except maybe keep their suspicions to themselves.

They heard Rachel crooning soothing words, and Lauren assumed she had scooped Cujo up as she headed for the door. The yapping was quickly stilled and Lauren smiled at Rachel's inherent affinity for animals. Even from the age of six, she could barely stand to squash a bug or swat a fly. She would bring home the most undesirable strays and beg "Doctor Dad" or "Miracle-Worker Mom" to make them all better. Maybe it was because she had become so aware of her own mortality at such a young age that she was so sympathetic to the plight of the helpless and afflicted. Rachel had been barely six years old when she ingested the tainted burger, but she had shown an awareness beyond her years. Even lying on a hospital bed, in intense pain and hovering at the edge of consciousness, Rachel's first thought had been for her new hamster. Lauren could vividly recall watching as her pale, fragile daughter reached for her father's hand and whispered, "If I don't get to go home again will you look after Peaches?" Tim had nodded, told her to go back to sleep and then had broken down in silent, body-racking sobs.

Lauren gazed longingly at Tim as he sipped coffee and stared out the window. He was so close, but lately it felt as if he were a thousand miles away. Sometimes she was so afraid—afraid that she was gradually losing him, and she just didn't know what to do about it.

"Mom?"

Lauren was wrenched out of her reverie as Rachel led two strangers into the kitchen. From the safety of Rachel's arms, Cujo was emitting a low, suspicious growl. It was directed at the small, imposing woman and tall, lanky man who had accompanied Rachel from the door. "Yes? What can we do for you?"

"Mom." Rachel cleared her throat and shifted Cujo to the other arm. "These are police officers. They wanted to talk to you."

Lauren raised her eyebrows, and sensed Tim tense beside her. "Police? What—" But then she stopped because there could only be one reason why the police would be there today.

The woman displayed a badge and said in a bright but businesslike voice, "Detective Sergeants Genevieve Turcotte and Will Ridgers. We're looking for Kira North. She wasn't at home and, because you're her closest neighbor, we thought you might have some idea where she's gone, and when she might be back."

Cujo yapped once, but a touch from Rachel silenced him. Tim shifted from one foot to the other as Lauren formulated her answer. The truth? What choice did she have? She'd always been a transparent liar. She cleared her throat. "Yes, actually. Cujo there," and she motioned toward the dog, "is hers. She asked us to look after him since she had to go away today."

Both detectives raised their eyebrows with obvious interest. When they spoke, they did so almost in unison.

"Away?"

"Cujo?"

Turcotte was professional and intense, while her partner seemed amused and incredulous. An interesting pair.

Lauren remained focused on the woman. "Yes. She said she was visiting her sister in Perth, and expected to be back to pick up her dog in the morning, before she headed off to work."

Turcotte had taken out a small notebook and was rapidly jotting down notes that made Lauren feel like a specimen under observation in a petri dish.

"Does she often visit her sister?" asked Turcotte, her pen poised and ready.

Her partner was busily tickling Cujo under the chin.

Lauren licked her lips and was glad to feel Tim's hand on her shoulder. "Occasionally. I-I think one of her sister's kids is sick. Kira's the first one she calls when that happens."

"She's a nurse, right?" asked the lanky man with the earring.

"Uh—yes." She shook her head. Oddly, the man's activities and easy demeanor were distracting her, keeping her from focusing clearly on the questions. "I mean, *yes*. She's a pediatric nurse, so works with children all the time."

"Would you like to sit down?" It was Tim's voice from behind her but, despite the benign words, it was laced with tension.

Lauren hastily urged them to sit, offered them coffee and soon the four of them were sitting around the table while Rachel chose to sit and observe from a stool a couple of feet away. She continued to cuddle and soothe the dog, but her eyes were wary, and her posture rigid.

Sergeant Turcotte tapped her pen on the notebook. "How much do you know about her relationship with Mr. Frechette?"

Lauren gripped Tim's hand for support. It was clammy and she could feel his pulse thudding against her palm. "They lived together in Montreal. They had a daughter who died of a congenital disease and they split up after her death." She swallowed but hastened to add, "That's very common when a child dies."

"Hmm." She made some notes.

"Do you know if she saw him since he came to Ottawa?" asked Sergeant Ridgers as he twirled his earring.

"Yes."

"And?"

Tim broke in. "Is Kira in some sort of trouble? Because that's just ridiculous. If you think—"

"No, no," said Turcotte with upheld hands. "Ms. North isn't under any suspicion. But surely you must have seen the news, and must know how urgent it is that we find Mr. Frechette. He's injured, and we have to talk to him to clear this up. We believe Ms. North may—"

"That's a load of crap!"

Lauren started at Rachel's tearful voice. She had sprung from her seat and was shaking with rage. "Rachel! That's no way—"

"They think he killed that girl! But he couldn't! How—" she wiped at her eyes, "how could he be so nice, make me feel so good, and then do that? It's crazy. You don't want to *talk* to him, you want to put him away!" She blinked furiously. "It's not fair!"

Tim stood and in two strides had enclosed Rachel in a hug as he softly encouraged her to control herself. But she would have none of it. "And…and he loved his little girl. And I know he loves Kira. I hope you never catch him!"

Lauren stood, but Tim had finally coaxed Rachel to silence and was leading her out of the room. "Can you handle this, Lauren?" he asked softly, indicating the police officers.

She nodded, and with a heavy heart watched him lead Rachel away. Meeting Alec had truly been a high point for Rachel—in a life that had far too few of them. It was a cruel twist of fate that the very next day she had to see him portrayed in the media as a murdering monster. Despite the evidence, Lauren found herself having great difficulty accepting that image of him as well. There had to be a mistake. There was something out of place and they just weren't seeing it. Maybe Kira saw it. Maybe she was working to fix it even as they spoke.

She turned to the officers. "I'm sorry about that. She's had a very traumatic week, and that little visit from Alec made her world sunny again…for a little while."

Sergeant Turcotte frowned. "Little visit? When was he here?"

Shit! "Last night. He made supper for Kira and then came over to cheer up Rachel."

"Are they reconciling?"

"Maybe rekindling the old fires?" asked Ridgers with a twinkle. Oddly, Lauren found herself drawn to Sergeant Ridgers. He wasn't much to look at, but still…

"No, not exactly. They were just sort of—" She sighed, unsure how much she should tell. "Just sorting through some old issues."

"Oh?" asked Turcotte. "Do you know what kind of issues?"

"I'd really rather not say. It's personal. Kira confided in me because she trusts me."

Turcotte seemed agitated and Lauren was sure the sergeant was going to press her when Ridgers stepped in. "Maybe we don't need to know details, but can you tell us what time he left? And perhaps you know something of his mood when they parted."

"I believe he left a little after nine-thirty. As to the other—"

"He peeled out of the driveway like a bat out of hell." Tim stood in the doorway, arms crossed, stance belligerent.

"Tim!"

"They have to know, Lauren!" He turned to the officers. "He left here angry. Lauren didn't tell me details, but she did say that Kira acknowledged some responsibility for hurting him years ago, and I can't see Frechette being the forgiving kind."

Lauren was speechless. She had never been so angry at Tim in her life.

"Do you think he's the Rideau Rapist?" asked Tim. His expression was almost hopeful. "I'd like to see that guy put away. If it's Frechette—"

Sergeant Turcotte was shaking her head. "No. We considered that, but the time line doesn't work. He was only in the country for one of the murders, and even then he had an ironclad alibi. The Governor General himself swears Alec was with him and his granddaughter the night of the last rapist attack."

Tim blinked. "Are—are you sure? I thought… It just would have made sense."

Lauren continued to puzzle over her husband. He sounded disappointed at this apparent development.

"Yes, it would have made things easy, but either Mr. Frechette intentionally mimicked the murders or it was purely coincidence."

"Or he didn't kill her at all," said Lauren softly.

Turcotte licked her lips and glanced uneasily at her partner. "Yes. Despite what the majority thinks, that is a distinct possibility."

Turcotte didn't think he did it. Lauren knew it. It was written all over the woman detective's face. Perhaps Alec had an ally after all.

The two officers stood to go. "However," said Ridgers. "It doesn't look good that he left here in a rage. It could add to motive. Maybe he took out his frustrations on Darcy."

Tim was gazing out the window, apparently retreating into his own world again.

"And it doesn't look good that Kira happened to disappear the day that he ran away," added Turcotte quietly.

"Kira is a law-abiding citizen," said Lauren tightly. "She cares for Alec, but I can't imagine—"

"Yes, I know," sighed Turcotte. "But even ex-cops can go bad."

"Ex-cops?"

"Do you have a number for this sister?"

"No. I'm afraid not." Lauren was still puzzling over the "ex-cop" comment.

"Well, if you see her, please tell her we urgently need to speak with her. And we'll be leaving a message with the hospital as well."

Lauren accepted a business card with their phone numbers emblazoned in faded black ink. "Yes, of course."

She ushered the odd couple to the door. But just as they were about to leave, Sergeant Turcotte turned to her. "If we don't speak to Kira ourselves soon, we may have to visit this sister, or possibly press you for the nature of her troubles with Mr. Frechette. I thought you should be prepared. It could be vital."

"I'll take that under advisement. Good night, officers." She shut the door firmly behind them.

She turned around and found herself bundled in Tim's arms.

"How's Rachel?" she murmured into his chest.

"She'll live. She's tough. I hugged her and tried to make it all better." He paused and stroked Lauren's back. "That used to be all it took. Funny how things change."

Lauren looked up at him. "Did you really think Alec was the Rideau Rapist?"

He shrugged. "It would have been nice and…neat, considering the Cromwell girl."

"I'm sorry I told you those things, Tim. I didn't want you to hate him. There's a lot more to his story."

"Yeah, maybe I was too hard on him. We've all got our own stories, don't we?" Tim's smile was sad and a little distant.

Feeling a need to reach out to him, Lauren touched his cheek. "We sure do. And Kira should be grateful for such good friends like us."

Tim traced her lips with a feather touch. "You're my best friend, Lauren. You know that, don't you?"

She merely nodded and melted against him as his lips molded with hers and his hands slid beneath her T-shirt. She didn't know where she'd be without him. She'd do whatever it took to hang onto Tim Nickle.

Chapter Fourteen

ꟃ

Kira glanced at her watch in the dim predawn glow. Five-thirty. She looked out the window with the cracked pane and the spider's web in the corner, and was greeted by gossamer ribbons of gold and pink tinting the morning sky. She had forgotten how beautiful sunrises could be, especially here.

Carefully, so as not to disturb her patient, she rolled over onto her side. The lumpy mattress creaked loudly in protest, but Alec didn't move. It had been about one a.m. when she finally acknowledged that she had to sleep. Her head had been lolling on her chest while she sat on the hard wooden chair she had dragged in from the kitchen. And there was no way she would be able to sleep in another room. She had to be close to Alec in case he needed her, or in case his fever spiked again. The solution had been obvious.

She had tried to maintain an appropriate distance from him in the cramped double bed. However, despite her best efforts, she found herself continually moving toward him in her sleep. Did she simply crave the physical comfort that came with sharing a bed with someone? It had been a very long time. Or was she drawn to Alec himself?

She tried to banish those thoughts from her mind as she touched his forehead. His skin was still clammy, but not nearly as warm as it had been at midnight. However, her relief was nominal. Fevers typically came down in the morning. Mid-afternoon was a danger zone, and she cringed at the thought of not being here with him then.

She slipped out of bed and reached for her shoes.

"Kira?" His voice was distant and weak.

She bent down and touched his hair. He was far too pale, and his jade green eyes were lusterless. His condition emphasized the innocent, Opie Taylor-side of his persona. His freckles stood out in stark contrast to the paleness of his complexion, and the scar under his eye looked a little bit pinker, a little bit fresher. Whenever she looked at him, every instinct in her cried out—*He's been through so much. He needs you. Take care of him. Help him and hold him and make it all better.* So that was exactly what she intended to do. "I need to change your dressing, but then I have to go."

He licked his lips. "Good. You've taken enough risks."

No, I haven't. In fact I've barely begun. Aloud she ventured, "I'm coming back, Alec."

He reached up to grab her hand, which was still hovering over his pillow. "If anything happens to you..."

"It will be my decision—my responsibility." She kneeled down so they were face-to-face. "I have to at least put in an appearance at work or they'll get suspicious. I should probably talk to the police, too. But as soon as I can clear things up there, I'm coming back."

He shook his head, but she stilled him with a gentle hand on his scruffy cheek.

"I'm afraid the antibiotics aren't doing the trick. I'm going to bring back some...things from the hospital that should aid your recovery."

"You're going to steal for me?"

She chuckled and reached for the dressing, peeling away the gauze and pads. "I'm already harboring a felon. I hardly think a little petty larceny will be my ticket to the big house." He seemed at a loss for words so she continued. "I'm worried. I don't like the look of you."

He managed a half smile. "You're the first woman to say that in a hell of a long time."

She tried to share his humor, but couldn't even crack a smile. She exposed the wound and it seeped a little more blood, but at least the gushing had ceased. She was nominally comforted. "I know you joke to cover up, Alec," she said as she rinsed the tissue with sterile saline. "You joke because you don't like to admit you're worried or vulnerable."

He endured the pain stoically and set his jaw at her insult to his invincibility.

"But that's okay. I'll worry enough for the both of us."

He ignored her and tried to sound cocky, but came off a slim notch above pathetic. "What if I've left by the time you get back?"

"You can't."

"You don't think I'm strong enough?"

"No, I'm quite sure you're strong and stupid enough to try to leave. So I've already disabled the BMW."

"You what?"

"Don't worry. I can fix it. But you're not going anywhere."

She could see the rage in his eyes. Alec didn't like not being in control. He had never liked taking orders, even when he was a cop. And he certainly had never liked Kira giving him instruction in anything. But, as usual, he remained his silent, stoic self, simmering in his own juices, and presenting his *Mr. Cool* face for the world to see.

Kira played along. "Good. We understand each other." She finished re-packing the wound and applied a fresh wrap to hold everything firmly in place. She stood and wiped her hands on a towel. "Now, I'm leaving the Tylenol and antibiotics right here with a jug of water. The bleeding seems to have slowed, but move as little as possible, and I'll try to be back by six o'clock tonight at the latest."

She studied his silent form critically. "Is that clear?"

She was pleased to see him fighting a grin. "Yes, ma'am."

"And don't do anything stupid while I'm gone, like black out or…"

"Or die?"

"Don't even joke about that, Alec."

He closed his eyes briefly before reaching for her hand, which dangled loosely at her side. Despite his condition, the fingers that enclosed hers were strong and vital…and possessive. "Kira, I…wanted to say I'm sorry for all those things I said at your place."

"Why?" She was genuinely puzzled. "They were the truth."

"Maybe I should have tried harder. I should have stuck around, tried to work it out. I don't know. I just gave up too easily."

"Maybe we both could have done things differently. Probably we're both to blame. I know I am." She smiled weakly. "But I think the time for regrets is over. Right now we have to work on clearing your name so we can get on with our lives."

"What if I did it?" His voice was so soft she wasn't sure if she had heard him correctly.

"What? What are you talking about? You couldn't have killed that girl any more than I could ignore a wounded kitten."

He let go of her hand and rubbed at his temple. "I don't know. I want to believe that. I have to believe that, but…"

"But what?" Kira knelt again. "What do you mean you *want* to believe it?"

"The whole time I've been lying here I've been going over it again and again in my head. But it seems the harder I try to remember, the more elusive the memories." He looked at her and his eyes were pleading. She had never seen him so uncertain, so vulnerable. Her heart ached for him. "It's like waking up from a dream, and you have these fleeting images of it, but the second you concentrate and try to recall the whole thing, it just vanishes, and then you can hardly remember what made you think you even had a dream in the first place."

"You mean you blacked out?"

"I guess...I mean, I must have. I did drink more than I should have. I was upset and angry. I felt entitled." He closed his eyes again. "Maybe I felt entitled to too much."

Kira licked her lips nervously. "Tell me exactly what you do remember."

What did he remember? He remembered feeling self-righteous and indignant and like a fool. Self-righteous because he had proven himself right. Kira had been exactly what he thought she was. He had been indignant because he had been used and taken for granted and he was damn sick of it. And he had felt like a fool for hoping that maybe he would be proven wrong.

But he didn't tell Kira all that. He told her about arriving at the mansion and having a couple of drinks. He told her about heading up to Darcy's room in search of a physical outlet for his passions and his anger. He told her about waking up next to a dead woman, and all the mayhem that had ensued.

"But you don't remember anything in between?"

"No." He had never been so miserable in his life. "Nothing."

She was silent for a few moments, and he thought his heart would stop beating altogether. If Kira believed him a murderer then it was most certainly true. And even if it weren't, the fact that she would *believe* it to be true would be a sentence worse than death by injection. He hesitated to acknowledge how much he needed her to believe in him. Maybe it was all the more important because he wasn't sure he believed in himself.

She stood slowly and said finally in slow, measured tones, "No. I don't care how it looks. You couldn't have done it. You just don't have it in you, Alec. I know you too well."

"But I fell asleep thinking how much I hated her, and everything she represents. I fell asleep thinking how much I hated..." He couldn't say it.

"Me?"

He nodded miserably. "Yes. And myself. What if I'm blocking it out because I can't bear to remember? What if—"

"That's enough!"

He started at the intensity in her voice. As he looked up at those amber eyes with the fiery emerald flecks, there was no doubt in his mind—she believed in him. That knowledge reassured and comforted him in a way that defied definition. In a way that was even a little bit disturbing. It had been a long time since he'd allowed himself to need someone—to trust someone. Trusting made him vulnerable, and he didn't like vulnerability. Unfortunately, in his current situation, he didn't seem to have much choice.

"Stop torturing yourself," she said with conviction. "You'll never get better if you keep beating yourself up like that." She checked her watch. "Now, I've got to go. I have to stop in at home to shower and check on Cujo before I head to the hospital." She kissed his forehead so lightly that it sent shivers down his spine. "Now remember my instructions, and I'll be back as soon as I can."

She headed for the door but his voice stopped her in her tracks. "Kira?"

"Yes?" she said impatiently. "I really need to get going."

"I wish things had been different."

The impatience evaporated like a puff of smoke on the breeze. "Yeah," she said, her voice thick and tight. "Me too. But wishing doesn't get us very far, does it?"

She walked out and he wondered if she knew how very true that was.

* * * * *

"I don't know what you expect to find," muttered Will.

"Stop whining like such a baby. Just because you didn't get any last night doesn't give you the right—"

"Hey!" He twirled his earring as he glanced around the crime scene with a disinterested air. "How do you know I didn't get any? Maybe I screwed her right into next Saturday."

Gen opened the closet door and flicked on the light, checking the contents for the umpteenth time, moving shoes, rearranging boxes. "Uh-huh. You're in a foul mood and I happen to know Paige went out with her girlfriends last night."

"Mmm." He leaned against the window frame and gazed out at the lush green carpet of grass and the fading sunrise.

Gen came out of the closet and sighed in frustration. "You *could* make yourself useful, you know. Last time I checked you had at least a few brain cells along with your hormones. *Use them!*"

"Which? The brains or the hormones?"

"Aaugh!"

He laughed, and started moving furniture. "All right, all right. It just seems so pointless. Forensics went over this place with a fine-tooth comb. I don't know what you think we'll pick up now."

"Neither do I. I won't know it until I see it."

"You're still convinced he's innocent."

"I'm not convinced either way. But I am convinced that if he did kill her it was vastly out of character for him, and we better have an ironclad case."

"I'd like to get to the hospital by ten and see if we can catch his ex."

"They were never married."

"Whatever."

A soft tap on the bedroom door interrupted their banter. They stopped what they were doing and looked up to see Carl Stuart's bespectacled face peering around the door. "Is there anything I can do to help you officers?" he asked sweetly.

"No," said Gen. "No, no. We're fine. But thanks for the offer."

"I thought we locked the suite door," said Will as he propped a foot up on the love seat.

"I have a master key."

"Oh? Do you now?"

Stuart scowled. "What are you implying?"

Will shrugged. "Nothing. It was an innocent question."

Gen knew all too well that absolutely nothing innocent made its way out of Will Ridgers' mouth. Even if it started out that way, it invariably became tainted somewhere along the route between his brain and his tongue.

Gen went into her usual post-Will damage control mode. "Thanks again, Mr. Stuart. And we want to thank you for being so cooperative, but we'd appreciate it if you don't disturb the crime scene further. I know you're security here, but this is strictly police business."

Stuart grunted, apparently unconvinced of the aptitude of the unlikely pair of cops who were conducting this highly sensitive investigation. "All right. But I hope you know that Mr. Cromwell is extremely anxious to see justice done. I trust everything is being done to bring Mr. Frechette in for a quick and efficient conviction."

"Yes," said Gen slowly, doling out her patience in small, well-proportioned servings. "We are doing everything we can to find Mr. Frechette in order to bring him in for *questioning*.

He has not yet been formally charged with the crime, and I'm afraid a trial and sentencing is well beyond thinking about, let alone discussing." She stepped over to the door and skillfully took Stuart's arm to lead him back to the hall. "When we do find him, you can tell Mr. Cromwell that he will be the first one we call. And I hope we can count on his assistance should we think of any more questions concerning his granddaughter."

They were at the doorway to the hall and, as Stuart stepped outside, he countered, "I should hardly think Darcy's past has anything to do with this. I should think your course would be clear, and that Mr. Frechette's arrest would be paramount."

"Why do you mention Darcy's past, Mr. Stuart? Is there something your boss neglected to tell us?"

Stuart seemed taken aback. "No, no, of course not. I merely thought…" He shook his head and regained his composure. "Don't change the subject. Just do your job and do it quickly." With that, he turned and strode purposefully toward the stairs.

Gen locked the door behind him, and walked thoughtfully back to the bedroom.

"That guy gives me the creeps," said Will the moment she returned.

"I couldn't agree more. But he might prove useful."

"Yeah, I could come up with a few good uses for him, and none of them are pretty."

"What I *mean* is, something he said makes me wonder if we have the whole story on Darcy Cromwell."

Will perked up. "What's this? Laying blame on the victim? How politically incorrect of you."

Gen stepped over to the antique triple dresser. "It's not called laying blame, it's called investigating. Speaking of which," she said with a meaningful lift of her eyebrows, "can we get back to it? That is what they pay us for."

Will grudgingly bent to prodding the cushion on the overstuffed chair in the corner.

Thankful for the silence, Gen systematically opened each drawer in the dresser. She rooted through underwear and shorts and—oh brother—tube tops. She had heard they were back in style, but she had hoped it was an evil rumor dreamed up by the *Stacked and Tacky Club*. Imagine her horror when she had begun to see twenty-five-year-old debutantes sporting the newly revived bane of her teenage years.

Unable to stop herself she asked, "Does Paige wear tube tops?"

Will blinked at her stupidly. "Only when she's chewing a wad of Double Bubble and balancing on her stiletto heels." He rolled his eyes. "What kind of stupid question was that? The closest Paige comes to a tube top is a strapless evening gown." Not a surprise, actually. What was amazing was that Paige had that level of class, and yet had chosen Will for a husband.

"You take her to a lot of black tie affairs, do you?"

Will ignored her. "Where the hell did that come from, anyway?"

"I was just thinking about Frechette—wondering if he went for that kind of style." *Or lack thereof.*

"Wondering if he'd go for you?" asked Will without batting an eye.

"Shut up!" She had made it to the nightstand, while Will checked beneath the cushions of the love seat. "I just wanna get into his head. Maybe it'll help us figure out where he went." She wasn't going to share the fact that Alec Frechette had made at least a cameo appearance in a few of her fantasies in the past few years. She was human, after all.

"I know who could get us into his head better than anybody."

"Yeah, I know." Will had a real gift for nagging when he had something on his mind. Some people would say he was tenacious, but Gen just thought he was stubborn and exasperating. "We'll go to the hospital as soon as we're finished here." She gazed at the bare, bloodstained mattress. The bedding had been stripped and sent to forensics for testing. She ignored the image of Darcy's sightless eyes and spread-eagled posture that sprang to mind. "If, that is, she shows up. Dollars to donuts she's keeping him alive somewhere."

Will shook his head in wonder. "I agree with you, but it boggles the mind how any sane woman could be so sucked in by his charms that she would risk everything to help a murderer."

Gen gritted her teeth, and bit back a response as she bent low and flashed her penlight under the mattress. "We have not yet established that he is. I'm sure Kira..."

Will flopped down on the love seat. When Gen didn't continue, he prompted. "You're sure Kira what?"

But Gen didn't answer. She was too busy retrieving something from beneath the bed. In her gloved fingers she finally displayed her prize.

"A glass?" asked Will, his tone reaching beyond bored. "So?"

Gen sniffed the contents before holding it up to the light. She turned it slowly, the intricately cut crystal of the tumbler casting prisms of light onto the walls. "So since when does forty-year-old Scotch leave a fine white powdery residue after it evaporates?"

"Huh?" Will got up and approached her to take a closer look.

She handed it to him wordlessly.

"Well, what do you know? Do you think it was hers or his?"

"Somehow I doubt Darcy was into Scotch. But the fingerprints will tell the tale, and I want to know what that powder is."

"You think he was on something? It would be a weird way to ingest coke, but anything's possible."

"Maybe. Or maybe somebody slipped him something."

"I think you're reaching."

She shook her head emphatically. "I don't think so. Right from the start this thing was too easy. It reeked like a setup. Maybe this will prove my theory."

"And maybe Mr. Frechette's glass happened to have a lot of residue from the dishwashing soap."

"Maybe." But she doubted it. Gen had good instincts. It was those instincts that had allowed her to fight her way up to detective through the ranks of the male-dominated Mounties. And her instincts were screaming that this whole thing stank like a week-old corpse. "But there's no point in arguing about it. Let's get it to the lab and then pay a visit to Ottawa General. If Kira isn't forthcoming, maybe her coworkers can be of assistance. I've heard that nurses gossip worse than cops."

Will's brown eyes widened and he blew out a short puff of air. "Wow! Hard to believe, but I guess anything's possible."

* * * * *

Kira checked her watch as her sneakers padded quickly down the long, familiar hallway. The enormous portraits of Big Bird and Elmo passed by in a blur. She was much later than she had intended. There had been construction on one of the highways between the cabin and her house, and then Cujo had yapped incessantly while she and Lauren had tried to talk.

Her palms were already sweating at the prospect of facing the two detectives Lauren had told her about. And her plans for the rest of the day did nothing to still the erratic beating of her heart. She hoped her anti-perspirant would live up to the ad campaign that had persuaded her to pick it up on her last trip to the supermarket.

For the moments your mother never warned you about. That was the slogan. The ads had depicted pilots landing a plane with only one engine, executives under the gun in a boardroom, even a dad coaching mom through the birth of their first child. She doubted they had considered the stress associated with harboring a murder suspect and lying to the RCMP while a career and a man's life hung in the balance.

She finally breezed into the oncology suite at 9:45. As she stashed her purse in her personal cupboard, she waited silently for the inevitable taunts from Jean. But they weren't what she was expecting at all.

"I'm surprised you came in today," said Jean under her breath.

Kira was confused by the lack of an edge to Jean's voice. "Why?"

Jean shrugged. "Well, that whole thing with your ex." She flicked her eyes to Mike's office door. "And there's somebody here to see you. I don't envy you that one."

"Why? Who is it?" She played innocent while her heart rate edged up another couple of notches.

"Cops. They're in talking with Mike right now."

"Mike?" Why on Earth would they want to talk to him?

Jean shrugged. "I think they just asked what he thought about your *sister* story."

Kira arched her eyebrows in feigned indignation. "Story?"

"Hey, it's not me you gotta convince." The door to Mike's office clicked open. "It's them, honey." Jean picked up a chart. "I'll look after Teddy for you while you're otherwise occupied."

Kira started to protest—she didn't like neglecting her patients, or heaven forbid, handing them over to Jean's callous touch. But the detectives didn't give her a choice. They walked directly to her, extending badges and hands, and completely sucking the oxygen out of the air.

"Kira North?" asked the small woman.

She nodded dumbly, but finally managed to croak out, "Yes, that's me."

Detective Genevieve Turcotte made the obligatory introductions, while her partner looked on with a quirky smile and an amused twinkle in his eye. "Dr. LaRocque here was kind enough to fill us in on your duties and a little bit about you while we waited for your arrival," the sergeant was saying.

"Oh? Well—"

"I also told them about how much your sister relies on your nursing skills." Mike turned to the officers. "She can be quite the pest. We've gotten calls from her in the middle of the day when her baby wakes up a half an hour earlier than usual from her nap. She needs a medical opinion on whether she should put her to bed at the usual time that night, or a half hour earlier." He chuckled. "It's all life and death with her, I'm afraid."

Kira was stunned. Mike knew nothing about her sister. She wasn't an obsessive mother, and they had certainly never gotten phone calls at work about anything so petty. Then it dawned on her—he was covering for her. She licked her lips. "Yes, I'm afraid it gets a bit embarrassing."

"Were you able to help her out yesterday?" asked Detective Ridgers.

"Uh—yes. We got the little one to eat his cereal at last." She tried an unconcerned smile. "Thank God the sun will rise again to greet another day."

Ridgers chuckled, but his partner didn't seem to appreciate the humor. "We really need to talk with you, Ms. North. Dr. LaRocque was kind enough to offer the use of his office."

"Must we do this now? I have patients and I hate to pawn my work off on the other nurses."

Ridgers smiled indulgently. "It won't take long. Surely you understand how urgent this is. There's a killer on the loose."

The heat rose to Kira's face as quickly as if someone had opened a steam valve. "Alec Frechette is *not* a murderer."

"How can you be so sure?" Ridgers' brows knitted and Kira got the sudden feeling that she had been deliberately goaded into that statement.

"I really think we should do this in the office," said Turcotte with an irritated glance at her partner.

Kira drew in a calming breath. "Fine." She stood and motioned toward the door. "Lead the way."

She noticed Mike looking on with concern as she followed the officers into his office. She tried to send him a silent *thank you* as she passed and, she thought, maybe he understood.

Kira settled herself in one of the three plush teal green chairs that faced Mike's desk. He had tried to pick furniture and decor that would make his patients and their parents as comfortable as possible. At the moment, however, it was doing nothing to soothe Kira's nerves. Turcotte settled down beside her, and Ridgers leaned against the corner of the warm mahogany desk. He picked up a pen and began to twirl it between his fingers.

Turcotte didn't waste any time. "Now, why are you so certain of Mr. Frechette's innocence?"

"Because I know him. He isn't capable of that."

"That's what Bernardo's family said too."

Kira turned a fierce glare on Ridgers. "Are you drawing a parallel between a serial killer like Paul Bernardo and Alec Frechette? Because if you are, that is simply ludicrous." Paul Bernardo was blond and blue-eyed, charming and intelligent. He was a model Canadian citizen who, with the help of his lovely wife, kidnapped, raped, tortured, murdered and dismembered several young girls—one of whom was his wife's sister. He had about as much in common with Alec Frechette as Will Ridgers did with James Bond.

"Is it?" said Ridgers with an annoying cock of one eyebrow. "Both were young and attractive and charming. Both cut up young women in their spare time."

Kira had to physically hold back from launching herself at Ridgers' throat.

"Will, take it easy," said Turcotte in a soothing voice.

And in a flash Kira understood. She leaned back in her chair, relaxed her clenched fists and casually traced the gold band of her ring. "Oh, I get it."

"Get what?" said Turcotte with a frown.

"You're playing the whole good cop-bad cop thing for my benefit. Really, guys, I thought you'd have a little more class."

Ridgers barely stifled a chuckle while Turcotte looked at him with undisguised irritation. "I realize that is how it may look, but actually we're not acting. I'm naturally even-tempered and professional, and Will here is naturally *obnoxious!*"

Ridgers put down the pen and held out his hands, palms skyward, "Guilty as charged. I do confess though to trying to catch you off guard, Ms. North."

Kira shook her head in mock exasperation. "I don't know why you're going to all this trouble. I have no idea where Alec is."

"We hadn't asked you that yet," said Turcotte quietly. "It's interesting that you would assume that's why we're here."

"Oh come on! I'm no imbecile. Ultimately you're hoping I'll lead you to him, if not directly, then by giving you insights into his thought processes. Well, I hate to burst your bubble, officers, but I haven't known Alec for the last seven years." She paused, trying to lend weight to what followed. "In fact I sometimes wonder if I ever knew him. And I certainly don't know where he would have gone."

"You saw him the night of the murder."

"Yes. We do have a history together, I'll acknowledge that much. I still care for him to a degree, and we had some old issues to sort through."

"Hmm. I believe Mrs. Nickle used that exact same wording."

"Hardly surprising, considering we rehearsed this whole thing months ago." Kira tried to shoot fires of indignation from her eyes along with the sarcasm. "It's all part of a grand conspiracy plan for Alec to leave a lucrative career as a bodyguard to the rich and famous, come back here, murder the Governor General's granddaughter, thus paving the way for…" She scrunched her eyes shut and rubbed at her temples. "For what exactly? What would be his motive in all this?"

Turcotte closed her eyes and took a deep breath, and Ridgers chewed on the inside of his cheek, apparently suppressing a smile. He seemed to find a lot of things funny.

Turcotte responded, "We know he left your house in a rage. It would be logical for him to take out his frustrations on Ms. Cromwell and, especially after drinking heavily, for things to go too far."

"Alec's too smart for that," she said simply.

"What was he angry about?"

"It's personal."

"Not anymore. It just became police business."

Kira allowed herself the luxury of looking out the window at the searing blue of the midmorning sky as she silently debated what to tell them. She decided on the truth—or at least the portion of it that wouldn't incriminate Alec by giving him an obvious reason to target Darcy Cromwell. "It had to do with our daughter," she said grudgingly. "He blamed me for not allowing him a role in her care. He resents me for shutting him out of her brief life, and I finally acknowledged the truth of it."

"If you acknowledged his accusations, why would he have left in a rage?"

"Those memories may be seven years old, but they are still very painful. He may have squealed his tires as he left my house, but I don't believe it was rage so much as anguish and grief that he was exhibiting." Once she got into the swing of it, lying wasn't so hard after all. Her palms had even stopped sweating. "He loved her very much, and I'm afraid I didn't give him an outlet for those feelings."

"What do you know about the incident in Montreal that preceded his resignation from the police force there?" It was Ridgers, breaking in with his usual brand of callous charm.

"What does that have to do with anything?"

"We're not sure. Maybe nothing. Maybe everything. A man died, Ms. North, and the public record on it is very fuzzy."

She stood and paced to the window, suddenly feeling claustrophobic. She wished she could lie about this one, but the truth was, she didn't know enough to make it worthwhile. "I'm afraid I don't know any more than what was in the papers. That incident happened a mere two days before our daughter died. We didn't have a lot of time to chat then, and the day after she died, he moved out. That was the last time we talked, since as soon as the internal investigation was concluded, he left the country."

"Tell us anyway."

She leaned heavily against the picture window and closed her eyes as she remembered how stricken Alec had looked when he had come home that night. But she hadn't had time to ask him what was wrong. She'd been far too busy looking after Cherisse to bother with him. It was only because a neighbor had watched the late-night news and had called out of concern that Kira knew anything had happened at all. At the time, she had been too exhausted to pursue it. Alec had always been able to look after himself. She had enough on her plate. Now she felt nauseous as she recalled those pathetic excuses. "His partner was killed in a shoot-out during a drug bust at an old factory."

"His partner was very young."

"Yes, he had only been on the force two years. Alec was his first partner."

"There was some question as to Alec's judgment in the situation, and that possibly he overestimated his partner's abilities, or sent him into a dangerous situation."

She licked her lips, which had gradually gone very dry over the course of this conversation. "I honestly can't comment on that. In the brief time we were partners on the force, I had no complaints. We worked well together. As to his state of mind at the time this happened, I am ashamed to say I didn't have enough interaction with him to offer an opinion."

"Ashamed?" Turcotte ceased a relentless binge of scribbling on her pad. "Why would you use that word in particular? You had a very ill child to look after, a certain degree of detachment from her father should be expected."

"I tend to take things to extremes," Kira said truthfully. Then sucking in a fortifying lungful of oxygen, she stood a little straighter and demanded, "Is that all? I do have patients to attend to."

"One last thing," ventured Turcotte. "Do you have any idea where he might have gone to recuperate? A friend? A special hideaway? A fishing shack or cottage perhaps?"

"No, I'm afraid I don't."

"And if you did, would you tell us?" Ridgers had slipped off the desk and was leaning his lanky form against the doorjamb.

"Honestly?" She paused and tapped her fingers against the window frame. "Probably not."

"If he came to you for help with his injuries, would you do it?" Ridgers just didn't let up.

Kira strode with purpose toward the door. "I think I've answered enough questions. If you think of anything else," she paused with her hand on the knob and with her eyes directed Ridgers to get out of the way, "call first." She opened the door and stepped out into the moderately less stifling air of the oncology suite.

Jean looked up warily from her position at the nursing station but said nothing.

"I'll go check in on Teddy before I start on the orders for today," said Kira matter-of-factly, hoping there was no tremor to her voice.

Jean merely nodded as Kira whirled around and headed for Teddy's room.

"Thanks for your cooperation," called Ridgers. "Say hello to Alec for us, and tell him we'll see him soon."

Kira stopped in her tracks and briefly considered going back and showing Ridgers exactly what she remembered from her days on the force, but instead she forced her steps to continue in the direction of a little boy who needed her. She also tried desperately to keep her mind off the man who no doubt needed her at that moment as well. She hoped he was following directions like a good little patient. The trouble was Alec had never been a good little anything.

* * * * *

"Do you buy it?" asked Will as they headed for the elevators.

"Mostly. I'm just not sure we've got the whole story."

"I'm sure we don't."

Gen punched the down button and watched the glowing numbers mark the elevator's progress toward their floor. "You've got a real way with women, you know, Will?"

He shrugged his bony shoulders. "What can I say? It's a gift."

"Well, next time you feel the urge to display your talents…" She looked up at his unapologetic grin. "Don't. Just shut up and let me do the talking."

"You're no fun at all, Gen. No wonder you don't got a man."

"You're all the man I can handle. You and our fugitive, that is. I want to find him before he skips the country or dies on us."

Ridgers patted her on the back as the elevator doors slid open. "And when we do nab him, don't worry, I'll let you question him in the back room *all by yourself*." He bobbed his eyebrows.

"You should be neutered."

"Ouch!"

"Let's go check on those lab results, Newt."

Chapter Fifteen

ꙮ

"Daddy?"

Alec took one more sip of coffee before looking up from his morning paper. "Morning, *chèrie*. You look ravishing this morning."

A flush of pink rose to Cherisse's tawny cheeks. With their fair complexions, redheads always had a raw deal when it came to the telltale rush of blood to the face. "You always say that," she said as she bent to kiss his cheek.

"It's always true." And it was. With each passing day her beauty grew, until he ached to look at her. And with each passing moment he lamented the speedy approach of the day she would leave them to forge her own life, alone in a harsh, cold world.

Cherisse sat down beside him and absently played with his fingers. The warmth of her touch never ceased to fill him with awe. The color in her cheeks didn't diminish as she continued to fidget nervously.

"What's on your mind?" he asked as he brushed a tendril of red silk off her forehead.

She laced her fingers with his. "Well…I was just wondering if—"

"Oui? Spit it out. You know I won't bite."

"Dirk Brown asked me out, and I was wondering if you'd let me go. I know I'm not quite sixteen yet, and I know how strict you and Mom are about that but—"

"Whoa!" he laughed at her anxious babbling. "Slow down there. Where exactly does he want to—oh, Christ!" A shooting pain in his side cut off his words and his breath.

"Daddy? What's wrong?"

He reached for her hand. He tried to anchor himself to her, but her hand seemed to dissolve in his like wet sand. The tighter his grip, the less substance he held. "Cherisse!" he pleaded. His surroundings wavered and swayed, as if he were viewing the world through layers of shimmering, shifting cellophane. "Don't go, *chérie*. Please."

"Daddy? Daddy, what's happening? Daddy, I'm scared!"

He could no longer see her. The room had gone murky and the air seemed thick—too thick to breathe. He could barely hear her, but still he fought through the haze, searching for the touch of that delicate hand.

"Daddy? Can't you help me?"

"I'm trying, *chérie*. God help me, I tried."

"Daddy?" And suddenly there was a frail wispy child sitting in his lap with a tiny, fairy voice and big searching eyes. "Will you read to me? Don't you like to read to me?"

"Of course. Of course I do, *chérie*." But he was confused and the pain was spreading. He reached for the book she held out and, despite the lack of oxygen in the room, he struggled to read the familiar words...

You knew she was going to die and you didn't wake me!

It was my one chance to be with her and I'm not sorry.

But I loved her and—

I loved her too, dammit! I loved her too!

Gut-wrenching sobs tore at him, and a fierce, mind-searing pain sliced through him, driving him relentlessly through the layers of semi-consciousness until his eyes flew open and he remembered.

He gasped for breath—for air that seemed determined to elude him. He sucked in lungful after lungful and couldn't seem to get enough. He raised his left hand to wipe away the dampness on his cheeks and realized it wasn't only tears that were soaking his skin. He was dripping with sweat, and yet the room seemed unbearably cold.

He pulled the blanket in a little tighter and closed his eyes to relive the fantasy. He couldn't believe how real it had seemed. And Cherisse had been almost sixteen. Even in a dream state, surely he should have realized how ridiculous that was. She would be barely ten now, if she had lived. And then he realized he had been living out one of the many little fantasies he had indulged in on their old deck back home in Montreal. Cherisse's first date, her graduation, dancing with her on her wedding day, even the birth of her first child—he had tortured himself over and over with images of things that could never be.

All those nights he had sat outside under the stars, with nothing better to do than make wishes that could never come true. The coughs and sobs and the murmurs of comfort would drift to him through the open windows from Cherisse's bed, and he would feel so useless and so helpless—and so guilty. It was his genes that had done this to her—his and Kira's. Perhaps Kira had an outlet for her guilt and grief. But he had none.

Only the stars could be trusted with his unanswerable desires and regrets. Only the stars would ever know the horror of his one, despicable wish. He lived with that guilt every day—wallowed in it, embraced it. It, perhaps more than anything, was the driving force in his life. It was what allowed him to forsake his pride and prostitute himself. That was all he deserved after the horrible thoughts he had allowed himself in a moment of weakness.

He closed his eyes as shivers racked his body, and a fresh pain lanced through his side. With an effort of will, he rolled over and reached for the water and pills that Kira had left him. And, for the first time in his life, he really wondered if he'd see another sunrise.

And for the thousandth time he wondered if that would really be such a bad thing.

* * * * *

Kira bent to retrieve a shabby teddy bear from beneath the bed in room seven.

"You almost finished?" Jean's voice reached her from the doorway.

Kira peered over the bed. Jean had been uncharacteristically accommodating and soft-spoken toward her all day. She appreciated it, but it had also lent an aura of disturbing surrealism to an already incomprehensible situation. "Yes. You go ahead, Jean. I'll finish and lock up."

Jean hesitated. "Are you sure? I wondered if maybe you wanted some company for supper."

Kira blinked slowly, and wondered briefly if she had lapsed into a hallucination. But Jean remained standing there, looking concerned and sincere. Kira latched her fingers around the teddy bear's throat and stood up. "No, thank you. That's very sweet, but I'd just like to get home and curl up with a hot tea."

"Okay." Jean still seemed hesitant to leave. Of all the days that Kira desperately wanted the place to herself, Jean had picked this one to play the Good Samaritan. "As long as you're sure you're okay."

Kira frowned and walked toward Jean, clutching the teddy to her chest. She decided to give in to curiosity. "That's very sweet, but I'm afraid I don't understand why you're suddenly so concerned for my welfare."

Jean stuffed her hands in the pockets of her uniform. She shrugged. "I don't know, really. I guess I never thought of you as having a life before. With you, it's always been work, and nothing else. And then I saw you with him, and realized you had a history with someone…" She sighed heavily. "And then that horrible stuff that happened at the mansion… I just figured you might be having a rough time."

Kira smiled in spite of herself. "Thanks. It's nice to know I've got friends behind me."

But Jean's next words managed to dampen the warm glow that had been kindled in her chest. "Do you think he did it? I mean, I can't really imagine it—he seems like such a nice guy and everything. But it sure doesn't look good, if you know what I mean."

Kira gritted her teeth. "Yes. I know all too well." She set the teddy down in his rightful place on the toy shelf. "Now, I'd actually like a little time alone, so why don't you head on out? I'll lock up."

Jean took one last look around before heading for her cupboard. "All right. But if you ever need someone to talk to—"

"You'll be the first one I call," said Kira, with a concerted effort to keep the sarcasm from completely saturating her voice.

Kira puttered around until Jean had finally gotten her purse, cleaned and put away her coffee cup, combed her hair, straightened her uniform and washed her hands in her own obsessive, compulsive, five-minute routine. As soon as Jean's footsteps had retreated down the hall, and Kira was sure she would not be disturbed, she sat down at the nursing station and picked up the phone.

The other end picked up on the third ring. "Transfusion Medicine, Nancy speaking."

Kira sighed with relief. She knew Nancy. That would make this a little bit easier. "Hi, Nancy, this is Kira from Pediatrics." She hoped the phone would hide the tremors in her voice. "Did you get the order I sent down earlier today for the blood on Josh Cooper?"

"Cooper," mused Nancy. "That's a new one."

"Yeah. He's a new ALL. His family just moved here a few weeks ago." Acute lymphocytic leukemia was one of the most common forms of cancer they dealt with, and also one that frequently demanded blood transfusions.

"Hang on a minute. I think we're finished, but let me check. It's been a crazy day down here."

"Sure." Kira waited while she was put on hold, and her heart beat a rapid tattoo against her chest. The lab demanded a blood sample on all patients that were to be transfused. Therefore, Kira had taken the necessary paraphernalia into the washroom with her and had drawn some of her own blood. She had, however, made a special request for O Negative blood for this new *patient* since she had long ago forgotten Alec's blood type and had no idea whether they matched. O Negative was the universal donor, so there was no doubt that the blood would be safe to give Alec, no matter what his blood group happened to be.

Nancy came back on the phone. "Yup. It's all ready. Two O Negs, CMV Neg, and they're even fresh." She paused briefly. "Mind if I ask why we had to cross O Negs? This kid is A Pos."

She took a deep breath to prepare for the next set of blatant lies. "Uh—he's a post-marrow transplant. He used to be O Neg, but the donor was A Pos, so his group changed. We just feel more comfortable sticking with the O Negs, especially since we're not sure if the graft is taking." This line of reasoning was the rationale for requesting that the blood be CMV negative as well.

The cytomegalovirus was very dangerous to transplant patients, and needed to be avoided at all costs. Since she had to give the transplant story to explain the different blood group, the CMV negative request logically had to follow. But it was merely a ruse to make her story sound believable.

"Oh," said Nancy slowly. "That's interesting. We don't get too many of those around here." Of course Nancy was referring to patients whose blood types had changed because of a transplant, but Kira had an irrational fear that Nancy might be referring to the deception, and the actual reason for the blood order. But, Kira reminded herself, that was ridiculous.

"No, I guess not." Kira rushed on in the hopes of getting this over with quickly. "So, I can come down and pick it up?"

"Now?"

"Yes. We're staying open late just to accommodate him. And I'd like to get both units right away to save time." They had a special, regulated fridge in the oncology suite just for this purpose, otherwise the Blood Bank would never let two units go out at a time. Sitting at room temperature was detrimental to the blood. Kira had a cooler stashed in her car for that very reason.

"Yeah, sure. Come on down. It's ready."

"Thanks." Kira hung up the phone and raked a set of rigid fingers through her hair. She quickly grabbed the oversized purse she had picked out to bring today, and stuffed it full of the tubing and paraphernalia that she would need to hang blood for Alec. She also grabbed the bag of IV antibiotics that she had covertly requisitioned from the pharmacy, and headed out the door. In her haste, she almost forgot to lock it. But finally she was riding the elevator down to the second floor where Nancy waited to unwittingly help Kira commit a federal offense.

She cruised into the subdued, after-hours atmosphere of the Blood Bank. With a decidedly blasé demeanor, she chatted with Nancy, told a few jokes and signed out the two units of blood that she hoped would help speed Alec to a complete recovery.

Once outside the Blood Bank doors, she slipped into a small alcove and stashed the units in her purse. It might draw attention if she was seen strolling out to her car with two units of blood dangling from her fingers.

She had just zipped up her bag and was about to step out into the hall when she felt a hand latch around her upper arm.

"What the hell do you think you're doing?"

Kira caught her breath and managed to keep from screaming. "Mike?" She turned around to face Mike's accusing stare.

He shook her in frustration. "Answer me! What the hell are you doing with two units of blood in your goddamn purse?"

She licked her lips and tried to come up with something, anything that would sound even remotely believable. But Mike's patience was wearing thin. "You're taking them to *him*, aren't you? You do have him stashed somewhere!" He released her arm and balled his hands into fists. "God, Kira! Are you insane? Do you have any idea—"

"Of course I do! You think I'm an idiot? He's innocent, Mike. I'm just trying to give him an opportunity to prove it."

"I never knew you were so gullible. Or does he just have some strange power over you?"

She gritted her teeth. "Of course not. Give me a little credit, will you? But if you feel this way why did you cover for me today? Why make up that whole load of crap about my sister?"

"Because I care about you! I may not agree with what you're doing but I don't want to see you doing time in Kingston Penitentiary either."

"Kingston doesn't take female prisoners."

"Kira!"

"What? What are you going to do, Mike? Are you going to turn me in?"

He studied her. He looked into her eyes for what seemed like an eternity, and then he framed her face with his hands. "Do you still love him? Is that why you're doing this?"

"I don't know. All I know is I owe him a lot. This is the least I can do for him. And I *am* convinced that he's innocent. I wouldn't be doing this if I weren't."

Mike dropped his hands from her face. "How bad is it?"

"He needs the blood. I'm sure of it. I'm just not sure if two units will be enough. I didn't like the wound, but he wouldn't let me take him anywhere. I cleaned it up as best I could, but—"

"Okay. I'll keep your secret on one condition."

She frowned. "What would that be?"

"Take me with you."

She stepped back, feeling as if she had been physically struck by the shock of his words. "You can't be serious! I can't let you get sucked into this as well."

"It's my choice, and you don't really have any other options. I'm a doctor, you know. Maybe I can do something for him that you can't. And maybe he'll be able to convince me of his innocence as well." He grabbed her hand to start leading her down the hall. "If you don't take me, I'll turn you in without batting an eye. And then you'll have to give up his location to make sure he doesn't die alone." He looked at her meaningfully. "Am I right?"

She nodded miserably and allowed Mike to lead her toward the exit. "Yes, you're right." They stepped outside and the early evening air felt fresh and cool on her hot skin. "Honestly, I'm glad you're coming. I'm scared for him, and I don't know if I could have handled it on my own."

"Good. That's good to hear. I just have to stop at a payphone somewhere to cancel my dinner date for tonight, but then, maybe together we can sort this whole mess out."

They headed for the parking lot. "Yeah, maybe."

"I think we work pretty well together—legally or otherwise," said Mike with a wink.

Kira couldn't help but smile back. The relief that washed through her at not having to shoulder this burden alone was sweet. It was good to have a friend like Mike that she could trust and count on, especially when she was so used to not counting on anyone but herself.

Alec wouldn't like it, but it seemed he wouldn't have much choice in the matter.

* * * * *

Carl Stuart removed his glasses from his nose and set them down precisely in the center of the small table beside his favorite leather recliner. He settled himself deeply into the chair, leaned back, kicked off his shoes and rubbed his eyes. The study was his favorite room in this modest, but well-designed bungalow in an upper middle-class section of Ottawa.

With a sigh of relief and pleasure, he finally dropped his hands to his lap and picked up the remote control for his big screen TV. He flicked through mindless sitcoms and sporting events. It never occurred to him to return his glasses to the bridge of his nose. He only needed them for reading. He merely kept them on throughout the day in order to perpetuate his image of a diligent security official who paid scrupulous attention to detail. He also found that glasses tended to make him look more trustworthy. They were just another part of the deception—a piece of the costume that could be donned or discarded as the need arose.

He scowled at the pathetic choice of programming. He had spent an obscene amount of money on this entertainment system, paid extra for all those special channels, and had even contemplated getting a satellite dish. His professional life and hectic evening schedule tended to find him at home alone much of the time. Besides that, such things were tangible evidence of his success. Just like his Mercedes and his well-tailored suits.

But still he had to budget. He had to watch his pennies in order to afford these luxuries. And it galled him no end that

Alec Frechette could afford his Armani and Versace suits, his BMW and gallons of overpriced French wine.

Alec Frechette had been a mediocre cop and, as far as Carl could tell, an even less remarkable bodyguard. The fact that he demanded a six-figure salary and apparently got to sleep with some of the most beautiful and powerful women in the world was an insult that cut through to the core of Carl's being.

Therefore, the opportunity to see Alec squirm, and hopefully put an end to his joke of a career, had been too sweet to resist. The fact that it had artfully taken care of that rich little bitch and effectively solved one other problem had been perks that had made the deal completely irresistible.

The trouble was, now that the heat was off and someone else was on the hook for the Rideau murders, Carl had a new set of problems. In order to keep the cops focused on Frechette, and hopefully suspicious of his involvement in those other murders, it logically followed that the attacks would have to stop now that he was on the run. Definitely once he was incarcerated. That made Carl Stuart extremely restless.

Just like the three-year-old who instantly develops a new interest in a toy that has been denied him, the fact that Carl would have to give up his favorite hobby was compounding his need to indulge exponentially.

It was all he could think about, all he could taste. It was interfering with his work and making him sloppy. But maybe there was a solution. Perhaps something that he had previously perceived as a puzzling twist of events would turn out to be his salvation.

He had to wait a little longer. Acting too soon would be pushing his luck to the breaking point. But before too long he hoped to feel the familiar rush again—the rush of adrenaline that came with finally having power over those arrogant bitches who seemed to take such great joy in ordering men like him around. Men who had the misfortune of not being born into the privileged elite. Men who had to work for a living and had no choice but to kowtow and grovel for every penny. Men who bowed and smiled and accepted tips like a puppy accepting scraps from the table.

The humiliation was that much greater because these were women who had no right to live such pampered lives. These were women who had done nothing to earn their money, other than to be born with the right genes, or to marry the right name. Some of them were beautiful, most of them were bitchy, all of them were doomed. And Carl Stuart derived great pleasure from being the vehicle of their destruction. Before they died, they always knew that, in his world at least, there was justice. They got what they deserved and, if they had earned their pearls and gold and furs with nothing more than luck or looks, then they had earned their grisly fate right along with their treasures.

And it was Carl's mission to see that justice was served.

* * * * *

Kira pulled the key from the ignition and reached for the door latch.

Mike's hand on her arm stayed her from launching herself out of the car. "Do you want me to wait in the car for a bit?" He flicked his eyes to the shabby structure surrounded by knee-high weeds. "So you can prepare him for my arrival?"

Kira considered it briefly. She had confiscated Alec's gun and hidden it underneath the kitchen sink. He hadn't asked for it and, even if he had managed to find it in her absence, she had removed the cartridges. Without a weapon, in his current condition, Alec was about as threatening as a Chihuahua on Prozac. She shook her head. "No. I doubt he's in any shape to put up much of a protest. Why don't you just wait outside the bedroom door for a minute while I talk to him." She squeezed Mike's hand. Their drive had been quiet, but the silence had been oddly comforting. Kira had not sensed any judgment or reproach from her friend, and that acceptance and support meant the world to her. "Besides, I want you in there. I'm not sure how he'll be. I hated to leave him alone so long, but I didn't feel I had a choice."

"You could have called an ambulance."

She turned away, for the first time questioning the wisdom of abiding by Alec's wishes. But Mike just didn't know the whole story. There was more than Alec's health at stake—there was his trust, and her debt. And they shared a bond that Mike could never understand. "No, I couldn't have. Not yet," she said simply. "Now, let's go."

She grabbed her purse and the cooler with the blood, and Mike grabbed the medical bag he had picked up from his car before they left, and they both walked with swift steps toward the front door.

They crossed the threshold and were greeted by an ominous silence. Kira didn't know what she expected to hear. Alec had no one to talk to, and there was no radio or television. Most certainly he was asleep, but there was a stillness in the air that she found foreboding.

"Back here," she said without giving Mike a chance to look around and take in the pathetic state of the structure. She led him to the second bedroom. She motioned for him to wait beside the doorway as she eased the door open, uncertain of what she would find.

Alec spoke immediately and relief washed through her. "Kira?"

She crossed the room and sat on the edge of the bed beside him. "I'm sorry I was gone so long," she whispered as she touched his forehead. He looked at her and her relief was instantly displaced by concern. His eyes were glazed and unfocused, and his forehead cool but clammy.

He licked cracked lips and closed his eyes again. "That's okay. It hardly seems like you left. I must have slept the day away."

She smiled. "That's good, sleep is the best thing for you. Alec, I have something to tell you—"

"You know I hate it when they put us on opposite shifts," he whispered.

Kira was confused. "What?"

"I know it's nicer for Cherisse if we don't need a sitter, but still—" He opened his eyes and Kira's heart sank to the pit of her stomach. "I miss you when we're apart. And I miss having you for a partner." He smiled weakly. "The new kid's okay, but—"

"Alec," she breathed. "Alec, we're not at home." Panic teased at the edges of her already tenuous emotional control. If he wasn't fevered, why was he hallucinating?

"Hmm?" he said, his voice sleepy and his eyes drooping heavily.

"Please, Alec," she urged. "Think. Listen to me. We're in my parents' cabin. You were shot."

His eyes had closed completely and he mumbled something incoherent.

"You quit the force. We split up." She nattered on, knowing full well he probably wasn't hearing her, but desperate to reach him. "You're suspected of murder, Alec."

He just shook his head and moved his hand as if trying to swat away an irritating insect.

"Cherisse is dead, Alec. Our baby died seven years ago."

He made an odd, strangled sound in his throat and, when his eyes opened again, she knew he had returned to the present.

"That was cruel," he whispered. "I was much happier back there."

Battling tears, Kira forged ahead in earnest. "I'm sorry, Alec. But you're very sick and," she swallowed and glanced at the door, "and I brought someone who can help."

He frowned. "Am I dreaming again? What did you say?"

She bent low to whisper in his ear so that Mike wouldn't hear. "I didn't have a choice. He caught me taking stuff from the hospital and he guessed. But he's a doctor," she paused and brushed her lips against his ear, "and he's a friend. I trust him."

When Alec didn't respond, she sat up and was concerned to see that his eyes were closed. But after a few deep breaths he said, "Did you bring drugs?" He opened his eyes. "For the pain, I mean."

"Is it bad?" Kira hoped it was the pain, and not fever that had sent him into la-la land. She already dreaded checking beneath the dressing.

"A little." In Alec's warped version of the universe that meant the pain was all-consuming. "And sometimes I have a little trouble breathing." *Severe shortness of breath.*

Mike took that as his cue, and stepped into the room. He immediately headed over to the bed and took charge. "Monsieur Frechette."

Alec regarded him with one half-lidded eye. *"Oui."*

"Dr. Mike LaRocque. We met at the restaurant last week. I'll state right up front that I'm not convinced you're innocent, but I care about Kira, and I'll do whatever she needs me to do." He popped open his bag. "Not to mention I can't stand to see a patient in pain." He tossed a small vial to Kira. "Here. Give him a shot of that. Fifteen milligrams."

"What is it?" Alec's voice was blatantly skeptical.

"Morphine."

That information silenced him. Temporarily.

Kira took the vial and found a small syringe.

Mike reached for the dressing. "I want to see what we're dealing with here, and then we can go ahead with the transfusion. His pallor and shortness of breath have me convinced."

"Transfusion?" Alec queried Kira with a glance.

"I convinced the Blood Bank that you needed it more than they did. Roll over."

"Huh?"

He seemed slightly muddled and confused by the activity, so she nudged him over on his side and within a few seconds had bared a nice little patch of skin on his hip. She drove the needle home.

He flinched but said nothing.

Mike, meanwhile, had apparently descended into his professional, no-nonsense, don't-take-any-crap mood. He explained, "She fabricated a patient, lied and stole for you, Frechette. You'd better be worth it."

Alec started to say something but Kira covered his mouth with her hand. "Don't say a word. You can bawl me out when you're well and free."

Any protests Alec would still have tried to make were lost in the sharp cry of pain as Mike pulled the gauze away from the wound.

"Christ," cursed Mike. "I may not have a lot of experience with gunshot wounds but this is ugly, and it's definitely infected." He felt Alec's forehead and frowned. "No fever now."

On an impulse, Kira slid a hand beneath Alec's back. "The sheet is sopping."

"I do seem to recall having occasional bouts of excessive perspiration," said Alec dryly. "But I just thought it was a severe case of post-murder, pre-death sentence jitters."

Kira ignored him. "I gave him antibiotics, but maybe they weren't enough."

"I took 'em just like you said," Alec mumbled, apparently disappointed that no one appreciated his attempt at humor. "And the Tylenols, too…I think." He shuddered at some unseen discomfort. "It's all a bit hazy."

Mike glanced at Kira. "Okay, we'll double up on the IVs and hang the antibiotics and the blood together. Did you bring any Ringers?"

Kira nodded.

"Okay, let's get going."

Alec watched them warily as they each picked a side of the bed and pulled out the tubing and needles. Mike's needle, with the large bore that was necessary for a transfusion, must have looked particularly foreboding. "You sure you guys know what you're—ouch!"

"Baby," chided Kira as she maneuvered the needle. "His pressure must be low, I'm having trouble threading the vein."

"Remind me never to let you help me make kabobs, *chérie,*" Alec grimaced. "You'd mangle the meat beyond—hey!"

A dribble of red backed up into Kira's tubing, thus indicating she had struck it rich. She finished threading the vein with the catheter, withdrew the needle and hooked up the antibiotics. "Never insult a woman who has a needle in your arm."

Alec's eyes were closed and sweat had beaded on his forehead. She regretted his discomfort as well as the jibe. "Sorry," she said softly, but she wasn't sure if he heard her.

"There." Mike had completed his own IV setup.

"*He's* good," mumbled Alec. "Didn't feel a thing."

Kira smiled. He couldn't be feeling too bad if he could still try to make her feel guilty.

Mike motioned toward the cooler. "Okay, let's get that blood hung. We'll use the bed-post, and let's not run it too quickly, just in case there's a problem."

Kira reached for the cooler and heard Alec's subdued voice. "Man, he's even bossier than you are."

"Doctors are naturally egomaniacs," quipped Mike. "It seems we have a lot in common."

Alec's chuckle was cut short, no doubt by the pain it induced. But Kira was glad to have heard it regardless.

Ten minutes later, the blood and antibiotics were dripping at a comfortable rate. Alec was resting more comfortably than he had in a while and Mike was irrigating and cleaning the wound. Kira watched the skilled and practiced movements of his hands as she bathed Alec's face and chest with tepid water. It was odd how Alec seemed so vulnerable here. She wondered how it was that she had missed it before. Even robust and healthy, everyone had weaknesses and needs. She had seen him as superman—strong and impenetrable as the fabled cartoon hero, because that was how she needed to see him. She hadn't had anything left to give him, so had told herself that there was nothing of hers that he needed. But she had no trouble taking from him. That thought stung with a ferocity that rivaled Alec's open wound.

Alec's whisper cut through her reverie. "This is almost as good as a Swedish spa. I should get shot more often."

"Shut up," said Mike and Kira in unison and then grinned at each other. In that moment, she felt closer to Mike than she ever remembered.

"Everybody's a critic," whined Alec.

At last the wound was dressed again and Mike stood to stretch.

"Thanks, Mike," said Kira as she dabbed at Alec with a small towel. "Why don't you bring in those sandwiches we picked up?"

Alec nodded mutely. "I could eat too."

Mike just stood there looking at them and Kira finally tore her eyes away from Alec to meet his gaze. He said nothing, just stood there, watching her—watching them.

"Mike?"

She saw his Adam's apple bob once and then he spoke. "Did you do it, Frechette?"

Alec managed to focus on the striking blond figure on the other side of the room. "I hope not," he muttered. "God, I hope not."

"What does that mean?"

"It means I don't believe I did, but I suppose I could have." Alec's words slurred slightly, indicating the morphine had begun to dull his awareness.

Mike frowned and turned his gaze to Kira, but she just looked away, unable to face the uncertainty in his eyes.

With a heavy sigh, he headed for the door. "I'll be back in a minute."

She stroked Alec's hair. "Have you remembered any more?"

"Not really." The words were sluggish. "Even if I did I wouldn't trust it. Today I remembered stuff that hasn't even happened yet."

"What?"

He blew out a long, slow breath. "Never mind. Just idle fantasies and old regrets."

Kira withdrew her hand and swallowed in preparation for her next statement. "I was thinking about you a lot today, Alec."

"Mmm."

"I was thinking about the mistakes I made—"

"We both made."

"Let me finish." He said nothing so she continued. "I know I've apologized for some of them, but I don't think I ever had a chance to tell you how sorry I was for what happened to Kent."

Alec's face registered pain, but Kira suspected it had nothing to do with the gunshot wound.

"I'm sorry I wasn't there for you through that, and I'm sorry I never asked you for your side of the story. The papers were cruel and you never disputed a word. I've often wondered if that was why you left the force and I wondered why you never defended yourself."

"It's complicated. The people who needed to know did."

"It's been seven years. Can't you tell me now?"

He opened his eyes and she thought maybe he was about to open up and share something with her when the door flew open and a flurry of activity erupted into the room. Suddenly there were people everywhere. Kira's heart was in her throat and she clutched Alec's hand in a feeble attempt to protect him. She watched, dumbstruck, as their tiny sanctuary was invaded by a legion of people in uniform.

"What the hell?" cried Alec as he made a feeble attempt to sit up and face the onslaught.

Kira felt herself being dragged from his side and heard the words that were all too familiar. Detective Turcotte was standing over Alec, flanked by her partner, and immediately behind them was an ambulance crew ready with a stretcher. She was quietly reading Alec his rights. Kira fought against the hands that held her and whirled around to see Mike hovering in the background. "Mike! You backstabbing son of a bitch! I trusted you and you lied to me!" Tears of rage and disappointment flooded her eyes. "He could've made it. Damn you!"

Mike ignored her and moved over to Sergeant Turcotte, who was now supervising Alec's transfer to the stretcher.

Even above the noise, she could easily hear what Mike said to the sergeant. "You're going to stick to our deal, right?"

Turcotte glanced at her and Kira felt a flush of indignation rise to her cheeks. "Yes. But you're responsible for her. We'll need to talk to her and she had better be available." She motioned for the officer who was holding Kira to bring her over. "I hope you realize how close you came to being charged, Ms. North. Dr. LaRocque was emphatic that the only way he would help us was if you were not prosecuted for your part in this."

"Don't do me any favors," she hissed at Mike.

"Kira, please." Mike's voice was tired. "You were vulnerable because of your history with him. You weren't thinking straight."

"Don't you *dare* tell me what I was or was not thinking. Why did you go through the charade of fixing him up and hanging the blood if you knew you were going to do this?"

Turcotte interrupted, "I'll leave her in your capable hands. Meet us at the hospital in a couple of hours so we can discuss this more fully, and so you can tell us what you learned."

Mike nodded and Turcotte turned her attention to her prisoner. Kira cringed at that word in association with Alec.

"I knew he needed the blood," Mike said in answer to her previous question. "And I knew that the ambulance attendants wouldn't consent to hang it since it wasn't through the proper channels. Once it was started there was nothing they could do."

"How big of you."

"I did this for you, you know. You were in over your head. You said so yourself."

Kira twirled her ring around her finger as she watched Alec's stretcher ease past her. On an impulse, she reached out and brushed a fingertip across his hand. "Don't worry, Alec. It'll be fine."

He just looked at her, his expression unreadable. But maybe she didn't want to know what he was thinking. Kira didn't envy him the session he was due for with Turcotte and Ridgers back at the hospital. She hoped he would be smart enough to insist on a lawyer. Thank God he could afford a good one.

As the stretcher disappeared through the door, she heard someone yell from the other end of the house, "I think I found it!" No doubt they had recovered the gun. Or should she say the "murder weapon". She experienced a faint wash of nausea. She had touched it. They would find her fingerprints on the gun. What would that mean for her? And then she scolded herself. Her worries were petty when compared to Alec's.

She felt a tug on her hand. "Come on. Let's get out of here."

She pulled back her hand as if she had been stung. "Don't touch me," she snarled. "How can I trust anything you ever say again? We had a good working relationship and I thought we were friends."

"I hope we can still be friends." He stuffed his hands in the pockets of his khakis. "But I doubt the working relationship will be a problem."

"What?"

"I can't sit on this, Kira. You're suspended until I can discuss things with Human Resources, but I sincerely doubt I'll be able to protect you from permanent termination."

Kira felt like the Earth had opened and swallowed her whole. "You can't be serious. My job is my life!"

Mike gritted his teeth.

Kira could hear the grating noise in the silence of the now empty bedroom.

"You must have known the risk you were taking. You went into this with your eyes wide open. You can't blame me for doing my job."

Kira looked away, treacherously close to tears. He was right, of course. She had known the risks, and had no right to fall apart now. She was just disillusioned at being betrayed by someone she thought she could trust, and by the fact that Alec had counted on her and she had let him down—again.

But then she frowned and looked up at Mike's familiar blue eyes. "Hang on a minute. What did Turcotte say? She wants to know what you learned?"

Mike's jaw clenched and she could see a vein pulsing in his temple. "I don't think I learned anything that the police won't eventually find out anyway. I hardly—"

"But you intended to. You would have used my trust to gain information," she considered her words, "if there had been any worth gaining."

"Well, he hardly confessed. What he said to me was ambiguous at best, so I think this argument is moot." He stepped toward the door. "Now, can we get out of this hole? I would think you'd want to be at the hospital and ready to comfort him when he's through with the police."

Kira didn't like his tone, but she didn't have the energy to argue further. She plodded after him, and didn't even bother locking the cabin behind her. All the other vehicles that surely must have been out there had already sped away. The forest seemed empty and unnaturally silent. She got in the passenger side, this time raising no objections to Mike's driving her car. She gazed at the cabin as it dwindled in the distance. They would have to send someone for Alec's Beemer tomorrow. She hoped he would have opportunity to drive it again.

"How did they know?" she asked, unable to keep from torturing herself.

"I called them from the phone booth. You had already given me a good idea of our destination and they hooked up with us shortly after that. You never noticed we were being followed."

Of course she hadn't. She wasn't used to looking over her shoulder, to mistrusting, to having anything to hide. Dammit, she still didn't. "He didn't do it, Mike. I know how it looks but he didn't." But even to her own ears, her voice sounded dead and her defense hollow and she wished she had just remained silent. Mike didn't deserve an explanation, and Alec certainly didn't need her to defend him.

"He didn't even sound convinced of that when I asked him. How can you be so sure?"

Kira did not deign to answer, and instead indulged in a few moments of quiet reflection. The car was a brief refuge, an island of stillness as it raced along the deserted highways that led back to civilization. She had a feeling the calm would be fleeting—the calm before the storm.

Chapter Sixteen

ഇ

"Are you comfortable, Monsieur Frechette?"

The nurse was so young, with stars in her eyes and, no doubt, lust on her mind. But Alec's upbringing wouldn't allow him to spew the fountain of profanity that was bubbling just out of sight. *"Oui."* He forced a sweet smile and instantly regretted it as the young woman practically melted into a puddle before his eyes. *"Merci.* I think I'll be fine." *Please leave now.*

She just stood there, gazing at him, oozing pheromones, and making Alec wish that Carl Stuart's aim had been just a bit better. Alec was being heaped with humiliation upon humiliation and he feared that it was but a prelude for things to come.

"Shelley." A man called to the nurse from the doorway. "Come on now." It was the doctor who had examined Alec upon his admission, and Alec had the distinct impression he was almost as impatient with his young assistant as Alec was. "The police need to speak to him, and we've done all we can for now."

"All right," said Shelley. "I'll be right there." But, instead of heading to the door, she made a show of tucking the blankets around Alec one more time. He thought if he was tucked in any tighter he wouldn't be able to breathe despite the third unit of blood that was now dripping its oxygen-rich nectar into his veins. "Don't worry," Shelley whispered under her breath. "Nobody believes you did it. I know you couldn't possibly—"

"Why?" he hissed as his hand snaked out to grab her wrist.

Shelley just frowned. "Why what?"

"Why couldn't I have done it?" he rasped, heedless of the needles of pain and the drag of fatigue.

Shelley shrugged. "I-I don't know. I just know you're—"

"You don't *know* me. What right do you have to think you *know* me?" He swallowed and felt a bead of sweat trickle down his forehead. But the words strained against his chest, demanding to be said. "You see a handsome face and flexing biceps and assume you would want me in your bed. But I might be Charles Manson, Junior for all you know. M-maybe..." He blinked as he gathered his thoughts. "Maybe after I'd screwed you I'd slice you up and dump you in the goddamn river!"

She tugged at her wrist in an attempt to dislodge it from his viselike grip. Her expression had changed from sympathetic to terrified.

"Please," she whined, but he couldn't make himself stop. He had held onto the rage and frustration for the past seven years, harboring it in his soul, trying to ignore it and pretending it didn't exist. But the murder, the pain, the uncertainty, the exhaustion and now his arrest had conspired to push him over the edge. Like a volcano that had awoken from dormancy, there was no going back.

"I'm sick of it! I'm sick of all of it." He was sick of people judging him on the basis of testosterone and genetics. He was a *person,* dammit, and there was more to him than what they saw in a glossy eight-by-ten photograph in *People.* "I don't need your sympathy or support." He'd managed alone for the last ten years of his life. He didn't *need* anyone. Even if he did, he certainly wouldn't pick a teenage nurse with a tight uniform and an overactive libido.

His energy was waning but he retained his grip on her just a moment longer. "You have absolutely no idea who I am, *Shelley.*" I *don't even know who I am anymore.* "And frankly I'd just as soon keep it that way."

He released her wrist and sank back into the pillows, exhausted.

Poor Shelley practically rammed into a tall blond man in her haste to get to the door. He was one of the arresting officers from the cabin but, for the life of him, Alec couldn't recall a name. Sergeant Something-or-other and his partner were standing in the open doorway and apparently had been for some time.

Shit! thought Alec. This just wasn't his day.

Shelley's hands fluttered about her like two epileptic moths. "Oh, oh. I'm so-so sorry. I—"

The man propelled her out into the hallway without a word, and the female officer let the door close quietly behind them as they entered the private hospital room. Alec caught a brief glimpse of the uniformed figure just outside the door—a vivid reminder of his new status as the scum of society.

"Well," drawled the sergeant. "Perhaps you don't want to fill Shelley in as to your true identity, but I'm afraid you're going to have to share it with us."

Alec merely closed his eyes in disgust—disgust with himself and the situation in general. "And you are?" he muttered in a weak attempt to change the subject.

The woman responded. "I'm Sergeant Genevieve Turcotte and this is Sergeant Will Ridgers. You met us at the cabin, but I suppose you might have missed—"

"You sounded extremely angry just then," interrupted Ridgers as he pulled up a chair. "Are you generally an angry person, Frechette?" Apparently he wasn't so easily distracted.

Turcotte tossed Ridgers an annoyed glance, but apparently decided not to intercede. She came around to the other side of the bed and leaned against the wall, watching him.

"Not generally," Alec conceded. "But somehow being the subject of a murder investigation has put me slightly on edge."

"Are you sure you don't want a lawyer present, Monsieur Frechette?" Turcotte's voice was soft and deferential and unfortunately it only served to irritate him further.

"No, goddamit! I told you I didn't, and I meant it." He took a deep breath and was grateful for the morphine coursing through his system. It seemed that was the only thing between him and a full-fledged rage like he had never experienced before. The even temper and cool outlook that he usually maintained had been frayed to within a hair's breadth of snapping. "I'm sorry. I'm just not myself."

"Then who are you?" asked Ridgers.

"Will—" warned Turcotte.

Alec blinked before reciting slowly and precisely, "My name is Alec Robert Frechette. My driver's license number is 4376599. I'm a Canadian citizen, and my preferred wine is Merlot." He managed a wry grin, suddenly feeling marginally more in control with the infusion of a little humor into the situation. "I believe that's all the Geneva Convention requires me to tell you."

Ridgers laughed aloud and Alec decided perhaps he wasn't a prick after all.

Turcotte was working hard at suppressing a grin, and maintaining the businesslike demeanor that hung about her like cheap cologne. Alec wondered idly what it would take to strip her of that rigid control.

"You actually know your driver's license number by heart?" asked Turcotte evenly.

"No. I improvised."

"You mean you lied," suggested Ridgers.

Alec's good humor burned away like mist in the sun. "I don't make a habit of it if that's what you're implying."

"But you did run from the authorities. Surely you know how guilty that makes you look." Ridgers twirled his earring absently.

"I thought the question was how guilty I actually *am*, not how guilty I look."

Ridgers' mouth twitched and Sergeant Turcotte apparently decided she'd had enough of the informal part of the interview. "I think we should start at the beginning, instead of somewhere around the middle." Her tone held a note of chastisement, which seemed to be lost on her partner.

Alec turned to meet her eyes, training his gaze on her and pouring on silent charms that had wilted heiresses and Duchesses alike. But Genevieve Turcotte seemed unmoved. "Why don't you begin with your trip to Ms. North's house and fill us in from there. We'll ask questions as you go if anything is unclear." She had pulled a steno pad out of her purse.

"Are you taking my statement yourself?"

As if on a silent cue the door opened and a small, frail-looking man with thinning hair, drooping chinos and carrying a small black laptop came in and sat quietly at the foot of the bed. He popped the notebook open on his lap and looked up expectantly.

"I see," said Alec simply. "All right." He took a deep breath and closed his eyes. "Let's take it from the top."

To Alec's relief, they did not interrupt and fifteen minutes later he was finished. His eyes were closed again, and his chest felt heavy. He had slept all day, and yet all he wanted at that moment was to turn over and descend into the world of dreams. He was bone-tired, and didn't know how he was going to face the endless questions he knew they were going to throw at him. Suddenly he longed for a friendly face, a loving touch, and ironically, the only person that he could at that moment call a friend was the woman he had spent seven years resenting.

When they were silent, he said dryly, "Any questions, boys and girls?"

"What did you and Kira argue about?" asked Turcotte.

"I thought I told you that."

"Tell me again."

Alec forcibly reined in the temper that was already straining at its barriers. He knew what they were doing, he had done it himself a hundred times, but it was different when he was on this side of the game. And, of course, it didn't help that his morphine was wearing off and he felt fatigued beyond human endurance. "I confronted her about how she had shut me out of my own daughter's life..." He sucked in extra oxygen. "And about how I had felt used by her sexually. She acknowledged—"

"That's very interesting," chimed in Ridgers. "You admitted to sleeping with Darcy Cromwell, as well as many of your previous clients. Did you feel used by them as well?"

"On occasion."

"But you were well paid, so—"

"So you can think whatever you like, Sergeant. I really don't give a damn." Despite his best efforts, Alec was unable to keep the edge out of his voice. This was all hitting just a little too close to home.

Turcotte entered the conversation, her tone agreeable, even conciliatory. "You said you sought her out for a physical outlet, and that you remember nothing after making love with her—"

"I had consensual sex with her," Alec said bluntly. "Love had absolutely nothing to do with it."

Turcotte looked slightly taken aback by the admission but she recovered quickly. "Is it possible you took out your frustrations on her in a moment of passion, and you are blocking it out as a defense mechanism?"

"Anything's possible, but I don't believe so." There was a voice inside his head screaming *Of course you did, you maniac! You're a monster and you've just finally shown your true colors. You hated her. Maybe you hated them all. Maybe it was just a matter of time before—*

"Do you socialize with Carl Stuart often?" asked Ridgers.

The question took him completely off guard. His eyes flew open as an indignant laugh erupted from his lips. "Hardly. Stuart and I have nothing in common. The only reason I sat with him that night was because he happened to be in the same vicinity as the booze."

Turcotte took over. "Did he pour the drinks?"

Alec blinked, suddenly astonished that he had not considered this possibility himself. "Yes. All of them."

"Did Mr. Stuart have reason to hate Ms. Cromwell?"

"I-I don't know. You'd have to ask him." Alec studied Turcotte's features. Her small brown eyes seemed to widen and her gaze softened even as he watched. As he studied her, his thoughts cleared and his mind opened to new possibilities. "Or maybe," he continued, "maybe I do. Once he alluded to her as being a spoiled brat who needed a good sound spanking more than she needed a bodyguard. And he certainly had no use for me. He resented my presence at the mansion, and made no bones about telling me so."

Turcotte nodded but never took her eyes away from his.

Suddenly uncomfortable with the attention, and irritated by it once again, Alec turned away. "Is it possible he drugged the whiskey?"

"We're just looking at all the angles," said Turcotte.

"I see." But Alec didn't believe them. There was something they weren't telling him.

"And what can you tell us about Darcy's past? Do you know if she had any other enemies?"

Alec suppressed a sardonic laugh, and had to press a hand to his side to dampen the pain. "Probably dozens. But you might want to pay a visit to Professor Dan Peters. He and Darcy didn't part on the best of terms." He frowned as Turcotte scribbled down the name. "Didn't her grandfather or Stuart give you that name?"

"No."

Alec closed his eyes and muttered. "Why doesn't that surprise me?"

The door opened and a tall slim man in a billowing lab coat breezed into the room. The doctor ignored the trio around the bed and checked Alec over quickly. "That's enough. He needs to rest. I want you out." He glanced pointedly at Ridgers. "Now."

Ridgers saluted him. "We were done anyway."

The odd little man with the laptop was already packed up and out the door. He hadn't uttered one word.

Turcotte stood and moved to go. "Thank you for being so cooperative. We'll be back tomorrow if we have any more questions, and I'm sure you understand the need for the guard outside."

"Yeah. I'm a definite flight risk."

She quirked a half smile. "Call me crazy."

Ridgers was already at the door and the doctor was taking Alec's pulse.

But, despite his drooping eyelids, Alec wasn't quite ready to end this interview. "Sergeant Turcotte, I'd like to speak to you alone for a moment, if that's all right?"

She frowned, but he could see the sparkle in her eye. She was probably wondering if he was going to confess or maybe confide some horrible secret to her—some wonderful little tidbit that would solve it for her, help her put away a killer and put her a step higher on the ladder to Mountie heaven. But that was the last thing on Alec's mind. He couldn't pinpoint the source of the need or why it had struck him so strongly today of all days, but it was as undeniable as the need for cool water on a hot day. He and Detective Turcotte had some business to attend to. And he wanted to get it out of the way now or it would eat away at him every time he laid eyes on her.

"All right. I'll meet you at the car," she said to Ridgers, who nodded and swaggered out without a word.

The doctor picked up on his cue. "Okay," he said as he headed for the door. "But no more than five minutes."

Alec nodded and waited for the door to swing closed behind him. Then he turned to Turcotte. "I'm sorry. I've forgotten your first name?"

She knitted her brows. "Genevieve."

"A beautiful name."

"What is it, Monsieur Frechette?" Her voice had an edge, but the pink tinge to her cheeks told another tale.

"I think you want something from me, Genevieve." His voice had turned as velvety and rich as Swiss milk chocolate.

"Yes. The truth."

"More than that. You're curious, aren't you?"

The color in her cheeks deepened as she swallowed. "Curious?"

Alec slid his hand around hers, which was dangling just within reach of the bed. She tensed but didn't pull away. "Yes. You can't help but wonder if the stories are true, and being here with me has only compounded the questions in your mind."

"I don't have the faintest idea—"

"I think maybe we should answer those questions so we can get past them, don't you?" He drew her hand to his mouth and brushed his lips across her knuckles as softly as the flutter of wings on the breeze. He was pleased to see the goose bumps travel up her arm.

"Mr. Frechette, this is completely inappropriate."

"Then why don't you leave?"

She licked her lips but still didn't move.

"You don't leave because you're dying to know. You've seen the pictures, indulged in the fantasies, and you're aching to know if I live up to the image."

She shook her head, but her eyes were windows to her thoughts. The cop was at war with the woman, but Alec knew too well how to direct the troops. In this man's army, the woman won out every time.

He pulled gently on her hand, regretting the fact that he was incapacitated and thus at a disadvantage. But what he lacked in physical ability he would make up in charisma.

She allowed herself to be drawn in even as she protested. "Are you trying to influence an officer?"

"No. I'm trying to clear the air so we can approach things like the professionals we are." In part that was true. He had seen the need in her eyes, and had already tired of it. He knew he would be dealing with this woman endlessly for the next few days, or months, and he couldn't abide the thought of facing that day in and day out. But perhaps it was also a show of power. She had power over him. In a very real way she held his life in her hand, and maybe this was a way to turn the tables on that—even it if was only briefly.

"This is absurd. I don't—"

But Alec's hand had cupped the back of her head and in the next instant her lips had joined with his.

It wasn't passionate. It was barely even sexual. It was experimental and sweet, and as chaste a kiss as he had ever bestowed on anyone. It merely hinted at promised pleasures and hidden treasures. It was a challenge he couldn't resist and, as his lips caressed hers, and his tongue flicked and teased at the perimeter of her mouth, he knew he was up to the task. Her eyes closed and her skin became dewy in those brief seconds of intimacy.

He was the one to break contact and, as she straightened up, he knew he had either made a friend or an enemy. Oddly he didn't care which. He had stripped Detective Sergeant

Turcotte down to the bare, raw essence of who she was—the woman she no doubt denied existed. Even if they sent him to prison for life, it was a little victory he would cherish.

She backed away. "That will be quite enough," she said haughtily, her face crimson and her eyes wide.

"Yes. I think that will do. Did I live up to expectations?"

She whirled around and headed for the door. "We'll be in touch, Alec. Ms. North will be allowed to visit you, but you will not be allowed out of your room." With that, the door banged shut behind her, an audible exclamation mark to her supposed indignation.

Alec smiled and laid his head back on the pillow. She had called him Alec. It was an unconscious concession to what they had shared. From that he deduced that, even if she worked to convict him, she would do so grudgingly. With that odd little kiss Alec had made a friend—or at the very least an ally.

Then his smile faded and he experienced the bitter aftertaste of his victory. That little triumph had landed him squarely back in the bottom of the pit that he had struggled so hard to escape. It had sucked him right back in and he hadn't so much as whimpered in protest.

He had performed just as expected. Like a trained poodle he had pranced around the ring and sat up and begged. He had jumped through the flaming hoop and won the ribbon. The trouble was that every time he jumped through that hoop he singed a little more of his fur, and lost another morsel of his dignity. And just whom was he performing for? There was no crowd to cheer, and no master to please. No one but himself. It had become a habit—a self-defeating addiction that he had no motivation to break. Or, more accurately, he had no one to break it for. The only person who counted wasn't worth the effort. He only had to look in the mirror to confirm it.

The nurse came back with another dose of morphine and soon sweet sleep stole over him like the darkness that crept across the sky. He fell into the abyss willingly despite the disturbing images that he knew awaited him there—disturbing images that were his only connection to a red-haired sprite who had made her home among the stars.

She belonged with the stars, of that he was certain. God knew she deserved that much. She had deserved so much more—more than what he gave her. Perhaps in his dreams he could seek her forgiveness. Only in his dreams did he deserve it.

* * * * *

Will's Mercury Capri was parked at the edge of the parking lot, directly under one of the old-fashioned carriage lamps that dotted the hospital grounds of Ottawa General. Bathed in the pool of yellow light, Will leaned against the car. He was drilling at his incisors with a wooden toothpick when Gen strolled up to him.

"So?" asked Will out of the corner of his mouth. "Did he confess? What did he say?"

"Nothing. Let's go. It's been a long day and I wanna get home." More than anything at that moment she wanted to get away from Will's inquiring stare. She got in the passenger side and tapped her fingers on her notepad while Will got the car underway.

"What do you mean, *nothing?*" That damn toothpick was still dangling from his lips. Gen didn't think he had even eaten anything in the last two hours. She cringed to think what he had dug out of that maw of his.

"Nothing. What's not to understand?"

"Well then, why did he call you in there? Did he make a pass at you?" Will grinned evilly.

"What the hell kind of question is that?"

"Hey! It was a joke. What's got your knickers in a knot?" Will glanced at her and she knew she was done for.

Why didn't she just keep her mouth shut and ignore him like usual? She had just tipped her hand with those few poorly chosen words, and the color she could feel creeping up her cheeks would do little to discourage Will's curiosity. So she just sat there and waited and tried to imagine a better place with balmy breezes, waving palms and—

"He did, didn't he?" Will laughed and Gen thought her own teeth would crack from the pressure she was exerting to keep her mouth shut. "Holy shit! The guy's got balls, I'll give him that." He shook his head and tried to stifle his chuckles. "Did you deck him?"

"Hardly. The man's in a hospital bed."

"Not to mention cute as hell." That irritating grin spread across Will's face like a malignant tumor.

"You're an asshole, Will. Or have I mentioned that before?"

He ignored her…as usual. "Oh, God." He actually wiped a tear of glee out of the corner of his eye. "I bet you enjoyed it. Little Ms. Liberated turns to jelly when the French Connection kisses her hand."

"I did *not* turn to jelly," she retorted, even though at that moment she doubted her legs' ability to support her if the need arose. "And it was *not* a French kiss."

"What?"

Oh God, oh shit, oh crap! she moaned to the merciless God of humiliation. She had *kiss* on the brain and her mangled thought processes had misinterpreted his words.

"He kissed you?"

"Can we ple-ease drop this? It's embarrassing enough without having you drag me through your own personal brand of muck. I can't explain how I let it happen, it just did. It won't happen again, and it won't have any bearing on how I treat him." She paused and glanced at her partner warily. "Okay?"

Will's expression had settled back into its usual irreverent, semi-serious mode. "Okay, okay. I believe you. Sorry."

Gen breathed a cautious sigh of relief. If she could just get home to bed, make herself a cup of chamomile tea and add a half a quart of rum she'd be just—

"Just tell me one thing."

"Will!"

"No, no, I'm serious. I really want to know."

"All right," she breathed, knowing he wouldn't let go of this willingly. "What is it?"

He frowned and twirled his earring. "What is it that makes him so special? Why do women swoon for him and fall all over each other to hire him? I can't think of anyone else that you would let get away with that." He looked away from the road for a moment and when his eyes met hers she knew he was in earnest. "I want to understand."

"Okay," she said thoughtfully. "That deserves a straight answer but I'm not sure what to say."

She gazed out the window and studied the glittering waters of the canal as it flashed past on her right. It reflected the moonlight and the stars and the lamps that illuminated its paths. Perhaps the true beauty of the Rideau Canal, or any body of water for that matter, was in the reflections on its surface. It took the simple light from a bulb or distant star, refracted it and magnified it on its shifting, rippling surface and that light became a thing of simple but eloquent beauty.

"It's complicated," she said at last. "Physically, he's attractive. I know that describes half the men in Hollywood, but he's unique. He's got this tough innocence thing going. All at once, he looks like the little boy you want to take home and cuddle and take care of, but with the rough edges and strength of the man who would slay a dragon for you. But that's not all."

Will was respectfully silent for a moment before prodding, "What's the rest?"

She looked at him and answered seriously. "When he looks at you, even if he's not talking directly to you, you get this feeling like you're his whole world. Like he's focusing on you and no one else. Like you are special and beautiful and sexy and..." She sighed. "And every woman in the world wants to feel like that."

Will shook his head in awe. "How does he do it?"

"Damned if I know."

"What serial killer wouldn't want to have that effect on women?"

"He didn't do it," she said simply. "I'll investigate impartially and look at the facts as they come in but, even if he's convicted I don't think I'll ever believe he did it."

"He *did* influence you. That son of a—"

"No. No, he didn't." She lapsed into silence and was grateful when Will decided not to pursue it further. She couldn't say for certain what it was, but that kiss had nothing to do with her apparent bias. Nothing.

Absolutely nothing.

And she would absolutely *not* think about it when she lay in bed alone tonight.

Sometimes being a career cop really sucked.

* * * * *

"So?" whispered a voice that was giddy with barely contained excitement. "What's he like?"

"He's an arrogant jerk," said the other with a sniff.

Instinctively Kira knew they were talking about Alec. Whether out of purely idle curiosity or a need to protect Alec's interests, she stayed in the shadows just beyond the nursing station and listened.

There was silence for a moment. "Really? But—but all the articles say—"

"Forget what they say. He was rude and insulting. He scared me. I'm starting to wonder if he actually did do it."

"Ah, come on, Shelley." Now the voice had turned skeptical and maybe a trifle bored. "You do have a tendency to overstate things. Are you sure you didn't come on to him, and now you're mad because he turned you down?"

Kira heard something slam. "I did *not* make a pass at him. I just told him I didn't believe he was guilty, and the next thing I know he's ranting on and on about how I don't know him, and about how he's sick of this and tired of that. He grabbed me and wouldn't let go." Kira heard the tap of computer keys. "Maybe the French Connection would like a few extra blood tests ordered on him in the morning, and maybe an enema would make him think twice about insulting us poor little nobodies who are only trying to save his miserable hide."

"Excuse me."

Shelley and her colleague glanced up in surprise. Visiting hours were long past over. Even the cleaning staff had gone home. Kira flashed her nametag that Mike had neglected to confiscate from her after he had taken her home and given her explicit instructions to stay put. These days Kira had better things to do with her time than listen to Mike LaRocque.

"Yes?" Shelley was oh-so young, with big brown eyes and a trim figure not yet ravaged by the trials of pregnancy and childbirth. Shelley did not yet know how cruel life could be. Kira felt it her duty to educate her.

Kira leaned her elbows on the chest-high counter that overlooked the two seated nurses. Kira smiled, coating her icy words in sugary tones like a razor dipped in chocolate. "Shelley. Is that right? Is that your name?"

Shelley nodded and smiled. She seemed uncertain but Kira also saw a flicker of recognition. She granted Shelley a warm we're-both-nurses-so-let's-be-buddies smile. "Shelley," she said again. "Has it ever occurred to you that you *don't* know Monsieur Frechette?"

Shelley frowned and cocked her head to consider the odd question. "Well, I guess—"

"I guess he's right. I guess you've just formed your opinion of him based on the fact that he's good-looking and successful." She paused and tapped her fingernails on the Formica. "And isn't there the teeniest possibility," Kira smiled and whispered intimately, "that you were being nice to him in the hopes that maybe—just maybe—he might notice you and you could..." Kira winked conspiratorially, "get into his pants."

Shelley giggled like an eighteen-year-old. "Well, okay, maybe I was thinking that...just a little."

Kira leaned in just a bit closer. "Well, honey, I've got news for you. I do know Alec Frechette. I've known him in ways you could only dream about. And Alec Frechette wouldn't touch you with a ten-foot pole. Alec has way too much class for a snot-nosed little smart-ass like you."

Shelley's mouth gaped and her eyes were wide with astonishment. Her colleague was leaning back in her chair, apparently enjoying the show.

Kira continued. "And if I *ever* hear that you performed any unnecessary procedures on Monsieur Frechette, or withheld his pain medications or did *anything* the least bit unprofessional, I'll have you up on negligence charges so fast it'll make your head spin." Kira stepped back to indicate she was almost finished. Almost. "And if I ever hear you say to anyone that Alec is capable of murder, I won't worry about going through official channels." Kira locked eyes with her unfortunate victim for an interminable moment before delivering the *coup de gras*. "I used to be a police officer and, needless to say, I know ways to hurt you that aren't even on the books—they don't leave marks, and I never leave clues. So don't mess with me, and don't mess with him. Got it?" It hadn't taken much for her to get into her old *bad cop* routine. She and Alec used to do that act pretty damn good. It always threw the bad guy for a loop when the lady played the bad cop, and Alec, restraining his mirth like the professional he was, would make a show of keeping Kira from clawing at some poor slob's eyeballs. Ah, those were the days—the days before everything went to hell.

Shelley swallowed and licked her lips. "You're insane. I'll report you—"

"Too late, sweetie. I'm already off the payroll. I've got nothing to lose. Trust me, that makes me even more lethal." With that, she whirled around, feeling smug and more self-satisfied than she had in years. She was finally doing what she should have done seven years ago. She was looking after Alec. She was putting him first, and to hell with the rest. Of course, she never could have neglected their child, but she had lost sight of the importance of balance and unity and mutual support. Now she had regained her perspective.

This was what she did best. She looked after people, and who better to be the focus of her talents than Alec, who had sacrificed so much for her. With that goal, with that objective in mind, she felt revitalized. She would stay beside him in the hospital, seeing to his needs and protecting him from vipers like *Shelley*. She would do everything in her power to make sure they found the real killer, and that Alec's name was cleared. If, heaven forbid, he was ever brought to trial, she would be right there beside him through that as well.

She would make up for everything. She would stick by him like she should have seven years ago. And maybe he would forgive her.

Walking on air, she approached the guard outside his door.

He raised one eyebrow. "Yes?" he asked.

"I'd like to see him please."

"Visiting hours are over." He tapped a finger on his thigh. "Who are you?"

"Kira North."

"You're the one who was hiding him."

"Yes. He's innocent."

Constable Whoever was unimpressed. "You used to be a cop?" Apparently he had overheard her tirade. No matter. She had no secrets.

"Yes."

"You should know better."

Kira frowned, took a deep breath and said slowly, "I know how police officers stick together. It's like a big brotherhood, and where everyone looks out for each other, sticks up for each other, no matter what. Right?"

He nodded slowly, uncertain where she was going with this.

"If you were falsely accused of pulling the trigger, or of doing so unprovoked or unnecessarily, you would expect your department and especially your partner, to stand behind you, right?"

"Yeah. I guess so."

"Well, Alec is kinda like my partner. In fact, we were partners years ago. That's all I was doing. I was looking out for him. Maybe I went about it the wrong way, maybe I made some poor choices, but I know he's innocent, and I reacted on a gut level. I tried to keep him safe." She watched the officer and allowed the words a little time to sink in. "Is that so horrible? Can you understand that?"

He stared back at her for a full minute before standing slowly and pushing open Alec's door. "Five minutes. After that you gotta come back at the regular visiting hours."

"Thank you," she said sincerely as she stepped across the threshold. The door closed behind her and the room was plunged into blackness. After a moment, her eyes adjusted and the light from the lamps on the street outside filtered in, casting the form on the bed in a silvery silhouette. He turned toward her and she thought she could see his eyes focused on her.

She walked over and touched his hand. "Alec?"

"Kira? What the hell are you doing here? It's after midnight."

"I had to see you. I had to know how it went with the detectives and I had to make sure you were all right."

"I'm fine. Now, you should go home and get some sleep. You must be exhausted too." His voice confused her. He seemed concerned but there was a harshness—an edge to it that disturbed her.

"I will. But I just… I-I was worried. I couldn't sleep until I made sure."

"Well, now you know. So go home."

She drew her hand away, disturbed that he hadn't returned the gesture, and at least closed his fingers around hers. "All right. But I'm coming back first thing. I'm hoping they'll let me take over some of your care. I can't work in oncology anyway, so—"

"What do you think you're doing?"

"Doing? I'm taking care of you."

"I heard you out there. I'm surprised you didn't wake the whole floor with that little speech."

Kira felt like she had been slapped in the face. "I was just defending you. I didn't think that was a crime."

"Well, I don't need you to defend me." His breathing was becoming ragged, and Kira didn't like to think what that was doing to his blood pressure. "You know, when you showed up at the cabin I couldn't believe it. I was so grateful that I wasn't alone and that you were on my side."

"I am, Alec. I've always been on your side."

He continued as if he hadn't heard her. "But now, I'm not so sure. I don't want to be just another cause for you, Kira. I don't want to be like the lost puppy with the broken leg that you take in just because you feel sorry for it."

Kira battled a rising flood of tears. This wasn't in the plan. Alec wasn't supposed to question her motives. He was supposed to accept her and love her because she had finally come to her senses and realized how important he was, and how thoughtless she had been. "That's not what this is about, Alec."

"Isn't it? If I hadn't gotten shot and become involved in the scandal, would you be here, wanting to take care of me, and make up for everything?"

She didn't answer, because suddenly she wasn't sure. Certainly she had felt horrible after Alec's accusations that night, and had planned to confront him. She had planned to apologize and admit her responsibility. But would she have been so committed to making amends if it hadn't been for the tragedy? She liked to think she would have. She liked to think that she was bigger than what Alec was making her out to be. But how could she know for certain?

"See? You don't know, do you? I heard your tirade outside and I thought right away, *Ah, Kira has a new project, a new cause to carry a torch for.*"

"That's ridiculous. You're much more to me than—"

"Well, I don't want to be anybody's charity case, Kira. Least of all yours. I don't need a mother, I need a friend. I don't need a nurse, I need a partner. I need somebody to share things with, not someone who'll take over my case like some damn social worker on a mission."

Kira's mouth worked around words that wouldn't come, and a lump in her throat that barely allowed air to flow to her lungs.

"Go home. I can deal with Shelley and her cohorts just fine on my own. I can deal with the cops and the accusations and the innuendo all by myself. God knows, it won't be the first time."

"Alec, please." Her voice cracked as she reached out to touch his hand again, but he just rolled over.

He turned away from her and muttered into the pillow, "Just go home. You've done your good deed for the day. Your merit badge is in the mail."

The darkness in the room was suddenly oppressive, the air so heavy and thick it felt as if she were sucking syrup into her lungs. "Alec?" she whispered. But he said nothing, just pulled the covers up a little higher. "I just..." She just what? She just made a fool of herself for nothing? She just alienated the one man she wanted to endear? She just screwed up and she had no idea how or why?

With a heavy heart and plodding steps, she turned and left the dark room. What should she have done differently? Then she knew. Once again, she had cared too much. She had gone overboard, taken it so far to the extreme that she had fallen right off the edge. The ground was rushing up at her and there was nothing to cushion her fall. There was no job to go to. There were no children to comfort and console. And now it seemed there was no Alec to focus her attentions on. What the hell was she supposed to do now? Go home and stare at the wall? Take Cujo for walks and cook him gourmet meals?

She walked past the nursing station, ignoring the hostile stare from Shelley and the evil smirk from her colleague. She punched the down button for the elevator and considered the fact that without a cause, without a project, her life had no purpose. Maybe Mike was right. Maybe she was just a Florence Nightingale wanna-be. Even as a cop she had spent less time tracking down perps than she had sympathizing with their victims. She had always thought that was a strength.

As she stepped into the cold gray elevator, however, she wasn't so sure. But how could caring about people be a weakness? By making you vulnerable, that's how. Caring meant you opened yourself up for daggers like the one Alec had just thrown at her—daggers that lodged in the heart, and sliced open the soul. She had to learn to develop a thicker skin. She had to stop wearing her heart on her sleeve and being so needy. She had to learn to distance herself a little from the suffering and the anguish around her. She had to stop caring so much.

And she would—right after the sun stopped shining and the moon fell into the sea. Old habits were hard to break.

* * * * *

Alec closed his eyes but the sleep that had come so easily just a few hours ago eluded him. Kira's voice in the hall had awoken him like a klaxon announcing a raging inferno. And now his brain churned with confusion and anger and questions he didn't want to answer. So instead he ignored them.

He told himself he had slept too much that day. He told himself it was the drugs and the pain and the worry over what he would face in the next few days. He told himself he'd had every right to speak to Kira that way, and he didn't need to feel guilty. But there was no denying it. He did.

He didn't know what had possessed him to turn her away like that. But when he heard her defending him to that cheeky little nurse, and then talking her way into his room, instead of kindling warmth in his heart, it had started a fire in his brain. He had meant every word, but now he wished he had reined in his tongue, given himself time to consider what he was doing, and maybe find another approach.

The fact was, he had just exiled his only friend. In many ways, he had been alone since the day Kira had decided to stay home full-time with Cherisse, but tonight he may as well have been drifting through the center of the Milky Way, for as connected as he felt to the world and the people around him.

He had lost his family years ago. His father and brother didn't scorn him, but neither did they understand him or his choices. The few times they had gotten together over the past few years the atmosphere had been strained and distant. They no longer had anything to talk about. They had nothing in common. So eventually Alec had stopped trying. And so had they.

He had abandoned his values and his scruples the day he had left the Montreal force and taken up his new and highly questionable vocation. He was a suspect in a volatile murder case…and he wasn't convinced that he wasn't guilty. He had likely lost his reputation and thus his career. And now he had thrown away the one person who had claimed allegiance and who had risked everything for him.

All he had left was a whopping bank account and a BMW with a bloodstain on the seat. Not exactly what he had envisioned for himself at this point in his life. He opened his eyes and glared at the cruel stars that were winking down on him so cheerfully. The one thing he had wanted most in his life—a family with a wife, and children bouncing on his knee—was the one thing he could never have.

So what was the point in even trying?

Chapter Seventeen

"Dr. Peters?" asked Gen.

The man in the doorway was bleary-eyed, and clad only in a gray terrycloth robe and foam tread slippers. He didn't look like a man capable of brutalizing and murdering a young girl. But, of course, that meant nothing.

He blinked and rubbed the sleep out of his eyes before repositioning a pair of small wire frame glasses on his nose. "I'm sorry, I don't have a class until eleven, so I was catching up on my sleep. Who did you say you were?"

"Detectives Turcotte and Ridgers," she repeated patiently. "We're investigating the murder of Darcy Cromwell."

There it was. A wave of panic washed across his features before being replaced by an expression that was guarded and uneasy. "I thought you caught the guy." His voice was a just a fraction higher than it had been a moment earlier. "I saw it on the news."

"Monsieur Frechette is in custody, but no formal charges have been laid. I'm afraid there are still a lot of unanswered questions."

"Hey," broke in Will impatiently, as he leaned a long, sinewy arm against the doorjamb. "Can we come in or what?"

Gen cast him a warning glance. "I must apologize for my partner, Dr. Peters. He and Emily Post are no longer on speaking terms."

Will quirked a half smile. "Actually, we never did talk much. Didn't need to. She taught me the kind of etiquette you don't discuss in mixed company."

Will's humor did little to alleviate the doctor's tension. He glanced up and down the street of his quiet, residential neighborhood, apparently wondering what the neighbors would think if they knew he was chatting with the police about a murder.

Considering what they had already learned about the man, she was hardly surprised to find him a little wary of public scrutiny. They had learned of the indiscretions at Queens in Kingston, and his current position at Ottawa's Carlton University seemed precarious. He taught very few classes and had taken a significant cut in salary. They still weren't entirely clear on the undisclosed details of the story, but she and Will found all these developments to be extremely interesting. It was also very interesting that the Governor General had neglected to mention the difficulties that Darcy had experienced in the months before her death.

The professor apparently decided this business would best be handled in private, after all. "Yes, of course. Please come in." He ushered them into a small, but neatly kept living room, decorated with an eclectic mix of furniture that ranged from African to antique. Oddly enough, it worked.

Gen always marveled at people who could decorate. She broke into a sweat if asked to hang pictures or pick out throw pillows. And heaven help her when faced with the paint display at the hardware store. The thought of choosing between those endless shades of sea green, pea green, tea green, lime and every conceivable shade in between, made her nauseous. She could face hostile bullets, rioting demonstrators and drug-crazed murderers, but show her a swatch of floral chintz and she dissolved into a quivering mass of aspic.

She and Will seated themselves on a futon couch, and Dan Peters settled across from them in a rattan chair with an enormous cushion.

He licked his lips and pulled the belt on his robe a little tighter. He looked from Will to Gen and back again before closing his eyes and whispering. "You found it, didn't you?

God! When I heard she was dead, I knew, even from the grave, she'd find a way to pin it on me. That conniving little bitch."

Gen blinked and swiveled her gaze to look at Will. They locked eyes for a moment before Will said uncertainly, "What is it you believe we found, Dr. Peters?"

Dan frowned. "The tape, of course." Then understanding dawned. "Ah, *shit*!" His head dropped back to rest on the high, fluffy cushion behind him.

"Perhaps you should start from the beginning, Professor." Gen pulled out her note pad as Will drew his legs up to sit cross-legged, yoga style. Strangely, in this setting, it didn't seem inappropriate in the slightest. "And I would suggest that you go slowly so you don't forget a single detail."

* * * * *

Kira dug in her heels. "I don't want to go in." She felt like a twelve-year-old whose mother was making her try on training bras.

"Kira, this is crazy," moaned Lauren. "You risked your life, probably lost your job, and are banned from leaving the city because of this man, and now you don't want to see him?"

"No, he doesn't want to see *me*."

"That's just ridiculous."

They were standing in front of the nursing station and Kira was grateful that the shift had changed so she didn't have to face Nurse Shelley. Kira didn't think she could face any more hostility, not even from a pathetic seductress wanna-be. Alec's rebuff had filled Kira's rejection quota and then some. Yet here she was.

The entire Nickle clan had dragged her down here against her will, and she hadn't had the strength to tell them why she didn't want to come. Or maybe she had really wanted them to do it. If she were forced into seeing Alec, it wouldn't seem nearly as pathetic as if she had come to him begging on hands and knees. *They made me come,* sounded much better than *Please Alec, let me be your love slave.*

"You had a fight," Lauren reasoned, "and you just need to talk it out."

"I wish it were that simple. I really do."

"Please, Kira?" begged Rachel who was holding a box of chocolate truffles that could have fed an entire regiment of Mounties. "I want to see him, and I don't want to go in alone."

"I'll go with you," offered Tim.

The three women turned to look at him with undisguised amazement.

"What?" he said defensively. "I need to talk to him about something."

Lauren reached for her husband's hand. "I think we should all go in."

Kira looked away, still putting up a token resistance, but she knew she'd follow them and she hated herself for it. She had spent yet another sleepless night, tossing and turning, staring at the clock and gazing out at the moon, and wondering what the hell was wrong with her. Was her life really so tied up in others, that now that she didn't have a job, or a child, or a man, she no longer had reason to get up in the morning? Was there nothing in her life that was just for *her?*

Even Cujo had been a charity case. There was no way Alec could have known, but she had picked Cujo out of all the other runts at the pound because she felt sorry for him. He had been hobbling around his cage with a splint on his injured leg. Her heart had melted at the forlorn, pathetic sight, and despite the fact that her original intent had been to pick up a guard dog, she had wound up instead with a lawn ornament with attitude.

Rachel tugged on her hand, those almond eyes pleading and innocent, and Kira was lost. "Oh, all right. But don't expect me to fawn all over him. He doesn't want that." She followed the group with heavy steps. "At least not from me," she mumbled to no one in particular.

The guard checked them out thoroughly before allowing them through the door. They walked in to find Alec sitting up, sipping from a huge latté cup, nibbling on an enormous cinnamon roll, and flipping through a copy of *McLean's*. He apparently didn't fall easily into the role of doomed desperado. No chains held him to the bed, and no stubble shadowed his chin. His hair looked just pleasantly rumpled, but his hospital gown looked crisp, and his bedclothes neat. He looked like he had just stepped out of an article in GQ—*How to stay perfectly pressed while a prisoner*. No doubt the latté and the cinnamon roll were compliments of an ardent fan. Probably one of the nurses. Kira absently wondered if he had shaved himself, and then she mentally slapped herself for caring.

He glanced up in surprise and took a moment to scan the group before his eyes rested on Rachel and a sunrise broke across his face.

Rachel blushed and Kira shook her head in amazement. Alec didn't even have to speak. He could charm the panties off a nun with merely a glance and a smile.

The smile was all the invitation Rachel needed. She approached the bed, holding out the chocolates and dripping with concern. "Hi, Alec. I…uh…I was so upset when I heard what happened, what with the murder and the police. And now this whole thing with Kira and getting shot and—"

Alec stilled her torrent was a fingertip against her lips. "That's very sweet of you, Rachel. But I hate for you to see me like this, with a guard at my door and—"

Rachel reached out and flicked a dribble of icing off his chin.

Alec grinned. "And no bib."

This time Rachel didn't smile. She just handed him the chocolates. "Are they going to put you in jail?" she asked quietly.

Alec just gazed at her and, for the first time in Kira's experience, he seemed at a loss for words.

Lauren came to his rescue. "You're looking pretty chipper for someone who was at death's door two days ago." She was right. He had color in his cheeks and his eyes had lost the dull, distant look that had accompanied his fever. But Kira still had to restrain herself from reaching out and touching his forehead to confirm for herself that his skin was once again cool and dry. *God! Stop it!*

The smile twitched at Alec's lips again. "It's amazing what a little blood transfusion and getting arrested can do for a guy."

"Stop joking about it, Alec," said Kira, and immediately regretted it. She sounded like a mother scolding an unruly child. But she had committed herself. "It's really not funny," she added more quietly.

Alec's glanced flitted across Kira's face before he focused on Rachel again. He tugged on her hand and motioned her to settle down on the bed beside him. "It may not be funny, but there's no point in dwelling on it and getting all depressed. Isn't it better to look on the bright side, and make the best of things?"

"Bright side?" asked Kira with a lift of her eyebrows.

"Well, I'm not officially charged with the murder yet and even in the worst-case scenario—"

"Prison."

"Yeah, that." He said it brightly but Kira could sense a darkness behind his eyes. "I would hardly be lonely. I'm sure even there I'd have no shortage of admirers anxious to be my *special* friend."

He winked to try and make light of it, but Rachel's face fell at that comment, and Kira could see that Alec regretted it. He was working very hard to stay strong, and not let anyone see weakness or vulnerability. He was overcompensating, losing his sense of propriety, and that told Kira that he was far more worried than he was letting on.

The silence hung in the room for a moment. Alec's eyes closed briefly, and Kira had no idea what to say.

Tim was the one who came to their rescue. "You're quite the celebrity, Frechette. You should see the swarm of reporters by the front doors. We had to sneak in through the laundry entrance."

"Doesn't it just figure," grunted Alec, "the one time in my life they're interested in *me* personally, it's because I'm wanted for a felony."

Tim's mouth cracked into an impish grin. "You know what they say, don't you? There's no such thing as bad publicity."

"Well, I don't know about that," said Lauren with an uncomfortable glance at her husband. Alec watched the duo's unspoken communications with a slightly whimsical glint in his eye. He seemed to be paying less attention to *what* they were saying, and concentrating more on *how* they were saying it. Kira suspected he was a little envious of the unity of spirit that Tim and Lauren seemed to share. Perhaps she was as well.

Tim ignored the unspoken reprimand and clapped his hands together. He rubbed them briskly as he eyed the box. "I think it's time we broke into those chocolates."

Lauren laughed, her irritation with her husband apparently forgotten. "It's barely ten o'clock in the morning."

"It's never too early for chocolate," said Tim with a grin.

"A man after my own heart," said Alec, but his tone was guarded. No doubt he was puzzled by Tim's apparent change of heart toward him. Kira was curious herself and intended to ask Lauren about it later.

They tore open the box and dug into the delicacies, enjoying the sugar-laden treats with gusto. The mood was almost festive, but every once in a while Kira's and Alec's eyes would meet and that horrible gnawing sensation would hit the pit of her stomach, despite the fact that it was saturated with French chocolate. The Nickles acted as a buffer, allowing her and Alec to avoid direct conversation with each other, but nothing could dispel the underlying tension between them.

Alec smacked his lips, and wiped his hands with a napkin. "Well, that's my sugar quotient for the day. If I get grief from the nurses for my poor diet, I fully intend to blame you, Rachel. You spoil me far too much."

Rachel beamed and her mother wrapped an arm around her shoulder. "Well, if they do, you can just refer them to us," said Lauren. "The Nickles take care of their own."

Kira had been gazing out the window at the gray, overcast sky that had been threatening rain all morning. At that comment, however, she turned around and saw something pass across Alec's features that tugged at her heart. She had silently wondered that his father and brother hadn't yet made an appearance at the hospital to show support for Alec. Alec's mother had died a year before they met, but Kira remembered him as being quite close to his dad and older brother. She was pretty sure they still lived in Montreal, just a few hours away. It was hardly a barrier to familial solidarity.

Kira was just about to ask him about it when it struck her that both Alec's dad and his brother were police officers. His dad may have retired, but Kira was sure his brother was still active on the Montreal force. Alec had gone into the family business. Perhaps his sudden career change had been perceived as a betrayal of their traditions. No doubt his being a suspect in a brutal murder would do little to endear him if he was already considered the black sheep.

But what about friends? If Alec had any friends, he would have made them overseas in the last seven years. But he had mentioned no one beyond casual acquaintances, and no one had made an appearance at his bedside. It was hard to fathom. Alec was charming and sensitive, intelligent with a keen sense of humor. He was loyal to those he loved and honest to a fault. He should be surrounded by friends and family. So why wasn't he?

"Thanks, Lauren," he was saying. "I appreciate the support but I'm sure this will all blow over soon." He glanced at Rachel. "And when it does I fully intend to take Rachel here, for a drive in my BMW to show her how grateful I am."

"Can I drive?" said Rachel with a coy flutter of her lashes.

Alec chuckled but his laughter was interrupted, first by a grimace of pain and a hand to his injury, and second by the police officer who poked his head inside the door. "You'll have to clear out, folks. The detectives are on their way up to speak to Monsieur Frechette."

Kira nodded. "We'll be right out."

Tim's voice cut in a moment later. With hands held up, palms outward, he commented, "I think I better use your facilities, Frechette. Those chocolates seemed determined to melt in my hot little hands."

"I'm sure your wife isn't complaining," teased Alec as Tim headed for the washroom.

Tim waved him off and tossed him a grin, and Kira found herself hoping that he and Alec might become friends.

While Tim washed up, Lauren and Rachel said their good-byes. Kira waited silently by the door and soon the women were back out in the hall.

"What about Dad?" asked Rachel as the door closed behind them.

"Maybe he wanted to talk to Alec a little before the detectives get there. Let's wait for him in the café by the doors."

The threesome walked toward the elevator and Kira punched the button. "He certainly had a change of heart about Alec. Do you know why?"

Lauren shook her head slightly as they stepped into the car. "I did talk to him but I'm not sure if that made the difference. He just suddenly seemed very intent on speaking to Alec. When Tim gets something in his head, he's as stubborn as a pit bull. Nothing gets in his way."

Kira nodded silently and stared at the shifting display of glowing numbers.

"So what on Earth was wrong with you back there?" The abrupt change in Lauren's voice startled her.

Kira's head jerked backward. "What?"

"You're just going to allow this to continue? Whatever is going on between you two needs resolution, and heaven knows nothing's going to happen if you're not talking."

Kira's anger suddenly flared far out of proportion to the criticism. "Who says we need to resolve it?"

"Admit it, you're miserable. And I don't believe you'll feel any better until you sort things out with him."

"He doesn't want to sort things out with me." Kira unclenched her fists and flexed her fingers. She had absolutely no reason to be so tense.

"Bull."

Kira's head drooped as she followed Lauren and Rachel off the elevator. She was startled to feel Lauren's hand on her elbow as she steered her toward the small tables in front of the wide picture windows. A fine spattering of rain now speckled the glass, and Kira thought she heard a distant rumble of thunder.

"Now, what's this all about?" demanded Lauren.

Rachel settled down and watched the two older women, no doubt completely fascinated by any discussion that revolved around men and relationships.

"I have no life," lamented Kira, her eyes riveted on the dreary landscape.

"What the heck is that supposed to mean?"

She finally looked at Lauren. "He doesn't want me near him because he thinks all I see is somebody who needs nurturing and mothering."

Lauren frowned. "Is that true?"

"A week ago I would have said no. But now he's made me wonder if it is true—if that's all I'm about. Without my job and those kids to look after, without a child to care for, what have I got? I don't have any hobbies. I have no other interests to speak of. I barely read anymore. The only television shows I watch are medical dramas, and even there I cry like a sap every time somebody gets the sniffles." She lowered her eyes. "Even my friendship with you started because I saw the need with Rachel. I knew you would need support, and that was why I started inviting you over for coffee and visiting Rachel in dialysis."

"Oh, Kira..."

She held up her hands as if erecting a glass wall. "No, no. Don't say it. I'm pathetic. He had every right to shove me out of his life, and I wouldn't blame you if you did exactly the same thing. I must have some sort of complex where I only get gratification through the suffering of others."

"Kira, stop it!" Lauren grabbed her hand. "That's ridiculous. Our friendship may have started out that way, but it didn't stop there."

Kira started to protest, but Lauren ignored her.

"When I look at you, I don't see a compulsive social worker or a live-in nurse. I see a friend, and friendship is a two-way street. You give a lot to us, but I believe we give a lot to you too. And I know your interest in our family is far more than sympathy or, heaven forbid, pity."

"No," Kira shook her head for emphasis, "of course not. You…you mean more to me than I can say. But what about the rest of it? And what about Alec? How do I change so that I'm more what he needs?"

Lauren tisked loudly. "See? There you go again. Maybe you need to make some changes, but not to be what he needs! It sounds like that's exactly what he doesn't want. He wants someone who is her own person, who is strong and independent, and who sees in him something more than merely an outlet for her compassion. When you look at him, you need to start to see what you can do for each other—not just what you can do for him."

Kira gazed down at her hands, folded on the table. "I'm just not used to counting on anyone. Even as a kid, I was always the one my mom asked to look after my little sister. And even if I could do it, how do I approach him?" She looked up. "I used to rely on him for things. He ran the house and supported us, but that wasn't enough for him."

"Kira, he needs you to need him emotionally. He wants you to be able to lean on him, look to him for comfort and support. But not just with caresses and hugs. He needs you to trust him with your fears and your dreams." Lauren sighed and bit on her lower lip. "Maybe you could start by telling him how uncertain you feel about where to go from here. Tell him how upset you are at the prospect of losing your job, and how you're struggling with the direction your life is taking." She granted Kira a half smile. "But I'm assuming a lot. Is he worth all the trouble? You've been apart a long time. Is he someone that you want to share your life with now?"

"Yes," Kira said quietly. "I've never felt a connection with anyone like I've felt with him. Maybe that's why I became so focused on my work and other people's problems. Maybe I couldn't face how much I was missing him, and how confused I was by his leaving." She tapped her fingernails on the table, a light staccato that blended with the gentle patter of the rain against the window. "When I was helping him with his injury and hiding him at the cabin, I kept thinking about how I owed him so much because of what had happened." The understanding had dawned like a flash of lightning. As if to underscore her thoughts, a low rumble of thunder echoed in the distance. "Maybe he sensed that. I shouldn't be with him because I *owe* him."

"You should be with him because you love him." It was Rachel's voice and they both started at the soft comment.

"Of course." Kira smiled at the girl, but a moment later, she launched from her chair. "Now, I just have to find out if he loves me."

"Where are you going? You can't see him now, he's with the police." Lauren checked her watch. "And where is Tim, anyway?"

But Kira didn't answer that last question. She called back. "I have some things to look after up in oncology. And then I'll camp out on his doorstep and he'll have to talk to me whether he likes it or not." Or at the very least he was going to listen. Confronting an invalid did have its advantages.

* * * * *

"Good morning," said Gen as she sauntered into the hospital room with a steaming coffee in a paper cup.

Alec cast a quick, puzzled glance at the bathroom door. Tim still hadn't made an appearance but, rather than risk embarrassing him, Alec remained silent. He couldn't care less what Tim heard anyway. He had no secrets. Or at least none that would be discussed in that room.

"*Bonjour,* Sergeant," Alec said with a polite dip of his head. "Where's your sidekick?" he tossed a meaningful glance toward the door. "Or are we going to be doing this *privately?*"

He tilted his head suggestively and exulted in the faint blush that rose to her cheeks. Making women blush was definitely one of his favorite things in life. It came in second, right behind making them do other, much less civilized things.

However, the moment couldn't last. Sergeant Turcotte pulled up a chair and by the time she sat down the color in her cheeks had faded to a pale peach. "He'll be here in a minute. He wanted to get a donut."

"Ah, *ma chèrie,* I thought you were bigger than that old cliché. Cops and donuts?"

"Monsieur Frechette," she said tightly. "Before he gets here I want your assurances that there will be no repeat of what happened yesterday. I don't want to have to press harassment charges."

Alec didn't quite see how harassment was the proper term for what had happened. Especially considering that she was the one who had all the power over his future, but he chose to humor her. "I promise I'll be good."

She frowned, apparently unconvinced, but he was saved from further discussion by Ridgers' entrance. He swaggered in, munching on a chocolate glazed donut, and carrying a bag, apparently bulging with a half dozen or so more. He flopped down, said good morning, and offered one to Alec.

"No, thanks. I already binged on chocolate this morning." He narrowed his eyes at Ridgers. "You're being awfully civil. What happened to the bad cop?"

"He's on vacation," said Ridgers around a mouthful of glaze and fat. "Besides, I don't do *Dirty Harry* on an empty stomach."

"Can we get down to business?" asked Turcotte impatiently.

It struck Alec that she generally had little patience with her partner's idiosyncrasies, but yet they appeared to have been together for a very long time. Despite their differences, they obviously made a good team. Being part of a team. He missed that about police work. He missed that period.

"What new questions do you have?" Alec asked with resignation. "Or are you here to officially charge me with the murder?"

"First things first," said Turcotte with a glance at her notes.

Alec's stomach clenched. It was only a matter of time before he was out of his nice cushy hospital bed and tossed behind bars in a bare detention cell. The thoughts of fending off other inmates had been cause for humor earlier, but actually the idea made him nauseous. He could hold his own in any barroom brawl, but defending his honor and defending his virtue were two entirely different things. And God help him if the other prisoners ever found out he used to be a police officer.

"We'd like to go over the evidence we have so far, Monsieur Frechette—"

"Please," said Alec with a raised hand. "Alec. I think we know each other well enough for first names, don't you?"

Turcotte blushed again, right on cue. And Ridgers' broad grin informed Alec that Turcotte's secret was out. She must trust her partner if she had told him that story. Alec sighed. How was it that his mood had soured so quickly?

"All right," she said without looking up. "Alec. Here is a summary of what we have to date." She read from her list. "We have a victim who died from gunshot wounds—one to her head and one to her chest. The bullets match your gun, and your fingerprints were on the casings."

She looked at Alec but he kept his face blank. "I don't deny loading the gun. I just deny pulling the trigger."

She looked back at her list. "We have motive in that you had come from a heated argument with Ms. North, and you even admitted to needing a physical outlet."

"Yes. My outlet was sex. I don't take out my frustrations by brutalizing women."

"Which brings up the fact that your semen was found on the body and your blood was found beneath her fingernails. The blood group leaves little doubt and we're waiting on DNA confirmation."

Alec winced internally at her bluntness, but merely restated the obvious. "Again, I don't deny having intercourse, and I confess that she tended to be rather…" He hedged as he searched for a suitable euphemism. "Her sexual appetite was definitely…enthusiastic. I don't deny that you'll find her nail imprints on my back, but they are hardly evidence of her trying to defend herself." He took a deep breath, glad that he had managed to pick his way through that little minefield. "I do deny raping and beating her."

Turcotte seemed to accept that, but then she fidgeted with her pen and glanced at Ridgers. "This is somewhat awkward…Alec. I—"

Ridgers broke in. "We wanted to know if the reason you quarreled with Ms. North was over the fact that you weren't the father of Cherisse Frechette."

That blew Alec away. He stared at Ridgers in silent shock for a few agonizing heartbeats before his temper spiked. "What the hell is that supposed to mean? Of course I was her father."

"Please Alec, don't play games with us," said Ridgers as he continued to munch. "That's impossible. Did you quarrel over Kira having an affair while you were together? Did you resent—"

"Hold on there just one second!" Alec had to restrain himself from leaping from the bed and wrapping his hands around Ridgers' scrawny neck. "I may have my complaints about my relationship with Kira, but I know she was faithful to me. Where the hell are you getting this *merde* anyway?"

"Come on, Frechette," said Ridgers as he leaned forward and rested his elbows on his knees. "You're shooting blanks, man. The coffee's got cream but no sugar. The plumbing's there but the well is dry."

"Christ, Ridgers!" interjected Turcotte. "Show a little sensitivity here. We know you're sterile, Alec. We're simply seeking to establish—"

Alec's laughter startled her. The pain shot through him with each chuckle, but he couldn't restrain himself. The thought of Kira fooling around, or of Cherisse belonging to another man had been so outrageous and insulting, he had come very close to pummeling Ridgers, even at the risk of an assault charge.

"Alec? What is so funny?"

"Ah, *ma chère,*" he sighed as he wiped his eyes. "I haven't laughed like that in a long time." Still grinning he added, "I may be *shooting blanks* now, but that was by choice. After I left Montreal, I got *snipped.*" He winked at Ridgers, whose face had turned pale at the thought.

Turcotte seemed shocked. "But—you're a young man. You could very well have married and still had a family. You obviously wanted children. I don't—"

"My reasons are my own," he said without trying to keep the edge out of his voice. "Can we please move on?"

She stared at him for a moment before consulting her notes. "All right," she said slowly. "You also admit to drinking heavily that night."

Alec was relieved to have left that topic behind. It had been his decision but it was very personal and not something that he wanted discussed openly. "Yes," he conceded. "But I believe that was why I passed out, and was unaware of the events that followed."

"We're not so sure of that...Alec." She cleared her throat nervously.

"Obviously. You think I killed her in a drunken rage."

"No. What I mean is, we're not so sure that you passed out because of the liquor."

"Oh yes, I forgot about your Carl Stuart questions. But I'm afraid that theory—"

"It is no longer merely a theory. We found traces of Haldol in your glass."

Alec frowned. The term was familiar but he wasn't exactly sure what it meant. "Haldol?"

"Yes. It's a powerful sedative. Mrs. Cromwell has a prescription for it for occasional bouts with severe insomnia. Carl Stuart would have had access to it."

"He drugged me?"

"There were no traces of Haldol in Darcy's system, and only your fingerprints and Carl's were on the glass."

Alec blinked, trying to grasp the significance of this. "But surely Carl Stuart is smarter than to leave a contaminated glass lying around."

"Are you trying to help your cause or help us get a conviction, Alec?" Turcotte's eyes were twinkling, and Alec knew she was just tickled by this development. Had his kiss had that much of an effect on her?

She continued, "The glass had been kicked far under the bed. A quick search of the room wouldn't have yielded it."

"Was his only motive to frame me?" The thought of Darcy dying merely as a pawn in some twisted pissing contest made him ill.

"We believe there could be more to it than that. But we can't comment on that, and we can't confirm it without speaking to Mr. Stuart."

"Why? Where is he?"

"He took the day off and we have been unable to contact him."

Unconsciously Alec covered his injury with a protective hand. "So, what are you telling me?"

"We're telling you that we cannot see our way clear to an indictment at this time."

"In other words, you're off the hook," said Ridgers with a grin. "For now."

"Keep in mind, though," cautioned Turcotte. "You still have things to answer for. You will have to face charges of leaving the scene of the crime, and possibly assault of the Governor General. Depending on the Crown Attorney's mood this could still have serious consequences for you." The words were grave but the fact that her lips seemed determined to twitch into a smile tended to lessen their impact. "And this doesn't mean you're free to leave the city. It just means we have to continue investigating."

But Alec's spirits had soared. Even her warning couldn't dampen his mood. In fact, if Turcotte had been within reach, he probably would have kissed her again, he was feeling so damn good.

"We dismissed the guard before we came in," said Ridgers as he stuffed a cruller in his mouth.

Turcotte stood. "So, stay close to your apartment or give us a number so we can reach you if needed. We don't want to have to send a cruiser looking for you."

"I'll check my answering machine like clockwork," said Alec as he stacked his hands behind his head and leaned back, feeling as if he might float right off the bed.

The twosome headed for the door. Ridgers sauntered out but Turcotte hesitated. She turned back and said seriously, "Keep in mind, Alec, if this *was* some sick revenge plot, Stuart may not be pleased to see you walking about free. He may feel slighted, and threatened by our questions. He may be severely pissed, and he may take it out on you."

"I'll watch my back." He winked at her. "And thanks for caring, *chèrie.*"

She snorted and stepped into the hallway. But not before Alec caught sight of the familiar crimson flush on her cheeks.

When he was sure they were gone, he called out, "Okay, you can come out now."

The washroom door cracked open and Tim stepped out looking somewhat sheepish. "Why didn't you blow the whistle on me?"

Alec shrugged. "I was feeling charitable."

Tim walked slowly over to the bed and leaned against the foot rail with rigid arms and an appraising stare. He fixed his almond eyes on Alec, his expression silent and intense. He stayed like that long enough to make Alec distinctly uncomfortable. Finally he spoke. "Why did you get a vasectomy?"

Alec winced. "What? No congratulations for not being a murderer? You hear all that and that's what you focus on?"

"Of course I'm glad you're not going to jail. Rachel will be happy, and I didn't really believe you did it anyway. Now, answer the question."

"I hardly know you!" said Alec in disbelief. "What makes you think I'm going to tell you something that personal?"

"How about if I guess?"

Alec had to admit he was intrigued by Tim's audacity. "All right," he said simply. "Guess away."

"Your daughter died of a genetic disorder, right?"

"Yes," Alec conceded softly, already stunned by that comment.

"Even if you and Kira had stayed together, the chance of you having another child with the same disease was one in four, assuming no contraceptives. Even then there's amniocentesis and genetic counseling, which would further decrease the risk of passing on the condition. However, such precautions carried the risk of a therapeutic abortion if the fetus tested positive and you were unwilling to resort to that."

"Yes."

"And then you left her, which even further reduced the risk since the chances of you linking up with another woman with that gene are astronomically low."

"True."

"But none of that mattered. The chance was still there, and you couldn't bear even a one in a million chance of facing all that again. But that's not all."

Alec felt numb. How could Tim possibly have known all that? "No?"

"No. You also blame yourself for all the suffering she went through. You wanted to fix it and you couldn't. All you could do was stand by and watch her die. Your genes were the reason she died, and you couldn't do anything to help her. So not only are you preventing it from happening again, you're also condemning yourself to a life without a family...in penance for failing her."

The tightness in Alec's chest prevented him from speaking. But Tim's comments required no affirmation. He was right on, and he obviously knew it.

A comfortable silence settled over the two men as Alec gazed out the window at what had turned into a raging tempest. Water coursed down the glass in wide, turbulent rivers. Lightning illuminated the landscape and a very close clap of thunder shook the floor, and made the glass shimmer.

Still gazing at the torrent outside, Alec said quietly, "I used to spend my time sitting on the back deck racking my brain for something that I could do to help. I called every goddamn clinic from here to Moscow but no one could help me. When I realized I was helpless, I started dividing my time between making useless wishes, and flogging myself with an invisible whip. *I should have known somehow. We should have checked. Our love was never meant to be. Just look at what I was putting both Cherisse and Kira through.* And all I could do was stand by and watch. I've never felt so impotent in my life."

He looked at Tim, his jaw and his throat tight. "That was the only thing I had power over. I had to take action and that was the only way I could assure that I never put anyone through that again. *I* couldn't live through that again." He looked to the horizon that was obscured by murky, gray clouds and uncertainty. "I just couldn't."

"I know," said Tim quietly.

Alec blinked and rested his eyes on the other man. Tim emanated a quiet assurance and sensitivity that Alec was sure had made him a wonderful father and husband. Alec envied him that. "How? How do you know?"

"I just do. I've made those same wishes, on those same stars, and had the same disappointments and guilt. But now's not the time for details." Tim swallowed with difficulty. "When are they letting you outta here? When they do, let me know, and I'll give you a ride." He paused and allowed a slow grin to spread across his face. "Maybe I'll even buy you lunch to make up for the lousy way I treated you."

It had been a long time since Alec had been acquainted with a man that he could really call a friend. Just maybe Tim Nickle could fill that role. "You're on." He tossed off the covers and gritted his teeth silently at the fierce reminder of his injury. But he stoically ignored the warning. "As a matter of fact, I've got the urge for a good plate of pasta and a big glass of Chianti right now."

Tim looked shocked and started to protest, but Alec ignored him. "I'm feeling better than I have in weeks. As charming as Lauren and your daughter may be, let's ditch the women and allow me to educate your palette, *mon ami.*"

"My palette?"

Alec reached for his clothes. *"Mais oui.* Be careful what you wish for," he said with a twinkle. "You just may get it."

Chapter Eighteen

ℌ

"Where's Mike? I need to see him immediately." Kira's voice mirrored the sudden strength of will that had found her after her conversation with Lauren. Lauren was barely ten years older than Kira and yet Kira constantly marveled at the wisdom that Lauren had accumulated in that short span of time. Or maybe some people were just naturally more in tune with human nature and the nuances of relationships.

Jean, seated at the nursing station and looking somewhat bedraggled and overworked, twitched a half smile that transformed her face. "You're awfully cocky for someone who just got the boot." Kira sympathized with the staff who would have to cope with the additional workload while she was away.

"I'm suspended, not terminated," Kira retorted. "Now where the hell is he?"

Jean's eyebrows lifted in disbelief and approval. Kira rarely used harsh language at work, nor was she so blunt about her needs. She had been known to be a tigress, but only when it came to her patients. It was about time that changed, thought Kira. Way past time.

"He went down to get a coffee and he promised me a sugar twist," said Jean evenly. "Why? What's so urgent?"

Kira clicked her fingernails on the desk. "I just need to talk to him, that's all. He may disapprove of what I did for Alec, but that doesn't mean he doesn't know I'm a good nurse. I need him to be my advocate with Human Resources. I'll take my licks, but they need to know that they'd be crazy to lose someone with my skills and dedication."

Suddenly Kira wondered why on Earth she was sharing this story with Jean. They had certainly never been kindred spirits, and she wasn't even sure if Jean agreed about Kira's nursing skills. But Jean's response surprised her.

"Good for you," she said with approval. "You're absolutely right. They'd be crazy to fire you."

Kira was stunned. "You mean you think I'm a good nurse? I didn't think—"

Jean waved away the question. "Of course you're good. You're one of the best I've worked with. You're a pain in the ass, but you're good for these kids and I'd be insane not to admit it."

Kira smiled and relaxed. "Thanks, Jean. That means a lot."

Jean looked back at her computer screen. "Don't go and get all mushy on me," she said gruffly. "It's nothing personal, you know."

Kira sat down to wait. "No, of course not. I can't stand you either."

"Right." But Kira thought she heard a muffled chuckle. They sat in silence for a moment before Jean said, "So, he turned you over to the cops, eh?"

"In a manner of speaking. But I suppose it's for the best. I don't know how long Alec could have stayed on the run, especially with his injury." She shrugged and drew a deep breath. "Mike says he did it for me. He made a deal with the cops so they wouldn't prosecute me. I suppose I should be grateful."

Jean snorted. "Huh! Man, he's a sweet talker. You sound just like his ex-wife."

Kira perked up. "You knew her?"

"I saw her a few times. She was a sweet little thing—kinda young, though, if you ask me. And gullible. By the time the divorce was final he had her convinced that it was all for the best. He practically had her thanking him for fooling around."

Kira blinked slowly and licked her lips. "Fooling around? I thought she left him and took their daughter."

Jean's head jerked back and swiveled to face Kira again. "Daughter? He doesn't have any kids—at least not legitimately. Who knows what seeds he's sown in distant ports."

Kira tried to sound only mildly concerned, and keep her voice even, while inside she was seething and on the verge of an explosion. "So, he cheated on his wife and leads a promiscuous lifestyle?"

"I think maybe Henry the Eighth slept with more women—but I don't think the gap is very big."

How had she missed this? How had she been so blind to his shortcomings? But then again how did Jean know all this? What if it was all hearsay and she was judging Mike unfairly? "How do you know?"

"I've seen him coming on to nurses in the cafeteria, and heard him bragging to the other doctors. You don't hang out in the cafeteria nearly enough, honey. It's a regular soap opera down there." Now she leaned close and whispered conspiratorially, "And, of course, there was the time I walked in on him and one of the clerical staff involved in a little *dictation* session in his office." She winked to drive her point home.

"He had sex with a secretary in his office?" Kira said in disbelief.

"Pretty cliché, eh? But that's our Mike—cliché to the bone." Jean shrugged. "He was awfully nice to me after that. He even brings me donuts sometimes. I'll take what I can get."

Jean began tapping out orders on the computer keyboard and Kira just sat there absorbing it all, and trying to tamp down the rage that continued to build inside her.

When Mike finally walked in, she was cool, calm and collected…and deadly.

He drew up short, almost sloshing coffee on his perfectly pleated chinos and Ralph Lauren golf shirt. "Kira!" His smile was bright and warm and Kira stifled the urge to slap it right off his lying, cheating face.

"Hi, Mike," she said sweetly.

He frowned. "Did you come to the hospital to visit *him*? I don't know how the police will feel…"

"Please," she interrupted. "Can we discuss this in your office?" Kira stood slowly, and indulged in a languorous stretch that she hoped would appear innocent but seductive. "I'm tired, but I really needed to see you." She dropped her voice a fraction until it hovered at husky without being overtly sexual. "Really."

His tongue flicked over his bottom lip and his eyes were unnaturally bright. "All right." He handed Jean her donut and motioned Kira to follow him back toward his private sanctuary.

Kira tossed Jean one meaningful glance as she ambled away. Jean merely watched silently, munching on her treat, the front of her uniform already speckled with sugar.

Mike closed the door behind them and sipped from his coffee as he leaned those tight little buns against his desk. He watched her through the steam. "So, how is he?"

"Doing much better. I wouldn't be surprised if they discharge him tomorrow or the next day."

"And where will he go from there?"

Kira gritted her teeth but kept smiling. "I really don't know, Mike. I'm hoping it won't be to the jailhouse but—"

"He's bad news, Kira. Surely you can see that. He hurt you before, and now he's involved in a highly questionable situation." He shook his head ruefully. "You should just stay away from him."

Kira plunked down in one of the plush chairs, her knees just inches from his. "You think I need someone more down-to-earth, more stable, more…honest."

He nodded, oblivious to her sarcasm. "Yes. You deserve that much. Even if he's acquitted, Alec Frechette will only bring you grief."

Kira nodded knowingly. "Right. Who knows what sordid secrets he's hiding in addition to all his conquests here and abroad?"

"Exactly."

Kira stood and moved very close to Mike, who continued to sip from his coffee and watch her curiously. "What I need is a hardworking, dedicated, stay-at-home type like you." She ran her fingers up his arm to rest on his shoulder.

"Uh…yes." He cleared his throat and set down his coffee. His breathing was beginning to respond to her advance, and she wasn't sure, but she thought there was other, more direct evidence of it as well.

"How could your wife possibly be such an idiot as to turn away that kind of stability and…commitment?"

"She was a very selfish woman," he lamented.

Kira had to restrain herself from rolling her eyes. "No doubt. Whatever did you see in her in the first place?" She walked her fingers around to the back of his neck, and moved in close enough so that her breath would be hot against his throat.

"I guess I was young and…" His Adam's apple bobbed. "Uh, Kira. I'm a little confused. I would have thought you'd be angry about what happened. I was hoping you'd come to understand, but…"

"Angry?" she crooned. "Why on Earth would I be angry? You only had my best interests at heart, right?"

He nodded uncertainly and she was pleased to see the hair on his arm rise as her fingers caressed the nape of his neck.

"You're a good friend, right, Mike? You would never mislead me about your motives, or your intentions."

He tilted his head against her hand, focusing more on her touch than on her words. "Mm-hmm," he mumbled. "That's absolutely ri—ouch!"

Kira's fingers had found the nerve bundle they had been seeking. As a female cop, it was very handy to have little tricks that gave her an edge over her larger, stronger, male counterparts. She had studied nerves and anatomy, and experimented on Alec, until she had perfected her own personal version of the *Spock Grip.* Mike's shoulders drew up around his ears, and his neck was in spasm, but Kira didn't relent. "You lied to me, Mike," she hissed. "You lied about your ex-wife, and you made up a child just to garner my sympathy and hopefully get me into bed."

Mike just whimpered helplessly.

"I don't take kindly to that kind of treatment, even from my boss. *Especially* from my boss. And don't give me this crap about turning in Alec for my own good. You took advantage of my trust in you and you did it because you saw an opportunity to get him out of the way." She twisted his flesh cruelly. "You wanted to get rid of the competition."

Mike managed to reach up and grab her wrist, wrenching it away from his neck and pushing her roughly away.

Kira stepped back, but retreat was the last thing on her mind. "I thought you had some class, Dr. LaRocque. I thought we were friends. Obviously I was wrong."

Mike rubbed the back of his neck, his face red with rage. "Oh, and I suppose Alec Frechette is your idea of a class act? Sure, he's got the looks and the bucks, but he's as horny as a hound dog in heat. He's just better at getting women to fall at his feet. And just look at what his latest conquest got for her trouble—a hole in her forehead and her picture on the cover of *Newsweek*."

"I told you," said Kira tightly. "He had nothing to do with that. And maybe Alec sleeps with his share of women, but at least he seduces them honestly." She couldn't believe she had just said that, but she ignored the chuckling devil on her shoulder and continued, "He doesn't have to lie to get them into his bed."

Mike just glared at her, but said nothing.

"Do you deny it? Do you deny making up that load of crap about your daughter?"

"No," he finally conceded. He moved around the desk and eased himself down into his plush executive chair. Kira suspected sitting in it gave him a certain sense of security and power in the face of her accusations. "I don't deny it."

"Why?" she asked, palms turned heavenward in a plea for divine understanding. "What could possibly have possessed you to go to such ridiculous lengths simply to seduce me? My God, if—"

"Dammit, Kira. I love you!"

If he had slammed a fist into her gut, she couldn't have been more stunned. "What?"

"You heard me. I've known you for two years. For two years, I've worked beside you. I've seen your strength and your compassion." He clasped his hands together and placed them in the center of his blotter. "And your beauty. But you refused to let me in. You barely even acknowledged my friendship, let alone considered me as a lover." He turned slightly and gazed out the window at the waning storm. "I guess I got a little desperate and went a little crazy when Alec showed up. I guess I was afraid that you might reconcile with him, and I thought it was my last chance to make you see what I had to offer."

Kira's eyes widened in astonishment. "You're telling me that you're justifying lying, deception and betrayal with *love*?

That's not love, that's objectification. You saw me as a challenge, a conquest that had eluded you. I was just a means to an end—another notch on your bedpost."

He shook his head. "That's not how it was at all. You just don't understand—"

"Oh, I understand all right. I understand all too well. I came up here to ask you to be my advocate and to help me get my job back. I was going to ask you as a friend, but now I know that's pointless because I don't believe you know the meaning of the word."

"Kira—" His tone was icy, a warning implied in that word. But she ignored it.

"So instead, I'll come at it from a different angle. I still want my job, even if it means working with you. So, if you don't do everything in your power to see that I keep it, I'll come after you with a sexual harassment suit, and I'll even go to the board about your conduct with that *secretary* Jean told me about."

"You're treading on dangerous ground here. I don't take kindly to threats."

"And I don't take kindly to lies. Alec may have left me, but he never lied to me. He never used me."

"You've got blinders on when it comes to him, Kira. You're going to regret this."

"Possibly. But not as much as you will if you don't come through for me in this." She whirled to go, and was startled to feel his hand on her arm. He must have practically vaulted over the desk in order to catch her at the door.

"Don't fuck with me, Kira, because I guarantee you'll lose."

"You can bet the only place I'll be fucking you, Doctor, is in your dreams." She glanced at his hand, still manacled around her arm. "Let go, or I'll scream rape and that won't exactly do wonders for your reputation either."

His hand recoiled as if she had drizzled acid on it. "Dammit, this is crazy. You're turning down a respected doctor for a murderer."

Kira refused to be goaded. She stepped out of the office and walked resolutely toward the door. She heard Mike's office door slam as she walked past the nursing station, now devoid of staff. No doubt Jean was tending to her patients. That thought made her ache in places too deep to identify.

But she took a deep breath, willed the ache away and strode toward the elevator. She might not have children to look after at the moment, but she did have business to attend to. Despite the situation, it felt good to take control again. She was on a roll. She was pumped and invigorated. It was the perfect time to confront Alec, and to take control of the rest of her life as well.

She sauntered past the nursing station on Alec's floor, and headed for his room. She was just about to push through unannounced when she realized that the guard was missing. The chair was still there, but it was vacant, and he was nowhere to be seen. Perhaps he had just gone to use the facilities. Even cops were human.

She stepped into Alec's room, and was astonished to find the bed empty. The covers were rumpled, obviously recently slept in. She checked the washroom, but found no one. And his clothes were missing. Feeling uneasy, she looked out into the hall again to see if the guard had returned. Had Alec slipped out and made a run for it again while the guard was otherwise occupied?

No, that was ridiculous. He knew better than that. Mind you, she thought he *had* run before.

She waited a few more minutes and when neither the guard nor Alec made an appearance, she approached the nursing station and asked tentatively, "Uh, is Monsieur Frechette out for tests?"

This nurse looked much more mature, with graying hair swept up in a youthful style. She blew an errant strand of hair out of her eyes with a well-directed puff. "Hardly. He signed himself out about ten minutes ago."

Kira felt her jaw hit the floor. "He did what?"

"The police said he was no longer in custody, and there was nothing they could do. We couldn't force him to stay." Her eyes twinkled in a way that was all too familiar to Kira. "And we tried. Believe me, we tried."

"But surely he wasn't fit—" Kira ignored the insinuations behind those words. She was beginning to see how quickly this attitude could become old and irritating.

Thankfully, the nurse resumed a more professional air. She held up her hands helplessly. "We tried to convince him of that but he just smiled and kissed me on the cheek and took off holding a hand to his side, and grinning like the cat that ate the canary."

Kira blew out a slow breath of fury. She was pleased that Alec seemed to be off the hook for the moment, but leaving the hospital was irresponsible and stupid. "Did he drive himself?"

The nurse frowned. "No. His friend said something about calling a cab."

"Friend?"

The phone rang. "Sorry, that's all I know." She shrugged as she reached for the phone. "He's a big boy. Let him make his own mistakes." She turned her attention to the phone, and Kira turned away and headed back toward the elevator.

"Right," she muttered. "If only he wasn't so darn good at it."

* * * * *

Mike tapped his pen on the blotter. His next appointment was waiting just outside the door, but he had other things on his mind.

He seethed with rage at Kira's shortsightedness and her misplaced loyalty to a man who was so obviously unworthy. Just like so many of the women Mike encountered, she couldn't see the big picture. She couldn't see all that he had to offer.

He tried to blow out his frustrations with a sigh, but the effect was nominal. His pulse still pounded in his throat and his heart still crashed against his chest. He wouldn't give up on Kira. Even if he wanted to, he couldn't. But in his current state of mind, he was in no condition to approach the problem rationally. This situation needed to be approached calmly and with a cool head. He needed to rediscover his focus, find a way to settle his mind and center his thinking.

Mike LaRocque knew only one way to do that. He gazed out through his wide picture window but he didn't see the spatters of rain or the angry blanket of clouds. Instead, he saw luminescent eyes and soft skin. In his mind, he caressed the curve of a breast and the silkiness of a thigh. At first the figure was anonymous, just a generic subject for his needs and desires. But gradually he narrowed down the choices and fixated on a specific subject and venue for his activity. Soon he had solidified his plans for the evening.

He had no doubt she would comply. They always did, and if they hesitated there were ways to tip the scales.

Mike LaRocque never went home disappointed.

Chapter Nineteen

ꟹ

Gen watched their visitor through the two-way glass. Mr. Stuart sat at the table, his expression rigid and his body motionless save for the occasional tap of his foot, and an annoying habit of adjusting his glasses.

She sensed a presence behind her. "Think he's sweated enough yet?" asked Will.

"He's not sweating."

"The guilty ones never do."

She glanced up at her partner. "You're so full of it."

"If you are referring to my ebullient wit and charisma, then you are absolutely correct."

"Ebullient? Did you read that on your box of Cap'n Crunch this morning?"

He grinned. "Actually, it was Count Chocula. Do you know what it means?"

"No, what?"

The grin flipped over to an exaggerated frown. "*I* don't know. Why do you think I asked *you*?"

She exhaled a long-suffering sigh. She would never admit to Will how much she enjoyed his antics and odd sense of humor. Never. "Okay, Shakespeare. I'm counting on your *ebullient* self to help me irritate the hell out of our suspect."

"No problem. He looks well worth the trouble to me."

"Let's go." Gen led the way into the tiny room.

Stuart watched their entrance warily. He said nothing as they took their respective seats, but his eyes followed their movements like a wounded animal watching a circling vulture. "Why am I here?" he asked at last.

"For questioning," said Gen. "I thought we made that clear."

"I already talked to you people at the mansion. I have nothing more to say."

"You sure you don't want a lawyer?" asked Will as he pulled a toothpick out of his pocket and proceeded to drill away at his molars.

Stuart scowled at him. "I told you I have nothing to say and I have nothing to hide."

"Right," snorted Will.

"You arrogant—"

"Mr. Stuart," interrupted Gen. "There are two items that we need to get your comments on."

Stuart tore indignant eyes away from Will and focused on Gen. "Yes? Let's get on with it, then."

"We recently interviewed a Professor Dan Peters."

Stuart's expression remained stony. He said nothing.

"Does that name mean anything to you?"

"I don't know why you need me to comment on this," said Stuart tightly. "You obviously know all the sordid details."

"Granted," said Gen with an ingratiating smile. "Did Ms. Cromwell pay you to help her?"

"No."

"You helped her willingly?"

Stuart's Adam's apple bobbed slowly, and his eyes remained riveted on Gen. "She was very persuasive."

"I'll bet," said Will with a sly smile. "She must have dished out some heavy-duty goods to persuade you to go along with that stunt."

Stuart turned murderous eyes on Will. "If you are implying that she granted me sexual favors, I find that insulting and I refuse to dignify such an accusation with an answer."

"Ah, come on, Stuart. Share. If she didn't go down on you, then what made you do it? What made you demean yourself like that?" Will shook his head mournfully and Gen enjoyed the rising flush in Stuart's cheeks. "That must have been humiliating for you." Will squinted his eyes, ducked his head and bunched up his shoulders in a cruel parody of a peeping Tom. "Watching her seduce this guy from your hiding spot in the closet." The toothpick dangled precariously from Will's lips. "Or maybe you get off on that stuff, eh, Stuart? Maybe you had your own private party in that closet while you watched. Just you and little *Hand-gela*."

Stuart launched from his chair, his fists clenched and the veins bulging on his forehead. "You sniveling, no good, son of a—"

Will held him at arm's length. "You better stop there," he said easily. "I might take offense."

"Mr. Stuart," interjected Gen smoothly. "Please have a seat. I must apologize for my partner. He has considerable trouble staying on the right side of propriety."

Stuart took a deep breath and stepped back, but the veins on his forehead continued to bulge like skinny, blue worms. He sat down and turned his attention to Gen. "All right," he said quietly. "Yes, she did have something on me."

He stopped there so Gen prompted him. "Go on."

"I don't see that it's relevant."

"Humor us."

He swallowed dryly. "She had caught me in something of an embarrassing situation, and she threatened to divulge that information to her father if I didn't help her."

Will leaned forward. "Let me guess. She caught you trying on her undies."

"Will!"

To his credit, Stuart kept his cool. "I refuse to go into any more detail on this. You said there was something else?"

Gen ignored him. "That must have infuriated you."

"How is that?"

"Oh, come on," laughed Will. "She blackmailed you into helping her blackmail somebody else. She forced you to break the law, hide out like a rat, take dirty pictures, and manhandle a naked man, and that didn't make you a *teensy* bit mad?"

The worms on Carl's forehead pulsed madly. "Perhaps a little. But I could never hurt Ms. Cromwell. My mandate is to protect her."

"We didn't accuse you of that," said Gen innocently.

"Oh, please. I'm no idiot. I can see where this is leading." Stuart leaned back and crossed his legs. "Now I must insist we go on to the next item or I will exercise my right to terminate this session. I have things to do."

"Well," Gen couldn't keep the tightness out of her voice. "We certainly wouldn't want to *inconvenience* you, Mr. Stuart. I'm sure your social calendar has been completely thrown askew by this pesky little murder. We'll certainly try and get this nasty business settled up so you can get back to the business of mansion parties and limo rides."

Will's eyebrows had lifted a notch at the display of irritation. Usually Gen left it to him to goad and bully the suspects but Stuart was getting under her skin. She couldn't shake the feeling that she was in the company of a toad, and she found herself battling an urge to squash him under the heel of her shoe.

But all Will said was, "*Askew*?"

She retained her focus on Stuart, and was startled to see the hate that had flared in his eyes. He spoke slowly, and with apparent difficulty. "I didn't mean to belittle her death or your investigation, but I would like to get this over with." He adjusted his tie. "If you don't mind."

"Why did you drug Frechette?" taunted Will.

Stuart's eyes riveted on him. "What?"

Gen had regained her composure. "We found Alec's glass under the bed. The glass that you had poured for him. It had only your and Alec's fingerprints on it. It appears the whiskey was laced with a drug."

Something akin to panic washed over Stuart's features. "That's ludicrous. So he took a little something to help him sleep. So what? He was obviously overwrought when he was with me. He—" Too late Stuart realized his slip.

Gen could smell the kill. "How did you know it was a sleeping medication, Mr. Stuart?"

"I—" He licked his lips. "I assumed...since he claims to have blacked out. It—It seemed logical."

Gen nodded knowingly. "We also found it very interesting that there were no fingerprints on Mrs. Cromwell's bottle of Haldol."

Stuart frowned. "I fail to see how that implicates me."

Gen shrugged. "I suppose it doesn't implicate you specifically, but it implies that someone handled the bottle and wiped it clean, since not even *her* prints were on it."

"She claims to have taken a couple just the night before," commented Will. "So, unless she's in the habit of wearing latex gloves to bed, it's all damn suspicious."

Stuart's eyes darted between them. "Why would I have just *happened* to take the pills that night? I had no way of knowing that Frechette would come in. He wasn't expected, and how would I have known he would head up to Darcy's room?" He leaned back, apparently feeling quite confident that they wouldn't have an answer for this one.

Gen leaned forward. "Perhaps Alec's visit was an unexpected windfall. But perhaps you had already planned to drug Darcy that night. Or perhaps you were upset over your part in Darcy's scheme with the professor, and you were in the habit of pilfering drugs from your employers to help you cope." She spread her hands and sat back again. "There could be any number of reasons for having those pills in your possession when Alec walked in that night."

Stuart squirmed. "That's ridiculous. You're making wild assumptions. Isn't it more likely that Frechette himself took them?"

"Alec didn't have a key to their suite." Gen kept her voice matter-of-fact.

Stuart's worms writhed across his forehead. "Neither do—"

"*You* have a master key."

Will snapped the toothpick in half. "Which would have also allowed you into Darcy's rooms while she and Frechette were asleep."

Stuart stood suddenly. "Am I under arrest?"

Gen watched him with interest. "We have no warrant at this time."

"But we're working on it," grinned Will.

"Well, I'm through here." Stuart seemed to be barely controlling his panic and rage. "You can be assured that I will be contacting my lawyer about these bogus allegations."

"Go right ahead," said Will grandly. "I'm sure you'll need him when you're headed up the river."

Gen remained silent.

Stuart turned to go, but then hesitated and turned around as if he intended to speak. He locked eyes with Gen, and she felt icy fingers skittering up her spine. His eyes were cold and—there was no other word for it—evil. She found her tongue just as he broke eye contact. "I'm sure we don't have to remind you not to leave the city, Mr. Stuart. You wouldn't want to give the appearance of evading the law, now would you?"

Without a word, he turned and strode from the room.

Will fished a fresh toothpick out of his pocket and began working at his incisors. "Think he's guilty?"

"As sin."

"When will we have the warrant?"

"We have a little more legwork to do, but I'm hoping by tomorrow."

"And then you think the investigation will be over."

Gen looked at him out of the corner of her eye. "Yes," she said slowly.

"There shouldn't be any more attacks."

She frowned. "What the hell are you getting at?"

"Nothing. I just want to be sure we're thinking the same thing."

"And are we?"

"I may have some…concerns."

Impatience began to eat away at her. "Would you care to share them with me?"

"I've noticed some inconsistencies at the murder scenes."

"I don't follow. I haven't noticed anything out of place."

"No, I know you haven't."

Gen waited but he said nothing further. Why couldn't he just say what he meant for a change? What was he afraid of? She didn't bite, for God's sake. At least…not literally. She sighed and asked, "What *kind* of inconsistencies?"

"Little things, really. But it's almost like there's two *sets* of murders."

She blinked as she tried to sort through the reams of evidence and information stored away in her mind. She couldn't think of any *inconsistencies.* "I don't know what you're talking about."

He shrugged and tossed the toothpick in the garbage. "Don't worry about it. I'm sure everything will come together. For now, let's just concentrate on Stuart. I do look forward to cuffing the bastard."

Gen decided it best to ignore Will's insinuations. For the most part his thought processes completely baffled her and she doubted there was any point in trying to figure him out now. She stood and headed for the door. "What did you have for lunch anyway?"

"Beef broth and a bun." He hesitated in the doorway. "Why?"

"No reason."

* * * * *

Alec leaned his head back against the supple leather of the carriage seat. "Fantastic plan, *mon ami,*" he said with closed eyes and a slow, comfortable slur.

"You're drunk," observed Tim. "It doesn't take much to impress you."

Alec shook his head and regretted it when the world began to spin. *"Au contraire.* I'm mush more dis-herning with a belly full of Chianti."

Tim snorted with laughter and Alec caught the carriage driver glancing back at them with an unmistakable look of disdain. Alec ignored him. He was feeling too good to care whether some frustrated English Lit grad approved of his social habits. Despite the nagging pain in his side, he couldn't remember the last time he had felt so damn good. Or maybe he did. During his time on the Montreal force, he'd had no shortage of drinking buddies and male bonding rituals. There he'd had people he could count on, friends he could trust with his life. Even his relationship with Kira had started on the basis of mutual respect and trust as partners and friends. Unfortunately, as a couple, they'd had trouble maintaining that standard. And then he had linked up with Kent and he thought he had found that kind of bond again. But he had been wrong. He'd forged a solid bond with Kent all right, it just wasn't the right one.

Regretting his train of thought and seeking a diversion, he nudged Tim in the ribs. Tim's whole body jerked and his eyes flew open in surprise.

"You got anything left in that flashk?" Alec lisped quietly.

"I wash shlee-ping," Tim complained as he rolled his eyes in irritation. "I thought we were going to try and use the long ride home to sober up a bit, not get even more plastered."

"Oh, yeah." Alec allowed his head to loll. "I forgot." But then he sat upright and studied Tim. And then he studied their surroundings as the horse's hooves gently tapped their comforting rhythm on the asphalt. "Hey!" He poked a finger in Tim's chest. "Thish isn't the way to my apartment."

"Damn right," said Tim without opening his eyes. "No way you're staying alone with that injury."

"I'm find," said Alec with conviction. "I don't need a baby-shitter." Alec blinked and then burst into laughter as he considered what he had just said.

Tim shook his head but couldn't keep the grin off his face. "No, you need a few gallons of coffee." The grin waned marginally. "And a nurse."

Alec lost his good humor. "You mean you're pawning me off on Kira, the good witch of the North?"

"Uh-huh. No way you're bunkin' with uth."

"Can't look after your friends, eh?" said Alec bitterly. "Too much trouble, I guesh."

"Nah." Tim waved a hand lazily in front of Alec's face and Alec found himself mesmerized by it. "I just don't want you around my women."

"You got nothing to worry about, Tim. They both love you too much." He sighed and gazed out at the sun sparkling on the canal. "You're a lucky man."

Silence settled over them, the hiss of the wheels and the clip-clop of the horse's hooves the only sounds to mar the stillness of the afternoon. They had sat at Dominico's long past the last of the lunch crowd. They had watched the storm wane as they guzzled wine and nibbled on bruschetta. The sun had finally peeked out and they had decided a carriage ride was a fitting end to a perfect afternoon.

"Kira loves you, Alec," whispered Tim. "Don't fuck with that 'cause you're trying to teach her a lesson, or because you can't let go of the past."

Alec was astounded at the sudden clarity of Tim's speech. He opened his eyes to find Tim staring at him from behind intense brown eyes. "There's a lot of water under that bridge. And sometimes I wonder if she loves *me*, or the idea of having someone to take care of." He raked his fingers through his hair. "I want what you've got. I want a best friend, and I'm not sure if she knows how to be that..." He sighed. "At least not for me."

"Maybe you gotta help her figure it out." Tim leaned his head back and closed his eyes again. "You told me you had something special for a while. And the two of you have history. Trust me, that's worth something. And *special* doesn't happen that often. It's worth working at to get that back again."

"Maybe," Alec conceded. "But there's still one thing I can never give her."

"If she loves you that won't matter."

Abruptly the carriage stopped.

"We're here," announced the driver, turning to face his charges. "That'll be eighty-five dollars."

Alec's eyes flew open. "What? That's outrageous!"

The young man merely shrugged. "I told you this was way off my route."

Alec was about to object but Tim shushed him with a frown and a hand that batted the air impatiently. "Shut up, Frechette. I think we can afford it, and it was a hell of a lot more fun than a cab."

Alec grudgingly pulled out his wallet and contributed his half of the fare. He had offered to cover it all at the outset, but Tim had been adamant they split it.

Tim struck him as a proud man, and the more Alec got to know him the more certain of it he became. Tim was intensely devoted to his family, and anyone he called a friend. Alec was beginning to entertain the notion that perhaps he fell into that last category. It had been too damn long.

They picked their way down from the carriage and struggled across Tim's front lawn. Tim insisted that Alec come in for coffee before facing the wrath of Kira. Alec had to agree that sounded like a good plan. However, he had to admit that at that moment running the bulls at Pamplona would have sounded like a good plan. He couldn't remember the last time he had been so drunk. Even the night of the murder he hadn't felt this completely out of control. Ironic.

Tim was just reaching for the knob when the door opened of its own accord, and they were both faced with their respective nemeses. Lauren and Kira stood in the doorway, with toes tapping impatiently, eyes narrowed suspiciously, and jaws set determinedly.

"Tim?"

Alec did not know Lauren very well, but the nuances in that one word were staggering. With a single syllable she had communicated, *Tim Nickle, you're drunk. What on Earth do you think you're doing dragging an invalid all over the city, and allowing him to endanger himself by overindulging? I expected better from you, Tim. You should be ashamed of yourself. And, by the way, I was worried sick. I'm glad you're okay.*

Tim just licked his lips and grinned. "Hi, honey. I love you too."

Lauren merely rolled her eyes.

"Don't give me that look," said Tim as he leaned against the doorjamb. Alec thought that too was a good plan so he followed suit. The only trouble was he miscalculated the distance to the support structure and had to catch himself before he careened to the ground. He ignored Kira's disapproving glare.

Tim continued his defense. "We were just celebrating Alec's good fortune. He's hardly on death's door, and I brought him here so he could be tended to by the two most beautiful and forgiving women in the world."

Kira and Lauren exchanged a glance, but Alec saw the smiles twitching at their lips. He nodded his enthusiastic affirmation. "*Oui.* Thass 'zactly right."

Kira stepped out the door and draped Alec's arm across her shoulders. "I'm surprised you can stand in your condition."

"Oh, I'm having no problem staying erect, *chérie.*" And then he giggled at the double entendre. That had to be one of the best jokes in history. Alec was sure of it.

"Oh, brother," lamented Kira as she watched Tim trying to suppress his own laughter. "I think we better get these two to bed before they make complete fools of themselves."

"I like the way you think," murmured Alec into her hair. He was trying to be flip, but at that moment she felt and smelled and tasted so good he was having trouble restraining himself from devouring her on the Nickles' front stoop.

Kira slapped his chest, but Alec felt the goose bumps on her arm, and knew that she was responding to his proximity in spite of herself. Part of him thought he should be angry or resentful about that, but another part of him was having extreme difficulty remembering why.

Before he could get his bearings, he realized Kira was leading him away from his friend. "Hey!" He glanced back at Tim, who was just waving at him with a stupid grin on his face, while his wife dragged him in through the front door. "I wass shupposed to have coffee with him."

"I'm glad you've got a buddy, Alec. But you need your rest. Coffee is contraindicated in your condition."

"You, sweet-talker, you," he teased.

She kept leading him toward her house and he followed willingly. "Are you really gonna let me sleep in your bed?"

"Who says I'm not putting you on the couch?"

"I know you too well, *chèrie*. You couldn't do that if your life depended on it."

"Well, maybe I'll be the one on the couch."

He chuckled as they reached her front door and Cujo greeted them with his usual enthusiasm. "I hope not," he said truthfully. "I really hope," he blinked as the Earth began to dissolve beneath his feet, "I won't be sick."

And that was the last thing he said before he passed out.

* * * * *

Bitch! Pushy, arrogant, conniving, manipulative, fucking little BITCH!

Carl Stuart prowled around his house like a lizard that had outgrown its cage. His session with Sergeants Turcotte and Ridgers had left him feeling panicky and out of control. He craved control. He lived for it, fed off it.

His position at the Mansion afforded him a certain degree of power. He had dominion over the other security staff and, to some extent, control over the Governor General himself. The job had its uses, but it also had limitations. As Darcy Cromwell had so effectively pointed out.

Carl dropped into his favorite recliner and kicked off his shoes, allowing himself to briefly relive those moments in Darcy's suite. He breathed deeply, imagining that he could smell her fear all over again. He relived the utter terror in her eyes and the moans of pain as he had struck and subdued the sniveling little simpleton!

But beneath Darcy's moans and cries he heard the echo of another voice. Angry and accusing, his father's familiar taunts ran through his head in an endless loop of torment. *You'll never amount to anything. Just look at you. Skinny as a rake, four eyes, and dumb as a stump. One of these days you'll wind up in the sewer, Carl. If you don't shape up and take control of your life, people will walk all over you. If only you weren't so stupid. Stupid. Stupid.*

Carl covered his ears to block out the taunts. But he couldn't escape one glaring fact. His father was right. He had made a mistake. A stupid one. A fatal one.

The glass. Carl had searched the room for anything that might link him with the murder, but he had apparently been too hasty. He had missed that damned glass, and that might prove to be his undoing. He refused to consider the possibility that he had made other mistakes. He had chosen a target that was too close to him, and he had let emotions like envy and rage get the better of him. None of his other victims could be linked to him in any way. He had been careful. Meticulous. Just as he had learned, he had always maintained a scrupulous attention to detail. *Color inside the lines, Carl. Your tie is lopsided. The table settings are crooked. Straighten them! Holy Mother of Jesus! If your father sees that, he'll take the belt to you. If you can't be smart, for God's sake be careful. Now, I'll forgive you if you rub your mother's back like a good little boy. No, no! A little lower. A little lower. Oh yes, that's it. Now give me your hand and…*

Carl snapped the chair upright and paced to the wall. He banished those heinous images from his childhood. He had no right to resent his parents. They had taught him well. He had learned his lessons. He knew about precision and accuracy and how to do things right. That was why he had eluded the authorities this long.

The authorities.

Genevieve Turcotte.

That name brought a fresh wash of fury. She had treated him like a common criminal. She had taunted and belittled him—Carl Stuart, distinguished employee of the Governor General of Canada, honors graduate of Queen's University and treasurer of the student council three years running in high school. How dare she treat him so shabbily!

He sneered as he recalled the interview in that dank, tiny room. Her partner had played the insensitive clod, but it had been obvious to Carl that she was the one who had directed the proceedings. Her partner was her pawn. She used him just like she no doubt used all the men in her life—scorning and humiliating them with impunity.

Carl had always focused his rage on the wealthy and the privileged—those who had been born into power or had acquired it by dubious means. Women who looked down their noses at the likes of him and those who raised him. Women who had achieved by design and deceit what Carl's parents had worked for their whole lives—only to be disappointed. These women hadn't earned their lot in life, and Carl had every right to strip their happiness away from them.

Perhaps someone like Genevieve Turcotte had much in common with these other women who used men for their pleasures and climbed over them on their steady ascent up the social and economic ladder.

She had used her partner to manipulate Carl, and then had insulted and belittled him.

Carl closed his eyes and gritted his teeth against the waves of rage and yearning that washed over him. He needed an outlet. He needed to regain control but, by throwing suspicion on Frechette, he had cut himself off. Another mistake.

Or was it?

They had obviously discounted Frechette as a suspect in the serial rapes. The ruse had failed. The playing field had opened up again. What was the harm in taking another? He had nothing to lose.

He opened his eyes and his path was clear. He *would* strike again. He would show the world what he was made of and that he wouldn't be led around by the nose by some puny, upstart female with a badge and a God complex.

Carl needed control, and Genevieve Turcotte needed to be taught a lesson. The plan was ingenious. It was perfect. What better way to dispense with the threat?

Carl refused to think beyond the act. By the time he headed to his room to prepare, he was too focused on the task at hand to consider anything beyond the anticipated moment of triumph. Consequences were irrelevant. Like a junkie seeking his next fix, Carl sought only immediate gratification. If he looked beyond that, into his future, he feared he might shrink in on himself in terror.

Terror was fear, and fear was weakness. Carl needed to feel strong. And he knew exactly how to go about it.

Chapter Twenty

ℵ

Kira snuggled a little more deeply into the plush cushions of her favorite reading chair. Her bedroom window was open a crack, allowing a soft summer breeze to flutter the curtains and cool her tea. Unfortunately, it did nothing to soothe her troubled mind.

She took a small sip, savoring the pungent aroma of honey and lemon as she watched the steady rise and fall of Alec's chest beneath the sheets. She had lost count of the hours. She knew it was late, but only because the television in the corner of her bedroom had shifted from old movies to the mindless drone of infomercials. A sales pitch on the wonders of instant hair removal had finally prompted her to rise from her cozy position cocooned inside a quilt, propped up on pillows, beside Alec. She was almost finished with the huge mug, and sleep still seemed an unlikely prospect. The images and thoughts that had been flitting through her mind were too intense and far too disturbing to allow that to happen.

Alec had collapsed just inside her front door and, after making a fruitless attempt to drag his unresponsive form to a more comfortable venue, she had finally relented and called on Tim for help. He had chuckled and staggered slightly as he had helped her maneuver Alec into her bedroom.

He had helped her tuck Alec in and then, on his way out, he had paused. "Talk to him, Kira," he'd said. "There are things you need to know."

And as she had puzzled over what that meant, she had found herself staring at Alec and drifting back across the years to their first years together. And she had come to some realizations. They weren't easy, and they weren't comfortable, but they were the truth. And she was at once eager and troubled at the thought of sharing her insights with him.

Lauren had asked that morning if he was worth it, and for a time she had also considered that question a little more seriously. The final answer had been a resounding *yes*. Perhaps her experience with Mike had been a blessing after all. It had shown her a stark contrast to what she had shared with Alec. It had given her a glimpse of the reality of the relationship world.

Perhaps Alec's and her relationship had been far from perfect, but it had been honest. They had never lied to each other. She blinked and looked away from Alec's face. Even with him asleep she had trouble facing him, because now she feared that perhaps she had lied to herself. And Alec had paid the price.

"Hey." She heard a faint whisper and turned to see him gazing up at her through bloodshot eyes that at that moment looked as innocent as a puppy's.

"Hey," she whispered back. She brushed a wisp of hair off his forehead. "How ya feelin'?"

"Like hell."

"Good. Maybe you learned your lesson."

"I doubt it. I've always been a poor student."

She should have smiled but she couldn't. "I'm so glad they didn't lock you up."

"Are you?" She started to protest but he continued as if he hadn't heard her. "I'd have thought you'd hate my guts after the way I talked to you the other night. I was rude and ungrateful, and—"

"No, you were right. I shouldn't be expecting gratitude for something I did by choice. And besides, I figured it's high time I stopped hating you for being honest."

"There's lots of other things to hate me for, right?"

That remark shocked Kira into silence. In the time it took her to struggle for words he managed to sit up and clutch at his head which no doubt felt like it was about to explode.

She finally found her voice. "I never hated you, Alec. I may have said some horrible things but I never hated you."

"Maybe not consciously, and maybe not overtly, but you did hate me." He lifted his head from his hands and met her gaze, and at last she understood. She had skirted the issue in her soul-searching because she had been unwilling to face that possibility. It had taken Alec's blatant accusation to shake her into facing it. "And I knew the exact moment it happened."

She licked her lips. "Yes, I think you're right." She tried to keep her voice even despite the fact that her heart had started fluttering like a swarm of butterflies.

"You admit it then? You admit that you blamed me for Cherisse's condition?"

Miserable, she nodded and gazed down at the half empty mug of tea she still held in her hands. "Yes. I admit it. I know it's totally irrational, and that my genetic makeup was just as responsible as yours, but..."

"But what?" His voice was tight with anxiety, and she hated herself for putting him through this. But it was necessary. And it was long overdue.

"But I think I needed to put the responsibility on someone—"

"And I was handy."

She closed her eyes and murmured, "Oh, God, Alec. I can't believe I didn't see it before. All my life I took on other people's causes, felt a responsibility to ease their suffering, or share their pain." She bit her lower lip so hard she thought she tasted blood. "And then, when I was faced with the possibility that I was partly responsible for my own child's suffering—"

"But it's nature, Kira! It was nobody's fault, for God's sake. There was no way we could have known."

She uncurled her legs from beneath her and set down her mug. She planted her bare feet on the rag rug beside the bed. Silently she stood and walked to the window.

"I know all that. God, don't you think I know that? But I know it...consciously. But emotionally, or subconsciously, or whatever you want to call it, I needed for it to be somebody's fault. I've never been religious so I couldn't blame God. I knew what I was in for when it came to caring for Cherisse and that I would have to watch her wither and die." She stuffed her hands in the pockets of her jeans and continued to gaze out at the moonlit landscape. "I knew I would have to bear that pain." She turned to look at Alec and felt a tear slip down her cheek. "I think I couldn't face shouldering the blame for her condition as well. You were close, and I trusted that you would stay and weather the storm with me no matter what. I think that I made an unconscious decision that it would be safe to punish you for her illness. I already knew that I would be taking on the majority of her care, so it was easy to shut you out of the rest of it."

"To shut me out of your life completely," he said bitterly.

"Maybe."

"But what about the sex? You didn't exactly shut me out of that." His tone was openly harsh and sarcastic, but she ignored it. He had every right to judge and condemn.

She took a deep breath. "I needed the physical comfort, and when we were together I could always shut everything else out. It was an escape and a haven and...and another way to punish you all rolled into one."

"By using me."

If Kira could have sunk into the floor and disappeared into a pit of black ooze she would have done so gladly. But that would have been too easy. She couldn't just disappear, or run from her problems. Or from Alec. But she couldn't quite bear to face him either. So instead she shifted her gaze back to the window. She studied the sky that had now cleared of cloud, leaving behind the twinkling, shimmering swathe of light that was the Milky Way. "I don't blame you for hating me, Alec. I could never expect you to forgive me for all that...and for the horrible things I said after Cherisse died. I don't know how you could ever live with what I did, especially when I don't know how I'll live with myself."

She was startled to feel his hands settle on her shoulders. She hadn't heard him get out of bed nor the sound of his bare feet on the old rag rug. But she felt the heat of his body against her back and she shivered slightly as his fingertips brushed over her skin. Then he rested his chin in the cradle of her neck and, when he spoke, his voice was husky and thick. "Do you know that's the first time you've ever really talked to me about how you felt about what happened?"

She was confused by his change of demeanor and intimate tone. She had expected him to rant and rave, throw accusations and possibly furniture. She had expected him to storm out of her house, and promise to never lay eyes on her again. She hadn't expected this. "Alec? I don't—"

"The day we got Cherisse's prognosis I saw it in your eyes," he continued, his chin still resting on her shoulder. "I doubt you realized it, but when I reached for your hand you pulled away from me. I saw you close yourself off to me and I saw the first glimmer of hate. Even then I knew you were focusing your hatred of what was happening onto me. I probably understood it better than you did yourself." She felt the warmth of his breath on her neck as he let out a long slow sigh. "I understood it, and to some extent accepted it. That kept me sane, but it didn't really make it any easier. The worst part was feeling so alone through all of it, not being able to share my grief—" His breath stilled against her skin. "And yours. Do you realize you never let me see you cry after that day?"

The question was rhetorical. She hadn't really thought about it, but it was true. Even on the day they were told that they were destined to lose their daughter within two years, even on the day that she died, and every day in between, Kira never cried in his presence.

Alec continued. "This is the first time since that day that you've let me back in."

"I'm so, so sorry, Alec." She just didn't know what else to say. She wanted to be eloquent and articulate, persuasive and charismatic—all the things he seemed to be so good at and she wasn't. She wanted to win him over with her charms and convince him of her love. But all she could do was apologize—empty, hollow, tired apologies that did nothing to assuage the way she had treated someone that she cared about.

He stood straight and with his hands placed firmly on her shoulders, turned her to face him. "Don't apologize, Kira. I don't want you with me because you feel obligated, or because you're settling some divine score. I want you with me because you want to be with me, because we're good together, and because we've got something special. You said before that you felt safe enough in our relationship to treat me that way. You trusted me to stick with you through the tough times."

She nodded weakly.

"Oddly enough, I think that's a good thing. You trusted me. Maybe you went about it all wrong, but that's something to build on. Just keep doing what you're doing—keep trusting me, and sharing with me. I think it's a step in the right direction."

"I'm scared…"

"See? That's the idea. You catch on quick."

She tried to smile as he drew her back to sit on the edge of the bed.

He sat down beside her and stroked her cheek so softly it sent chills to her toes. "Scared of what?"

"That I'll try and fail and hurt you all over again. I don't know if I'm strong enough to do this." She picked up his hand. "I don't even know if I deserve the chance."

"I'm hardly blameless in all this, you know. I could have tried harder, pushed you, threatened you, done whatever it took to make you see what was happening, and to let me have a part in Cherisse's life. But I took the easy way. I let you do it because it was simpler to just wallow in my own misery, and hate you right back."

She continued to stroke his hand, exploring the subtleties of form and texture that she used to know so intimately, but that she had almost forgotten existed. "How is it possible to hate someone that you love so intensely?" she mused quietly. It was more to herself than to Alec, a profound observation on human nature. She didn't expect a response, but she immediately felt the tensing of his fingers, and heard him catch his breath.

She looked at his face and his features were taut. Before she could question him about it, he pulled his hand from hers, stood and walked to the wall. He turned to face her and leaned back against the nutmeg-colored drywall, his left hand absently covering the injury that she knew must still be very painful.

"Why don't I get you something for the pain? Surely between your headache and that—"

"No!" He wouldn't look at her. "No," he said again, more softly. "There's something you need to know before we start blindly pursuing this new and wonderful world of love and forgiveness."

"What? What are you talking about?"

He still wouldn't look at her, and when he spoke his words were halting and uncertain and the anguish behind them tugged at her heart. "I meant it when I said I wasn't perfect you know. I-I thought my share of horrible things, too."

"You were allowed."

He shook his head viciously. "No, let me finish." He took a very long, deep breath before continuing. "That last year, in the evenings after I had finished with the cooking and the dishes and paying the bills, when they wouldn't let me work anymore, and I had nothing else to do but drink and worry, I started sitting out on the back deck to do just that. Then I started making these endless wishes as I watched each new star pop out every night."

He rubbed at the wound again and Kira stifled the urge to go to him. He wasn't finished and she needed to respect his needs even when they went against every instinct she had to comfort and intercede.

"Mostly they were pointless wishes for Cherisse to miraculously get better and for us to have a family like we dreamed of. Then they got even more specific and outrageous. I'd wish for Cherisse to graduate as valedictorian. I'd wish for the perfect wedding for her and, of course, the perfect husband."

Kira thought all this was sweet and endearing. She was confused by his apparent turmoil over his dreams, even if he knew they were destined to elude him.

"But toward the end they changed. I was getting so frustrated and tired and…and angry—angry at her for being sick, and angry at you for not being there for me." He closed his eyes and his Adam's apple bobbed slowly. "And then one night, just about a week before—before the end, I found myself wishing that she would just get it over with and die."

Kira bit her lower lip and winced when she aggravated the spot that had already been almost gnawed through earlier.

He continued blithely on, his words a stream of self-deprecation and guilt. "I just wanted my life back. I wanted a home without the constant moans and the hiss of the oxygen. I wanted to be able to sit and watch the hockey game without worrying that it would disturb somebody's fragile sleep."

At last he looked at her. "I knew I could never have my daughter back, but God help me, I wanted you back. If she had to die I wanted her to do it and put me out of my misery, and let us get to know each other again."

Kira watched helplessly as he sank to the floor, his back plastered against the wall, his knees up around his ears and his face contorted as he fought to hold back tears. "And then I realized what I had done—what I had thought. But I couldn't take it back. I felt as if Cherisse must have heard. At that moment I knew that she would always hate me for wishing such a horrible thing, and then of course a few days later she obliged me—she died."

Kira knelt beside him, feeling so powerless and uncertain. She wished she were big and strong enough to gather him up, and hold him and put everything back together the right way. It felt as if their life together was a puzzle that someone had dropped and reassembled all wrong. The pieces were all there, but they were distorted and mismatched, and the task of sorting through it all was daunting.

She decided the only way was to start small—one piece at a time. She laid a hand on his and whispered. "I don't think that was so horrible Alec, and I don't think it's so uncommon."

"Did you? Did you ever wish for her to die so you could get on with your life?"

"No," she said truthfully. "But all my energy was focused on getting her through. You had nothing to focus your anxiety on. And from what I've seen of my chemo kids' parents, I don't think that's an uncommon reaction. It's so hard to see your child in that kind of pain, and to face such a prolonged grief. I don't think it's a completely selfish thing to wish for it to be over." She stood and tugged on his hand, pleading with him to stand. "Especially when you know there's no hope." She led him back to the bed. He followed grudgingly, his footfalls so heavy they sounded like blocks of oak striking the floor.

She urged him to lay down and shuddered to see him wince as he hit the mattress. She leaned down and kissed the fine stubble of his cheek. "Don't be so hard on yourself. You're only human, prone to mistakes." She smiled. He met her eyes, and she felt an old familiar warmth spread through her chest. She had forgotten what it was like to share of herself—to share things with Alec. "Just like somebody else I know."

"Lay with me," he said quietly.

"I hardly think you're up to that, Mr. French Connection."

He didn't smile. "No, I just want to hold you." His voice was sleepy and soft like velvet. "I haven't held you in so long. I haven't held anyone in so long."

His eyes drooped and suddenly Kira was infinitely tired. Without a second thought, she slipped out of her jeans, and with a little bit of female magic removed the bra from beneath her T-shirt. She slid between the covers and nestled herself against him. He wrapped an arm around her and drew her in tight with her bottom against his middle, like spoons in a drawer.

She drifted off quickly, feeling more secure and content and deliciously tired than she could ever remember. The last thing she was aware of before sleep stole over her completely was his breath on the back of her neck, and the soft brush of his lips against her skin—the touch exquisitely intimate, yet oddly chaste and even more fulfilling than a night of carnal passions. Perhaps this was the first time they had truly been together since the day of Cherisse's diagnosis—without walls of anger and guilt and blame. With only a blanket of trust wrapped about them, and an infinity of possibilities before them.

Chapter Twenty-One

ꟿ

Gen jerked violently and her eyes flew open. "Shit," she hissed into the darkness.

She turned over and glared at the glowing green digits on her clock radio. But she was so bleary-eyed that even from a scant twelve inches away she couldn't make them out. She blinked and tried to clear her vision. But then she frowned, rolled her eyes and moved the highball glass that had been distorting her view of the numbers.

1:37.

She had finally drifted off after an hour and a half of tossing and turning, when that annoying *slip on the ice and fall on your butt* sensation had hit. The experts had some fancy name for it, but the term eluded her at the moment. All she knew was that it was annoying as hell to be that close to dreamland only to have it snatched away from her so rudely.

The last few nights she had been plagued by an uncharacteristic insomnia. The drink had been intended as a sleep aid but, unfortunately, the vodka with a splash of orange juice had turned out to be an inadequate remedy. She was painfully aware that the cause of her affliction couldn't be cured with a shot of liquor or a glass of wine.

She sniffed and looked out the window at the stars that continually taunted her sleeplessness with their glittering luminescence. Gazing out at them at this time of night was a vivid reminder that such things were the domain of poets and lovers.

She wondered if she would ever find herself privy to the heartfelt sighs, gentle caresses and bittersweet turmoil that apparently saturated the world of love and infatuation.

Infatuation. Perhaps that wasn't the correct term. Infatuation implied a one-sided, unhealthy, obsessive love affair. Like the way she felt about Alec Frechette.

She grimaced and rolled over so she wouldn't have to face those twinkling points of light.

In the privacy of her own bedroom, she could freely admit it to herself. Like a lovesick teenager who had homed in on a new heartthrob soap star, she had lost all touch with reality. She had indulged in the requisite fantasies and had snuggled up to shapeless pillows in a pathetic attempt to mimic the warm comfort of a sensuous male embrace. The fact that Alec's lips had actually been on hers had been fodder for her fantasy mill, and she resented him immensely for that. The fact that it could never—*never*—happen again stung like lemon juice on a paper cut. Not that she'd have a hope in hell of seducing him anyway. He loved another. That much was obvious, and oddly, in her own way, she wished him well. She wished it for both of them.

She sighed deeply. Perhaps some day she'd encounter her own version of The French Connection. Perhaps—

She heard the creak of a door. She bolted up in bed, instantly wide-awake and alert. *Someone's in the house.* The hinges on the swinging door between the kitchen and the hallway had squeaked for the past six months, and she had been meaning to buy a can of WD-40 in order to remedy the problem. Suddenly she was grateful for her tendency toward procrastination.

Adrenaline flushed into her system as she slipped out of bed and groped toward the dresser where her purse was stashed. She strained to hear the approach of footsteps, but feared that the brand-new carpet in the hall would provide an irritatingly effective barrier to such a warning.

Unfortunately, her bedroom door was wide open. She never closed the damn thing because it made her feel claustrophobic. She hated the feeling of being cut off. Funny how suddenly she craved it.

She rounded the foot of her bed and peered warily out the open doorway into the hall. She always left a small night light on in the bathroom next door. It was out, leaving only ominous blackness, affording her no hint as to the nature of the prowler. Fearing he was near, and fighting a wash of panic, she lunged for the dresser and the comfort of the Lady Smith and Wesson that was hidden inside the imitation leather handbag.

She latched onto the shoulder strap just as a leather-clad hand clamped over her mouth. Clutching the strap in a tight fist, she instinctively rammed her elbow back into her attacker's gut. She heard a gratifying grunt as her elbow sank deeply into his stomach. His hold loosened marginally, but when she hitched her hips to the side and landed a fist soundly against his testicles, his strength apparently abandoned him. He yelped in pain and let go as she scrambled away toward the open door. She continued to work at the clasp on her purse.

"Bitch!" he yelled, and she could feel his oily presence close on her heels.

He clutched at her oversized T-shirt and, for once in her life, she was grateful she hadn't bought new pajamas in the last decade. The worn material ripped away in his grasp, and she was free to stumble into the hall.

With sweaty hands and ragged breaths, she grappled with the clasp as she headed for the front door and the dubious safety of a residential neighborhood at one in the morning. She was just reaching for the knob when a body slammed into her from behind, plastering her to the door and knocking the breath clean out of her.

Gloved fingers snuck around her throat and he hissed in her ear as she struggled for breath, "Now you pay, bitch." He knocked her head forward against the oak. Her skull cracked painfully against the wood and the world wavered about her. But years of training paid off. She kept her wits about her. She kept alert. Kept thinking.

She could sense his form against her. He wasn't big, but still he was stronger than her, and possessed by forces she had no wish to imagine.

One hand tightened around her throat just as her fingers latched around the butt of the pistol inside her purse. But his other arm encircled her and pinned her arms to her sides, limiting movement and diminishing options. She struggled for breath and the presence of mind to angle the gun so as not to shoot herself even as she tried to disable her attacker.

"You think you're so special," he hissed. "But you're just another stupid, upstart bitch. Another whore. And you'll learn..." She tuned out his demented rhetoric and focused on saving her life.

Her bare feet were virtually useless and, in her current position, so was the gun.

As she struggled for breath, he leaned in and whispered fervently in her ear. "You want it, don't you? Just like all of them. Just like—"

He groaned as her skull crashed squarely into his temple. He didn't let go, but his hold relaxed enough to allow her to twist around in his arms and aim the pistol.

For a flash, she considered taking him in alive and unharmed. But only for a moment. Nobody called Sergeant Genevieve Turcotte a stupid bitch and got away with it.

* * * * *

She couldn't stop shivering.

Gen hugged herself tightly. She clutched at the soft cotton of her sweatshirt, and pressed her knees together to conserve heat. She had donned the sweat suit immediately, even before calling in the cavalry, but the thick, fleece material wasn't providing its usual level of insulation.

She gazed down the long, sterile corridor and tried by a sheer act of will to make him appear. But the only figures she could discern were the usual overworked nursing staff with their dull green scrubs, and intense expressions as they flitted about tending to patients and paperwork. A couple of officers in uniform stood a few feet away, discussing the evening's events in hushed tones, and occasionally tossing a wary glance in her direction.

The younger one with the knife-edge crease in his trousers ventured to speak to her. "You sure one of us can't take you home, Sergeant? There's nothing more for you to do here. The captain said—"

"I told you," she said irritably. "I'm waiting until he gets here. I need…" She dropped her eyes to her running shoes and swallowed the words that had formed on her tongue. "I need to discuss this with him."

"But—"

"I *said* I'm waiting for him."

"Yes, ma'am," said the young officer, somewhat sheepishly.

Ma'am. Gen hated that term. She knew it was a term of respect, but it made her feel like an old spinster on the verge of senility. *Ma'am* conjured up images of graying hair pulled back in a tight bun, double chins, and paper-thin skin. Instead of instilling her with confidence and authority, it made her feel weak and frail. For years she had held to the firm belief that the word *ma'am* should be reserved for women in supermarket checkouts and nursing homes. Her subordinates should be required to refer to her exactly as they referred to her male counterparts. Her femininity would not be threatened by the title *Sir.*

Sir implied respect, authority and control. It brought to mind a distinguished carriage and a decisive manner. The words "*Yes Sir!*" were followed by a sharp salute and a click of the heels.

The words "*Yes Ma'am,*" were followed by a warm smile and a book of coupons.

Sir should be a gender-neutral address. A slow, sly smile spread over her lips at the images those words brought to mind.

"Well, howdy, Mrs. Bobbitt!"

Gen's head snapped up at Will's familiar voice. "Where the hell have you been? I've been waiting here half the damn night. And I'm not in the mood for your snide remarks and tasteless humor."

Will stopped in his tracks and held up his hands in self-defense. "Whoa there! Sorry. I just meant—"

"I know what you meant." She stood abruptly. "Now can we get out of this hole. I'm sick of the smell of antiseptic, and I'm tired. I've had a rather trying evening," she said dryly. "I'll fill you in while we drive." She strode with purpose toward the exit doors, and heard Will's rapid footsteps catch up and fall in beside her.

"I'm parked just over here," he said in an uncharacteristically mellow tone. He motioned her toward his Mercury Capri parked just outside the Emergency Room doors.

Still hugging herself against that all-pervasive chill, she followed and waited in silence while he unlocked the passenger side door. She allowed him to open it for her, and she slid gratefully into the comforting warmth of the plush bucket seat.

Will took his position behind the wheel, and a moment later they were cruising beside the canal, lazily making their way back toward her house. The silence hung heavily in the car, and she knew he was waiting for her to speak first. They had almost reached her neighborhood when she finally found her voice.

"So where were you?" she ventured at last.

"Busy. I'll tell you about it in a minute. But for now I wanna know how you're doing."

"Fine."

"Mmm." He didn't sound convinced. "How about Stuart? Will he be peeing sitting down for the rest of his life?"

"I don't know, and I don't care. He got out of surgery an hour ago. He'll live, and he should be darn grateful."

She caught a grin flit across Will's face. "I'll say. You sure can take care of yourself. Remind me not to sneak up on you in the dark. Paige would never forgive me."

A ghost of a smile passed across her lips, but her face couldn't sustain it. She shrugged because she didn't know what else to say.

"You did good," he continued. "I'm glad you blasted him in the balls. The bastard had it coming."

"Yeah, well, it-it wasn't enough." Something surged within her that she didn't want to acknowledge. "But..." She cleared her throat because for some reason the words seemed determined to clog there. "But at least he won't be able to hurt anybody else."

"You sure you're okay? That must've been scary as hell, having him sneak up on you like that. Cop or no, that's enough to give anybody a severe case of the shakes."

She clasped her hands together to still the tremors. She took a breath and marshaled her defenses. "I don't need your condescending remarks, Will. Just because I'm a woman, it doesn't mean I'm weak and vulnerable. I'm a professional. I don't need—" To her horror a sob burst from her throat. "I don't—" She shook her head in a feeble attempt to regain control. "I just—"

The car had stopped in her driveway and, even as she fought back the unruly and humiliating tears that spilled out of her eyes, she heard her car door open, and felt Will's hands drawing her out of her seat. He wrapped her in his arms, and she made a weak attempt to push him away before conceding defeat and allowing herself to sob freely against his chest. All the terror and anguish and exhaustion washed out of her in wave after wave of unchecked emotion.

She had held herself together through the aftermath—questions and reports, the trip to the hospital and the limited paperwork that she could manage at three a.m. She had held onto her usual cool cop persona through all that, and had barely flinched at the knowledge that she had come *that close* to becoming another statistic. But suddenly and unexpectedly the *woman* who hid behind Detective Sergeant Genevieve Turcotte's carefully honed image had peeked out. For one terrifying, liberating moment she let herself be vulnerable. And, oddly enough, Will was the only one she could trust with that.

Sobs racked her lungs and spasms clutched at her body. The tears streamed down her cheeks and wet his shirt. She allowed herself to sink into his supporting arms as she purged the emotional toxins from her system. She had never before been so grateful for a warm embrace.

He held her in silence. His hands neither stroked nor placated, he just allowed her to cry and vent without question or interference. And she acknowledged to herself that this was the real reason she had insisted on waiting for him to take her home.

He was her partner, and he was a pain in the ass, but he was also a friend and someone she had learned to count on. Strong arms and a firm chest were a bonus, and she allowed herself to soak up his strength and compassion.

When the sobs subsided, he led her wordlessly toward her front door and unlocked it with the spare key she had given him a year ago when he had come in to look after her cat. Her cat had died a month later, but he had kept the key. Typical.

As the door closed behind them, she found herself smiling. She wiped at her eyes. "Sorry about that."

He frowned. "About what? Now you gonna offer me a coffee or what? We've got a lot of shit to go over, and I'm about ready to pass out from exhaustion."

She nodded meekly and led him toward the kitchen, ignoring the fingerprint dust and the police tape. The crime scene had been released and she intended to take that down soon. It had been ludicrous to put it up in the first place. What the hell were they thinking?

As she wiped away the layer of dust and assembled the makings for coffee, she felt her strength return, and the shivers ebb. Will would never speak of her emotional display again. He was an insensitive clod, but he was a good friend. And, oddly enough, he knew where to draw the line with his quips and insults.

She switched on the drip and settled down across from him at the kitchen table. After a few moments she said, "I gather you heard the story?"

He grinned. "Yep. Sergeant Matzold filled me in when he called and asked me to pick you up."

She nodded grimly. "I'm afraid I'll have a lot of shit to deal with, considering my method of self-defense."

Will shrugged. "You didn't kill him. I think they should give you a medal for exercising such incredible restraint."

She determinedly kept the smile off her face. "At least it's over. I suppose I should be glad he targeted me this time. I had the training and the presence of mind to defend myself, and now he's off the streets." The coffee had already ceased its sputtering. "The Rideau Rapist prowls no more."

"Well, not exactly."

"What?" Her eyes snapped to his. "What does that mean?"

He cleared his throat, apparently hesitant to share his news. "It seems we have a copycat after all."

She blinked stupidly. "A what?"

"You heard me."

"What are you saying? You mean there was *another* rape?"

He nodded, his expression bleak. "Yes, it happened almost simultaneously with Stuart's hit on you. That's where I was tonight."

"Jesus," she muttered, trying to assimilate this assault on her sense of plausibility.

"So, it seems I was right."

"Right?" Her mental processes seemed to have slowed. She was having trouble sorting through everything. Will's logic was twisted at the best of times but tonight she found it incomprehensible.

He just stared at her, and then slowly shook his head. "You really don't hear me half the time, do you?"

"What?" The one-word answers were irritating even to her, but they seemed to be all she could manage.

"I *told* you about my suspicions. I *told* you that I thought there were two sets of crimes."

"You never used the word *copycat!*" She was feeling unusually defensive.

"How else would you interpret it?"

"I..." Her mouth hung open. And then slowly she closed it.

"You never really thought about it, did you? You never even considered the possibility that I might have an insight, or see something that you didn't."

"No," she said too quickly. "It's—it's not like that at all."

But he just kept looking at her, his eyes intense and solemn. They weren't Will's eyes at all. They weren't the eyes of Will the Jokester, or Will the Irreverent. They were the intelligent, soulful eyes of a man she didn't think she knew. And gradually, as she gazed into those warm, gray depths she came to a realization. A disturbing realization.

She dropped her gaze to her hands clasped in front of her. "Oh God, Will, I'm sorry." She wanted to reach out to him but couldn't find the strength. She continued softly, "I guess I've always had this image of you as…" She didn't want to say it, but he said it for her.

"As a screwup?"

Her head hung just a little bit lower. "Yes," she whispered. "I know you're not. I mean…I see that you're smart and capable and…" She waved her hand weakly in the air as if trying to catch the words that had escaped her. "…and all that. But, with the way you act, I've gotten into the habit of treating you that way. And I guess…" She managed to lift her gaze to his. "And I guess I started to really believe it."

To her relief he smiled and shrugged. "I guess I can't complain. I've worked pretty hard at honing that image. I can't very well fault you for buying into it."

"Why?" she asked.

"Why what?"

"Why do you never let anyone see your serious side? Why work so hard at being a 'screwup'?"

He managed to look incredulous. "Are you kidding? If I let the world know how truly incredible I am, I'd have to beat the women off with a stick. I have enough trouble keeping Paige satisfied." He sighed deeply. "Besides, look what happened to Frechette. You think I wanna end up like him?"

"Right." She nodded grandly, deciding it safest to play along. Will's insecurities were his own. "I can definitely see your point." She got up to pour the coffee. "So what did you notice that alerted you to this possibility?" She filled Will's mug and placed it in front of him. "What did I miss?"

"There were just little things that didn't seem to fit. It was like there were two separate patterns. They were close enough that at first glance the differences were negligible, as if we were dealing with one perp and once or twice he just got a little careless, or maybe had to rush." He shrugged, as if he were a little uncomfortable in this new role. "But the main thing I noticed was that the bullet wounds weren't completely consistent. In all of the cases but two they were shot in the forehead."

Gen sat down at the table with her own mug. "The other two were shot in the temple."

"Yeah. And in those two cases the shots to the chest were just a bit off. He didn't quite hit the heart."

"Both of those women were still alive when they were found."

"Technically. It looks like our copycat doesn't know his anatomy very well. He's not a terribly efficient killer."

Gen closed her eyes in misery, not looking forward to asking this next question, but knowing she had to. She didn't want to believe this whole thing wasn't over. She didn't want to think about more women suffering. "So he struck again tonight?" Maybe saying it again would help make it seem real.

He nodded. "That's where I was when they called me to come get you. They didn't want to burden you with it just then, so I handled it alone."

Gen sighed heavily. "Who was it this time? Was she still warm when they found her?"

"Christine Brinston, the daughter of one of the MPs. She lives out near the airport. Same MO down to a tee." He finally reached for his cup and took a sip before adding as an afterthought. "Oh—except for one thing."

Gen looked at him suspiciously. He was being too cavalier. Something was up. "Yes?"

"She's alive and kicking."

Gen smiled broadly. "You're kidding, right? You're just trying to screw with my mind."

He shook his head grandly. "Nope. It seems Miss Brinston has taken some self-defense classes. She put up quite a fight." He peered at Gen out of the corner of his eye. "Seems like it was a good night for feisty broads."

"Finish the story." She tried to sound impatient but came off closer to giddy.

"She had a baseball bat under the bed and managed to knock the gun out of his hand. It flew out an open window. The one that he had climbed in through, apparently."

"Did he run?"

"No, he wrestled the bat away from her and tried to beat her to death with it."

"Christ."

"I guess he thought he succeeded when she lost consciousness."

"But?"

"But he never got a chance to rape her and she woke up in the ambulance, mad as a hatter, and eager to put the sucker away. She pulled off his ski mask in the struggle. She's working with a sketch artist even as we speak to come up with a composite."

"Did you find the gun?"

"No. There were some footprints in the flowerbed. Looks like he had the presence of mind to search for it. He must've found it because we couldn't find a trace."

Despite the setback, she could barely contain her excitement. Instead of being faced with another endless and daunting investigation, success was in their grasp. An eyewitness and a sketch. It wasn't a conviction but it was a damn good start.

She landed a hand on Will's shoulder and squeezed. "We'll get him, Will. Finally…we'll nail him. We'll nail them both."

"To the wall," he said cheerfully. "By the way, you got any sugar? You make lousy coffee, Turcotte. This stuff could singe the hair off my chest." Then, abruptly, he looked down and feigned surprise. "Oops. Too late."

Gen had to turn away so that he wouldn't see her laugh.

Chapter Twenty-Two

Mike LaRocque glanced at his watch. He had forty-five minutes before he was due at the hospital for his first appointment of the morning. He wove his Nissan Altima through rush hour traffic, quickly but efficiently slipping under yellow lights and swerving around anyone who dared take more than their allotted time to make a left turn, or pull into a parking space.

Mike felt sufficiently recovered from his encounter with Kira the day before. He had found his comfort elsewhere. He had sought solace and renewed his strength the only way he knew how. He sighed contentedly as he remembered and relived yet another triumph.

And so, he had awoken this morning, refreshed and rejuvenated and ready to face the task at hand. With calmed nerves and a quiet mind, he was able to reexamine the situation with Kira and had devised a new approach.

Kira's discovery of his lies had been unfortunate, but the damage was not irreparable. There was always another approach, another tactic. He had never before been unsuccessful when it came to setting his sights on a woman and luring her into his life, and eventually into his bed. Kira had been more of a challenge than most, and there had been an inordinate number of obstacles placed in his path, but even this setback could be overcome.

He had been caught off guard by her accusations and threats. He had been uncharacteristically paralyzed by this new development. But now he was more sure of himself. He'd had time to consider Kira's state of mind at the time, as well as his options.

In fact, with the recent developments, the challenge had taken on new and exciting dimensions. The thrill lay not only in the victory, but in the contest itself. What was the point of bagging the prey without the chase? Reeling in the fish held much more satisfaction if one's arms were weary from playing the line and battling the odds. And Mike *would* beat these odds. It was a matter of principle. A matter of pride.

But he needed to act quickly. He needed to act while Alec was still in custody, and her access to him was limited. He feared that the longer Kira was exposed to her old flame, the less likely she could be lured away.

Mike gritted his teeth as he thought of his competition. He had always admired Frechette. Alec lived the life that Mike could only dream of—a life replete with international adventure and luxuries too numerous to catalogue. Alec had his pick of the fastest cars, the finest wines, and the most beautiful and wealthy women in the world. And, thanks to Alec's inferior social position, none of them wanted an emotional attachment. All they wanted was an attractive man on their arm, and an adept lover in their bed. They didn't want commitment or children or fidelity, and he was rewarded with a six-figure salary and holidays on the Mediterranean. What man wouldn't salivate at the prospect of such a life?

Sure, Mike liked his work. He enjoyed helping those afflicted children, and even grew attached to them occasionally. But for him, medicine was essentially a means to an end. The prestige and lifestyle that went along with being a doctor was the real reason he had entered the profession.

Medicine was a business, pure and simple. Helping people and the rush that came with seeing a patient walk out the door a little bit healthier than when they walked in was often just a bonus—a perk in a profession that was all too often laced with stress and disappointment. No matter how selfish his motives for going into the *business,* losing a patient was never easy. Mike wasn't unfeeling, he was just realistic about the ways of the world.

His life might be lucrative but it wasn't easy. And the least he could expect was a little respect from his colleagues and the nurses and clerical staff who worked under him. And he'd be damned if Kira North was going to get away with judging and threatening him. She owed him. And, dammit, but she was going to pay.

* * * * *

Kira's eyes flickered open as a shaft of sunlight lanced through the blinds on her bedroom window and speared her retinas. She immediately closed them again and rolled over in search of a warm body and a gentle caress. But the other side of the bed was empty. Still groggy from sleep, she fluttered her hands across the mattress, thinking that he must be hiding somewhere amidst the rumpled mass of linens. But her search was fruitless.

As wakefulness stole up on her, she gradually accepted that he was definitely not in the bed with her, and then she glanced at the clock. It was eight-thirty, long past her usual wake-up call. She rarely needed an alarm clock as she almost always awoke on the dot of seven, and rolled out of bed eager to face the day, and anxious to focus her energies on those precious lives that needed her so desperately.

She indulged in a moment of regret for the patients who would ask for her that day but were destined to be disappointed. It was small wonder she had slept past her usual time, considering what time she had finally fallen asleep the night before, and considering that her day seemed to lack purpose.

But then she smelled the telltale aromas of baking and coffee and she smiled to herself. Perhaps today had a purpose after all.

She dragged herself from bed, slipped on a light cotton robe, and headed to the bathroom to tame the wild wreath of hair that tended to greet her every morning. Even satin pillowcases weren't able to coax her short hair into making it through a night without ending up in a wild tangle of spikes and horns.

She didn't want to take the time to douse her hair in the shower, so instead she wet it down as best she could before sauntering into the kitchen, her bare feet slapping quietly against the terra-cotta tiles.

She walked into the kitchen and smiled. Alec stood at the stove, tending to some mysterious creation, with a spatula in one hand and Cujo tucked snugly under his arm.

She was able to approach him, unnoticed, from behind, and wrap an affectionate but careful arm around his waist.

"Good morning, handsome," she said softly, her voice still laced with sleep.

"'Morning, beautiful." He turned and kissed the top of her head.

"You're up early," she observed. "I was supposed to wake up to your usual morning snorts and snores."

He laughed. "You're the one who snores, as I recall."

"I just never told you how noisy you are. I was trying to preserve your fragile male ego."

He drew up a little straighter. "There is absolutely nothing fragile about me." His voice dropped drastically, landing soundly in the macho male range. "I'm a man's man, virility personified, strong and tough, masculine through and through."

She rolled her eyes at his bravado and realized how much she had missed this familiar banter and teasing. "Oh, yeah, and you would never eat quiche or bake blueberry muffins."

"They're banana," he said defensively. "And the bananas were starting to rot. It was the only prudent thing to do." He popped a piece of bacon into Cujo's mouth.

"Did you put in chocolate chips?" she asked as he set Cujo down and the dog scooted over to his dog dish.

"Of course. How could I forget?" He put the last of the bacon onto a paper towel to drain and turned to face her.

She snuggled instinctively against him, her face against his chest and his arms wrapped firmly around her. "I've missed you, Alec." She murmured as she breathed in his familiar musky scent. "I didn't realize how much until just now."

He gently pulled away and tipped up her face with a finger under her chin. "You know that none of those women meant anything to me."

She quirked a half smile. "That sounds terribly cliché, Alec. Surely you can do better than that."

He didn't smile. His eyes were full, and his expression earnest. "No, really. I need you to understand that. I slept with them, and maybe even grew fond of some of them. But they were all using me and I knew it. I never allowed them to become a part of my life—a part of me."

"I understand that. But it wouldn't matter anyway. We weren't together, Alec. I didn't expect fidelity. I would never judge you for that."

To her surprise, he dipped his head and settled his mouth over hers. His lips stroked and caressed, his tongue barely flicking the perimeter of her defenses. The kiss was gentle but insistent, and it made her knees weak with anticipation. He separated only enough to murmur, "But I was faithful, Kira. Despite how angry and betrayed I felt, despite the women I gave myself to, despite everything, I was always faithful to you in my heart."

With those few words, he stole the breath from her very soul. She barely managed to whisper, "You do have a way with words, Monsieur Frechette. If you weren't injured I'd take you to bed right this minute."

He waggled his eyebrows, but his response was cut off by the buzz of the oven timer. "Ah, the muffins," he said as he let her go and regretfully reached for the oven mitts. As he pulled open the oven door he tossed her a glance from the corner of his eye and said huskily, "Don't underestimate me, *ma chère*. I just might surprise you."

Kira's insides coiled at the implication. She was oddly uneasy at the prospect of making love with Alec again, but her thoughts were rudely interrupted by the doorbell.

"Damn," said Alec quietly. "I hope the press haven't figured out I'm here. Tim and I had a hell of a time getting away from the hospital unnoticed."

"I'll be careful," said Kira as she headed for the door.

"And I'll pour the coffee," he called back. "Half a quart of cream, right?"

"Right," she replied, laughing. As if there was ever any question. Alec always remembered the little things, like what she took in her coffee and that she liked chocolate chips in her banana muffins. He had always known that she was a size five long and that she didn't like her lingerie to be too lacy. He remembered birthdays and anniversaries, and brought her flowers just because. She had been a fool to toss that all away. And she was damn lucky that he saw something in her that had tugged him back to her doorstep.

With that thought on her mind, she forgot her promise to be careful. Without checking the peephole, she swung open the front door, and her heart sank. "Mike."

"Good morning, Kira." Mike dropped his eyes and looked suspiciously contrite. He held out a paper sack. "I brought some pastries. I thought—"

"You thought you could bribe me with butter and blueberries?"

He lifted his eyes to hers and his jaw flexed. "I'm your friend, Kira. I just thought it was about time we addressed our differences. I think we both made mistakes. I would hate to lose you."

Kira had to restrain herself from slamming the door, literally in his face. "You never had me, Mike. That is what this has all been about, isn't it? *Having* me?"

Mike's eyes closed briefly, as he apparently worked at moderating his temper. "Can I come in so we can talk like civilized people?"

"That would imply that you're civilized."

Mike gripped the paper bag a little tighter, his knuckles whitening around the wrapper. "You haven't exactly been the model of honesty and integrity, Kira. Can't we—"

"No. Assuming you manage to get me my job back, I'll work with you, Mike. But, like I said before, we'll never be friends again. Friends don't lie and use each other." She felt a presence behind her.

"Truer words were never spoken," said Alec silkily.

The expression that passed across Mike's face at Alec's appearance wouldn't have been out of place at a vaudeville show. *Outraged and stupefied* barely grazed the surface of what Mike seemed to be experiencing. "Frechette?" croaked Mike. "You're—you're *out*?"

"Technically I was never *in*." Alec wrapped a possessive arm around Kira's shoulders. "But if you mean I'm no longer in custody, then you would be correct. The police have decided they have other suspects to investigate."

Mike blinked. "Other suspects?"

Kira felt a smug satisfaction in Mike's apparent confusion. "Sorry to disappoint you, Mike. But it seems that all your machinations were in vain. Alec is in the clear."

Alec cleared his throat uncomfortably. "I wouldn't go quite that far. As long as Darcy's murder is under investigation, I'm hardly off the hook."

Kira waved away his objections. "As far as I'm concerned, you're in the clear."

Mike's expression barely masked his irritation. "You're so quick to forgive murder and you won't even consider forgiving a few white lies?"

Kira's jaw dropped. "White lies?"

"Can we talk privately?" Mike's voice was low and intimate, and shaded with desperation.

Kira shook her head in disbelief. "You just don't get it, do you, Mike? We have nothing to talk about. You're not what I thought you were. You're not—"

"What I *am* is fed up!" The rage in Mike's voice shocked her.

She just looked up at him in astonishment, barely registering the tightening of Alec's hand around her shoulder.

Mike pointed a finely manicured finger in her direction. "You're willing to throw away a friendship and a potential for something wonderful, all because you've got the opportunity to have Alec Frechette back in your pants."

"LaRocque." Alec's words were a quiet warning that Mike chose not to hear.

He continued his tirade. "You criticize me for being promiscuous and for skirting the edge of ethics when it comes to trying to make you see how much I care about you."

Kira scoffed but Mike wouldn't allow her to speak.

"And yet *you* lie, steal, take advantage of your position at the hospital, harbor a felon—" He threw up his hands in exasperation. "I can't even list it all in one breath. You won't even give me a chance to tell you how I pulled out every stop in order to get you your job back. I risked my own job and my reputation with the board in order to get them to merely *consider* reinstating you. You should be on your knees thanking me, and yet you still have the nerve to cast stones at *my* integrity." He sneered at her and growled out the words, "You don't deserve me."

"Thank God." Kira set her jaw and clenched her fists. Any joy at the news that she had a chance at being reinstated was lost on the waves of rage.

Mike poked her in the chest. "Maybe you got what you deserved after all. Maybe a lowlife gigolo like Frechette is exactly what you nee—"

Kira had been so caught up in Mike's venting session that she hadn't noticed Alec let go of her shoulder and step toward Mike. She certainly hadn't expected Alec to land a fist squarely in the center of Mike's face.

Mike landed on the grass, groaning and pressing a palm to a gash on his lip.

Shaking with rage, Alec stood over him. Alec held his side, obviously in pain from the exertion but, when he spoke, his voice was strong and focused. "Get the hell out, LaRocque. When I first met you, I thought you had class. I even considered that maybe Kira *did* deserve somebody like you, instead of what I had become. But now I know the truth. You're lower than a snake's belly, and I don't let anybody talk to Kira like that." He sucked in a fortifying breath. "Or to me."

"You're nothing but a brute, Frechette," slurred Mike through his fingers. "You may have a Swiss bank account and a BMW, but you've got no class at all. In the end you'll get what you deserve."

"I certainly hope so," said Kira as she tugged Alec back toward the doorway. "I hope you both do."

She drew him inside and slammed the door. She flipped the dead bolt and turned her attention to Alec. A thin sheen of sweat coated his forehead and upper lip, and she wasn't convinced that it was due to anger. "Come with me," she commanded, drawing him toward the back bedrooms.

"But…what about breakfast?"

Kira was running on pure adrenaline and righteous indignation. Mike had maligned and insulted Alec, and indirectly caused him physical pain. Perhaps her decision to continue to work with the man had been premature. There were other hospitals. Other jobs. Other kids she could help. And right now she had a commitment to the man she was dragging back toward the bedroom. "Breakfast will keep. You're obviously in pain. I want to make sure you didn't damage yourself again."

He let her lead him and when he got to the bed he lay down gratefully. "God, that felt good," he breathed, referring to the feel of LaRocque's skin splitting beneath his fist. However, the adventure had its downside. That little burst of activity had sent a sharp pain cutting through his side, and he was still having difficulty breathing through it.

Kira lifted his shirt and began to check the dressing. "I have to admit I kind of enjoyed it myself. I could get used to having a bodyguard." She grinned but Alec didn't return the sentiment.

He studied her thoughtfully. "I get the feeling, though, that I'm missing something. Did something else happen between you two?"

Kira gently touched the gauze and satisfied herself that all was well. She re-taped the dressing. "It's not worth going into. He's not worth the trouble." He caught a glint of mischief in her eyes. "You sort of lost your cool there for a minute."

He chuckled quietly. Kira had a gift for understatement. "I guess I did. I find that's been happening with alarming frequency lately."

He still didn't feel quite up to heading back to the kitchen so he remained where he was and studied her face.

As usual, she sensed what her patient needed. Cautiously, she lay down beside him and examined his profile. "I'm not complaining. I like it."

"You'd rather be around a hot-head than a cool cucumber?"

"Yes. I think I would. I like knowing what you're feeling. I used to feel like I was guessing all the time."

Alec gazed at the ceiling. "I guess we both made a lot of mistakes back then. I thought you wanted me to be strong. So that's what I was."

"Tears don't make you weak."

Puzzled, he frowned and looked at her. "Tears?"

"You know how I never let you see me cry? Now that I think about it, it was mutual. The night she died, I walked in and found you holding her. I remember that you had tears in your eyes, but the moment you saw me it was like they evaporated."

"They dried up because you immediately threw your accusations at me." He said it quietly, with no edge and no judgment. He didn't intend to sound harsh or angry. It was the simple, honest truth.

She dipped her head in silent acceptance of his words. "Yes. I suppose I got very good at throwing out accusations." She sighed and lifted her eyes to his again. "But other than that I don't remember ever seeing a tear in your eye. I guess I didn't think anything of it, because you had been so stoic for so long. Plus men aren't supposed to cry so easily. But, you know, we never grieved together." She touched his cheek. "We shared Cherisse. We shared something wonderful, but then when we lost her, we couldn't share that."

"I did cry." Alec's whisper was barely audible as the memories clogged in his throat and misted in his eyes. "After we argued that day I got a motel room. I—" His breathing caught. "It hit me so hard I was afraid I'd never be able to stop. I'd lost Cherisse. I'd lost you. I'd lost my career."

She stroked his cheek, silently encouraging him to continue.

"I remember stepping in the shower. I had the water so hot I was afraid it would burn my skin, but I stayed because somehow the steam and the sound of the shower helped me pretend it wasn't happening. I don't know how long I was in there, but by the time I got out the water was cold." He had leaned against the tiles and let the pounding water wash away the river of tears that he had been so unwilling to admit existed. Eventually he had sunk to the floor of the tub, spent and exhausted, and still the river refused to run dry. He had felt like his whole world had evaporated in a single, mind-shattering explosion that left behind nothing but a great, gaping void. The tears hadn't healed him. They had only left him feeling more empty. And infinitely alone.

"And you didn't cry again after that, did you?"

He shook his head. "I decided I'd wallowed enough. I had to find a new direction for my life." *I had to try to fill the void. I couldn't bear to be alone again.* "That afternoon I placed the call to the French embassy."

"Wait a minute!"

Her sudden exclamation startled him. His eyebrows pulled together. "What?"

"What do you mean you'd *lost* your career?"

He didn't answer her.

She sat up, and fixed him with a steely stare. "I know that business with Kent was difficult, but surely you didn't take responsibility for it! It couldn't have been your fault. There's no way—"

"Kira."

She stopped and watched as he propped himself up on a stack of pillows.

He sighed heavily. "No, they didn't fault me. But the truth of the situation had to remain undisclosed, and I knew that with the shroud of secrecy I would always be looked at with suspicion by my colleagues. Kent died bloody, and I got away unscathed. It looked damn suspicious. I didn't blame them for mistrusting me. Even the captain wasn't privy to the whole story. I wasn't forced out, but I decided I didn't want to face that. With everything else that had happened, my path was clear. I made the decision to leave."

"What? Why on Earth was it such a big secret?"

"I told Internal Affairs, and no one else. I couldn't take the chance of the story leaking out to Kent's family. I owed him that."

"Owed him? You're talking in riddles, Alec. What the hell happened that you had to go to such lengths to protect a dead man?"

He looked at her and decided that perhaps he'd protected a ghost long enough. He owed Kent a lot, but perhaps he owed Kira more. "Do you really want to know?"

"Yes! Of course I do. It's obviously painful for you, and I want to be there for you now." She swallowed against a lump that had apparently formed in her throat. "Especially since I wasn't back then."

"Kent stepped into the line of fire intentionally."

Her mouth opened but no sound came out. Finally she managed to croak out, "He killed himself?"

"Not with his own gun, but...essentially yes." He closed his eyes in misery, and let the images play against the backs of his eyelids. "I watched it happen. I thought he was behind me as we were making a retreat out of the warehouse. We had stumbled across the smuggling operation by accident, and had decided it best to get out and call for backup. The thugs hadn't seen us yet, and we could have gotten out no problem. But I had gone about twenty feet—I was almost to the door—when I heard Kent shout." He opened his eyes and his voice trembled as he recalled the images. "I turned around to see him standing in the middle of the floor, surrounded by a half a dozen armed drug dealers. He trained his gun on the head honcho and said, 'You're gonna die, motherfucker'." Kent's voice had been strong and authoritative, but the sweat on his forehead and the quivering of the gun had told the true story. Kent was terrified, and Alec had never felt so impotent in his life. "He looked over at me, and in that moment I understood what he was doing."

"They shot him," she whispered.

He nodded miserably. "Fifteen rounds hit him. He never even got off a shot. I watched helplessly as…" His voice trailed off as he pictured the last moments of his partner's life. He could see that young, vital body shuddering as the bullets drilled into him. The youthful persona that was Kent Elliott—bright and funny, tough yet compassionate—had ceased to exist. Kent was the quintessential boy next door and he hadn't deserved such an end. He hadn't deserved it, but that was the end he had sought. And in achieving success he had doomed Alec to relive that moment of absolute helplessness and anguish, over and over, in his dreams.

He forced himself to continue, "And I had to run like a coward before they trained their AK-47s on me. But I had no choice. He was dead."

"You don't have to explain to me. You did what you had to do."

He remained silent. That was true, but it didn't change the facts or take away the nightmares. But perhaps sharing the story, and sharing a little of the grief was a positive step toward healing—toward filling the void.

He felt her fingers stroke his arm. "You said you understood. Did you know he was considering suicide?"

"Not exactly. But—" Alec chuckled nervously. The story he had just told was a breeze compared to what came next. "He-he died for love. He had confided in me that he had fallen in love with someone. Head over heels, fireworks and earthquakes kind of love. But his feelings weren't returned. He'd been despondent over it for weeks. So in a way…" He shrugged. "I guess I should have expected it."

"You can never expect something like that, Alec. You can't hold yourself responsible because he lost his heart to a woman and made a rash decision."

Alec formulated the most difficult words he'd ever spoken in his life. "Not a woman, Kira. Me. Kent had fallen in love with *me*."

"Oh, God," moaned Kira. Her stomach coiled into knots at the implications of what Alec had just told her. "Kent was gay?"

He nodded. "I had worked with him for almost two years and had no idea. The day he confessed to me I was just as shocked as you are now."

Kira suspected she had blanched, since she felt somewhat lightheaded. She couldn't imagine Alec facing something like that, knowing that Kent had likely felt an attraction to him almost from the beginning. "But..." She struggled to understand. "What did he hope to gain by telling you? He knew you were heterosexual. He knew—"

"He knew you and I were having problems. I confess that I had begun confiding in him—leaning on him quite a bit in the weeks before he told me. I knew he was young, but I was with him so much of the time, and I desperately needed somebody..." His voice trailed off and Kira felt sick that Alec hadn't been able to count on her when he'd needed her.

He sighed. "I'm afraid he misread my friendship and the trust that I placed in him. He had wondered if I was bisexual. Or maybe I should say he hoped I was."

"I take it no one else knew of his preferences."

"No. Not his fellow officers or friends. Not his family. He took a big risk by coming out to me."

"How did you handle it?"

"I was stunned. I'm afraid I wasn't as sensitive as I should have been. But I wasn't exactly cruel either. After the initial shock, I calmed down and tried to let him down easy. But I had to make him understand that nothing could *ever* come of his feelings."

"He was devastated," Kira observed.

"To put it mildly." Alec adjusted himself on the pillow and focused his gaze on the ceiling. "He sank into a depression. He became difficult to work with, and I was considering requesting a new partner assignment, especially since it had become awkward. I suspect he was also worried that I would spill his secret. I take it his family wasn't very tolerant, and he lived in mortal fear of them finding out."

"I think he had a lot of other problems besides a broken heart, Alec."

"Maybe." He turned to look at her again. "But I was the last straw. I suspect he was even trying to save his family the embarrassment of a suicide. So he saw an opportunity and he took it."

"So you kept his secret to protect his family from embarrassment."

"Not just embarrassment. They had lost a son and a brother. There was no need for their memories of him to be tainted as well. He was a good kid. He was just mixed up." And Alec had sacrificed the trust of his peers and likely the respect of his own family.

She laid a hand gently on his shoulder, wishing that she could lift just a little bit of the weight that rested there. "Except that it left you shouldering his burden. It looked like you had acted rashly and had endangered him."

Alec shrugged. "Like I said, I had decided to leave anyway." He looked away. "In a way Kent's confession helped me make that decision even before he was killed."

Kira already felt somewhat overwhelmed by the whole story, and that cryptic comment only served to heighten her anxiety. She shook her head and gave him a quizzical look.

"The fact that he saw me that way just confirmed the way I had begun to see myself. As a sexual object. It made it that much easier to hire myself out and let those women use me."

He smiled a sad smile that tore open Kira's heart. "He helped me find my niche."

Kira wanted to sink through the floor. "I'm so sorry. Alec, I—"

He grabbed her shoulders and shook her. "No, Kira. *I'm* sorry. I didn't tell you that to make you feel guilty. We've been through this and, as far as I'm concerned, it's over. We're starting fresh. Besides, I made my own decisions. I take responsibility for them."

"Still..."

He stroked her cheek. "Still what?"

"I wish things could have been different."

"Wishing doesn't change anything. Believe me, I know. You have to make your own dreams come true."

She studied him in the late morning sunshine. His eyes glistened with the sunlight and a few unshed tears. They were so green they didn't seem real. "What are your dreams now, Alec? Where do we go from here?"

He leaned into her until his forehead rested against hers and their noses touched. "I'm not sure. But I know one thing. I want to go there together."

She laced her fingers through the hair at the nape of his neck.

He closed his eyes but didn't touch her.

"I've missed you, Alec," she whispered. "Have I told you that yet?"

"Actually, I think you have." He opened his eyes and gazed into hers. "What happens now?"

She dropped her hands to the hem of his shirt and proceeded to peel it over his head. "Now I make love to you," she said when he was bare-chested.

He smiled with his eyes. "I thought that was 'contraindicated' in my condition."

"Oh, I think you're up for what I have I mind."

"Oh?" She could tell he was intrigued and she had to work hard to suppress her own smile. "What does that mean?"

"It means you don't exert yourself. And you let me do all the work." She pushed him back onto the pillows. "And I won't take no for an answer."

"Who's arguing?" Mischief danced in his eyes and she didn't think she'd ever loved him so much.

But then she sobered. "Don't make light of this, Alec. I—"

He shushed her with a finger on her lips. When she was silent, he cupped her jaw in his hand and drew her close. His hands were warm on her cheeks and his breath as sweet as the memories she had tried to forget.

"I didn't mean to," he whispered. "I've missed you, too, Kira. It's been too long since I've made love with someone."

Her heart clenched as she grasped the full spectrum of his life over the last years. Maybe for some men recreational sex was a dream come true. Great sex with no strings and no commitments sounded like a man's idea of heaven. But not all men were ruled so completely by their hormones. Not men like Tim Nickle. And not men like Alec. He'd had a gaping hole in his life the last seven years—a hole that she had drilled, and perhaps a hole that she alone could fill.

She bent low and lavished a delicate kiss on his lips. She shared her breath with him and teased his lips with her tongue. The familiarity of the touch and the melding of their souls settled inside her and grew until she ached with a profound need to be with him.

She drew away just enough to be able to focus on his eyes. "You're mine now, Alec Frechette. As of this moment, the French Connection is *dis*connected."

She didn't give him a chance to respond, but homed in on his mouth again, this time the contact fervent and possessive. She crushed his mouth beneath hers as her hands massaged his chest and her tongue sought his. He groaned in pleasure and the warm reverberations set up housekeeping in her heart. The kiss took on dimensions of ferocity that almost frightened her, and she felt his arms lock around her back.

With some effort, she withdrew her tongue from the recesses of his mouth and nipped at his lips. She peppered kisses across his eyelids and cheekbones and then whispered, "I've always loved your cheekbones. Did I ever tell you that?"

He tried to shake his head, but she had already lowered her mouth to his chin. She gently raked her teeth across the sharp angles of his jaw. "And your jaw. You have a wonderful jaw."

"You talk far too much," he groaned. "And you have far too much clothing on."

He slipped his hands inside her robe and snuck them up under her T-shirt. The feel of his hands on her bare skin sizzled through her, stoking the long dormant fires of passion. His fingers skimmed her ribs and massaged her breasts until a moan of pleasure escaped her own lips.

She obliged the unspoken request and sat up to shed the robe and T-shirt. They landed in a rumpled heap in the corner, and left her clad only in a pair of white cotton underwear. She hadn't owned a pair of frilly panties for six years. She had a feeling her lingerie closet was about to undergo a dramatic overhaul.

She raked her eyes down his torso, taking in the gauze and tape, the rippling abs and the feathering of auburn hair that trailed down into the waist of his jeans. She traced a finger across his ribs and followed the slight crease down the center of his abdomen. She bent to kiss his navel. "You've let yourself go, Alec," she murmured as she tasted the familiar saltiness of his sweat. "We'll have to start working out together again." She unsnapped the button of his jeans.

He chuckled as she worked the denim down over his hips. "Yes, ma'am," he said through his grin. "I—" He sucked in his breath. "Christ!"

She slid her lips up and down his shaft, alternately stroking and allowing her teeth to hint at hidden dangers. She tasted and taunted, laved and loved.

He muttered a few more expletives in French, and she could see his knuckles gripping the bedcovers.

She gloried in his pleasure. She had never done this before. She had always let him take the upper hand in lovemaking, and allowed him to please her. It wasn't because the idea had repulsed her, but it had never seemed necessary before. Now it did.

She reached around him and clutched at his buttocks. He raised himself slightly to meet her, and she lost herself in the thrill of her gift.

But a moment later she was startled to feel his hands on her shoulders. He bodily dragged her away from her mission, and pulled her up until they were eye to eye again.

"You're a devil," he breathed.

"Why did you stop me?"

"Because I want to share this with you." He grazed his thumbs across her nipples and she felt them tighten at his touch. "I want to be inside you."

"I live to please you," she said with a smile. She wriggled out of her underwear and straddled him. Slowly, deliciously she slid over him, encasing him inside her and letting him fill the hole in her own soul. She had sought healing in her chemo kids, sought to ease her own suffering by easing theirs. But the remedy had been inadequate. Perhaps she had been too quick to overlook the one person who had shared her pain and who could complete her healing—who could fit the puzzle pieces back together.

He began to undulate his hips in response to her, but she leaned down and whispered against his lips, "That's my job. Relax and let me do it."

He smiled up at her, his eyes glazed and dreamy. She kissed him, urgently but quickly. Then she sat up and began to move her hips in a provocative rhythm that teased and cajoled and excited. His eyes closed and his jaw muscles flexed.

The memories of old pleasures crashed over her like a tidal wave, but mixed in with the tide was a new sensation of sharing and singularity—as if they had truly joined together as one for the first time in their lives. The barriers of grief and blame and guilt had tumbled, allowing them to truly touch each other again—allowing them to cross the void of the years and find what they had lost on the day their future had been snatched away so cruelly. Perhaps they had a future after all. It was just a different one.

Alec opened his eyes and locked her gaze with his. She could feel the wave approaching and could see it in Alec's eyes as well.

He found her hands and laced his fingers with hers. He squeezed as the wave crashed over them, leaving them both breathless and glowing with sweat and satisfaction. She collapsed over him, her breasts grinding into the damp, curly hairs of his chest, and she heard him whisper into her hair, "All right, you've convinced me."

She smiled and flicked her tongue at his nipple. "Convinced you of what?"

"That I'm yours for keeps. Wild horses couldn't drag me away from you now."

She stacked her hands and propped her chin on her knuckles. She studied him intently, allowing the warmth of his skin to seep into her like the heat of a sauna on a cold winter day. "I figured it was about time I took my turn. From now on, it's fifty-fifty. In everything."

He stroked her back. "Does that mean you'll help with the cooking?"

She stifled a chuckle. "I don't know about that! I think—" Her breath caught in her throat and she sat up abruptly. "Oh, God, Alec. What have we done?"

He frowned at her. "I thought that was fairly obvious."

"No, no!" Her heart was beating double-time as she considered the possible consequences of her recklessness. "It's the middle of the month." Panic rose up inside her like fresh lava in a long dormant volcano—searing hot and deadly. "We didn't take any precautions. Oh, God!" She covered her mouth. "I can't do that again. I can't—"

"Kira!" He practically shouted the word at her, and he was gripping her shoulders so tight she almost winced at the pressure.

"What? We just—"

"Stop it! It's all right. There's no reason to worry."

"What the hell are you talking about? There's every reason to worry!"

"Just relax and listen to me for a minute. There's something I need to tell you, and I need you to hear what I have to say. All of it." He waited while she steadied her breathing. "Okay?"

She battled confusion and panic but conceded. "Okay. I'm listening."

Chapter Twenty-Three

ℌ

Lauren glanced at the forlorn form on the couch. "How ya doin', sweetie?"

"I'm fine, Mom. You need help with the dishes?"

"No, no. There isn't much. Most of it will fit in the dishwasher."

"Okay." But Rachel's voice sounded far from okay. She sounded weak and exhausted. It was dialysis day. Dialysis runs were scheduled for every other day, and invariably by the time the second day of the cycle was drawing to a close and the time of her run approached, Rachel had begun to feel the effects of the toxins that her dormant kidneys were unable to purge from her system. As the waste products steadily built up in her bloodstream, Rachel's energy level and sense of well-being declined. But she seemed even more withered and drawn than usual. She had barely sipped at her soup and hadn't touched the loaf of fresh French bread that was usually one of her favorite indulgences.

Lauren wondered if Rachel's worry over Kira and Alec's adventures over the last few days had taken its toll. Rachel's ability to cope with all the challenges she faced continually astounded Lauren but stress could not be ignored as a factor that wore on the body. No doubt Rachel's youth and naturally optimistic outlook helped matters. But everyone had limits.

Lauren poured soap into the dishwasher and flipped the soap holder closed. She snapped the seal shut and began the cycle. How would she ever have coped without the modern conveniences of a dishwasher and a microwave? How did people cope with this kind of illness back in the days of outhouses and ringer washers? Then she smiled grimly. Back in those days, Rachel would never have survived this long. They would likely have lost her twelve years ago. They would have lost so much.

She strode into the family room and planted a kiss soundly on Rachel's forehead.

"Checking for a fever?" asked her daughter suspiciously.

Lauren granted her a half smile. "You know me too well." She sat down beside her daughter and focused on the noon-hour newscast. "Actually, I just felt the urge to kiss you. Sometimes I love you so much it scares me."

"Oh, *Mom*."

"You'll understand someday—someday when you have a child of your own."

"Dialysis patients are poor pregnancy risks, Mom. You know that."

"Not after they get a transplant."

"I don't know. There's all those anti-rejection drugs and..." Rachel shrugged listlessly. "And I've got to get a kidney first."

"It'll happen. I know it." Lauren stroked her hair. "You have to think positive. You have to—"

"Mom!" Rachel pointed to the television. "Are you listening?"

Lauren switched her attention to the urgent words of the anchorman on the screen. They both listened with rapt attention as the events of the previous evening were related to Ottawa's concerned citizenry.

"There were *two*?" repeated Lauren incredulously.

"Shh!" hissed Rachel, but a moment later, she giggled at the news that one of the perpetrators had effectively been castrated by a well-aimed bullet.

"That should be mandatory in these cases," whispered Lauren, who had just gained a new respect for Detective Sergeant Turcotte.

But she quieted again as the anchor continued. "The police are confident that an arrest is imminent. The latest survivor of the atrocities is battling her injuries to work with a sketch artist and come up with an accurate rendition of her attacker. Hopefully this image will be available later today so that it can be released at a press conference this evening."

"Wow!" Suddenly Rachel's fatigue seemed to evaporate. "So that means Alec is off the hook for good!"

"So it would seem," said Lauren through a grin.

"I wonder if they know. We should call them right away."

"I'm sure they know. But maybe we can stop by later this afternoon to offer our congratulations."

"Really? Could we?"

Lauren laughed. "You are completely transparent, you know."

The sound of the front door startled them both. They looked up to see Tim drop his briefcase in the kitchen and settle himself heavily at the table.

Instantly on alert, Lauren rose from the couch and crossed over to him. "Tim? Are you okay? I thought you had appointments all afternoon."

He dropped his head into his hands. "I canceled. I think it's the stomach flu." He swallowed audibly. "I think I need to spend the day in bed."

Lauren touched his cheek. His skin was clammy. She tipped up his chin and, when he looked at her, she thought she'd never seen him so miserable. His complexion was waxy and his eyes dull and listless. "You're right. You look terrible."

He smiled weakly. "You sure know how to kick a guy when he's down."

"You okay, Daddy?" Rachel had entered the kitchen.

He looked at her and Lauren could swear a wave of pain washed over his face.

"I'll be fine." But his voice was thin. "It's nothing a little peace and quiet can't cure."

"Did you hear the news?" asked Rachel brightly.

He licked his lips. "News?"

"Yeah. Alec's off the hook."

Tim smiled and for a moment a spark of vitality returned to his features. "Oh, that. Yes. I'm glad he doesn't have anything to worry about. He deserves some happiness."

"That's enough chattering," said Lauren with authority. "Let's get your father to bed."

He let them lead him from the kitchen, an arm draped over each of their shoulders. Lauren thought he must be feeling very weak indeed, considering how heavily he leaned on them. But when they got him into the bedroom he shooed them away.

"Let us tuck you in, Daddy," pleaded Rachel. "You always look after me. Now it's my turn."

"Next time," he placated. "I'd just like to soak in a hot tub and slip between the sheets. I don't think I've ever been so tired."

"Can I get you anything?" asked Lauren as she helped him out of his suit jacket.

"No, but there is one thing you can do for me." He settled himself on the edge of the bed.

"Name it."

"Go away."

Lauren frowned. "What? You're kicking us out?"

He grinned but his eyes weren't in it. "Uh-huh. I meant it when I said I wanted peace and quiet. Besides…"

"Besides what?"

"Rachel has her run this afternoon anyway. Why don't you two head out a little early and buy yourselves something frilly. Or maybe get yourselves some new earrings or something. A big investment is paying off in a few days, and it's been ages since I've gotten you anything extravagant."

Lauren was skeptical. "What big investment?"

He waved away the question. "None of your business. Now get out of here." He was trying to sound flippant, but the effort at levity seemed to cost him. His shoulders sagged further, and his smile slipped away, leaving behind an expression shadowed by pain.

"I don't know," hedged Lauren, as she continued to evaluate her husband and weigh his words. "Rachel wasn't feeling the best."

"I'm better now, Mom. And I *did* see a really cool pair of earrings down on Spark Street."

Tim was staring at her, his eyes pleading and…searching. She felt oddly uncomfortable under his stare. She shifted her gaze to Rachel and frowned. "Well…"

"Ple-ease." Tim and Rachel chorused in unison. They had practiced that particular ploy for years until they got it down just right. Whenever they ganged up on her like that, she didn't have a prayer.

"All right." She walked over to Tim and cupped his cheeks in her hands. "Promise me you'll sleep and won't work on that darn laptop?"

"I promise."

"I'll hold you to your word, Tim Nickle."

He grabbed her hand and pressed a kiss to her palm. "I've never broken my promises to you, Lauren. You have to believe that."

That confused her. "What?"

He stood and pointed toward the bedroom door. "Now go. But I want a big kiss and hug before you leave."

Rachel moved toward him, but Lauren stayed her with a hand on her arm. She looked at her husband. "You know better than that, Tim. If you're sick—"

"Mom!" cut in Rachel as she shook of Lauren's restraining hand. "If he's contagious he probably gave me the germs two days ago." She turned toward her father, and said with authority, "Let me look after myself."

To Lauren's surprise Tim didn't protest when Rachel wrapped her arms around his neck and planted a big wet kiss on his cheek. This lack of concern wasn't like him at all. Lauren's sense of unease mounted, but she didn't interfere.

The hug lingered but at last Rachel pulled away and said, "You take it easy and get better, Daddy, and I'll bring you home a surprise."

"You got it, angel." He stroked her cheek and traced the line of her jaw. He seemed to be studying her face, looking at her in a way that reminded Lauren of the way he used to gaze at his brand-new daughter as she lay snuggled in her crib—with awe and a trace of wonder. He said softly, "I'd do anything for you." He swallowed and dropped his hand to his side. "Anything."

Rachel pulled away and hustled toward her own room to gather up her things.

Lauren approached him and was surprised by the fierceness of the hug that greeted her. He mumbled into her hair. "Do you know how much I love you both?"

"Of course, Tim. What's wrong?"

He kissed her cheek and stroked her hair. "Nothing."

She pulled away and held him at arm's length. "That's nonsense. There's something going on. You're not acting like yourself at all."

He shook his head. "Don't worry so much, honey. I'll be fine. It's just this damn flu making me all emotional." He chuckled but the sound was weak. "I threw up at work and I swear I thought I was dying. I haven't felt this sick in ages. I just need to be alone for a while, that's all."

Lauren frowned again. "If you're sick, being alone is the last thing you need."

"Just trust me, okay?" His voice was a little stronger, his expression set. "I know what I'm doing. And besides, Rachel needs you."

"I don't know..."

He chuckled and drew her close. "Will you take your life in your hands and let me kiss you?"

She found herself smiling. "We've shared enough viruses over the years. I guess I'll risk it."

He settled his mouth on hers and kissed her deeply. His embrace was tender yet intense, the kiss laced with passion. And in that moment she sensed none of the fatigue and misery that had so concerned her just moments before. It reassured her, if only a little.

When he pulled away she started to speak, but he had already propelled her toward the door. "Now go and let me get some rest."

She stepped into the hall, and he had already closed the door behind her.

"Ready, Mom?" called Rachel.

Lauren studied the bedroom door. Despite his reassurances, something struck her as being not quite right. Something was wrong with Tim and she suspected there was more to it than a simple case of the stomach flu. But he often needed time to himself. Perhaps it was best to let him work it out on his own. He'd share it with her eventually. He always did.

"Yeah, I'm ready. But let's stop in on Kira and Alec before we go."

Rachel appeared with her purse and a smile. "I hope they get married. It'd be neat to have them both for neighbors."

"Yes. That it would."

* * * * *

Alec flipped a pancake expertly onto a plate.

Unwilling to leave their sanctuary, they had picnicked in bed on fruit and muffins and coffee, but eventually hunger had spurred them out of the bedroom and into the kitchen. It had been years since Kira had tasted his fluffy creations and she had insisted on pancakes and bacon for lunch. She had decided against sharing the fact that she'd gone shopping the previous afternoon, stocking up on the ingredients on the off chance Alec would feel up to satisfying her craving. He didn't need to know exactly how *much* she missed his cooking.

With the tongs, he plucked up a slice of bacon from the paper towel and laid it on the plate beside the golden disks.

Kira snatched the plate away and drowned the entire thing in maple syrup. "Well, it's about time," she complained as she settled down at the table with her treasure and a glass of milk. "It sure took you long enough."

"Haute cuisine takes time, *ma chère*."

She snorted. "Blueberry pancakes are hardly haute cuisine." She stuffed an enormous morsel into her mouth—and sighed in ecstasy.

"Perhaps not *regular* pancakes. But mine approach nirvana." He relished the ecstasy on her face as she downed the first bite and dug in for another.

"You think very highly of yourself."

"Perhaps. But I seem to recall that Cherisse ate my pancakes long before she ate any other solid food."

Kira's chewing slowed and a warm smile tickled at her lips. "Granted. But I'm sure the fact that they were dripping in maple syrup had absolutely nothing to do with it."

"She did have quite the sweet tooth, didn't she?" Alec ladled more batter onto the griddle, but his mind was lost in his memories. Ever the politically correct parents, they had tried so hard to shield the toddler from the terrors of sugar and candy. But despite their efforts, by the age of one she had already managed to taste a variety of sinful delights and had reveled in each and every one. Once she was diagnosed, however, they had thrown caution to the wind and, as long as she could chew and swallow, she was free to eat as many suckers and chocolates and as much ice cream as she could handle. She had handled quite a bit. Most of the smiles that Alec remembered were sticky ones. And every one filled his heart.

"Mmm. Can't imagine where she got it." Kira pointed a crisp strip of bacon at him like an accusatory finger.

"I have a very discerning sweet tooth," he said smoothly.

Kira chuckled and crunched into the salty treat. "Can you believe I had already worried that she would have to watch her sweet tooth when she got to be a teenager?" She looked up at Alec and he met her gaze. "I worried that she'd always have to watch her weight." She shook her head sadly. "Funny how those concerns seem so ridiculous now."

"She wasn't pudgy as a baby, though," he said quietly.

"No. She was perfect."

"All green eyes and fiery hair and man, could she wail!" Alec's eyes flitted mischievously toward Kira. "Can't imagine where she got *that*."

"I don't scream that loud," she said defensively.

"No. Only on roller coasters."

"That's half the fun."

Alec flipped another pancake. "God, this feels good."

Apparently Kira knew exactly what he meant. "Yeah." She sopped up the last of her syrup and stuffed a dripping hunk of dough into her mouth. "We never really had a chance to remember together. At least not the happy stuff."

"I'd give anything to make more happy memories, Kira. I'm sorry you were so angry."

She sighed heavily and pushed her chair back. She crossed over to him and wrapped her arms around his waist. "I wasn't angry. I was surprised."

"You were angry."

"Okay, I was angry. Making the decision to deny yourself children forever, whether with or without me, was very rash and very hasty." She nuzzled her face against his chest. "But I suppose I have to forgive you since I love you so much my chest hurts."

"I did what I had to do, Kira. I don't regret it. If you want children you shouldn't be with me anyway."

"I do want children. But I want you too."

She said them lightly, but those words cut him. "You can't have both. It's as simple as that."

"There's always adoption," she said hopefully.

"You know what the waiting lists are like for that, and anyway…"

"What?" she whispered. "We're sharing everything now, remember?"

He hated to say this, since it sounded so selfish and shallow. But he had to be honest with Kira, and he had to be honest with himself. "Honestly, I've heard too many horror stories about adoption. Even if you manage to get an infant, often you're inheriting someone else's problems, and you face endless turmoil as they hit their teens and twenties. I've been through one heartbreak. I don't think I could face another."

"Okay."

He looked down at her and blinked. "Okay, what?"

"I pick you."

"Just like that? What about your maternal urges? Your biological clock? Your dreams?"

"Honestly, I pretty much gave up on the idea of children years ago, but I had to be sure of your feelings. We can be happy without children, Alec. But I—" She looked at him with an expression that wrapped around his heart. "But I can't be happy without *you*."

He closed his eyes and hugged her tight.

"Besides, I don't think I could face those risks either. But you have to grant me one concession."

The mischief glinting in her eyes worried him but he had to ask. "Yes?"

"I will need something to focus my caregiver energies on, so we might just have to adopt an army of Chihuahuas."

"Oh, God," he groaned. "I'll never get any peace."

The phone rang.

"See what I mean?"

Kira pushed away from him and picked up the receiver as he refocused on the last of the creations on the grill.

"Uh…Alec?" said Kira as she held out the receiver. "It's for you."

He frowned. Who knew he was here? The cops. Dammit, he didn't want to deal with that right now. But apparently there was no avoiding it. He took the receiver with a sense of resignation. "Yes?"

"Monsieur Frechette?"

The voice sounded vaguely familiar. "Yes, that's me."

"This is Ted Bridges. I'm the executive secretary for the Right Honorable Jonathan Cromwell."

Alec vaguely remembered the man who had flitted about the mansion booking appointments and shuffling schedules. Alec had barely spoken to him, but apparently it was enough that he recognized the voice. But then he found himself wondering why on Earth Cromwell would feel the need to contact him. "Yes?" he said tentatively. "What can I do for you?"

"His Honor is requesting a private meeting with you."

Alec's eyebrows lifted and he noticed Kira watching him intently. "Now, why would he want to do that? He thinks I killed his granddaughter. Is he planning to shoot me?" Or perhaps he was packing that infamous butter knife.

"Quite the contrary, Monsieur Frechette. In light of recent developments he would like to extend a formal apology, and he wants to do it in person."

"Recent developments?"

The other end paused. "Haven't you heard?"

"Heard what?"

"About the arrest. They've caught the rapist. One of two, actually. But they are confident they'll find him soon. And the victim has confirmed that it *wasn't* you."

Alec blinked dumbly as he absorbed this information.

"Monsieur Frechette?"

He shook his head to clear the cobwebs. "Th-the victim?" he stuttered. "You mean she's alive?"

"Yes."

"Well…who did they catch?"

The other end sighed, and Alec caught a hint of impatience. "I'm not sure if they've released a name yet. But must we go into all this now? The Governor General would like an answer."

Alec still felt somewhat off balance, but he managed to say, "Uh…when does he want to see me?"

"Whenever is convenient, but he was really hoping to do it soon. This afternoon if possible. His Honor is mortified by the horrible circumstances you found yourself in and, while he bears no responsibility for them, he regrets that such events transpired under his roof, and he feels a responsibility for the pain you experienced."

It shocked Alec that the Governor General could see beyond his own pain, considering he had lost his granddaughter mere days ago. But in light of that, perhaps

Alec should make an effort to comply with the man's wishes. "All right. How's two o'clock?"

"Fine. He'll look forward to seeing you."

They bade each other farewell and Alec set the receiver back in its cradle.

"Well?" asked Kira impatiently.

He briefly summarized the conversation for her, and was pleased to see the radiance burst across her face at the news that he was indeed free and clear of suspicion.

After the requisite whoop of joy and a few hugs and kisses, she glanced at her watch. "It's one o'clock already. Are you going to go in that?"

He glanced down at his faded jeans and T-shirt. "Uh—I guess I should head back to my place and change first."

"Do you want me to come?"

"No. I'm pretty sure he expects to meet with me alone. You clean up the kitchen while I'm gone."

"Gee, thanks."

"It's the least you can do after I've fed you. Fifty-fifty, remember?"

"How cruel of you to use my own promise against me."

He lavished a slow kiss on her lips. "I'll be very grateful if I return to sparkling counters."

She waggled her eyebrows. "I do like the sound of that."

Moments later he had donned his shoes and pulled open the front door. He was just about to kiss Kira good-bye when he noticed the approach of two familiar figures.

Lauren and Rachel, faces glowing with pleasure, were striding down the front walk.

"It would appear that you heard the good news," said Kira as they reached the door.

"Yup," said Rachel brightly, with a soft blush for Alec's benefit.

Lauren extended a hand. "We wanted to offer our congratulations."

Alec shook it and bowed smartly. "I appreciate the courtesy, but I'm afraid I have to make tracks, ladies. I have a mansion engagement to attend."

"Oh, really?" asked Lauren with a curious lilt.

Alec pecked Kira on the cheek and edged past the two women. "Kira can fill you in. I really have to go."

As he left he overheard Lauren say to Kira, "Good, and then I've got a favor to ask of you. I'm worried about—"

Alec slipped in behind the wheel of his BMW, which Kira'd had delivered there after his hospitalization. He glanced at the three women and thought absently that they made a very handsome group. Tim Nickle had been damn lucky to have them to himself all these years. But now he was going to have to share them. It was damn well about time.

* * * * *

Dr. Mike LaRocque folded the handkerchief and stuffed it back in his pocket. Apparently he had disguised his voice sufficiently to fool dear Monsieur Frechette.

Alec would be occupied for quite some time. It would be at least two hours before he figured out that the summons had been bogus. And in that time Mike would have had ample time to persuade Kira that she had made a mistake.

All he needed was a little time alone with her. Surely he could make her understand.

Mike's fingers flexed and relaxed. His palms were damp and clammy. Despite the respite of the previous night, the stress of the past few days was wearing on him. He wanted Kira North, and he was used to getting what he wanted.

If it didn't come to him willingly, then he took it. He made things happen. He was a man of consequence. Not someone to be trifled with, and Kira had to understand that.

She *would* understand that. Or she would pay the price. Just as another had done just a few short hours ago. Others had denied him and felt the sting of his fury. She would be no different.

He dabbed at the sweat that dribbled down his forehead. He would hate to do that to Kira. Her future was so bright and promising. But he couldn't allow her to walk all over him. Nobody screwed with Mike LaRocque and got away with it.

Nobody.

Chapter Twenty-Four

Kira tried in vain to stuff the pancake griddle into the dishwasher. She tried moving a few plates and changing the pitch, adjusting the angle—maybe if she took out a rack…

She laughed at herself. In the time she had spent trying to fit the stupid thing into the automatic appliance she could have washed it by hand twice over. She plopped it in the sink to soak and snapped the dishwasher shut.

She glanced around the kitchen. Bacon crumbs littered the table, and little dribbles of batter and grease speckled the stove. This was the reason she never cooked. She hated cleaning up. Eating a sandwich over the sink demanded very little in the way of cleanup time. *Mind you, it was also lonely and pathetic.*

Resigning herself to years of scrubbing and whining, she grabbed a dishcloth and soaked it in hot water. She was just about to brave the greasy stove when Cujo's frantic yapping alerted her to the possible arrival of a visitor.

Without hesitation, and secretly glad of the interruption, she tossed the cloth in the sink and headed for the front door. No one had knocked yet, so she peeked out the front window, and let out a string of curses that would have made a Merchant Marine blush.

"Mike," she whispered under her breath. Who *was* he? Tenacious didn't begin to describe his behavior over the past few days. "Stubborn" barely scratched the surface. Perhaps "obsessive" was the correct label for her former friend and confidante. She made sure the dead bolt was engaged before stepping back from the door and considering her options. If she opened the door to him, she had little doubt he might actually force his way inside in order to facilitate persuading her to reconsider her decision.

Wasn't it convenient that he had found her alone? Had he been watching the house, just waiting for an opportunity to catch her without her newly acquired lover slash bodyguard? The idea made her shudder.

She heard his clipped steps on the flagstone walkway, and knew she had to make a decision, and she had to do it quickly. Either grab the gun out of the coffee can, and threaten his manhood in order to convince him of her sincerity or…

Just as the doorbells chimed and Cujo erupted in a frenzy of indignant yaps, an idea struck her. She knew exactly what to do.

*****

"Here." Will held out an enormous Styrofoam cup and a plain paper bag.

Gen glanced up from her computer screen. "What's this?" she asked suspiciously.

"A hefty dose of sugar, fat and caffeine. Just what the doctor ordered."

She frowned at the mysterious bag that likely contained enough calories to balloon her out to the size of a pregnant hippopotamus. "Eclairs?"

Will nodded.

"All right. If it makes you happy." Keeping her face poker straight, she snatched the goodies away from him. "But you owe me one."

Will chuckled as he settled down with his own treats. "Did you get any sleep after I left last night?"

"A little."

"How's our resident wart-faced slime-bag doing?"

"He'll have a catheter for weeks," she said through a sugary grin.

Will grimaced and crossed his legs. "That hits just a little too close to home, you know."

She shrugged. "Funny, but the captain also looked awfully uncomfortable while we were having our little chat a few minutes ago."

"I don't know what he's got to worry about," snorted Will. "Even at close range you'd have a hell of a time hitting that tiny—"

"Will!" She put a stop to his tasteless humor, but she couldn't shake the odd sensation of euphoria that accompanied a good sound indictment. She let out a light sigh. "Stuart's case is ironclad," she said in an effort to stay on track. "Now that we've got him, we'll see about matching his DNA to some hair samples found at the other scenes."

"Too bad he didn't leave prints. That would be so much quicker."

She nodded. He had been careful. But not quite careful enough.

"Any word on the sketch?" mumbled Will, his lips already ringed with icing.

She nodded and took a sip of gloriously hot coffee that had been liberally diluted with cream and sugar. "I just talked to Chip. He called to say he was bringing it right over. He just finished with our courageous victim a few minutes ago. She seems pleased with the rendition."

"Good," nodded Will approvingly. "I just hope it gets us somewhere."

"Hi ya, Gen," warbled a high-pitched voice that set her teeth on edge.

Chip Heyer, the resident artist, strode in, oozing charm.

The coffee soured slightly in Gen's stomach. It was common knowledge that Chip had designs on her. But the thought of actually touching him set her skin to crawling. She was of the private opinion that he was gay, but just hadn't quite figured it out yet. He was in denial, and Gen figured that he saw her as a convenient way to prove his heterosexuality. In other words, she might just be desperate enough to go out with him.

It figured that the one man who was attracted to her was apparently hunting down his dates among the wrong sex. Could her life *get* any worse? "Hi, Chip. You got the picture?"

"You bet!" He was already handing the computer-enhanced sketch across the desk.

"Thanks. We'll call if we need anything else."

His face fell at the obvious dismissal. "All right. Hope it helps." He tossed Will a contemptuous glance before leaving their office and closing the door softly behind him.

"Guy hates me," lamented Will. "It's been three years since I laced his sketch pad with itching powder. Some people just can't take a joke." He had already rounded the desk to take stock of the picture over Gen's shoulder.

The moment he caught sight of it he breathed, "Holy shit!"

His sentiment mirrored Gen's. She swallowed thickly. "Dammit! He seemed like such a nice guy."

"Yeah. This one's not gonna be as much fun as I thought."

She stood and grabbed her purse. "We better get going."

For once Will had no witticisms to share as they exited the office in silence and headed for the car.

* * * * *

Kira slipped in through the sliding glass doors off the Nickles' back deck. Just as promised, Lauren had left it unlocked to allow her to get in without disturbing Tim's fragile sleep. She locked the door behind her, and stepped into the kitchen, her footsteps echoing on the sparkling tile floor. The house seemed quiet. Unnaturally so. Of course it was empty, save for a sick man who was supposed to be snoozing quietly in his bed, but still…

She hugged herself against an odd chill that shimmered over her skin. She looked around the room, and peeked into the family room, half expecting to find a ghoul watching her from the dim corners.

She shook her head in self-deprecation. The last few days had no doubt gotten her paranoia juices flowing. She brushed herself off as if she could physically wipe away the odd sensation of foreboding.

She made one final visual sweep of the room before heading toward the master bedroom.

She hoped it had been long enough to allow Tim to finish with his bath and slip into bed. Lauren had informed her of her husband's plans, but had worried that either he would end up working in bed on his laptop, or that he would be so sick that he wouldn't be able to care for himself. She had asked Kira to check on him to make sure he was resting peacefully, and not locked in battle with his insides while he worshiped at the porcelain pedestal.

Kira smiled as she recalled Lauren's mildly fretful tone as she spoke of her husband. She had tried to sound flippant but the genuine concern in her eyes had been all too evident.

Kira reached her destination and knocked ever so gently at the bedroom door before pushing it open. She really hoped he was in bed. The last thing she wanted was to walk in on him, soaking, naked and vulnerable, in his Jacuzzi tub. But when she stepped into the bedroom she found it empty, the bedcovers undisturbed. She listened cautiously for the swish of water from the en suite bath, but all was silent.

She frowned and was just about to turn around when she sensed a presence behind her.

"Kira?"

Tim's voice startled her. She whirled around and looked up in surprise to see the face of a stranger. His face was haggard and etched with lines of fatigue. His eyes were dull and his shoulders drooped. He looked ten years older than the last time she had seen him. "Tim? Why on Earth aren't you in bed?"

He just looked at her, his chest rising and falling heavily as if every breath required a supreme effort of will.

Kira began to feel uncomfortable. "I'm sorry I came in without knocking. But Lauren asked me to check on you, and she didn't want me to disturb you by ringing the bell. "

"You shouldn't have come," he said simply. He swallowed, his Adam's apple rising and falling as heavily as his chest. "God, Kira. Today of all days, couldn't you have minded your own damn business?"

She chewed on her lip, suddenly feeling like an intruder in the dwelling that had been almost as much of a home for her as her own house. "I'm sorry. But she asked and—"

"You have to go, Kira. Now."

"I-I can't. I was hoping to stay for just a few minutes, and anyway…" She tried to read him but couldn't. "You don't look well. I think I should stay and—" At that moment she registered the fact that Tim was holding something in his hand.

Clutched at his side, his knuckles whitening around the dark, gleaming metal, was a Beretta Cougar—a sleek, semi-automatic weapon that had no business being in this house, let alone in his hand.

Her eyes riveted to the pistol, she spoke through her confusion, "Tim, why are you holding that? I didn't even know you owned a gun."

He didn't answer for a long time, and when she finally lifted her eyes to meet his, tiny shards of ice pricked at the back of her neck. His eyes shimmered with unshed tears and he sighed so heavily she thought she would wilt from the sadness on his breath.

"Tim?"

"I'm sorry, Kira. But you...being here changes things. But, then again, maybe it's better this way after all."

"Better what way? What on Earth are you talking about?"

But he didn't answer the question. Instead he muttered, "I hate to do this to you, but—"

Too late, she sensed the movement of the gun and a moment later stars blasted across her retinas and pain lanced through her brain. The world went dark, but her last thoughts weren't of fear. Her last conscious thought was that something was terribly wrong with Tim, and she hoped that he would be okay.

* * * * *

Alec tapped his foot impatiently as he stared out the picture window at the expansive green carpet and abundant flowerbeds.

The Governor General had called him there to apologize and now he insisted on making him wait? Somehow, the etiquette of such a scenario struck Alec as faulty. But then he chastised himself. The man was grieving. What right did Alec have to complain about a little breach of protocol?

Alec brushed at nonexistent lint on his black khaki trousers, and double-checked that the white polo shirt was relatively stain- and wrinkle-free. He had decided he was taking a break from suits and tuxes. He was taking a break, period. He had decided that he was taking Kira on an extended, and much deserved vacation. Other than the week at her parents' cabin, they'd never really had a holiday together. Maybe somewhere tropical, but not the Mediterranean. He'd had his fill of those particular azure waters.

He fought a grin as he considered the problem. Perhaps a honeymoon in Hawaii…

He heard the creak of the heavy, oak doors and he turned to greet his former employer.

Jonathan Cromwell stalked into the room. As he strode toward him, Alec mused that the man had aged significantly in the days since his granddaughter's death. There were lines around his eyes and mouth that seemed to have deepened. His pallor was gray and wan. Actually, the hard, cold set of the Governor General's face and the deeply etched lines reminded Alec of cracked gray granite. Except for his eyes. Jonathan Cromwell's eyes burned hot with what Alec could only describe as hatred.

Cromwell stopped mere inches from an already wary Alec. "What the hell are you doing here?" he spat. "You've got a lot of nerve, setting foot in this house again, after what you did!"

Alec shook his head in confusion and tried to step back a foot or so to gain a feeling of control over his personal space. "I was *asked* to come. I was under the impression that you wanted to make a formal apology."

A flurry of emotions passed over Cromwell's face. "A-apology?" he sputtered. "Are you insane?"

Alec had to remind himself to close his mouth, which had involuntarily gaped open. He reined in his temper and spoke evenly. "Yes. I was told that in light of the arrest last night, you regretted the fact that I had gotten sucked into such an ugly situation."

"*Situation?* Is that how you refer to my granddaughter's rape and murder? You arrogant, pompous, self-absorbed…" The words sputtered and died on the waves of fury.

"Are you saying…sir," Alec said the word with difficulty and measured his irritation out in manageable doses, "that you did *not* summon me here today?"

"Of course not. You're not only a pervert and a sex fiend, but you're delusional as well."

Alec stepped away another few feet. He crossed his arms over his chest and leaned back against the enormous maple desk. "I'll ignore those insults since I know you're grieving and not completely responsible for your actions."

"I meant every word, Frechette. You may not have killed her, but you slept with her against my explicit instructions. You took advantage of Darcy's innocence—"

Alec's loud guffaw drowned out the rest of his speech. "Darcy Cromwell was about as innocent as a rabbit in heat."

"You son of a bitch," growled Cromwell. "How dare you ravage the memory of my flesh and blood?"

Alec held up his hands impatiently. "Forget it. You can put her up on a pedestal and give her a half a dozen halos for all I care, but I want to get one thing straight."

"Make it quick, before I have security throw you out."

"You are telling me that your personal secretary did *not* call me a little over an hour ago and request this meeting?"

"I really don't see how he could have done that," said Cromwell as he strode toward the door, "since I excused him from duties until we've had a decent period of mourning. He left for a vacation in Australia yesterday." Cromwell thrust open the door. "Now get the hell out of my house, and I don't ever want to lay eyes on you again."

Alec stuffed his hands in his pockets and took his time walking toward the door. He held his head high as he passed, but hesitated a moment to say with sincerity, "I hope you never find out the truth about Darcy." He met the other man's gaze. "It's funny how the truth has a way of shattering our illusions."

"Get out."

Alec left the mansion in silence, grateful to leave behind the memories of death and pain and uncertainty. He looked forward to a future without such things. He decided it was high time he started focusing on hope for the future, instead of regrets from the past.

But as he drove a nagging question plagued him. Who would have wanted to lure him to the Governor General's mansion? Had someone merely wished to humiliate him or perhaps cause Cromwell more pain? And if it wasn't the secretary, then why did that voice sound so familiar?

He played the telephone conversation over and over in his head. He squinted his eyes in concentration, as if that could help him hear the voice more clearly in his mind. Then he sifted through all the people he'd met since his arrival in Ottawa. He went over a half a dozen conversations before it struck him. *LaRocque!* That son of a bitch! Alec floored the accelerator. The dear doctor hadn't wanted to lure Alec *to* the mansion. He had wanted to lure Alec *away* from Kira.

What did he have planned, anyway? Did he really think he could persuade Kira that he wasn't slime? Or was he thinking of something a little more direct? That thought made Alec's stomach twist into knots.

He pressed the accelerator a little harder and vowed to persuade Mike LaRocque, once and for all, that he was sniffing up the wrong tree. Sometimes the only commands a stupid mutt understood were those that were accompanied by a good sound whack from a rolled-up newspaper.

* * * * *

Kira's temples throbbed and her eyes felt like lead weights had been stitched to the lids. She tried to rub her forehead and her eyes, but her hands seemed loath to cooperate.

She managed to crack open one eye, and then the other. She opened them wider and instantly recognized the pale gray tiles and warm cherry cupboards of the Nickles' kitchen. That was not so unusual. However the fact that she was tied securely to one of their dinette chairs was.

"Thank God," muttered a familiar voice. "I was afraid you'd never wake up."

She blinked away the cobwebs and gazed down at herself. Smooth nylon cord had secured her torso and shoulders to the high-backed chair. She sensed that the same cord bound her wrists together, and held her ankles to the chair legs. She turned bleary eyes on her friend. "What—I—" She shook her head in confusion. "I don't understand!"

Looking like he barely had the strength to move, Tim dragged one of the other chairs over so that he sat knee to knee with her. He still held the gun. He cradled it in his hand like he was comfortable with it. Like it was an old friend. His thumb stroked the butt occasionally, as if to reassure himself that it was close and accessible.

He studied her. "Yes. That's why I waited for you to wake up. You're my friend, Kira, and you need to understand."

She tugged at her bindings and tried to ignore the pounding in her temples. "Understand what? What the hell has gotten into you? Guns and ropes? Are you having a nervous breakdown? Is the fever making you delirious?"

"No, Kira." His voice was low and sad. "I'm completely in control of my faculties." He smiled wanly. "Maybe not sane, but I *do* know exactly what I'm doing. And…" He looked away as if he couldn't bear to meet her gaze. "And it is important to me that you understand why I have to do this."

"Do what?" she said as panic and confusion swirled through her.

He reached out as if he wanted to touch her, but then he pulled away. His hand shook visibly. "I'm the copycat killer, Kira. My picture is the one that is going to be broadcast all over the city tonight. I don't have much time, and I need to make you see—"

"What? You're talking crazy! You couldn't hurt a fly, let alone rape and murder anyone. You're delusional, Tim. You're—"

"*Quiet!*"

The absolute rage in his voice halted the words on her tongue. But as quickly as he had lapsed into fury, his face smoothed over, and the anger was replaced by sorrow.

"Just…just let me explain."

She waited, fighting to keep her breathing steady and her heart from leaping from her chest.

"I did it for Rachel."

"Rachel?"

"Yes." He stood and paced to the counter. He turned to face her and leaned back against it. He gazed at the gun as he spoke. "After the second murder I got this crazy idea in my head." He actually smiled at the apparent irony of his words. "One of my clients knew the family of the woman who had died and he told me that she had been an avid supporter of organ donation. He figured I'd be interested because of Rachel's situation." He sighed deeply. "Of course he was right." His thumb stroked the gun. "Anyway, none of her organs were usable, of course, because it was too long between the time of death and the time that she was found. In my research, I found that organ donation is not reserved for those who are deemed to be brain-dead. There is actually a two-hour window from the time of death until the organs are no longer usable. Even a little longer in the case of the more stable organs like the heart and kidney." He met her eyes and Kira fought a chill at his words. "Of course, I decided I couldn't leave it all to chance. I had to take steps to make sure the odds were as much in favor of organ harvesting as possible."

"Tim," she breathed. "This is insane. You can't possibly be telling me—"

"Of course I can, Kira. I'm not making this up. It's all real. Painfully real." He spoke so calmly, so confidently. Her mind balked at the possibility he could be telling the truth.

"You—" Her mind struggled to get a grasp on these developments. "You mimicked the murders?"

He nodded. "I pulled in some markers. Some of my clients were cops, or had connections in the police department. Feigning concerned curiosity, I managed to get details on the murders that weren't available to the general public." He crossed to her and sat down in the chair again, his knees brushing against hers. "The papers printed that the victims were raped and shot. They didn't divulge the level of brutality, or the details of the shooting."

"D-details?"

"Yes. He always shot them twice, in a very specific manner. He shot them first in the forehead and then in the heart." He managed a sardonic smile. "It was almost like he wanted to be damn sure they were dead."

She shook her head and pain speared through her.

"You see—" His manner changed. He leaned forward and his eyes were earnest, almost eager. He actually seemed excited about sharing these details with her. "It was so simple. It was perfect because he wasn't targeting whores or hookers. He targeted high-class, healthy women who were low risks for AIDS and other diseases that would have precluded them from donation. He was smart enough to wear a condom and not leave semen for DNA identification, and he never left fingerprints. I couldn't have asked for better.

"So I had to come up with a way to increase the chances. Eventually I figured that if I shot them in the chest, but deliberately missed the heart, and then shot them in the temple so as to miss the brain stem…" He leaned back and shrugged as if to say the rest was obvious.

Kira finished for him. "It still looked like the Rideau killer and they were more likely to live a little longer."

"Long enough to make it to hospital. Especially if I called 911 immediately after the attack. I would call from the house but not speak or give them any information. They'd trace the call, and send cops and ambulance to those kinds of calls as a precaution. So it looked as if the victim called just as she was attacked or just before succumbing to her injuries."

She swallowed, her mouth suddenly as dry as Death Valley. He had thought it all out so thoroughly, with such calculated precision. The fact that Tim was capable of such analytical madness terrified her. "And it worked?"

He nodded miserably. "Yes. Twice." He stood and pounded a fist against the counter in rage. "The first one wasn't a match. That kidney ended up going… God knows where. After all my hard work—" He spoke as if the victim had owed him something. As if his methods were legitimate and valid. As if he weren't completely insane. "And then the second one…"

"Rachel was sick and couldn't go under anaesthetic."

He whirled on her. "Yes, goddamit! That would have been it, you know. I wouldn't have had to do it anymore." He paced the length of the room, gripping the gun until his knuckles went white again. "Do you know how much I hated doing it? Beating and raping those women? But I had to! I had to throw suspicion off myself by making the crime as accurate as possible."

"Tim!" she shouted. "This isn't you! The man who married Lauren and is a wonderful father to Rachel could never perform such horrors!"

He took a menacing step toward her. "Don't you see? I did it for them! It was my fault that Rachel ended up on dialysis in the first place. She's young and vital. She has her whole life ahead of her."

"And what about those other women? Didn't they deserve to live too?" She shouted the words and immediately regretted it, fearing it would antagonize him into doing something even more outrageous than tie her to a chair.

But he continued as if she hadn't spoken. Apparently, the victims were of no consequence. To Tim Nickle, his family was everything. They were, quite literally, the whole world. "She deserves a chance," he said with passion. "She deserves a life without machines and feeling like her life is always going to be on hold." He stabbed himself in the chest with a rigid finger. "I had the opportunity to give that to her, and I took it. Because of me she almost died. It was my responsibility to give her a chance to live." Sweat beaded on his forehead and trickled down his temples, past that finely sculpted brow and those almond-shaped eyes that Lauren always said could melt her heart like no other man's ever could. But this wasn't the husband that she loved or the father that Rachel adored. This was some new entity—a monster forged in the fires of guilt and rage and a twisted sense of responsibility. "She has to *live*, goddammit. She *has* to. And I need you to make sure that happens."

Kira watched in fascination as he crossed back to her and sank down onto the chair, his knees touching hers. He hung his head and supported it with his free hand. The gun dangled, almost forgotten, at his side.

She tugged feebly at her bindings, but the cord just cut more deeply into her flesh. She relented and suddenly something struck her. "Lauren mentioned that you were eager to accuse Alec of the crimes at one point."

He nodded miserably and looked up through bloodshot eyes. "I found myself hoping he was the rapist, because if they caught the real one then I would be forced to stop. It would have been stupid to continue if the real one was in custody." He shook his head and looked back at his hands—hands that had done unspeakable things in the name of love and commitment. "I was relieved when it wasn't him because Rachel took to him so well. But then…" He shrugged.

"Then you felt you had to try again."

Again he nodded.

She spoke softly, intimately. "She wouldn't have wanted you to do it, Tim. You must know that."

"Of course I know that," he mumbled into his hand. "That's why I have to do this now, before they catch me and put me away. Before I disappoint Lauren and Rachel and shatter their world."

Kira's stomach knotted as she recalled what he had said. *He needed her to make sure Rachel lived.* What did that mean? "Do what? What are you planning, Tim?"

He straightened in the chair and took a deep breath. His chest had to work so hard it seemed that he was breathing in liquid oxygen instead of air. He reached out and touched her cheek. His hand no longer trembled. An eerie calm seemed to settle over him as he spoke. "You're a good friend, Kira. You'll do this for us, won't you? It's for Rachel, after all. You understand why it's necessary."

She felt her heart leap into triple time and felt a bead of sweat trickle down between her breasts. He couldn't possibly— Not after all that they had shared—

But his eyes were sad and fevered. "I need you, Kira. I don't have much time. The police will recognize my picture. They could come any minute. I know it. I can't run. That's the coward's way out. And I have to make it all count for something. Rachel *must* have a kidney. She'll take it. She has to."

Kira struggled in vain. She whimpered but couldn't seem to form words.

He reached for a cordless phone that lay on the kitchen counter beside him. "I'll call and make sure they come immediately." He swallowed and a tear squeezed out of his eye and trickled down his cheek.

Out of the corner of her eye, she saw him click on the phone.

"Tim," she whispered, battling terror and confusion. "Please, God, don't do this."

"I'm sorry, Kira. I'm really so sorry." He raised the gun and she found the strength to scream.

* * * * *

Alec's BMW screamed into the driveway. Just as expected, Mike LaRocque's Altima was parked at the curb. Alec erupted from his car and stalked toward the front door. "No good, slimy, manipulative, conniving—" He muttered a steady stream of epithets as he approached the entrance. If he found the dear doctor in anything approaching a compromising or threatening position with Kira, he swore he'd teach that doctor a few new uses for his stethoscope. Alec was nothing if not imaginative.

He reached for the knob, but the door was ajar. It swung in easily, and he was astonished to find that the dead bolt had been ripped off the wall. "What the hell?" Was LaRocque really desperate enough to break through a door to get to her? Then he struck himself in the forehead with an open palm. What was he thinking? LaRocque was desperate enough to impersonate the Governor General's secretary. Was B&E really such a stretch?

He rammed through the door calling loudly, "Kira? Are you okay?"

"She's not here." Mike's voice reached him from the kitchen.

Alec blasted into the room, still pumped on indignation and adrenaline. He found LaRocque leaning against the counter sipping on something he had obviously pilfered out of the liquor cabinet. Cujo was munching contentedly on a stack of doggie biscuits that the intruder had probably used to bribe him into silence.

Alec swatted the drink out of Mike's hand and the tumbler shattered against the tiles.

"Hey!" yelled Mike over the barrage of canine yapping that the noise had set off.

"Quiet!" bellowed Alec. Apparently Cujo accepted Alec's authority because he skulked back to his treats with barely a whimper.

That taken care of, Alec grabbed Mike by the shirt. "Now what the hell do you mean, *she's not here*?"

"Take your hands off me."

Alec dug his fingers in a little deeper. "What did you do with her?" he growled.

"I didn't *do* anything."

"You lured me out of here and broke into her house. I'd say that qualifies as *something*. Now tell me where she is before I pound your face in with a kitchen mallet."

Mike's jaw muscles worked furiously. "I admit I went a little overboard with my scheme."

"*A little?*" Alec was incredulous. "You're obsessed, man. You're—"

"But I came in here and she was gone. I swear. I waited, hoping she'd come back."

Alec struggled to control his breathing, and he forced his fingers to uncurl from Mike's shirt. "Where could she have gone?"

Mike shrugged, and sank into a kitchen chair. He dropped his head into his hands. "I've been sitting here trying to figure out what the hell was going through my head the last few months. After I broke through the door and couldn't find her, I realized she might have slipped out the back because she was actually afraid of me." He looked up and Alec could see misery gleaming in his eyes. "That hit me hard. I've been on some kind of trip the last few months. I've been acting like a pig with the nurses and clerical staff. I've been—"

"Will you shut up, LaRocque!" Alec shouted with impatience. "I don't give a damn about your personal pity party. Right now I want to find Kira. I want—"

The crack of a gunshot echoed through the kitchen.

Mike's and Alec's eyes riveted on one another. Almost in unison they said, "That came from next door."

Both men scrambled for the front door. They had exited the house and were halfway across the lawn that separated the two units when Alec noticed a car stopped at the curb. Two familiar figures were just exiting their vehicle. "Gen!" he yelled and waved frantically.

The little woman looked up and a smile briefly lit her face, but Alec hardly had time for niceties. "We heard a gunshot!" He pointed toward the Nickles' as he ran. "From in there."

He and Mike reached the front door just as Gen and Will broke into a run. He heard Gen yelling something at him, but he chose to ignore her. He ignored her, and he ignored years of police training, when unarmed, and unprepared, he burst into an unknown, and very possibly, dangerous situation.

But the second he entered the house he knew he had done the right thing. He heard Kira's frantic cries from somewhere in the depths of the house. He stumbled through, vaguely aware of the other three rescuers, hot on his tail. He followed the sobs and pleas for help toward the kitchen at the back of the house.

But when he stepped through into the familiar room where he had shared coffee with Kira's good friends just a few days before, he halted in his tracks. A sickening mix of horror and disbelief washed through him.

Tears streamed down Kira's face as she looked up at him. She had ceased her screaming, and gazed at him with eyes full of misery and pain. She was okay. She was tied to a chair, but physically she appeared to be fine.

At her feet, however, immersed in a pool of his own blood, his eyes wide and sightless, lay the one man that Alec had deemed worthy to call a friend.

He heard the wail of sirens and locked eyes with Kira… And felt something inside him die.

Chapter Twenty-Five

ꟗ

Kira and Alec walked slowly down the familiar hallway toward the ICU. Their steps echoed off the cold tile and bare walls.

She was grateful for the arm that hugged her shoulders and the feel of Alec's hips shifting next to her own. She needed his strength. Just as he needed hers. Perhaps, for the first time in their lives, they were sharing a crisis as equals—leaning on each other and seeking comfort and solace instead of pointing fingers and assigning blame.

She rested her head against his shoulder and wrapped her arm lightly around his waist. The devastation on his face upon finding Tim that way had mirrored her own. Anger and disappointment warred within her, interlaced with mind-numbing grief and heartache.

She couldn't close her eyes without seeing a slow-motion replay—Tim, sitting tall and straight in his chair, his eyes locked with hers as he lifted the gun to his temple. An intense sorrow settled across his eyes and he had smiled a sad farewell as he pulled the trigger in his one final attempt to give his daughter the gift that had thus far eluded him. Kira had watched helplessly as he fell to the floor and blood had gushed from the wound. It had spread over the pale gray tiles but its essence had stained her soul.

She ached for her loss, as well as for Alec's. But most of all she ached for what Lauren and Rachel were going through.

Rachel. Kira closed her eyes and tried not to think about what Rachel faced over the next few hours. No one should be faced with such a dilemma, least of all someone like Rachel Nickle. A girl who brimmed with the beauty and innocence of youth, and now ached with the pain of a loss that should have been beyond her years.

They had almost reached the little room where Lauren had said they would be waiting, when Kira heard a familiar, raspy voice.

"Hey, Kira!"

With a heavy sigh, Kira stopped and turned to see Jean bearing down on them, her steps uncharacteristically quick and purposeful.

Breathless from her exertion, Jean waddled up to them and said with excitement, "Did you hear?"

Battling a weariness so deep it seemed that words took too much effort, Kira merely shook her head.

Jean stood up a little straighter. "Mike LaRocque is being suspended."

That shocked Kira enough to give her a much needed dose of energy. "Suspended?"

Jean nodded proudly. "He tried to screw me over, and I don't take kindly to being treated like a peon."

Kira shook her head in confusion. "What are you talking about?"

"He figured out that I'm the one who ratted him out to you. So he tried to get me fired!" She propped her hands on ample hips. "Can you believe it? That little prick invented some tall tale about me neglecting my patients."

Kira caught a smile twitching at Alec's lips. "I take it the ruse didn't work."

"No sir-ree! I had reams of stuff on reserve for just such a development. I came back at them with all kinds of stories of sexual harassment and generally slimy behavior."

"Wow," was all Kira could think to say, but Jean's tirade hardly allowed for more.

"He'd threatened all kinds of women with dismissal if they wouldn't sleep with him. And a few that stood up to him actually got the boot!" She took a deep breath, obviously feeling quite smug and proud of herself. But then she leaned forward and whispered covertly, "It helped that he made the mistake of mentioning my name to Kim Witzel last night."

Kira shook her head in confusion. "Kim Witzel?"

"Yeah. She's a practical nurse down in Emergency. I guess Mike had been making the moves on her for a while. She's been trying to get transferred to Day Surgery because the shifts in Emerg are killing her, what with her being a single mom and all. Mike knew that and basically implied that if she slept with him he'd pull strings for her and get her in."

Kira just blinked stupidly at the scope of Mike LaRocque's corruption.

"I guess she gave in to him last night. But when he was leaving he made some kind of snide comment about me and that I'd *get what was coming to me*. So when she heard about my troubles this morning she called me up right away." Jean sniffed as she smoothed a nonexistent wrinkle out of her uniform. "It was the icing on the cake. That together with all my other dirt on him—"

"You've been collecting information for quite a while?" asked Kira in disbelief. "Why didn't you say something sooner?"

"Sooner?" Jean looked at Kira and frowned as if to imply that Kira was a little dim for not knowing the reason already. "I waited until it was in my best interests to bring the charges to light, and I figured *now* was the time."

"You're such a humanitarian," quipped Alec.

She shrugged, oblivious to his sarcasm. "They've suspended him pending investigation of the charges and I say good riddance. I'm tired of his huge head parading around up there, anyway. It's time for some new blood."

Kira idly hoped it would be that easy to find a new oncologist. "Thanks, Jean," she said in an attempt to dismiss her colleague. "It's good to know, but—"

"But we have friends who are expecting us," filled in Alec.

Jean glanced toward the ICU. "In there?"

Kira found herself battling tears and was grateful for Alec's strong presence.

"Yes," he said quietly. "So, if you'll excuse us?"

"Yeah, sure." Jean's eyebrows pulled together slightly. She was obviously curious as to the circumstances, but she must have sensed their anxiety enough to respect their privacy. She turned around and waddled off. "See you in the trenches, Kira."

Kira didn't respond.

"Will she?" asked Alec.

"See me in the trenches?"

He nodded.

"I don't know. I *will* nurse again I'm just not sure how or where." She shook her head to clear the web of emotions that muddled her thinking. "But I can't think about that right now." They had reached the doorway to the little waiting room. Kira was about to step inside when Alec pulled her to the side and wrapped his arms around her.

He whispered in her ear, "Are you sure you're okay?"

She nodded mutely, but savored the softness of his shirt against her cheek.

"I mean," he continued, "you barely finished with the police, and then you had to relate all that..." He blew out a breath in lieu of words that couldn't begin to scratch the surface of what Kira had experienced. "Everything to Lauren and Rachel." He shook his head in wonder. "I can't imagine facing them and telling them those things about him." He pulled away and she looked up at him. "You didn't have to, you know."

"Yes, I did. No matter what he did, that doesn't change what he was to me. To them. He told me things that they had to know." In the aftermath, they had found a suicide note that Tim had apparently been in the midst of writing when Kira interrupted him. He had apparently been struggling with words that were inadequate to express his feelings and regrets. Kira had finally understood why he had needed her to help save Rachel's life.

She had become his confessor—his intermediary. He had told her his story in the hopes that she could relate it to his family, and hopefully convince Rachel to take his kidney. He had loved her so much, and he had known the struggle she would face. But even as Kira had relayed the message, she had seen the disillusionment and disappointment in Rachel's eyes. Kira feared that she had been a poor choice. She had never been eloquent. Her skills of communication and persuasion had fallen short of the mark. Oddly, even considering what Tim Nickle had done and what he had become, she hated to let him down.

Rachel was still adamantly refusing the transplant.

And Lauren was as torn as her daughter. Perhaps more so.

She returned her gaze to Alec who had been watching her patiently. "It helped having you with me when I talked to them." Alec had held her hand and silently supported her as she retold her story.

"Just doing my job." He smiled but it was thin and weak. So many people were hurting over this. It staggered the imagination.

"Kira?" Lauren had stepped out into the hall. Her eyes were red and swollen, but dry...for now. "Thanks..." She glanced back into the waiting room. "Thanks for coming."

Kira stepped away from Alec and reached for her friend. Lauren fell into her arms, as worn and tattered as a tissue that had been swept up in a tornado. Silent sobs racked her body, and Kira wondered that Lauren had any tears left to shed. And then she wondered how her own body had managed to squeeze out yet another manifestation of grief.

At last, they pulled apart and Lauren wiped impatiently at her eyes, as if she were self-conscious about her display. As if she were unsure that the man beyond those doors deserved to be mourned. Kira regretted that. But she felt powerless to assuage such a profound pain.

"How's Rachel?" asked Kira.

"Not so good," said Lauren. "She's been sitting in there for the last hour. She won't go in to see him. She's hardly spoken. She won't even talk about what's going to happen, or what could happen. She—" She shook her head as if to express the inadequacy of words. "I don't know what to tell her, Kira. Dear God! How does a nineteen-year-old deal with something like this? She's been wanting a kidney for so long. It could save her life. But not like *this!* How could she live with this for the rest of her life? I..." Her voice faded away to nothing. When she spoke, it was barely above a whisper. "I just don't know. I don't understand this. I don't understand him. I loved him and I thought I knew him, but obviously I was wrong."

"Let me talk to her." Alec's voice startled them both.

"Alec?" asked Kira. "Are you sure?"

He nodded, his expression sober and intense. He looked to Lauren. "Please. I need to speak to her. Privately."

Lauren considered him for a moment, her eyes once again dry but her face drawn and tired. "All right. If you think you can help..."

But Alec was already through the door.

Kira laid a hand on Lauren's arm. "I think maybe he understands Tim better than any of us. They shared something yesterday. In those few hours they shared something profound."

"Maybe," was all Lauren could say. "But I look at Tim in there," she motioned toward the doors, "hooked up to all those machines, barely alive, his spirit gone, his body an empty shell, and I recognize the face. But I wonder if in twenty years of marriage—I wonder if I ever really knew him."

"You did, Lauren." She steered her friend toward the coffee shop where they could sit and sip and try to recapture just a little bit of normalcy. "You can't erase all the good because of what happened. That would be cheating yourself." She wrapped an arm around Lauren's drooping shoulders. "And that would be cheating him."

* * * * *

"Hi, Rachel." Alec settled himself beside her on the worn Naugahyde couch. She was curled up in the corner—her knees drawn up to her chin and her face tight with misery and suffering.

She didn't answer him.

He gazed at her and relived the moment they had broken the news. They had waited until Rachel finished her dialysis run, knowing she would need all her strength and resources to face the mountain of grief that loomed. He and Kira, flanked by two uniformed police officers, had been waiting outside the dialysis unit doors when Rachel and Lauren stepped into the hall. He had looked on in mute desperation as she had listened to Kira's tearful words. He had tried to lend his silent support as Rachel and Lauren's world had been brutally knocked out from under them. He had watched helplessly as Rachel and her mother had wept and crumpled from the weight of their pain and disappointment. All he had to offer was a strong shoulder and a sympathetic embrace. That had done little to ease their suffering, but maybe there was a way he could help.

He sighed deeply as he sorted through his thoughts and the brief memories of his time with Tim. What could he say to make her open up and listen to him? How could he help her to understand and see the truth?

He took a chance and reached for her hand that lay limp and lifeless on her knee. To his relief she didn't pull away. He cradled those delicate bones in his palm, trying to impart a trace of warmth into a soul that seemed so cold and alone. He licked shaking lips and decided to just plunge right in. "You have to do it, Rachel."

That got her attention. Her head swiveled around and her eyes drilled into his. "Do what?"

"You have to take his kidney."

"I don't *have* to do anything. Are you saying you agree with what he did?"

"Of course not," he said softly.

She swallowed, visibly fighting a fresh wash of tears. "Then what *are* you saying?"

He didn't answer immediately, and she used that time to vent some of her anger.

"He *killed* people, Alec! He...he beat them and killed them." Alec suspected she couldn't bring herself to face what else her father had done, supposedly in her name. He suspected the guilt associated with that knowledge fed her misery like kerosene on a bonfire. "He did all that and then he abandoned me." She wiped at her eyes with a wadded-up tissue. "I'm just supposed to forget all that? I'm just supposed to say, *Oh well, shit happens. My daddy was insane. He lied to me about who he was. He turned his back on every value he ever taught me. He was a hypocrite and a killer. But since he's going to die anyway he may as well help me while he's at it.*"

"He never lied to you, Rachel."

"What are you talking about? Of course he did."

"He may have lied to you about where he went at night. He may have lied to the police and done hideous, unspeakable things. But he never lied to you about who he was. And he never lied about how much he loved you."

She looked away. "How can someone who kills so viciously love anyone?"

"He didn't kill those women out of a need for power, or an obsession with pain or cruelty. He hated what he was doing and what he had become. He knew it was evil and unspeakable, and he did it out of guilt and shame, but those feelings had their seeds in the deep and abiding love of a parent for a child."

She still refused to look at him. "You talk as if you knew him. You and he were friends for a day. How can you possibly presume to understand him?"

"You're wrong, Rachel." He spoke with enough intensity to demand her attention. She finally met his eyes. "We may not have known each other long but we understood each other. We shared something few men have to face—a mortal threat to our children."

The set of her face eased slightly. "Your daughter?"

"Yes. I would have done anything—legal or otherwise—if it would have given her a chance to live."

"You wouldn't have killed, though. Normal people don't do that."

"No. I don't think I would have. But I think that when he saw what Stuart was doing and he saw the possibilities, no matter how outrageous, something warped inside him. All he saw was an opportunity to *do* something." Alec smiled sadly. "For men there's nothing worse than powerlessness. It just about killed me that I couldn't do anything to help Cherisse. I know that your dad was the same."

She looked away but he could tell that she was considering what he was saying.

"He was sick, Rachel. In his heart, he was sick—sick with guilt and grief and worry. Don't punish him for his illness. Don't punish yourself." He held her hand a little tighter. "Remember how much he loved you. Remember how he hugged you when you cried and listened to you when you needed to talk. Remember how he laughed with you and read to you, and remember how much he loved your mother. Make his love count for something. Take his offering and let a little piece of his soul melt into yours." He saw a tear squeeze out of her eye but he didn't relent. "It may take years, but eventually you'll forgive him. If you miss this opportunity now, you'll never forgive *yourself*."

She turned to him and her bottom lip quivered as she struggled through what must have been a vortex of pain. "I just want my daddy back, Alec." A sob burst from her throat and Alec wrapped her in his arms. "I loved him so much. And I hate him for going away."

"I know you do," he murmured into her hair as her tears soaked into his soft white polo shirt. "I know you do."

Epilogue

One year later

ℰ𝓃

Kira lounged back and gazed up at the luminescence of a thousand distant suns.

"More wine?" asked her husband.

She held out her glass and allowed him to fill the crystal goblet with his favorite French Merlot. She was gradually developing a taste for it but, for now, she drank it because Alec enjoyed it, and because she wanted to share that with him. "Are you trying to get me drunk?" she asked with a grin.

"Maybe." He settled down beside her on a lounge chair. "God knows I don't get enough sex."

She chuckled. "A month of passionate encounters in the surf of the South Pacific isn't *enough sex?"*

"Nope." He sipped his wine. "There's no such thing as *enough sex*."

"Will you two stop talking about boinking each other?" Rachel gathered up the last of the plates from the patio table. "You're starting to make me nauseous."

Alec sighed deeply. "You need a boyfriend, Rachel. Maybe I could set you up with—"

She placed delicate fingers firmly over his mouth. "Don't go there, Alec." Her smile was warm and her face glowed with good health. She bent low and pecked him on the forehead. "You're all the man I can handle." She retrieved her load of dishes and headed for the kitchen. "For now."

Both Kira and Alec chuckled as she stepped through the wide-open patio doors.

Lauren's voice reached them from the depths of the house. "Do Rachel and I have to do these dishes all by ourselves? Honestly, I just don't know about you two. Sometimes it's like I've got three children instead of one. I swear—"

Kira tuned out the familiar lighthearted complaining and leaned over to whisper in Alec's ear. "She loves us, you know."

"I know. Everybody loves me."

She leaned back in her chair and linked her hand with his. "Your head is getting too big again. What, with a new wife worshiping the ground you walk on, and your business taking off—" Alec had started up a firm that offered private security to visiting dignitaries. His name and the flurry of publicity around the events of the previous year had guaranteed his success.

Kira, on the other hand, had begun taking the occasional temporary private nursing job for chronically ill children. She enjoyed the personal touch and the flexibility of such an arrangement. They both seemed to have found their niche. Individually, as well as together.

She shook her head in mock sorrow as she sipped from her wine. "Yes, your ego has swelled to mammoth proportions. You need to be taken down a peg or two."

"Rachel keeps me in line."

The warmth in his voice when he referred to his surrogate daughter filled Kira's heart. He and Rachel had both felt a void in their lives. They had looked to each other to fill it.

While Lauren wept on Kira's shoulder, Rachel had looked to Alec. She had leaned heavily on him in the days after her surgery, through the mourning of her father and the months of recovery. In her, Alec had found a young friend, and hope for the future. She had stood up for Alec at their tiny wedding, right alongside her mother, who had witnessed for Kira. The foursome shared a special bond. They shared precious memories of a man who, despite his mistakes, had touched all their lives. And hence they shared a unique outlook on life.

Kira heard the clatter of plates and squeezed Alec's hand. "We should really go in and help."

"In a minute." His gaze was lost amongst the endless expanse of stars.

"When you look at them now, what do you wish for, Alec?"

He turned to her and a smile lit up his face. "Why, nothing. I look at them because they're beautiful." He leaned over and whisked a kiss across her lips. It was quick but warm and full of promise. "I have everything a man could want. There's nothing left to wish for."

Why an electronic book?

We live in the Information Age—an exciting time in the history of human civilization, in which technology rules supreme and continues to progress in leaps and bounds every minute of every day. For a multitude of reasons, more and more avid literary fans are opting to purchase e-books instead of paper books. The question from those not yet initiated into the world of electronic reading is simply: *Why?*

1. ***Price.*** An electronic title at Ellora's Cave Publishing and Cerridwen Press runs anywhere from 40% to 75% less than the cover price of the exact same title in paperback format. Why? Basic mathematics and cost. It is less expensive to publish an e-book (no paper and printing, no warehousing and shipping) than it is to publish a paperback, so the savings are passed along to the consumer.
2. ***Space.*** Running out of room in your house for your books? That is one worry you will never have with electronic books. For a low one-time cost, you can purchase a handheld device specifically designed for e-reading. Many e-readers have large, convenient screens for viewing. Better yet, hundreds of titles can be stored within your new library—on a single microchip. There are a variety of e-readers from different manufacturers. You can also read e-books on your PC or laptop computer. (Please note that Ellora's Cave does not endorse any specific brands. You can check our websites at www.ellorascave.com

or www.cerridwenpress.com for information we make available to new consumers.)

3. ***Mobility***. Because your new e-library consists of only a microchip within a small, easily transportable e-reader, your entire cache of books can be taken with you wherever you go.
4. ***Personal Viewing Preferences.*** Are the words you are currently reading too small? Too large? Too... ANNOYING? Paperback books cannot be modified according to personal preferences, but e-books can.
5. ***Instant Gratification.*** Is it the middle of the night and all the bookstores near you are closed? Are you tired of waiting days, sometimes weeks, for bookstores to ship the novels you bought? Ellora's Cave Publishing sells instantaneous downloads twenty-four hours a day, seven days a week, every day of the year. Our webstore is never closed. Our e-book delivery system is 100% automated, meaning your order is filled as soon as you pay for it.

Those are a few of the top reasons why electronic books are replacing paperbacks for many avid readers.

As always, Ellora's Cave and Cerridwen Press welcome your questions and comments. We invite you to email us at Comments@ellorascave.com or write to us directly at Ellora's Cave Publishing Inc., 1056 Home Avenue, Akron, OH 44310-3502.